Song of the White Swan

FIRST EDITION
First Printing, 1997

Cover art and design: Laughing Owl Publishing, Inc.

ISBN: 0-9659701-6-7
LCCN : 97-073404

Laughing Owl Publishing, Inc.
12610 Hwy 90 West
Grand Bay, AL 36541

Song of the White Swan

Aleta Boudreaux

Laughing Owl Publishing, Inc.

AUTHOR'S NOTE

When John Cabot arrived on the shores of Cape Breton, Nova Scotia in 1497, he was greeted by native people anxious to trade with the white men from across the sea. Many of the native people did not survive the Europeans invasion of the 16th century, but the Mi'kmaq, the People of Nova Scotia had a friendly relationship with the French well into the 1700's.

One wonders how the Mi'kmaq came to be so well prepared and what kind of leader they possessed who had the ability to guide them safely into the new Era of their homeland.

One also wonders what drove the Europeans to seek the New World. Historians say it was riches and gold. Perhaps there were other things more precious that made men cross the uncharted waters.

There is little information available on the Mi'kmaq Indians of Nova Scotia prior to European contact; however through diligent research by Dr. Ruth Holmes Whitehead and the staff of the Nova Scotia Museum, much of the Mi'kmaq heritage has been accurately catalogued for posterity.

Though the Knights Templar were formally disbanded in the 13th century, many sources claim that they remain active and influential even in today's culture. The Druid Sisterhood of the Moon, the legendary priestesses of the Île du Sein, off the Western coast of Brittany, are waiting to be discovered.

I wish to thank my husband, Hamilton, for his patience and constant support, my son Hamilton IV for his timely revelations and his boat models and my mother, Iris, who has always encouraged me to be a writer. I thank my sister, Louise, for listening to my early attempts at dialogue and all my friends for their research, invaluable critique and encouragement during the birthing of my first novel.

I am indebted to Dr. Ruth Holmes Whitehead, for without her research and knowledge, my representation of the Mi'kmaq culture would be completely fictitious.

To Lady Mu Kalysto, my teacher and Connald Fraoch Eilean, my friend, I give my thanks for sharing their secrets.

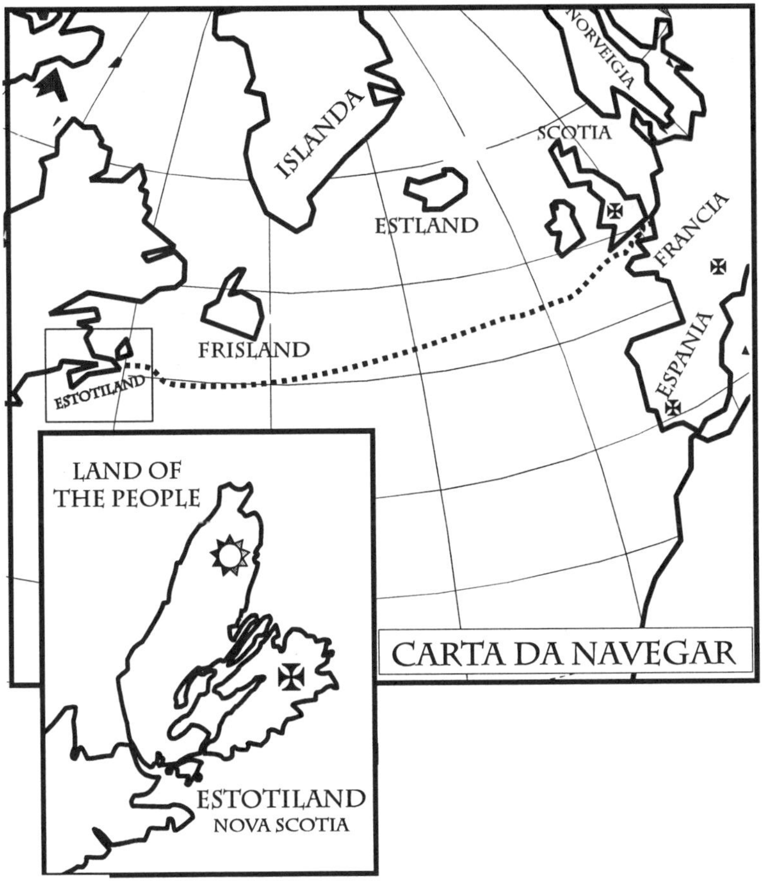
NORVEIGIA
ISLANDA
SCOTIA
ESTLAND
FRANCIA
FRISLAND
ESPANIA
ESTOTILAND
CARTA DA NAVEGAR
LAND OF
THE PEOPLE
ESTOTILAND
NOVA SCOTIA

Oiseaux de Passage

Birds of Passage

Chapter I

Château Rennes
Brittany, Mid-June 1491

Heathen. Pagan. Blasphemer.

Words used to condemn; to accuse.

Antoinette Charboneau knew the man sitting on the low dais in front of her would say all these words before her interrogation was over. She wondered why the words had not yet escaped from Cardinal Visconti's lips and why he had not locked her in some dark *oubliette* beneath the *château* to await her death at a more auspicious time.

Yes. From the Christian Church's point of view she was certainly a pagan. A heathen? Perhaps. But never a blasphemer. She had never shown irreverence toward anyone's religion; only to those who professed to act on their favored deity's behalf. Egotistical, pompous and vindictive people like Cardinal Marcello Visconti.

Antoinette searched the faces of the men standing beside the Cardinal. She knew them all. Some she had laid her healing hands upon. She had delivered the heirs of others at frantic midnight callings. They were men who from childhood had worshipped the Ancient Ones and the Great Goddess, as well as the One God of the Christians. No doubt they were here to stand witness to her powers.

"*Mademoiselle* Charboneau." The Cardinal raised his opulently robed arm and waved a gloved hand toward the men standing by his side. "We have called you here to discuss a problem facing both the Church and the Crown of France."

"I beg pardon, Your Grace. I am not privy to the problems of your Church, though I am sure there are many that vex you," Antoinette said. "You must realize that even though I am advisor to Lady Anne, I am not at liberty to speak for her in her absence. Shall I send for her? I'm certain she is in her chambers."

Visconti leaned back in his chair, his arms perched on the padded armrests. He tented his hands across his prominent belly. He might be master at this game, but he was on Antoinette's ground—he was in Brittany, in her domain, and he was powerless to harm her if he wanted the young Duchess Anne's agreement to marry the King of France.

"I do not feel it appropriate to discuss this matter with her Ladyship. It is a question of propriety, I assure you. This problem can be solved without involving King Charles or Lady Anne."

Visconti did not tarry with niceties, but he was wasting his breath. For the last hundred years, Brittany had been under a Breton's rule, separate from France, distanced from the politics of Rome. The ancient ways and the old gods were still revered, kept alive by the strong will and the enduring faith of the Bretons.

The Cardinal bent forward on one elbow and his dark brows creased together in a long thin line. He looked like a hawk surveying his prey, ready to strike her at the earliest sign of weakness.

"Unless you wish to make trouble and bring hardship upon everyone you represent," he said, "I suggest we talk."

"Am I to understand you are threatening Anne de Bretagne? And my order?"

"I would not call it a threat, *Mademoiselle*. Simply a warning."

"Warnings often precede disaster." Antoinette narrowed her eyes and locked her gaze with his, seeing beyond his facade of piety. He hid his true thoughts, but the energy circling around him, bright with orange streaks, vibrating with flares of green, betrayed him. She wondered what drove him to be so full of hatred.

"What do you require of me, Your Eminence? I am but one person. I cannot act or answer for an entire community." She motioned to the men standing beside the Cardinal. "Perhaps you should ask your assembly their true feelings about King Charles' trespass in our province. Ask these men how much they will enjoy the Church's total control of their lives."

Visconti stood and dismissed his entourage. The men scurried across the black and white checkerboard floor of the great hall like frightened sheep. None of them looked back toward Antoinette. She knew they had been carefully chosen for this interrogation. They had been bought, but not paid well enough to keep silent if she revealed too much about Visconti's mission.

As the last man exited, the Cardinal stepped off the dais in a flurry of red and black fabric. Startled at the little man's quick movement, Antoinette remained calm.

"Don't play games with me." His words were awkward,

thickly laced with his Italian accent. "I know *what* you are. And you know what I have the authority to do if you give me even the slightest provocation."

His robes reeked of frankincense. The energy around him encircled her with buffeting waves of anger. His gaze traveled the length of her body and Antoinette stiffened, holding away the malice that touched her.

I must not show my anxiety. He must see me as Anne's advisor, not just a young woman. He must understand I will not back down.

"You have no power here," she said. "Not as long as Anne is regent." *Not as long as the people respect the Sisterhood and honor the Goddess.*

"You mean not as long as you are her counselor." Visconti let out a long dramatic sigh. "Why do you make this so hard for us?" He waved to the window where campfires were visible, scattered like tiny flickering stars across the open expanse beyond the keep. "Look at your situation. It is hopeless. King Charles' mercenaries are camped just outside the château's walls. Who knows how much they will abuse the good people of Rennes until the King arrives? The way I see it, Lady Anne has no choice but to marry him and honor her father's treaty. And you, my dear..." He raised a short stubby finger to Antoinette's face and traced it down the length of her cheek. "...your presence and influence will not be tolerated when King Charles rules Brittany."

Antoinette grabbed his wrist and dug her fingernails into his satin glove. Her gaze burned in defiance.

"How dare you threaten me!"

Visconti looked down at her hand. The edges of his mouth turned up in a thin mocking smile.

"How dare *you* not respect my intelligence. You are not a mindless handmaiden whispering gossip into the ear of her mistress. You are Anne's trusted advisor and—a pagan. I wonder why she listens to you."

Antoinette released his wrist and took a half step back. "You have no authority to remove me from Anne's court."

"No. Indeed I do not." He straightened his gloves, adjusting the large ring resting on his index finger. "I do not have that power—not yet."

"You will never have it. Anne will never acquiesce to such a demand."

"Perhaps not; but when she is Queen, she will obey Charles."

"Obey Charles?" Antoinette smiled and made a small

laugh. "Anne did not even obey her father."

"Duke François was not the King of France."

"No, he was not King, but he was our ruler, as Anne is now. The Duke took no dictate from King Louis, nor will Anne be commanded by his son."

"You underestimate our power, my dear. No matter how faithful she is to her people or how tolerant she is of your ancient gods, Anne is still a Catholic. When she marries Charles, she will be forced to listen to our demands or she will risk the wrath of the Church."

"So you *are* threatening Her Ladyship."

"If you believe the truth to be a threat—then so be it."

"The truth, Your Grace, is something you have yet to speak." Antoinette held back her anger. She had to let him reveal his secrets along with his display of vanity.

"You want the truth, my dear? The truth is the Church will not allow you to remain in the Queen's court. Nor will we permit the Sisterhood and your ancient gods to influence any part of Brittany."

"Surely you mean that *you* will not permit it. Your Church has always allowed the Bretons the freedom to worship as they choose." Antoinette's voice echoed off the high ceiling. "Your God has prospered here. Why disturb the people now? Why take away what little remains of their ancient ways, their *pardons,* their innocent petitions to the Ancient Ones?"

Visconti turned, and his robes swished against the marble floor. His eyes glared with a passion deeper than she could have imagined. "It is the Church's will. As Brittany becomes one with France, so it will become one with the Holy Christian Church. The Sisterhood of the Moon will be destroyed and the ancient gods you force upon the Bretons will vanish."

"Never!" Antoinette stepped back from him. "The Ancient Ones have always existed. They will not disappear, simply because you wish it. Nor will the Sisterhood."

Visconti laughed. "We are prepared to assimilate your gods into the bosom of the Church as we have for many centuries. After several generations, no one will even remember them. Do you know the names of the gods of the people before the Romans conquered the Gauls? Before the Romans conquered Britain?"

She wanted to say yes, but she would not give Visconti the gift of knowing that the legacy of the ancient gods and goddesses remained intact. It was best to let him think his church had been successful.

"I see by your silence that you understand."

Let him think so. Let him think I am powerless to defend my faith, my people, my regent.

"If I consent to your requests Your Grace, what then? Will the Sisterhood simply cease to exist? I believe you would not stop at our mere submission. I have seen the Inquisitors' fires burn too often."

"The Inquisitors can be kept away. I know someone who has the power to stay their hands, but his grace comes with a price."

"Which is?"

"Anne's compliance to the King."

"You do not know Her Ladyship. She refuses to be handled like chattel."

Visconti stepped closer. So close she could thrust her dirk into his belly and be done with him. So close she could see a tiny fleck of black in the white part of his left eye, smell the garlic on his breath and the rancid oil of his perfume.

"She has no choice," he said coldly.

Antoinette stared into his dark eyes, knowing he would stop at nothing to secure Brittany. He would crush the Sisterhood if they interfered further in his politics and he would not hesitate to petition for Anne's expulsion from the Church. Even though she accepted the Ancient Ones and the Goddess, Anne was still devoted to the Blessed Virgin. She would be as lost without her faith as much as Antoinette would be without her own.

"I will not betray the Sisterhood or my people." Antoinette turned from him and walked to the outer door leading to Anne's private chambers. In a final act of defiance she turned back to face her adversary.

"The Church will never control Brittany, Your Grace," she said. "Not while I live and breathe."

Château Rennes

The darkness had a life of its own.

Beyond the window, in the emptiness of the night, the demons of doubt and the shadows of chaos danced together to keep away the dawn. The harsh shriek of a seabird tore through that emptiness with a preternatural cry.

Antoinette's heart pounded as she sprang from her bed and ran to the window. She looked toward the horizon, straining to see into the dawning sky. "An omen. A messenger sent by the

Goddess."

But there was no sign of bird winging its way to the heavens, only the haunting shadow of morning light looming above the small stone cottages and ripening fields of summer grain. Perhaps the pre-dawn visitor had only been in her dreams. Nevertheless, she would consider it a forewarning.

After the confrontation with the Cardinal, she had to be cautious. Visconti was not above murder to achieve his goal. He would order it in the name of his Christian Church and believe himself absolved of his crime.

Antoinette opened the neck of her gown to catch the light breeze drifting across the open fields. Even though the ocean lay some fifty leagues to the North, the humid air smelled of salt and sea. In all her eighteen years, she could not remember the heat of summer being this stifling.

Like a vigilant sentinel guarding first light, she leaned against the window frame, feeling the stone's cool texture against her skin. She imagined the moist air flowing around her, inside her, softening the tense muscles in her legs and arms. It had been a long time since she'd slept soundly, a long time since she'd felt the blessings of the Goddess.

"Beloved Mother, I need you. I need to feel you, to hear you, to be comforted by your words of strength and hope. Let me know that what I am doing is right for the people, for my sisters and for myself."

Only the barking of dogs on the hillside beyond the keep replied to her request and Antoinette laughed. What made her think the Goddess would answer her now? She had petitioned the Goddess before, and her prayers had not yet been answered. Visconti and his men were still in Rennes.

She believed in the power of the gods, but belief was no longer enough. She needed to *know* they were with her, *know* without doubt that she should fulfill her obligations to the Sisterhood of the Moon by remaining at Anne's side.

Even ritual had become an empty ceremony for Antoinette. The words, the movements no longer held the same meaning. Even when she summoned the forces of nature, the spectral powers that once flowed through no longer touched her.

Only once had she experienced the true bliss and ecstasy of the embrace of the Goddess, of being enfolded in a weightless, timeless, moment of rapport. A feeling, said by many, to be like the instant of passion's release.

Now, Antoinette wondered if that momentary rapture had been an illusion, if she would ever feel the touch of the Goddess again. She felt like an impatient witness to life.

Waiting for something that might not exist.

Antoinette took a deep breath, letting out her frustration. She was nearly eighteen and had been chosen from early childhood to continue the legacy of the Sisterhood's counsel to the duchy of Brittany. It was too late to have second thoughts.

She wondered if it was Visconti's threats that had made her question the wisdom of the Sisterhood. He had placed her in the position of defending not only her faith but the ancient traditions of the Breton people. Was there something else that caused her to be out of step with the rest of her kind? To question and not to blindly obey?

Even with the strength of the Sisterhood behind her, Antoinette felt powerless. What few visions she'd had told her nothing of Brittany's future, nothing about her own destiny. Perhaps it was time to try again.

Withdrawing a small candle from her pocket, she placed it in a silver holder and set it upon her writing desk, then lit it with a firebrand from her hearth. She took a long, deep breath to begin her magic.

"Candle of light—Candle of power—First burn to honor the Blessed Mother. Give me strength with your fire, and burn to bring my heart's desire."

Antoinette closed her eyes and whispered anxiously. "Beloved Goddess. Show me what lies ahead."

After a suspended heartbeat she let out her breath with a long sigh. Still no answers. She had to have faith, patience. Wanting was not enough to make the magic work.

Once more she focused on the sounds of the dawn; to the warm wind whispering through the tall oaks and lofty aspens surrounding the château and to the sound of sentries moving along the balustrade above her.

The singing of morning birds beckoning the dawn faded in and out of her hearing. She watched the candle flicker and flare as she slipped into a space between sleep and awareness. The scent of lavender drifted on a rare cool breeze. Then the vision came.

A rocky shoreline extended far beyond a fog-laced headland. The gray outline of majestic trees loomed in the distance.

She could hear the sound of waves lapping the shoreline, smell the salt air and feel the dampness of a misty, early morning.

From out of the mist, a man appeared. He was tall and dark, outlined by the growing dawn behind him. His eyes reflected in the candlelight behind her, but his other features were indistinct. His eyes were black, and as deep and mysterious as the sacred caves of Lascaux. Their gazes locked and a sudden warmth spread around her, filled her with a longing to reach out to him. As if drawn by her thoughts, the man lifted his arm, beckoning her to his side. Entranced, Antoinette took a step forward and extended her hand into the swirling mists.

A sound behind her snapped her awareness back into the room. The otherworldly vision instantly faded.

Instinctively Antoinette extinguished the candle and moved against the far wall. She looked toward the door where a shape hovered just outside her sight.

"Who's there?" she demanded.

"Hush *Chère*. 'Tis only I." A small woman emerged from the shadows.

Rushing across the cold slate floor, Antoinette pulled her grandmother into the room. "What are you doing here, Ursule? You should be with the Sisters. Cardinal Visconti's men are everywhere."

"Tsk," Ursule muttered, pushing Antoinette away with the side of her wrinkled hand. "You know I am safe. I haven't lived all these years to die at a witch's stake."

Antoinette could not deny Ursule's magic was greater than her own. Ursule was a High Priestess of the Sisterhood. Her skills in ceremony and ritual were legendary among the acolytes of the Goddess. She had been companion and advisor to Duke François, but with his death she had withdrawn to live on the Île du Sein, off the western coast of Brittany. The island was home to the Sisterhood of the Moon. Women dedicated to do the work of the Goddess.

What could Ursule be thinking, wandering the dark hallways of Château Rennes? Antoinette wondered.

"I've come to give you a message." Ursule picked up a gray feather from the floor. Looking first toward the window, then at the smoldering candle, she handed the feather to Antoinette. "It seems I'm not the only one concerned about you."

Antoinette took the proffered feather and laid it on the bed.

"I'm not sure what all this means, *Grand-mère*. What am I supposed to do? Surely the Sisterhood has not placed Brittany's future in my hands."

"And why not?" The old woman sidled to the bed and gingerly climbed onto the mattress, patting the empty space beside her.

The lines on Ursule's face ran together into fine delicate patterns like streams of water washing across silky white sand.

Her face showed the wisdom and passing memories of a lifetime. Her silver-streaked hair was pulled back from her face. She no longer wore the blue robes of the Mother, but the honored dark robes of the Crone, the wise woman. Ursule's voice was still sweet and youthful. "You are the only one we can trust. You are chosen by the Goddess to defend us, to delay the dissolution of the Sisterhood as long as possible."

"Delay?" Antoinette was astonished at the woman's choice of words. She sat down beside her. "Dissolution?"

"Yes," the old woman conceded. "We know the days of open worship are waning, but there are still many things we must do before we seem to disappear. Many things must happen before the Ancient Ones step aside for the one god of men."

Visconti's threats to the Sisterhood echoed in Antoinette's mind.

"What do you mean step aside?" she asked. "I can't believe the Mother would willingly give way to such an unforgiving god."

"Only in the eyes of men, Antoinette. The Goddess and the Ancient Ones have always been, always will be. They are eternal." She waved her hand toward the window. "Like moonset and sunrise. I do not need to tell you that the Ancient Ones must often take the names and guises of those gods most comfortable to the minds of men." She shook her head and sighed. "But I fear, this time, the goddess will sleep for many centuries. The followers of the Christ are spreading from here to the edges of the earth."

Antoinette hopped down from the bed and extended her arms wide. "What am I supposed to do, Ursule? What does the Goddess want of me?"

"That my dear, *I* cannot tell you. I came to remind you to be cautious and not to sacrifice that lovely neck of yours to this Christian god. The King's emissary is quite a ruthless man."

"Visconti." Antoinette spat out the name like a bitter tonic. "He is a snake, Ursule. A snake that I would like to feed to Hecate's hounds."

"Be patient, Antoinette. You must tread lightly and bide your time. Things are moving quickly. There may yet be a place for the Goddess."

"Anne promises she will do whatever she can to keep the Sisterhood safe."

"And she will honor her promise, as her father did. But she will not be the only ruler in Brittany if she marries King Charles. He will have a say in her affairs and Visconti will be by his side. The Church wants Brittany's wealth along with the souls of her people."

The rattle of armor outside Antoinette's chamber startled both women. Antoinette ran to lock her door, her long gown flowing like shimmering wings against the dark stone walls.

"You must go now." She turned to her grandmother. "The guard is changing."

Unhurried, Ursule slid down from the bed and walked toward a heavy tapestry hanging behind Antoinette's bed. She shoved on the corner of a discolored stone and a hidden passageway appeared.

"Don't worry about me," she whispered. "I know this palace's secrets. I will blend with the scenery."

An odd feeling of loss swept over Antoinette and she touched her grandmother's cheek. She wanted to talk about her doubts and her recurring dreams, but there was no time.

"Be careful. Listen to your heart," Ursule whispered as she stepped into the dark corridor. The stone slid shut behind her and Antoinette heard Ursule's words in her mind.

Follow your visions.

"Follow my visions?" Antoinette sighed as she backed away and leaned against the hard oak door. Her visions were the problem and her heart spoke in riddles. Neither was reliable.

Suddenly, the latch moved beside Antoinette's hand and she stepped away from the door. The heart she'd just dismissed leapt up and lodged securely in her throat.

Chapter 2

St. Malo
A seaport on the Brittany coast

"Take off your clothes!"

A woman's voice came from beneath the shadows of a hooded cloak. The command was full of authority.

Étienne's black eyes blinked against the lantern light thrust at his face. He took a hasty half-step back and found a cold stone wall beneath his fingertips, blocking his retreat from the alley.

"*Pardon*?" Étienne struggled to keep his voice from cracking.

"You heard M'lady, boy!" A swarthy young man stepped forward, threatening to enforce the cloaked woman's unusual request. "Take them off."

Étienne looked in disbelief at his assailant who towered over him like an ancient oak. The foreign accent, the shoulder length curls and the sheathed sword hanging at the man's side were surely the trappings of a pirate.

Étienne's gaze settled on an immense pistol waving before his face and his heart skipped a half-beat. He was a dead man.

"But *Mademoiselle—Monsieur,*" he pleaded, turning from one adversary to the other. He wished he could see the woman better. "I—I have nothing on underneath."

"*Écoutez!*" The woman's voice, cool and clear, demanded immediate respect, as though one would not dare to countermand her power. "Listen!" The woman settled the lantern near her feet. "There is nothing you have that I have not seen before. We have no time to argue with you."

A wave of soft perfume drifted toward Étienne as she stretched her gloved hand toward his trews.

"All right! All right!" Étienne threw up his arms in defeat. He could step back no further. "But I promise you, the King will hear of this outrage."

The woman stifled a giddy laugh and lifted her head to reveal glittering blue eyes against a pale, yet simple, face.

"The King, indeed!" She snapped. "What would the King care about a ship's boy losing his clothes in a back alley?"

Étienne sighed. She was right. King Charles would not care about a peasant boy; he had other worries now that the English had gone from France.

Reluctantly, Étienne pulled the linen tunic over his head and handed it to the woman. "*Mademoiselle!* I am not a ship's boy. I am an apprentice to the navigator aboard His Majesty King Charles' ship, *La Réale.*"

The woman nodded to her conspirator and the pirate waved the pistol at Étienne's pants.

Étienne hesitated before reaching for the rope belt that held up his loose-legged trews, hoping for a miraculous reprieve from his embarrassing and dangerous situation. He made a final pleading glance toward the edge of the alleyway where another woman stood in the safety of the shadows.

She had betrayed him. How could he have been so stupid as to believe her promise of kisses and caresses in the seclusion of the dim passageway? Moments ago in the tavern, she'd spoken to him sweetly and tenderly, promising him things he'd only dreamed about. Her skin was as soft silk, her lips as sweet as his father's apple brandy. Now he could barely see her standing in the shadows. But he knew she was watching his degradation through eyes he remembered as deep and green, and treacherous, like the sea on a moonless night.

He cursed as he balanced on one foot and then the other, pulling off his pants. What a fool he'd been on his first, and surely his last, adventure.

He held his pants discreetly in front of him. There was no way to hide his humiliation or his nakedness from the cloaked woman who would not turn her head aside. The man with her slowly extended his arm.

In the tenseness of the moment, Étienne glanced at the rakish pirate. For the first time he noticed the quality of the man's silk shirt, the ruffled sleeves and heavily embroidered cuffs, and the rich texture of his long velvet tunic. The woman, though dressed in a simple dark gown, wore a lush cloak trimmed in ermine. The faint light revealed shoes gilded in gold and tied with ribbons of silk. Even for a country boy, he knew something was amiss.

"*Mademoiselle,* why are my clothes so important? Surely you can afford to purchase better than you can steal from me."

The pirate waved his weapon toward Étienne's nose. "It's not only your clothes, lad. We need your name as well."

"My name? How can you steal someone's name?"

"*Mon Dieu*!" The woman reached beneath her cloak, then produced a coin and pressed it hard into Étienne's hand. "We are not thieves, boy. I'll pay for the use of your clothes and your name."

With a quick snap of her wrist she snatched the ragged pants from his grasp, then disappeared into the recess of the alley where the green-eyed temptress lurked.

Étienne's eyes widened with astonishment. A year's wages—a gold ducat lay in his palm. It was more, much more than he would earn in several months at sea. Recovering his senses, he grabbed his knapsack from the ground, and held it in front of him. "I—I don't understand."

The tall pirate took off his cape and threw it around Étienne's shoulders. "This is the first time you've been aboard *La Réale?*"

Étienne nodded and pulled the cloak tightly around him. He strained to look past the man toward the shadows moving in the darkness. He could hear fabric shifting, feet scraping the stone walk. What were the women doing?

A light tap on his shoulder with the cold barrel of the pistol recaptured his attention to the foreigner's words.

"*Ah—Oui, Monsieur,*" Étienne remarked.

"Have you ever met any of the crew, the officers?"

"*Non, Monsieur.* I have just arrived from St. Brieuc. This is my first voyage aboard a merchant vessel, my first job as apprentice." Étienne straightened his shoulders. "I have waited a long time for a position such as this. To work aboard the King's ship—"

"Well, you will have to wait a little longer to test your manhood." The ermine cloaked woman spoke from the shadows. "Be certain of his identity, Sebastian."

Étienne looked up into the man's face, trying to find a clue to the mystery surrounding him. Perhaps this Sebastian was not a pirate after all. Étienne took a deep, relieved breath and made a brave step toward the women. He would reason with the lady one last time. "M'lady?"

The foreigner side-stepped hastily between them, lifting the pistol to remind his captive of his situation.

"Your name, boy! What is your name?"

Étienne stopped still. "My name is Étienne. Étienne Clement."

"He's the one, M'lady," Sebastian whispered over his shoulder.

A prescient shiver swept over Étienne and he pulled the cloak tightly around him, realizing his mistake. This was no simple robbery. These people, whoever they were, were looking for him. They had been waiting for him. The green eyed woman was merely a ruse to obtain his possessions. But what could he possibly own that was worth all this trouble?

"Please *Monsieur.* I have no clothes, I will miss my ship's departure."

Sebastian placed one hand on the hilt of his sword, the other on Étienne's shoulder. He turned Étienne away from the alley and from the women.

"*Oui,* Étienne," he said. "*Quel dommage.* It is a shame that you will most definitely miss your ship."

Swelling apprehension choked Étienne's words. *La Réale,* the ship he'd waited for all his life, would leave Brittany without him. Was Sebastian going to kill him after all? "What are you going to do with me, *Monsieur?*"

Sebastian stepped back and shoved the pistol into the band of his pants. He placed a strong hand on Étienne's arm.

"Don't be afraid, *mon petit ami.*" The man's eyes twinkled in the reflected light from the tavern and when he smiled, Étienne instantly felt at ease.

"First," Sebastian said. "We will get you some other clothes, perhaps even a hot meal. Then, most likely, we will let you go. But after *La Réale* sails."

"What about my job, my position?"

Sebastian's voice remained calm.

"Well, we will just have to ask the King to find you a good job aboard another ship."

Étienne looked up with confusion at the mysterious foreigner with his dark hair and smiling face. Could Sebastian be a pirate and also know the King of France?

"You have influence with King Charles?" he asked.

"*Mais Oui*!" Sebastian gave a light touch of camaraderie to Étienne's shoulder as he steered him toward the nearby tavern. "Doesn't everyone?"

Antoinette stifled a grimace as she pulled Étienne's threadworn tunic over her head. Though it was clean, it held a lingering odor of greasy meat, stale wine and sweat. But it would do. For the little time she must wear it, it would do.

Her companion, Anne de Bretagne, Duchess of Brittany turned to face her. She pulled back the hood of her cloak and dark silky tresses drifted down over her shoulders. "Are you afraid?" Anne asked.

Antoinette looked up at her friend, straining to see Anne's blue eyes in the dim light of the lantern on the nearby ledge. She forced her voice not to waver. It would do no good to frighten Anne any more than necessary, but she had to be honest.

"Of course I'm afraid. You've just committed a crime and I'm running away from my duty."

"No. You are on a mission for me," Anne insisted. "To ask King Henry to come to my aid. He is my last hope and I can't entrust my message to anyone else."

Anne smoothed a lock of brown hair from Antoinette's face and held it briefly within her fingers, then she opened the shade of the lantern to shine more light on her friend. Antoinette was indeed beginning to look like the young boy she had tempted into the alley.

Anne shook her head. "I did not think of this before. Your lashes are too long, your skin is too fair, too fine. I should have sent you disguised as my handmaiden to sail with Sebastian to Dover, but I cannot wait for his ship to travel the coastline. You must leave tonight for England. I will wait in Rennes for your message from Henry. Whether he comes or not, I assure you Cardinal Visconti will be gone from our land by the time you return."

"Charles' emissary will not leave Brittany, Anne. Even if you do not marry Charles, the Church is securely established here. They will never rest until they have complete control over us. If you are successful in forcing Visconti to go, some other vicar of the Church will take his place. Perhaps someone without even his disguise of diplomacy."

Antoinette took a shallow breath and willed herself to be calm. She would remember to be angry as soon as she stopped being so damned scared. How did things get so complicated? Two days ago she'd been in Rennes, safe within the walls of the castle. Now, no matter what Anne wanted her to believe, Antoinette felt like she was being sent into exile. Away from Visconti, away from her duty to Anne and to the Sisterhood.

"It will be all right," Antoinette said calmly. "By tomorrow I will be safe in England and in a few weeks I will be back with you in Rennes."

She brushed her hand across the rough fabric of the tunic, wiping away the certain-to-exist crumbs of bread and Goddess knew what. She would not even think about the vermin living deep within the warp and woof of the trews. Her small fingers fumbled with the rope belt at her waist and she cursed.

By the gods! Shc shouldn't have to suffer through this masquerade. Being a friend and counselor to the Duchess of Brittany and her status as a priestess was the only protection she'd ever needed. She pulled a small dagger from her shoulder pack, cut a length of the rope from her belt, then tied her hair back in a tight braid.

"I must go now or I'll miss the ship and this deception will be for naught." She bent down to the ground, picked up a handful of dirt and smeared it on her hands and face. "There, that should do it."

"Ugh! You're disgusting," Anne said. "Just like Étienne."

They shared a brief smile, but there was nothing either woman could say to ease the sadness of the moment.

Breaking the tension between them, Antoinette cautiously stepped out into the street and chanced a glimpse toward the tavern.

What was keeping Sebastian? Time and the ship would not wait.

As if summoned by her thoughts, Sebastian, tall and elegant, sauntered toward her. His cape billowed behind him in the stiffening breeze off the water. She could tell by his easy gait that he'd downed a cup or two of ale in the short time he'd been away. There was a slight look of mischief on the young Italian's face as he ventured into the light.

"Is the boy all right?" Antoinette asked.

"*Si, Señorina.* I have locked him in a room with a hot meal, a full jug of ale and the tavernkeeper's daughter. He will be asleep with a big smile on his face when I return." He handed her a small loaf of bread and a half empty bottle of ale. With a quick word of thanks she shoved both into a knapsack.

"Did you get his papers?" Anne asked.

Sebastian pulled out a rumpled piece of parchment from his tunic and waved it in the air.

"Orders signed by King Charles himself."

"*Très bien.*" Antoinette took the paper from Sebastian, stuffed it into her pocket. She slung her own black pack over her shoulder, then wrapped her arms around Anne and pulled her close. She would miss her friend, her sister, even the few days she would be away.

"Goddess be with you," she whispered, holding back the tears she felt creeping to the surface. "I will be back before the moon is full."

Anne caught her as she pulled away. "Wait!"

Unfastening a small brooch from her gown, she handed it to Antoinette. "Keep this with you. If you need me, send it at once."

Antoinette felt the intertwining silver circles as she clutched the talisman tightly in her hand. She nodded her thanks to Sebastian and stepped out from the alleyway into the faint light from the open tavern door.

Anne watched her friend walk across the uneven docks, amazed at the subtle changes in her appearance as she neared the ship. There was a difference in her stride, a relaxing of her stature. Ever so slowly Antoinette became a young gangly boy. For an instant she thought she saw Étienne Clement step onto the dock and stand beside *La Réale.*

The wind was suddenly still, like the first moment before a storm. Anne echoed the air's hesitation, holding her breath. Would Antoinette make it safely past the sentry, or would he be suspicious? The eyelashes would surely give her away.

Sebastian doused the lantern and placed his hand on his sword. He was ready to spring into action at the slightest hint of danger.

A tense moment passed. The sentry looked at Antoinette, then at the parchment, then back to Antoinette. Apparently satisfied, he waved her aboard. Without a backward glance, she stepped off the gangplank and onto the ship.

Anne sighed with relief. Tomorrow Antoinette would be standing on a dock in St. Albens, away from the menacing Cardinal. But Anne would not go back to Rennes as she'd promised; she would go directly to Langeais to speak with Charles. This insult to her sovereignty had gone on too long. She would surprise him and meet him in person to discuss the future of her country, without the interference of the Catholic Church.

Without warning, Sebastian's strong hand seized Anne's arm, pulling her back into the shadows. Before she could voice her protest, he motioned her to silence with a finger pressed against his lips. His pistol was cocked, ready. She heard the slow, almost silent scratching of metal against leather as he slipped his rapier from its sheath. Anne strained her neck to look beyond him to see what danger awaited them now.

Two soldiers dressed in the red and white mantle of the Cardinal's guard stood before the open tavern door. The light twinkled on the hilts of their swords. They turned toward the dark alleyway and slowly walked forward.

Impulsively, Anne threw her arms around Sebastian's neck and looked up into his eyes.

"Be silent," she commanded in a whisper. "Kiss me. Let the guards think we are lovers."

Sebastian smiled, his eyes wide with amusement. A more pleasant order he'd never received, although perhaps it was not the wisest one. He pulled her close, keeping his pistol hidden under the fold of her cloak, lowered his head and kissed her. His gaze followed the guards as they ambled past.

When they rounded the corner, the kiss lingered until Anne pushed away from an increasingly ardent embrace.

"Very convincing." Her dark eyes flickered as she straightened her gown. "Thank you for your cooperation."

Sebastian lifted his shoulder. "*Mon plaisir*, M'lady. I hope I did not offend. I *have* had a bit to drink. And well—"

She waved away his concern with the swift lift of her hand. "Our actions served our purpose. And we will not speak of it again."

Cautiously she walked into the light and threw her hood up to cover her hair.

"Now we must go. We must ride to Langeais."

Chapter 3

Château de Langeais - France

The heavy summer air was rich with the smell of smoldering frankincense.

Cardinal Marcello Visconti paced the marbled floor of his private chambers. His thoughts raced in anticipation. The damned witch had to be dead by now. He smiled to himself, his upper lip curling across his broad face in a small sneer of triumph. By now Anne's sorceress, Antoinette, was roasting in hell.

He'd planned her death carefully and cautiously, and at sufficient distance so no one could blame him or his office. She would die, away from the protective arms of the duchess and the far reaching eyes of her pagan Sisterhood on the Île du Seine. They were the root of his problems; a flock of godless heathens, women that cursed his life, and yet, made his otherwise solemn existence so exciting. And he could not touch them, for Anne de Bretagne's authority was still resolute. The Inquisition had no stronghold in her realm. At least not yet.

But with the witch out of the way he could ferret them out one by one. By destroying them, he would put an end to the Bretons' pagan beliefs, take down the shrines and monuments to the Goddess and replace them with the tall spires of Christianity.

He wished he'd had the pleasure of forcing a confession from the beautiful pagan priestess. He should have been the one to lay the blade to Antoinette Charboneau's pale and fragile neck. But, given time, there would be others.

The chase—the hunt—the capture—the torture. Visconti could feel the excitement mounting within him, his fists tightening with supreme pleasure as he thought of the intense moment when the condemned submitted to the inquisitor's influence.

"Confess!" he whispered under his breath.

Visconti wiped the sweat from his tainted hands onto his heavy velvet robe and breathed a small sigh of imperfect contentment. He had not been given the pleasure of absolving *Mademoiselle* Charboneau of her most grievous sin of heresy before she died. It was a shame that her impure soul had been destroyed before she was given the opportunity for absolution and salvation. Another sheep lost from the fold, he thought dryly. But one less pagan to burn.

Would it be wise to tell the King of Antoinette's possible demise? Perhaps not yet. He should wait until he heard directly from his mercenary. Yes. He would tell Charles that the woman had fled Rennes. Let the news of her death come from another source; from the King's spies or from Anne herself. Only he would know that the church had any hand in the witch's demise.

Visconti stopped in front of a gilded mirror and straightened the scapula resting on his thick shock of dark hair.

"Oh, Your Highness," he said, whispering to his reflection. A surprised and appalled look appeared on his mirrored face. He moved his hand to hover over his heart. "A most unfortunate incident has occurred—most unfortunate. The young counselor to the duchess has disappeared. What a tragedy!"

He shifted his weight from one foot to the other, his heavy vestment pulling him down like an anchor. The sooner Anne's ships and Brittany's treasury were at his disposal, the sooner his friend Cardinal Guliano Della Rovere would sit on the papal throne.

Della Rovere was a powerful and influential cardinal. He had tactfully arranged for King Charles to claim the duchess as his bride, assuring the loyalty of the Bretons toward the King. Visconti had arranged events within Brittany, but the headstrong willfulness of the young duchess and her steadfast refusal to accede her country continually impeded his plans. Until he found Anne's weakness. It was her undying love for the Breton people, a virtue to her credit and one he would use to his advantage.

Now that he had succeeded in taking away her support, both from Maximilian of Austria and from the Sisterhood, it was only a matter of time before she yielded to the King's demands to marry. Then Brittany and her treasury would belong to France and eventually to the Church.

Visconti was skilled at manipulation. It was ludicrously easy to shape Charles and his egotistical ideas of his heritage and bloodlines. As a descendant of the glorious Charlemagne, he believed it was his destiny to become Emperor of the Holy Roman Empire. But it was the hand of God guiding the hand of Visconti that would make it all happen.

How shocked Charles would be, Visconti thought, if he knew the depravity that ran rampant among the See of the Holy Church.

The Holy Father, Innocent VIII, had allied himself with Roderigo Borgia and with Lorenzo de Medici. Innocent was losing control of the Papacy as well as the government of Rome.

It was a perfect time for Cardinal Della Rovere, a dissenter among the Curia, to step into the Papacy. All Della Rovere needed to begin his campaign was Charles' money, his hungry army of mercenaries and total command of Brittany's impressive seaways. When the Princes of Europe elected Charles to the throne, instead of the Hapsburg King, Maximilian, Della Rovere could secure the Holy Office of the Papacy for himself. The crusades against the Turks could begin again and the treasures and the gold of the infidels would flow into the coffers of the Vatican like rich summer wine.

The Church would mount the expeditions to find the New World, to claim it in the name of Christ. Not the monarchs of Spain. Not the Knights of the Cross.

With a swish of his robe, Visconti motioned for the guard to open the massive oak door. The submission of Brittany could wait no longer. It was time to counsel the King on the wisdom of his imminent marriage.

ରା

A ray of sunlight streamed through a pane of the rose patterned window, flickering off Anne's needle as she carefully stitched the hem of a fine silk scarf. Tiny stitches caught the threads of the delicate fabric and bound the edges in a tight, even seam. She was honoring a time-old tradition, giving her husband a symbol of her purity and faithfulness to wear at their betrothal.

Mid-stitch she ran her hands over the smooth flawless fabric. Never in her wildest dreams did she imagine she would marry Charles VIII, the King of France, nor that she would be forced to be a wife to someone she did not love or desire.

And as for sharing Charles' bed? Anne grimaced at the thought. He was a repulsive little man. She would lock her bedchamber door and encourage him to keep a mistress. If she was artful and cautious, she might never have to bed him. It was, after all, a *mariage de convenance,* a marriage of politics for the King; the symbolic uniting of the duchy of Brittany with the House of Valois. A House long beset by chaos. Charles' father, Louis XI, had been a cruel king and his grandfather, Charles VII, had honored and then condemned the Maid of Orleans, Joan.

Since Charles had claimed her to be his queen nearly a year ago, her life had been in turmoil. In a desperate act she'd married Maximilian of Austria, but the marriage had been annulled before she had even seen her husband. The capital city of Nantes had been treacherously handed over to the King by her father's late advisor, and she had fled to Rennes.

When she'd come to Langeais to bargain with Charles, he had sequestered her, in the Loire Valley, away from her people and her court. No one had been allowed an audience. Hopefully Antoinette would soon send word that King Henry would intervene to prevent the marriage.

Anne lay her sewing in her lap, sighed and looked over at Miriam, her new lady-in-waiting. She was not a Breton, but a maid hand-picked by Charles as her companion. There was no one she could talk with, no one to notice the strangling, invisible chains that bound her to the side of the King of France.

"Is there anything M'lady requires?" Miriam asked. "Do you wish me to send for wine, open the window?"

"Oh, yes! Have the window opened. Send for fruit and wine."

Miriam rose, curtsied then disappeared behind the heavy oak doors with a swish of her long gown.

Anne listened intently until the sound of the tiny silver bells tinkling at Miriam's waist disappeared down the corridor, then she took a deep breath.

"Ah—Blessed Mother — I'm finally alone."

She swept away the snippets of thread from her green brocade overskirt and stood, spreading out the wrinkles of her day gown then waved her finger at her reflection in the mirror.

"You may rule my activities in France, Charles, but you will not rule me in Brittany. I am Anne de Bretagne," she said mockingly. "Sovereign of my own province. Ruler of my own heart."

Miriam burst into the room, excitement spreading across her face. "M'lady. You have a—visitor."

Turning, Anne looked behind her attendant. She knew her visitor would not be Antoinette, but it might be someone from home.

"It is a young bard, M'lady. His name is Alain Bodrot. He insists on seeing you." Miriam hesitated, a grimace spread across her plain featured face. "But—he smells more like a fish monger, than a troubadour."

Anne composed her response, not wishing to appear too anxious for news from Brittany. She chose her words carefully, knowing that Miriam would report her every word and action to Charles.

"We will be happy to grant him an audience. See to his comfort and cleanliness and I will accept him in the rose garden. Tell the bard he may play for my pleasure."

"*Oui*, M'lady." Miriam made a light curtsey and the bells at her waist tinkled in response. "I'll see that he washes behind his ears before he eats, even if I have to do it myself."

Anne opened the tall glass doors leading to her garden and smiled to herself. Alain was indeed a bard, a singer of tales and fables. He was able to come and go in the courts of England and Europe without question, and he was Anne's personal courier.

☙

The weather had been wet and dismal, yet the aroma of late summer roses filled the air with a tart sweetness. Anne strolled through her rose garden, lost in thoughts of home, until a rustle at the gateway alerted her and a tall valet appeared with a young man in tow.

Alain now suitably dressed, followed the servant into the garden, struggling to keep pace with the man's long legged stride. The bard's pale shoulder length hair bobbed up and down and the red feather in his soft-crowned velvet cap kept rhythm with his steps. He was dressed in appropriate court attire, and a cloak of blue silk, folded back over about his shoulders, softened the weight of an exquisite harp.

The attendant announced with all formality. "Alain Bodrot, Bard of Rennes to play for your pleasure."

"*Merci.*" Anne regally dismissed the valet with a wave of her hand.

Alain made a low, exaggerated bow and rose with a wide grin across his face, showing a slightly chipped tooth in an otherwise flawless smile. He was only a year or two older than she, nearly seventeen. He was well schooled and well traveled.

"I see you have been cleaned to a presentable state." She patted the edge of the bench and motioned him to sit beside her. In the seclusion of her garden, there would be no formalities between old friends and it was good to see a friendly face.

"Yes." He rubbed his neck. "Your housekeeper must have

sent the stable groom to wash my back. I hardly have a hide left."

She leaned back and looked him over. "What is this I hear of your taking up fishing as a profession?"

"Ugh—I spent the last two days on a cargo ship crossing the channel, then I traveled to Langeais with a market cart of fish. It was the only transportation I could afford from St. Malo."

"Well, you are exonerated, Alain." She touched his hand in friendship. "But tell me why you are making such haste. All went well, I assume."

Alain lowered his eyes. "I fear that our beloved friend has been lost."

"Lost?" Anne shook her head in disbelief. "How could she be lost? I personally saw her go aboard ship. I watched *La Réale* leave the harbor for St. Albens."

"*Oui.* She went aboard the ship, but it did not dock at St. Albens. I waited through three days of rain and squalls, but *La Réale* made no landing."

"But, Alain," she leaned close to him. "It must have docked somewhere."

"Not along the coast of England. I spent the last three weeks and all the money you sent with me searching from port to port along the coastline. She did not dock in England."

"Do you know where the ship was going?"

"I spoke with Sebastian when he returned from Dover. Her ship was scheduled to dock at St. Albens, but for some reason they made a change of route. He discovered that the ship headed west after it passed Cornwall. He believes it was sailing to Ireland." Alain hesitated, looking down at his shoes. "He said if he had known *La Réale's* destination, he would never have allowed her to board the ship."

Anne's turned her gaze away from Alain and took a deep breath of the still air. What cruel games Fate was playing on them, she thought. Because of her desire for freedom, her friend, Antoinette, might be dead, dashed to bits on breakers along the wild Irish coast.

Alain's soft voice retrieved her from her melancholy. "Sebastian also said the captain of the ship is a Templar, a Knight of Christ."

Anne twisted the rose in her hand until the bud snapped from the stem like a dry summer twig.

"Holy Mother," she sighed. "What have I done? I have placed Antoinette in the very midst of her adversaries. The Templars are opposed to everything the Sisterhood believes. He will kill Antoinette if he discovers who she is."

Alain took the dismantled rose from her hand and touched the young duchess' arm in consolation. "Antoinette is now in the hands of the Goddess. Only She can control her destiny."

Chapter 4

La Réale - At Sea

The tall ship headed for the distant horizon, a white speck against an azure sky. Her seasoned wood moaned as she plowed through the cresting waves, parting the sea with a salty spray across her bow. The billowing canvas sails, taut and full, strained against the rigging and pushed her westward.

Antoinette sat behind the mizzenmast, gazing out at the spreading wake behind the ship. There had been no land for what seemed an eternity. No birds, no ships and no hope of seeing either. She wondered how far she had traveled in these endless summer days that stretched from well before sunrise until long after moon set.

Why had everything gone so wrong? She should now be safe and secure behind the walls of King Henry's castle, waiting to return home to Brittany.

Antoinette let her body sway with the rocking of the ship and hummed an ancient prayer to please the gods of the winds. A cool breeze mixed with the warm July air, and kissed her face with a smell of freshness and sunshine. She smiled, knowing though she was far from her home, the Ancient Ones still watched over her. She wished they would tell her where *La Réale* was going and how much longer she had to pretend to be someone else.

It seemed ironic that she was a visible stowaway on a ship whose very sails boasted the red cross pateé of the Order of Christ, a branch of the secret order of the Knights Templar. These men secretly ruled the waters of the world and controlled the money behind the monarchs of Europe.

But the Templars were the least of her worries. She dared not tell anyone who she was, or why she was aboard *La Réale*. If the crew discovered she was not a mere boy—not Étienne Clement—but a woman, a priestess of the Goddess, it would mean her certain death. They would brand her as a witch for having deceived them so well and then it would begin again, the accusations, the interrogations and the threat of things worse than death.

It had been an unwise move, to leave Anne to defy both Cardinal Visconti and King Charles on her own. By leaving Brittany for longer than the fortnight she'd intended, Antoinette had put Anne in danger. But, she reminded herself, Anne was a survivor; she would listen to her heart and follow her intuition.

Taking in a long breath of the bittersweet air, Antoinette closed her eyes and settled back against the mast. The power of the wind vibrated through the ship's rigging, rhythmically humming a mournful song through the solid wood. Slowly, she began to slip toward a quiet place within her mind. It had taken her years to develop this peaceful center, and without it she would surely have gone mad.

With skilled precision, she calmed her thoughts and turned her attention back to the elusive task of learning her location. If she knew where she was, or even where she was going, things might not seem so hopeless.

From the narrow shadow of the sails, Antoinette watched the captain as he stood firmly on the quarter-deck, his legs braced against the rolling ship. He was a man accustomed to the sea. Tall and lean, his body barely shifted as the ship broke through the waves. She had heard his name before, DuPrey—Jacques DuPrey—but she could not remember where, or when. It really didn't matter. She knew enough about him to know she needed his knowledge to survive.

She studied his movements as he worked his mysterious instruments of navigation, aligning the polished wood cross-staff with the midday sun, then carefully transcribed his sightings to a leather bound book. The pages fluttered back and forth in the wind and the feather quill pen quivered helplessly as if it wished to soar to the heavens.

He wields his magic well, she thought, determined to learn his arcane craft. She wondered which god or goddess ruled over the magic of navigation, then decided it was best to pray to all the Ancient Ones. She needed as much magic as she could summon.

The gusty wind blew annoying wisps of hair from its ribboned bounds at the nape of Jacques' neck and he moved his hand to push them back. The lightweight fabric of his white cotton shirt stretched across his broad shoulders as he reached upward to take his reading and Antoinette wondered if his delicate hands were accustomed to handling the sword as well as his fragile instruments of navigation.

As he turned to transfer his notations to his *rutter*, his navigational log book, a small crucifix slid from its hiding place against his chest. It dangled from a black satin cord and glittered in the sunlight. Nonchalantly, he reached up to caress the solid and comforting shape. Was it a gesture of habit, she wondered, or an action of great faith?

He was soft-spoken, and even though he was not more than thirty-four or thirty-five, his manner demanded respect. He had certainly shown great patience with her and empathy with the crew during these past few weeks. She wondered why he never wore his official uniform, but always dressed simply in the dark hose and linen tunic of the merchant class.

Antoinette looked down at her stained clothing and rubbed at the spots of dirt held fast within the weave of the coarse linen tunic and longed for the touch of fine silk and velvet. She wondered as she looked at her rough and blistered hands if they would ever become smooth enough to handle fine fabrics again.

As though echoing her thoughts, Jacques sighed. He set down his pen and looked up at the sky, a frown darkening his otherwise cheerful face. Antoinette knew from his audible signal that she could speak to him without disturbing his work and she moved closer.

"The weather is clear today, *Monsieur* DuPrey." Antoinette smiled and followed his gaze up toward the rigging.

Jacques wrinkled his brow, then looked out at the whitecapped waves in the distance. "Yes, lad. But it may be the calm before the storm."

Her smile faded as she remembered the gale, the driving rain and the turbulent seas that kept them from docking at St. Alben's Harbor. She had been afraid when the ship's keel skimmed past the rocky coastlines of England and headed out to sea. Not of her death, for she knew that her life was in the hands of the Goddess, but the fact that once they passed the last remnants of land there would be little chance to escape.

"Do you see the high clouds to the west? They are pulling the wind toward them, building their strength as they travel across the water."

"How can you tell, *Monsieur*?"

"Knowledge and experience, Étienne. Most weather builds from the west." Jacques lifted his hand toward the horizon with a graceful gesture. "If you wish to be a navigator you must learn to read the skies as well as the sea and the stars."

"There is so much to learn."

Jacques looked at her with a wisp of a smile, his

expression suggesting that her statement was obvious. "*Oui* Étienne, that is why there are so few navigators."

Although Jacques was not a boastful man, Antoinette could tell he was proud of his accomplishments and took his commission aboard *La Réale* seriously.

La Réale, the King's ship, was the prize of His Majesty's fleet and the first of her class, running one-hundred feet from the bowsprit to the stern and thirty-five feet in breadth. Borrowing the best from both the Venetian and Portuguese, the Breton shipbuilders made a ship designed for long distance travel. Besides the mainmast and foremast, it boasted a mizzen and a bonaventure, sails designed to catch the shifting winds. Her polished wood and brass gleamed in the sunlight and the full sails glimmered with the sparkling reflection of the sea. But her genteel curves were deceptive, for within those swells were guns, mounted on each side of the deck and atop the mainmast lookout. *La Réale* was laden with goods and armed for protection.

A voice yelled from the main deck, pulling Antoinette away from her thoughts.

"Étienne! Étienne! Fetch the water bucket, boy. We're dying of thirst from settin' the sails."

She looked at the men with disdain. They could not be expected to respect her in her present disguise, but they had no right to order her about. She was not the ship's steward.

"Don't dally like a lady's maid now!" another shouted. "Be quick or we'll feed you to the sharks."

"Go on," Jacques said with a quick nod toward the lower deck. "We shall learn more about navigation at midnight. *Oui*?"

"*Oui, Monsieur.*" The men would be asleep at midnight and her studies would be uninterrupted.

She scurried down the ladder, collecting the water bucket from the lower deck. She was accustomed to the crew's light-hearted taunts and jests, but stayed away from fighting. If she were challenged, she knew she would lose more than the argument.

Antoinette tugged at the coarse britches that rubbed rudely against her skin and walked with the clumsy stride of a young man. Her body language, clothing and manner had been quite convincing. In the nearly four weeks at sea, through the sweltering mid-summer heat and tight living quarters, her imposture had not been discovered. Even Jacques, with whom she spent many hours as his apprentice, did not seem to suspect her age or her masquerade.

After the first week, Antoinette had been tempted to cut her hair; but instead, she secured her unruly brown curls with a tight braid. The loose linen tunic and baggy britches disguised her blossoming figure, but she could not hide the dark green eyes and long lashes that were all too feminine, even for a girl. She made a valiant effort to look aside as often as possible, hardly making direct eye contact with anyone. Her voice was soft like a lad entering early manhood, and she spoke in the short, easy sentences of the commoners, hoping she would not betray her vast education. Changed most of all was her skin. Once ivory white, it now glowed with the golden tones of long days spent in the summer sun.

Sometimes, the thought of spending another day in her unwashed clothes made her wish she'd stayed in France and faced Cardinal Visconti and his inquisition. At least the abuse he gave would end in death and not in the extended agony of sleeping near forty sweating, snoring sailors.

She had never been in the company of so many men. As a child she had played with the small boys who lived near the château, but they were not at all like these seasoned veterans of the sea, men with brine in their blood, who lived a hard life seeking adventure and fortune. Many were from the outlying provinces along the French coastline. Though some were the King's men, displaced from the long war with England, hired and well paid to work the ship, defend the Crown and ask no questions. Their silence suited her well, for few spoke to her, except when they needed something.

When the weather permitted, Antoinette slept topside and stayed out of the way of trouble. As she was Jacques' assistant, no one questioned her comings and goings. She would often steal a few minutes in his cabin for a quick washbasin bath, but her spirit longed for a hot luxurious soak, to melt away her ever-present aches and pains.

Antoinette returned topside with the fresh water bucket and held it as the men took turns drinking from a long wooden dipper. She looked at each one, wondering what sort of family or loved one waited for his return, and tried desperately to overlook their rugged appearances, to see them all as merely unpolished jewels in the Mother's heart.

She knew some by name but most only by reputation. Living in such close quarters, she knew how they slept, ate and cried. She'd heard their dreams and guessed their vices, and counted herself lucky she'd made a few friends and, as yet, no enemies.

There was Pierre, a burly man from the Burgundy coast, hot tempered and strong. François, from La Rochelle, shy and morose. And Paul, a mere boy, only a few years younger than she. Far too young, she thought, to serve on such a rugged ship. There were others with whom she shared the long days and nights at sea, but there was no one to share her secret.

Turning from the men, lost in her thoughts, she headed toward the hatchway with the remaining fresh water.

As if someone opened a door to winter, a cold chill engulfed her and she shuddered. Glancing up from the hatchway she met the harsh glare of the first officer, Lawrence Bernard.

Antoinette looked away, yet she felt his piercing eyes staring at her as she descended the stairs. She would need to be more careful, she thought. Bernard had the eyes of a hawk and the nose of a hound. If he caught her gaze too long, he would surely see through her disguise.

He was perhaps thirty years old, but he looked as though he had been robbed of his youth. He was not among the aristocracy of France, but he took the liberty of dressing in the rich brocades and fine fabrics of the nobility. The crewmen despised his arrogance, but obeyed his commands. She had heard he was ruthless with his discipline and that his whip-hand was fierce.

Antoinette thanked the Goddess that things aboard ship were calm. There had been no need for Jacques to call for discipline. Only Paul, the young steward who served the first mate, nursed a swollen black eye.

Antoinette surmised that Lawrence Bernard could vent his rage most accurately if desired. Had she known of his demeanor, she would have insisted on a more inventive disguise. Perhaps a friar's robe would have been a safer choice for her passage. She knew of the Christian church's rites and ceremonies, even learned a few words of their litany as a child when she listened to her mother's prayers. But that was long ago, before Antoinette was accepted into the Sisterhood, before she was taken from home.

Now, honoring the Great Mother and the Ancient Ones, her beliefs revolved around the ebb and flow of nature in all its myriad forms. She had dedicated her life and heart to the service of Brighid, the goddess of healing. Antoinette knew of other worlds, of fairy spirits and elementals, but the god of the Christians was as unfamiliar to her as the sea.

There was nothing she could do. She was at sea, aboard *La Réale,* and she must act out her masquerade as Étienne.

Once safely away from Bernard's scrutiny, Antoinette headed for Jacques' cabin. He would not be finished with his sightings until the sun was lower in the sky and she needed get away from the prying eyes that always seemed to follow her.

For much of the day Antoinette had the run of the ship. She knew when the men came and went, where things were stored, and most of all where she could be by herself to make her daily invocations to the Ancient Ones. She unlocked Jacques' room, then latched the door behind her.

The captain's quarters, located at the stern of the ship, just below the quarter deck, were large. Under a large shuttered window, an ornately trimmed berth dominated one entire end of the room. On each side of the berth, equally ornate storage lockers held Jacques' personal belongings, his dress clothing, shoes and sword. Secondary portholes along the port and starboard walls were decorated with intricate carvings. A small writing desk, table and chair hugged the interior wall. A navigation table sat against the opposite wall. It was a wonderful room, quite adequate for Jacques' work and her meditation.

Antoinette closed her eyes and listened to the rhythm of the sea as the waves lapped against the sides of the ship. It was a comforting sound, even though it meant she was still far from land.

"Mother Ocean." Her whisper was anxious. "Where does this vessel take your daughter?"

Antoinette's right hand strayed to her left forearm and to the pink crescent-shaped birthmark she kept well hidden. All the devotees of the Great Goddess bore the moon shape somewhere on their person or on their clothing. But it was a special gift to be born with the mark of the Mother, the mark of the moon. Right now Antoinette didn't want special gifts, she wanted answers — knowledge.

She opened her eyes to a misty vision.

A rugged shoreline was shrouded in fog.

Home. Surely this means the Mother is taking me home.

The shoreline faded and a shadowy figure walked toward her. It was the man from her visions. She could see him clearer than before though his features were still obscured by the swirling mists around him. This time his unbound hair fell straight and black, surrounding his face like dark clouds around a full moon. As he walked he extended his arms, beckoning her to come to him. Strange lines of a black and red design twisted around his wrists. His hands were bronzed, his fingers long and tapered. Not a gentleman's hands, but not a slave's.

I will go with him this time and leave this ship. His spirit calls me to cross over.

A sudden chill passed over her as she reached into the mists to touch him. She stopped, then shook her head. She had no time for this now. No time to deal with some mysterious spirit that pulled at her heart. She would follow her desires later, when she was safe and at home.

Waving her hand into the air, she dispelled the vision. The phantom and the mists disappeared. Sometimes the strength of her sight was too strong. Sometimes it overlapped into reality with a frightening force. She must be more careful lest the visions come at an inappropriate time.

At home, in Brittany, she had always been able to step back, to stop the unwanted visions and shield herself from the images she conjured. But this phantom—this man with the dark eyes—was becoming harder to resist. It worried her that she had been willing to give in to his haunting charm and follow him. But what if he was truly part of her destiny? What if she was refusing her fate by her stubborn resistance?

She had been taught that Fate was dictated by the gods and could not be changed. Though she believed this, Antoinette often wondered if Fate could be redirected like a ball rolling down a hill. A light nudge here, a shove there. Fate would change. The path would still be the same, but Destiny would be channeled to a path of her own choosing.

A movement from outside the door reminded her that Jacques would soon return. Her hands shook as she lit the small oil lamp on the table. Its sudden brightness chased away the eerie chill. She made a quick glance around the room. Except for the menagerie of objects on his navigation table, nothing was out of place.

Bemused at the disarray in the otherwise meticulous cabin, Antoinette crossed the short distance, her curiosity building with each step.

The table was layered with several navigational charts, their curling parchment edges held down with an odd assortment of silver and glass paperweights. Maps had always intrigued her, and at a very young age she had learned the shapes of Brittany, of England, Scotland and Spain from her brother Gaston's charts. He had once been a navigator, though now he lived in Scotland.

Sweeping her hands across the smooth parchment, she contemplated the familiar curving shorelines of Finistère, the inlet harbor of Brest and rocky coastline of Douarnenez. She could almost feel the lonely distance through her slender fingers as they followed the colored inks that labeled the land in broad swirling pen strokes.

How far away?

There were no scales of reference.

After some moments she realized this was the chart Jacques labored over every evening and often until dawn. The left and top sides of the chart were incomplete. Penciled outlines suggested a broad expanse of land at the top. On the left edge of the chart strange symbols and lightly penciled-in words were written in the vacant spaces. She traced the shape again with her finger. The shape of these coastlines were uniquely different. Perhaps this was their destination. She let the chart's image burn into her memory. A place without a name.

She felt a tingle in her fingers and pulled them away. This uncharted land was somehow important to her destiny.

Two bells signaled the changing of the watch and Antoinette ran for the door, hoping she had not spent too much time in her daydreaming.

She whispered a quick reverent prayer. "Thank you, Great Goddess, for your blessing." *And for one more glimpse of my future.*

She threw the latch just as the door flew open. Her breath vanished as she stood face to face with Jacques.

"*Pardon Monsieur,*" she said, attempting to recover her composure. "I—I was clearing for your supper."

He gave her a long sideways glance and stepped past her into the room, his broad shoulders brushing against her as he maneuvered the narrow doorway.

"Ah." He surveyed the room with a slight turn of his head. "*Bon!*"

"Shall I bring your wine before your evening meal?"

"Oh—please." Jacques began to remove his tunic and shoes, indicating that he would rest before dinner.

Antoinette turned away and moved toward the door as he disrobed. Something must weigh heavy on his mind, she thought. He never rested this early. But she would not ask him now. After his meal he would be more pleasant.

"*Oui, Monsieur*, I'll bring your wine." Antoinette lifted the latch and slipped through the door.

As the door closed, Jacques glanced around the room. The light from the lamp flickered in a steady flame, casting shadows of distant memories on the wall. He walked to a small writing desk and slipped a chain holding a silver key from around his neck. Unlocking the drawer, he placed his log book inside. He had no reason to doubt his steward's honesty, but this expedition was too important to leave anything to chance. Étienne's curiosity and thirst for knowledge about navigation was justified, yet Jacques made a mental note to watch the boy more closely. He would speak with Étienne and ask him about his family.

In their discussions, Jacques had been frugal with the secrets of his craft, offering, he hoped, just enough to pique Étienne's interest. He delighted in seeing the spark of wonder in the young lad's eyes as he spoke of the vast beauty and mysterious intrigue of the East. It reminded him of the adventurous anticipation of his own youth and his insatiable desire for a life at sea. He wished that he could explain to Étienne the stark loneliness which offset the pleasures. But that was part of the quest, and Étienne would need to learn those truths on his own. Those were the things that brought one into manhood. Now he was content to share the excitement of his past and enjoy the companionship of the boy on the long and tiresome voyage.

Something about him intrigued Jacques, opened doors to memories he'd long tried to forget. Étienne's eagerness brought back emotions that kept Jacques on the edge of his senses. When they talked and worked together it reminded him of old friends and his youth as he studied with the masters of navigation at Sagre. He, too, had started his career early in his life, and he was accepted into the Order of the Knights of Christ at the age of seventeen and into the Navigator's Guild. He had traveled to the remote ends of the earth for them and for the King of France. He had learned more in service to the Crown than he ever had at school in Sagres. It was because of his discoveries in navigation and his unquestionable loyalty to the Order that allowed him the privilege to command this important mission.

Perhaps, if this voyage proved successful, he would approach Étienne about coming with him to Sagres. After all, he was entitled to a respite from the King's service and a season at Sagres would be ideal. To discuss discoveries with the master navigators was just what he needed. Perhaps there would be new things to discuss with Señor Columbus.

For now, he must remember to stow the charts before he left the cabin and make sure his desk was locked. Étienne may be honest, but anyone aboard could be a spy. The Portuguese and the English would pay dearly to know the true destination of the King's ship.

He sighed in relief as he closed his eyes, settling into a well-deserved rest. Nothing was out of order, yet he could feel a sense of otherworldliness tugging at the edge of his mind. It was not a disturbing feeling, merely different. Like a prayer. Like a blessing surrounding him.

One of his hands strayed beneath his pillow, confirming the location of a small pistol. The other hand moved to his crucifix. He would be glad when this voyage was over. There was too much at stake to relax.

Taking a deep breath, he drifted away on waves of exhaustion, faintly wondering how he could smell the wild lavender and mint from his mother's garden so far away from home.

He dreamed, and in his dream he was not alone. He stood on a ship's deck, arms linked in friendship with another youth. They were on an adventure to see the world.

Chapter 5

Antoinette's work started before sunrise. Assisting the cook, she dispensed the morning meal of thick grain porridge, hard biscuits and heavily watered wine to a hungry crew. After the meager fare was devoured and the galley deck cleared, she would take Jacques his food.

Not to be idle, she took on other duties, one of those being the cook's assistant. This assured her that she would have at least one good meal every day and she could see just what she was eating.

This night, with the officers and crew fed and back topside, she ladled out her soup into a wooden bowl then sat down next to the cook. She closed her eyes briefly.

"Ye be a good Christian?" Cook's question roused her from a stolen moment of peace.

"Ah well." She shrugged her shoulders as she slid a piece of fat to the edge of her bowl.

"Myself, I been at sea so long I pray to them that controls the weather." Cook chuckled and sopped up his soup with an end of dried biscuit.

A kindred spirit, she thought. "How much further do you think we have until landfall?"

Cook lifted his eyebrows then rubbed his bristly chin.

"Well... we're carrying so many supplies, it's hard to tell. But the fresh water, aye, that's the key. There's about ten to fifteen barrels left, so I'd say we have about five or six days to landfall, then enough for the return trip."

He paused and took another sop of soup. "That's if my prayers be any good and the weather holds true."

"And if it doesn't?"

Cook took a swig of wine and shrugged his shoulders in mock resignation. "Then we best pray to all the Gods for their pardon." He ended their conversation with a loud belch and left the table.

ʚ

Near the change of the midnight watch Antoinette walked the mizzen deck. The winds were steady and from the west and a small crew held the late night duty. During these hot July nights, many of the men joined her on the deck. With the lower portholes sealed shut, there was little fresh air below and even less in the lower storage holds.

Tonight Lawrence Bernard commanded the midnight watch. She did not speak to him, though they greeted each other with a cordial nod. Antoinette had no desire to befriend *Monsieur* Bernard and no obligation to do so.

Antoinette slipped away to sit beside the mizzenmast to wait for Jacques. Leaning against the solid wood, she could feel the wind's force filling the lanteen sail, pushing them onward. The night sky was brilliant with stars and the waxing moon peeked from behind straying clouds above the eastern horizon. The wake from the stern churned the seemingly peaceful sea, marking the ship's passage with a white bubbly foam.

Antoinette dreamed of her beloved homeland, struggling to hold back her tears. She longed for the rich green hills and flowered valleys of Brittany, her country, her people. Torn by generations of war, shuffled between French and British loyalties, it was now at peace, but that peace had cost the lives of many friends and family members. Antoinette felt like a casualty of war as well. Only exile from all that she knew and loved had robbed Death of one more victory.

She reached for the comforting medallion sewn safely within the seams of her britches. The round brooch of fine silver that Anne had pressed into her hand as a parting gift gave her comfort. It was the symbol of the unending spiral of life, the Celtic Circle. A token for Antoinette's safe passage in England and a remembrance of Anne's friendship.

Antoinette felt as though her heart would burst with a sudden engulfing despair. She burrowed her head into her folded arms and rocked back and forth in rhythm with the ship, refusing to give in to the emotional turmoil that swelled inside her. If she ever allowed herself to feel the loneliness, feel the anger or the fear, she knew she would lose herself completely in remorse and self-pity.

A comforting voice broke into her sadness and a warm hand descended with a light pat to her shoulder.

"*Mon ami.*" Jacques stood above her.

How long had he been there? she wondered.

"I too, weep for my country and my loved ones. That is the sorrow of a life at sea."

His voice was soothing, yet oddly disconcerting. He looked out past the stern, letting the sound of the ship's wake finish his sentence. She knew he had left his homeland as well, but to serve his King and country. He would return to the welcome arms and gratitude of his regent.

"Come. It is almost midnight and we must take the reading on time."

Antoinette watched in silence as Jacques unrolled a chart onto the table, placing the lighted oil lamp on one corner, his ink well on the other and his astrolabe in the middle.

"You must tell me of your family," he said nonchalantly, arranging the instruments on the table. "How did you come to be an apprentice on this ship? Surely you must have longed for adventure to journey so far from home. And to be placed aboard the King's ship as a first assignment, you must know some high officials at court."

Something cautioned her to choose her words with care. With a deep breath, Antoinette regained her composure and began a reply, keeping her explanation close to the truth in case she was questioned again.

"*Monsieur.* I was too young to fight for my country with the King's regiment. But I have always had an adventurous spirit." She didn't mention that her grandmother had locked her in the cellar so she wouldn't run away to Alsasce to fight the Capetians. Antoinette refused to listen to her brother Gaston when he told her that women had no place in battle. He was a fool. She knew that the stories Ursule told of Joan of Arc were true. The maiden was one of the Great Mother's most steadfast warriors.

"I understand your frustration, *mon ami.*" Jacques' voice was deep and warm, and the rich tone brought a smile to her face. "I tried to fight for King Louis, but was barred from combat by my pending oath to the Navigator's Guild. My knowledge of the sea was too important for the Guild to risk me on the battlefields of Burgundy. But tell me who recommended you to this position?"

The twelfth hour sounded the change of watch and Antoinette thanked the gods for the well timed interruption. Jacques took up the astrolabe and turned it skyward. She would remain silent until he finished the midnight readings and by then she would have found an answer for his prying questions.

As he took the sightings through his quadrant, she watched his graceful movements, wishing that she could find a way to confide in him. He was becoming her friend, and he was kind to her.

Jacques worked for the better part of an hour, then he motioned for Antoinette to come over to the table.

"Here." He held up the shining astrolabe. "It's time you had a closer look at the stars."

Antoinette could feel his eyes following her movement. Does he know? she wondered, looking at his face as he placed the prized astrolabe in her hand and arranged her fingers on the cool golden metal. He held the instrument up in front of her and turned her around to look up at the sky.

As he reached up to steady her arms, Antoinette was certain she felt a hesitancy in his behavior, a slight delay in his movement, a sharp intake of his breath. Yet when his hands reached her arms his grip was firm and confident.

"Look through this." Jacques pointed to the viewfinder on the glass. "Find the brightest star in the Northern sky."

Looking through the instrument, Antoinette saw tiny lights blur past her eyes as she moved the astrolabe around the sky.

"Slowly." Jacques' voice was calm and instructive. He moved behind her, carefully guiding the astrolabe with precision to the correct area of the sky.

She could feel his warm breath on her neck as he positioned the instrument. Light shivers ran down her back and through her arms. She felt as though someone had walked on her shadow.

Abruptly, Jacques stepped back.

"I—I think I've found it," she quickly exclaimed as the bright light of the Northern Star finally beamed through the lens.

"Now, hold it steady. Place your finger on the pendulum where it rests on the scale."

Antoinette found the dangling ball and pressed it hard to the metal gauge.

"*Bon.*" Jacques said. "Now, tell me the number on the rule."

She held it out to the oil light with excitement. "It reads

forty-four degrees. Should we turn northward to adjust our course?" Antoinette checked her words as she saw the look of astonishment in Jacques' eyes. She had revealed more than she should know. He had taught her how to chart the sky with degrees and angles, but knowing their destination lay to the west meant she had undoubtedly studied his maps.

Jacques didn't give her the chance to explain. There was a cold look of disappointment in his eyes as he took the instrument from her hands. He placed the astrolabe securely in his pocket and slipped his hand around her arm.

"I think we should go below now. You owe me an explanation. You know too much about my craft."

She looked at Jacques with desperation. "*Monsieur,* I can explain. I beg you, hear me before you judge me harshly."

Her gaze locked with Jacques' momentarily, then he released her arm. He turned to collect his chart and instruments, giving Antoinette a slow sideways glance.

"Very well! Come with me to my cabin and I will hear you out. If what you tell me proves false, I will not hesitate to turn you over to the authorities when we return to France."

"*Mais oui, Monsieur.* I will speak nothing but the truth."

What a fool she had been, she thought, as they walked silently across the deck. Her pulse pounded harder with every step and she was sure that Jacques could hear her heart beat as loudly as the waves that slapped against the sides of the ship.

As they climbed down the hatchway ladder she felt as though she was descending into the depths of the sea itself. Her visions of freedom quickly faded.

It took an eternity to walk the few steps from the ladder to Jacques' cabin door. There was no way out of her dilemma.

Dear Brighid, she prayed as she lit the small oil lantern beside his door. *Will I ever learn to be silent?*

☙

Surely the boy had a good explanation for his education, Jacque reasoned. Étienne had been sent by the King to serve as his apprentice. He could not be guilty of treason. Perhaps he was from a ducal estate or the son of one of the King's men. This would explain his knowledge of navigation.

The thought of handing Étienne over to the Knights of Christ made Jacques uneasy. If they found Étienne to be a spy they would not hesitate to kill him. And he was too young to die; there was not even a shade of a youthful beard on his cheeks. And his eyes, they were too sad to be deceitful, his voice too honest to be criminal.

The sweet scent of cooking herbs wafting up from Antoinette's hair and Jacques felt disoriented.

Why did Étienne's nearness suddenly disturb him? he wondered. Why did he care so much for the boy?

Jacques pushed open the door to his cabin and the darkness sprang to light. He motioned for Antoinette to sit on the cushioned chair, then he walked toward the navigation table.

In his haste, he had once again left his charts unrolled. Placing another chart atop the desk, Jacques cautiously touched the stiff parchment, smoothing out the wrinkles. Then his expression hardened.

"Tell me now." He looked over his shoulder at Antoinette. "If you lie, it will only fare you worse punishment. How much do you know of this voyage?"

"*Monsieur*, I do not know what you mean. I only know that *La Réale* is a merchant ship."

"Stop your trickery, boy!" Jacques turned to face her. "You have too much education to be a novice apprentice. Were you a cleric before you signed onto his majesty's ship?"

"*Mais non, Monsieur*. It—it is not what you think." She paused in a long silence and contemplated her next statement with a great deal of indecision. "My *grand-mère* taught me to read and write and to interpret maps."

She could tell by the hard look in his eyes this was not enough. "My uncle is a navigator. He is a member of your Guild. I learned about the stars and about navigation from him."

"One of my guild?" Jacques slammed his hand down on the table, knocking over an empty wine glass. "Who teaches a youth the secrets of navigation without the Guild's permission?"

Jacques crossed the small room in a quick stride and took hold of the collar of her tunic, looking into her eyes with a piercing stare of which she could never have believed him capable. "Did he take you as apprentice? *Parlez-moi*! Speak to me!"

Antoinette was silent, his sudden anger frightened her. How could she explain? The questions came too fast for her to form any coherent lies.

"Who is he?" Jacques let go of her tunic in a sudden shift of emotion. "Tell me his name and I might believe your story." He waved his arm toward the door. "Or it's straight to the prison hold."

Perhaps she could still bluff her way through this ordeal. "My uncle is Gaston Charboneau."

Jacques let out a soft laugh and threw back his head. His teeth gleamed in the lamp light as a smile crossed his face.

"Charboneau? He, of all our navigators, would be the most unlikely person to take on an apprentice without our permission."

He walked calmly to his writing desk, unstopped a bottle of claret and slowly poured himself a glass of the wine. "A well-informed spy would know of Charboneau's reputation." Jacques drained the glass of claret with a swift tilt of his head, then looked once more into her eyes.

"*Monsieur*, I assure you that I am not a spy, but a loyal subject of King Charles."

"No!" He stepped before her and grabbed her by the shoulders, bringing her up to face him. "You are *not* a well informed spy or you would know that Gaston is now is exile and that we went to school together. Furthermore, his only sibling is a girl too young to have a child your age."

Jacques stared into her eyes, then with a sudden jerk released his grip and stepped back.

"*Mon Dieu!* You—you are the young sister!"

Antoinette calmly returned his gaze, holding her head and shoulders erect. It was too late to back down now. He knew her name, knew her family.

"*Oui, Monsieur.* I am Antoinette Charboneau."

They looked at each other in silence for many moments then Jacques sat down on the edge of his berth, debating his new discovery. It was beginning to make sense. His instincts told him that the boy was not a simple apprentice. He attributed Étienne's graceful movements and naiveté to his youth. Jacques breathed a sigh of relief. He was not, after all, attracted to the young boy Étienne, but to a lovely young woman. And she was a Charboneau.

Jacques rose and walked to his locker. He took out a silver goblet, poured it full with claret and offered it to Antoinette.

"You have my complete attention, *Mademoiselle* Charboneau." Her name slid off from his lips in a slow rhythm.

Antoinette sat down and stared into the oil lamp-light. She felt a close kinship with a moth fluttering near the flame. For the first time since she left Brittany she found it difficult to control her emotions. The days leading up to her departure had been too hectic to concentrate on fear. Now, one person held her life in his hands and she wanted so badly to trust him, to pour out all her frustration and anxiety to someone who cared.

"Please, tell me why you are here." His voice was warm but insistent when he spoke. "What evidence do you have that you are not a spy?"

Antoinette looked down at the trembling glass in her hand. She wondered how well he knew her brother, Gaston, and if so, would his honor toward a fellow navigator be stronger than his honor to the king. She took a deep breath and raised her head and looked resolutely into his eyes. She had no choice but to trust him.

"I am a member of the household of the Duchess. I am a companion to Anne de Bretagne."

Jacques leaned forward. His hand braced against his desk steadied him against the rolling ship and the turbulent thoughts coursing through his mind.

"I am not one of her maids of honor; I am her most trusted friend." Antoinette took a sip of the claret, hoping for the right words to explain her situation, silently praying for guidance. "It is because of my association with Anne that I am now exiled from my home." She continued softly, slowly, her words weaving her story into intricate patterns, telling him of the events that led her to *La Réale's* deck.

Jacques looked at her inquisitively, his pale blue eyes twinkling in the lamp light. Antoinette had his full attention. She knew she could cast a spell to make him forget her deception, but she needed to save her magic for greater emergencies.

"*Monsieur,*" she whispered, leaning forward in her chair. "The things you ask me to tell you may put your life at risk. I beg you to accept the fact that I am here, and—that if I live to see land, I will leave this ship and your life forever."

Jacques wrenched his eyes away from the glance that held him. He looked through the opened porthole into the dark night, trying to still the myriad questions running through his mind. Things had already gone too far. As a loyal officer, he should stop her now and turn her over to his first mate, but he owed too much to her family to betray her without thought.

There was no doubt in his mind that she was a Charboneau. She shared her brother Gaston's rugged spirit, his strong will and determination, and hopefully, his integrity. As he listened to her words, he recalled a voice from his youth and remembered the delicate features of Antoinette's mother.

"Marguerite." Jacques said her name in an inaudible,

reverent whisper. Then he focused his attention on the young woman beside him. “I am sure we both share enough secrets to sink this ship, but I must know beyond doubt that you are a victim of circumstances and not a spy.”

He slowly crossed the room, then turned to face her. “Are you aware that I am personally employed by the Navigator’s Guild to map this voyage?”

“No, *Monsieur.* I told you. Who you work for is none of my concern.”

“But you *have* studied my charts.” He turned toward the objects of discussion. He fingered the chart’s edge, then hastily rolled them all and tied them together. He could not risk her knowing more, not until he knew where she placed her loyalty. “Do you have any idea where we are going?”

“Yes. A fool could tell we are always heading west, always steering northward. But you must believe that I am not here by my own wish and I would very much like to know where I will be allowed to disembark.”

Jacques looked at her with growing uneasiness, not wanting to crush her hopes for returning to France quickly. He paused for a moment, not sure if he should tell her the whole truth.

“First, you must tell me how you got aboard this ship and why you are posing as my apprentice.” Jacques' voice was insistent. He crossed the room and circled behind her, this time looking at her as a woman and not a young boy. He settled once again on the edge of his berth and looked directly into her eyes. “I can be trusted with your secrets.”

Could he? she wondered. Could he be trusted with the knowledge that Anne listened to the counsel of a pagan priestess? Would he understand that the King’s counselor was attempting to manipulate the Crown’s power for the Church?

No. She could not tell him all the secrets. Not yet.

“I came aboard your ship simply to cross the channel,” she said. She thought of young Étienne and how wickedly she pretended to seduce him and how Anne and Sebastian had taken his clothing. “I borrowed Étienne Clement’s position with the full intent to redeem his name and honor as soon as I landed safely in England. We did not consider the possibility that the ship would never make landfall.”

“We, *Mademoiselle*? You said ‘*we*’. Who is your companion in this charade? To whom do you owe your allegiance?”

How much more could she tell him, she wondered and still keep her life and her word of trust to Anne and to the Sisterhood?

"I know you are a devoted follower of the Christ and I am hesitant to speak further of my beliefs."

"If I am to judge your innocence or guilt, I must know who has placed your life in such a precarious position. I have traveled to places where there are so many beliefs that men have personal names for god, and worship fire. I will not judge your faith, unless it directly affects the mission of this vessel."

She hesitated, searching for the right words, the right way to tell him everything without placing her head on the block. If she told him she was, by the Cardinal Visconti's definition, a heathen and a witch, she would surely hang, even if he determined she was not a spy. A knot of confusion writhed in her stomach as she looked at Jacques' expectant face.

Mother help me, she prayed.

A light breeze came in through the porthole and flickered the lamp's flame. Then a whisper of calmness enveloped her and Antoinette knew that Jacques could be trusted.

"Very well, *Monsieur.* You will have the truth. I am a member of the Sisterhood of the Moon, a priestess of the Great Goddess, the Great Mother. I am a humble servant to the Ancient Ones, oath-bound to use my healing skills in the name of Blessed Brighid."

Antoinette paused and stared at Jacques, looking for the signs of shock and disgust she saw so often, but his face was expressionless and patient. "I am not only Anne's friend, I am her counselor and advisor. She has placed me aboard your ship."

He leaned forward and looked at her with disbelief. Not at her pronouncement of her faith, or that Anne de Bretagne would willingly listen to a pagan, but at the fact that there was a heathen in the household of Guillaume Charboneau, the late King Louis' most honored champion *d'ordonnance.*

Jacques touched the crucifix hidden beneath his shirt. "But your mother, Marguerite and your brother Gaston—they are very devoted to Christ and to the Catholic Church. And your father... he fought at King Louis' side for the glory of France. Why ... you even have a French name, not a Breton's."

"*Oui.*" She sighed. "Marguerite refused to continue the matriarchal lineage into the Sisterhood when she married my father. She promised her son would be raised as a Christian, as a Frenchman and not as a Breton.

"Only by promising her first daughter to take her place with the Sisterhood was she allowed release from her inherited legacy." Antoinette paused and turned her eyes away from Jacques. She forced the sad memories of her early childhood away. "I was four years old when my father died, then I left home when I was ten. I have not seen her, or Gaston, in many years."

Jacques was intrigued. Even beneath the layer of dirt on her face he could see Antoinette's delicate features. She was indeed Marguerite's child, yet she held an air of mystery that made her unique. She was the child he had watched playing with her toys, the child he had given little attention when he had visited the Charboneau home.

Jacques recalled more distant memories. Marguerite had once shown him a great kindness and now, he realized, he owed it to her daughter to hear her explanation. The circle had come full round.

The sounds of the waves against the hull filled the awkward silence hovering between them. Antoinette looked down at the neglected glass of claret in her hand then took a long, slow drink. She must tell him everything before she lost her nerve.

"Until Duke François' death, my grandmother, Marguerite's mother, Ursule, was his housekeeper and companion. She is also a High Priestess of the Sisterhood, placed in the Duke's household to counsel him, as I do Anne. Ursule taught me respect for the old traditions, the rituals, the magic and the invocations to the Ancient Ones."

Jacques watched her intently, the intoxicating haze of the claret disappearing with the intensity of her story. The question of her belief was not a problem to him. He long suspected the ancient Druid traditions were still practiced in Brittany. The people openly worshipped the pagan gods and their local saints along with the Christian ones. But until now, his suspicions had been unconfirmed. Jacques knew his beloved Christ was not accepted by all men. There were many other ways to worship God.

"You see," Antoinette continued. "We believe the essence of life is in everything. It is in the earth, the wind, the stars, the sea. The powers of the elements and the Ancient Ones can be summoned to heal, to protect or to destroy. They are to be honored and respected, for they protect and nurture their earthly children."

Jacques understood much of what Antoinette told him, but his mind wandered as she spoke. Not to his travels, but to Antoinette's enchanting beauty.

As he looked closer, he wondered how he could have missed such elegance. He marveled at her rich, fawn-like grace as she moved her hands to emphasize a word or to make a point. And though her hair was windswept and loosely tied behind her neck, he could not help but imagine it flowing over her shoulders.

Jacques shook his head to clear away the fantasies he was beginning to create. "Why were you going to England?"

"To petition King Henry to come to Anne's aid. He does not care for Charles and would surely help her." She laughed lightly. "My voyage was supposed to be short."

Antoinette's explanation was far from what Jacques expected but it was believable, and it was no mystery why King Charles wanted her out of the way. He needed no new problems with the Pope. If Innocent VII knew the future Queen of France was counseled by a priestess of a pagan goddess, he would not hesitate to use that information to further divide the clergy.

Jacques could not help but wonder why Anne was involved in this religious turmoil. "Why does Anne listen to your counsel? Why does she choose to continue with the old ways, instead of embracing the view of the Church?"

"*Monsieur,* Anne is a Breton! She believes as her ancestors believed."

"*Mais oui.*" Jacques said. The Bretons were a proud and independent people. Their Duchess Anne de Bretagne, would be no different.

Chapter 6

Château de Langeais - France

"You will not speak to me in that manner!"

King Charles slammed his hand against the thick oak dining table, rattling the plates in his anger. He glared past the flames of the flickering candelabra, rising from his chair to look straight on at his adversary. His voice was deep and commanding. "Not now! Not ever!"

Anne had held her words over dinner, trying to gather enough courage to confront him with her news of Antoinette. Now was the time to see how much his Highness actually knew. She changed her voice to a cool resonance, attempting to calm his agitation. She was glad that they were dining alone and that he could not see her hands tremble as she grasped them tightly in her lap.

"My Lord, perhaps I have not made myself clear. My subjects are *my* concern and I do not appreciate your advisor's interference in the affairs of my Breton court."

Charles waved his hand to dismiss the servants in attendance. He saw no reason to let them carry tales throughout the castle. The atmosphere in the elaborately decorated dining hall was suddenly close and oppressive. Ignoring Anne's determined face, he walked to the window and pushed it open wide. Perhaps the night air would moderate his temper, then he would be able to make it through the meal without blunder.

This lovely black-haired vixen was pushing him farther than any woman ever dared. Why did he let her get away with it? First she defied him in battle and now she reprimanded him in his own dining hall.

Casually, he looked back toward the graceful maiden sitting at the end of the long dining table and quickly remembered why he was willing to give her almost anything in his power.

She was so delicate, so desirable, too good of a prize for a man as unattractive as himself. Her demure countenance—when she was obliged to show it—could win any man's desire and make him do her bidding uncontested.

By God and Heaven, he thought. He had even delayed the wedding to suit her temperament.

This stubborn and willful young girl was the regent of her own province and would soon become a powerful headstrong woman, and the Queen of France. How could he ever make her understand that Visconti looked out for the good of the crown that she would soon share?

He breathed in the heavy damp air drifting in from the window, restraining his words until the last servant disappeared behind the ornately carved doors. Slowly he turned to address his future wife.

"Cardinal Visconti looks out for our best interests. He watches the affairs of the Crown. That is his obligation. When you are Queen, he will— ."

"He will *not* be my advisor!" Anne stood, meeting Charles' gaze with a look of defiance. She would have him know that she would not be manipulated. Especially not by a repulsive little man like Cardinal Visconti. "You have made it very clear that *my* choice of counselor is not welcomed in Your Highness' court."

Anne's gown swayed with the shifting of her weight as she

walked around the table to meet her opposition. It was time she knew what kind of man she was marrying and this was the moment to test his strengths, to find out if he ruled the throne or if the Church had already usurped his power.

Charles stood his ground, watching her walk the distance, noticing the slight limp that marred her otherwise flawless beauty.

Anne stopped an arm's length from him, her blue eyes set sternly in her demanding face—a face that could entice a man with a smile as easily as it could send an army to war. She will be a powerful queen, Charles thought, but if she was looking for a confrontation now, he would certainly oblige her. He set his chin, holding back thoughts of a possible married life in hell, and proceeded with all the elite decorum he possessed.

"I thought this topic of your friend, Antoinette, had long ago been set aside. You agreed she would be detached from the court."

"*Mais oui.*" There was a touch of animosity in Anne's voice. "I agreed that she would not be counsel in my court, but I never believed that you would silence her words with murder."

"What?" Charles' controlled features could hardly hide the surprise at her impudence. "I gave no orders for her execution."

"I do not speak of execution, my Lord, but assassination."

Charles stifled a flush of anger and he took on a practiced stance of authority.

"*Mademoiselle*, we have been through this debate before. I find your implications in very poor judgment. Do you know what you are saying—and furthermore have you forgotten that *I* am the King and that you are not *yet* Queen?"

Holding back his growing temper he turned toward the window, away from the accusation in her fiery blue eyes. Outside, the Loire River drifted on in silence, a light rain speckling the surface of the unblemished water.

"Charles," Anne said, softening her voice as if to soothe a babe. "I am well aware that you are King. What I wish to know is—if you are still the ruler?"

"*Pardon*?" Her statement brought Charles' thoughts back into the room. "What did you say?"

"Do you *know* what goes on within your court?" she demanded. "Do you know who is making the decisions *for* you?"

Oh, Grand Dieu! Will this woman ever back down?

"*Mademoiselle*, you go too far!"

"*Mais non*!" Anne took a step toward him, fully aware that if she did not proceed with caution, Charles could have her neck on the block before sunrise. Even though she was the future queen, she was not safe from execution. "It is best we speak of these things before we go any farther."

"Very well." Charles poured a goblet of wine from the nearby decanter. He watched the blood red wine fill to the top of the silver rim, wondering how he should react to her questioning. "What are you implying?"

Anne gave an unnoticeable sigh of relief as he motioned for her to sit beside him and proffered her the wine. *Will he listen? Open his heart, Beloved Mother. Make him see the wrong that has been done.*

She slowed her breathing, choosing her next move carefully. "My Lord, Antoinette vowed to me that she would resign herself from the affairs of court. She was making arrangements to remove her belongings from Rennes. But Visconti wasted no time making decisions in your absence. Were it not for the whisperings of the servants, Antoinette would have been..."

She stopped, realizing that she must stay with the facts and not let her emotions cloud the issue. "Antoinette left Rennes, but when she attempted to leave Brittany from St. Malo, Visconti's guards were already in position at the docks. She was forced to leave her homeland as a fugitive."

Charles listened patiently, his eyes taking in the beauty of the woman who so passionately told him a story quite different from Cardinal Visconti's uneventful accounts. He kept his voice even and non-committal when he spoke.

"Where do you get this information?"

Anne hesitated. She could not tell him that she was there with Antoinette. That she and Sebastian hid from the guards and watched Antoinette board *La Réale*. But she must tell him the truth. She would not begin their relationship with lies.

"My Lord, Brittany is still my country. My ears and eyes are everywhere."

Charles nodded his head. He understood her need for a network of informants. He possessed his own spies throughout the Empire.

"Ah. But, M'lady, you accuse the Crown of murder. This you must explain."

"Antoinette boarded the ship, but she did not cross to St. Albens. I have received word that the ship she boarded headed out to sea." She waited for any response to her words. When none came, she placed her hand lightly on his arm. "Charles, she was on *La Réale —your* ship."

This time there was no mistaking his reaction.

"*Mon Dieu!*" Charles' chair tumbled back against the stone floor as he lifted his weight. "*Mon Dieu*! What will you women do to me?" He paced the length of the table. "How in the name of heaven did she get aboard *La Réale?* Why?"

"The how is—unimportant." Anne stood slowly, keeping her eyes level with his. Then she turned and walked to the window. The rain was falling in light transparent sheets. A summer storm was settling over the small houses across the river. "The why—was in desperation," she said with a heavy sigh. "A desperation brought on by *your* counselor."

"So—we are back to Cardinal Visconti."

"*Oui*, Cardinal Visconti." She almost spat his name. "Do you deny his involvement in my affairs?"

"No." Charles stopped and looked straight into Anne's accusing eyes. "No, I do not deny his interest to protect the Crown and to some degree I do not deny his watching Antoinette's movements. Although his explanation did not include interference by his guards— other than a watchful eye for her departure from Brittany."

"Then you *knew* she left on *La Réale?*"

"No, I know she left Brittany. Visconti made no mention of *La Réale.*" Damn the man, he thought. The cardinal had sealed Antoinette's fate as surely as if he swung the executioner's ax. Charles reproached himself for allowing Visconti to get involved with Antoinette at all. But he could not admit this to Anne.

He had deliberately and painstakingly kept *La Réale's* mission from the meddling eyes of the Church. They need not know *all* his business. Now, with Antoinette's involvement, he wondered if the mission had been discovered by the Sisterhood or by the Church. Either way it was doomed to failure.

"Anne, you must believe that I had nothing to do with Antoinette's forced exile." His voice was conciliatory as he walked to stand beside her at the window. Together they overlooked their domain. He wished that he could put his arms around her and enjoy the evening of rain together. But the privileges of a husband were not yet his, and he would not tread where he was not invited.

Charles turned his thoughts back to the problems at hand. "Your friend brings these events upon herself with her archaic ideas of gods and goddesses. I heard how she goaded Visconti with her visions and prophecies."

Anne delicately withdrew from his side and paced across

the room to stand by the blazing fire. The air was suddenly chilly. She knew he was right. Antoinette's tongue was sharp and her resolve unwavering. If she had just stepped quietly aside and disappeared into the country, she would have been less of an outward threat to Charles and to the Church.

Anne could never begin to explain the intricate balance the Goddess held on all events or the necessity of leaving the religious practices of her people alone. She searched for a word to describe Antoinette's strong will, but none surfaced. A headache began to swim around her forehead and she pressed her fingers to her temple to ease the pain, then turned to Charles.

"Antoinette is gone. If there is nothing that you can do to insure her safe return, surely you will at least deal with Visconti's offense."

Charles crossed the room, acutely aware of Anne's sudden weakness. He placed his hand beneath her elbow and escorted her to the soft padded chaise, then sat beside her. "*Ma petite chère*, you have my word that I will look into the matter."

"Charles." Her voice was strained from the release of so many emotions. "If we do not resolve this issue, how can we ever hope to build a union of trust and love between us?"

He looked at her with anticipation. Did she really hope to love him? "Anne, love is not something that is required to satisfy our responsibilities to the Crown."

"Perhaps, not. But trust, Charles—we must learn to trust each other or we will have nothing."

"Yes," he said, boldly reaching to smooth a stray lock of hair from her forehead. "We will work on the trust and perhaps love will surprise us."

Chapter 7

La Réale - At Sea

The ship's bell broke the silence of the sultry night air. It was early morning and hard to concentrate. The interview with Jacques seemed to go on for hours as Antoinette attempted to explain the delicate balance of power that Anne maintained within her Duchy in Brittany.

"With a careful blending of the teachings of the Catholic Church—honoring the Blessed Virgin Mary and the Great

Goddess side by side—both the nobility and the peasants were satisfied. At least, until Cardinal Visconti stepped in as Counselor to the King. Now the Church demands a stop to all the old practices."

"Wait," Jacques interrupted her, leaning forward, his hands on his knees. He sat opposite her on the edge of his sleeping berth. "This Goddess that you speak of, you call her Brighid? I have heard of her before. St. Brighid is the patron saint of England. Do you mean to tell me that they are one and the same?"

"Not exactly." Her explanation would take careful thought. This man was a Christian.

She straightened her back against the chair and handed the empty wine glass to Jacques for refilling.

"When St. Augustine went to England hundreds of years ago, Pope Gregory instructed him to replace the Celtic customs with Christian tradition so the people would accept the Christian church with greater ease. He transformed our gods and goddesses into the saints of the church. He replaced our Sabbats with Christian holidays and built abbeys and churches at many of our sacred meeting places." Antoinette smiled, and her eyes sparkled with mischief as he handed her the filled goblet. She lifted it in a toast.

"Thanks to Gregory, many things were preserved that might have been lost or destroyed. You see, in the Celtic tradition the Great Mother is known by many names. I honor her as Brighid, the patroness of healers. The Christians see her as the Blessed Virgin. She has been known as Hera, Juno, Isis and many other names throughout the centuries."

She took a sip of the wine and looked at Jacques, trying to determine if she overstepped her boundaries. She could tell that her foreign ideas touched a sensitive nerve in him and that his thoughts were elsewhere.

"I do not expect you to completely understand my explanation. These things are not widely known among the followers of the Christ."

Jacques sat on the edge of his berth and looked past her. He had said nothing disparaging and she was surprised he had not taken her by the scruff of her collar and hauled her topside to punish her blasphemy and arrogance. But Jacques was not like other Christian men she had met. Perhaps he was a mystic, like her brother Gaston was alleged to be.

After a long moment, Jacques leaned back against the carved wooden edge of his berth. He stretched out his long legs and folded his arms across his chest. Antoinette looked deeply into his eyes, but could not read his thoughts.

"*Monsieur*, I have told you all I can. You—you look as if you don't believe a word."

Then he leaned forward. "*Mon amie*, I have traveled to many countries, witnessed many things on my voyages. I believe you. But, I must tell you that I find it uncomfortable to discuss such deep philosophies with women."

Antoinette gave a light laugh. "Then you must never have spoken with my *grand-mère*. She is widely known for her speeches."

A grin spread across Jacques' face. "Oh yes, I knew your *grand-mère*. I spoke with her on many occasions and on most of them I ended up on the wrong side of her walking stick."

He picked up a small container of dried fruit, uncapped it and offered a portion to Antoinette. She shook her head in refusal. She looked at him with wide curious eyes.

"In my youth, I would often call on your family. Gaston would invite me home with him from Navarre."

Antoinette was surprised. She had no idea Jacques knew her family or that he knew Gaston. No one had ever spoken of Jacques. Then she realized that if he had visited Rennes when Gaston was in school, she would have been a small child.

In truth, she would not recognize Gaston as a fully grown man, for she had not seen him since she was ten years old, before she went to Nantes with Ursule.

"Is he still alive?" Jacques rose from the berth and slowly paced the room.

"Yes." She followed him with her gaze. She felt no need to tell him of Gaston's present life in exile. She did not want to think of Gaston at all, the memories were still too painful. "As far as I know."

They were both silent once more. Antoinette looked past the darkened window and Jacques took advantage of his position behind her to look at her features in the lamplight. For the first time he looked at the soft shape of her shoulder and the curve of her neck, sweeping upward to her chin. He noticed the rich texture of her hair and the delicate shape of her ears.

Abruptly, he chided himself for thinking of her so intimately. She was just a child, half his age at best.

"Tell me of Anne," he said, deliberately setting his other thoughts aside. "How is she able to keep the Church from interfering in her government?"

Antoinette was thankful he had changed the subject. She did not wish to speak of her family. Instead she told him of the events that occurred before she left Rennes.

"Anne did not make religious beliefs an issue at her court. She made a deliberate effort to keep Church and State separate. She did not encourage or discourage any beliefs. Anne is very private about her philosophy and few people know her true feelings about the Goddess.

"It was when Cardinal Visconti, King Charles' emissary, arrived in Rennes that we began to have problems. He stirred up the long extinguished fires of heresy and threatened to bring his new Inquisitors into Brittany. Anne let him rant and rave, knowing he had little power to enforce his threats."

Antoinette stopped and took a drink of the wine. She could feel her anger at King Charles building by the moment and knew she must temper her feelings in front of Jacques. Until she knew how much allegiance he owed to the King, she would not speak against him.

Jacques' face was expressionless, though she knew he listened with rapt attention. "Anne is young. But I hear she can be persuasive."

Antoinette smiled, remembering the many arguments she had lost to Anne's quick wit.

"Yes, she will resist the King until he agrees to Brittany's continued independence. Before I left, Charles was insisting that if he dies before her, Anne must marry the heir to his throne. Consequently, if Anne dies without any children, Charles will have Brittany entirely."

Antoinette looked at Jacques, leaning slightly forward, giving emphasis to her words. "Obviously this arrangement is not to my liking, for it places Anne's life in constant danger. At any time, Charles can secure her death and have Brittany without question."

"Do you think him so very ruthless?"

"It is Cardinal Visconti that I do not trust. He insists the Bretons give up their *Pardons*, their tributes to their local saints, and that they must embrace the Catholic Church completely. Anne will never agree to this. I have told Visconti as much and—well, you see where it has landed me."

Jacques nodded his head. "Has Anne made her position clear to the King?"

"Yes. He publicly acknowledged her wishes. He told her he would not allow the Church to disturb the Breton's manner of worship, but in exchange for his leniency I must leave her counsel and she must cut all ties to the Sisterhood.

"When it became apparent that Visconti planned to enforce Charles' demands, Anne decided to send me to seek King

Henry's aid. I boarded *La Réale*, the storm came and the rest of my life in now in your hands."

Antoinette drank the last of the claret with a swift backward tilt of her head and handed the glass to Jacques.

He had listened patiently to her story, already knowing much of the political background about the marriage, but none of the religious intrigue. He let her give her account of the events, absorbing her every movement, the toss of her hair, the slow blink of her deep green eyes. When she began her story, he wondered how this small girl could be involved in such a grand scheme. But now as he looked at her, sitting across from him, he saw a woman with strong confidence and a deep commitment to her faith. Antoinette Charboneau would be a very powerful adversary and a definite thorn in any monarch's side.

Now that he knew Antoinette was a woman, Jacques wondered if he could continue to treat her like a boy. He wasn't sure he could refrain from showing her the gentle graces due her gender; the simple actions of respect, the polite necessities of civilized life.

He stood abruptly and walked the short distance across the room, hoping that the small space he placed between them would help him think more clearly.

When he finally spoke his voice was calm and strong.

"Antoinette, I believe your story. You see, I too have my differences with the Church. I know firsthand how treacherous its vicars can be. Many times the College of Cardinals has denounced my Order, threatening excommunication for all its heretics. Especially those of us at Prince Henry's Institute at Sagres.

"The Church is not happy that we are gleaning the treasures of countries she has yet to conquer by the cross. If His Holiness did not have such a lust for gold, we explorers would be rotting in Avignon's prisons."

Antoinette was taken aback by Jacques' near-blasphemous attitude. "But, I understood you to be devoted to the Church."

"To God, *Mademoiselle*! To Jesus Christ and the Blessed Holy Mother," Jacques hand strayed to the medallion around his neck. "To the Heavenly Father, yes. But not to Rome and not necessarily to the King of France."

"Then you won't send me back to face the Church?"

"*Non!* They are the *last* ones who need to know you are here."

Antoinette watched in silence as Jacques paced the small room, his hands fretting at the ribbon in his hair. She remembered her older brother Gaston, acting as the head of her family after her father died. He'd made the same gestures when he was making decisions. Perhaps, she thought, it was a particular trait of men, that they walked to work out their problems. She hoped Jacques was kinder to her than Gaston had been.

Jacques stopped. He couldn't think straight with Antoinette watching his every movement. He couldn't focus on a solution until she was out of his sight. He walked to his charts, but they offered no security.

"Leave me now." He dismissed her with a wave. "I'll not turn you over to the Church or to my order nor will I be part of your deception."

"*Monsieur*, I know that I have placed myself in great danger and I won't ask any more of you than your silence."

Jacques did not look up from his charts as she rose from her chair.

"The Blessed Brighid has me under her protective cloak," Antoinette said, reaching for the door. "She will aid me when I call upon her."

"Would that I had so much faith," he sighed.

As Antoinette silently closed the door Jacques allowed himself to collapse into the nearby chair. His head pounded from the intensity of her visit. Too much wine, he thought. But then he realized there were too many memories as well.

He looked pensively at the closed door. "*Dieu vous ait en sa sainte garde!*" he whispered. "God have you in His holy keeping."

The aftershock of the long meeting with Jacques lodged in the pit of Antoinette's stomach and she leaned back for a long moment against the hard cabin door. Every nerve was tightly strung. She desperately needed to release the overpowering energy swelling inside her. She had to breathe fresh air and to feel the freedom of the wind, to liberate herself from the emotions tangling within her before she burst.

Antoinette headed for the moonlight streaming through the hatchway. It would be cool topside. Except for the few men tending the sails, everyone would be asleep.

Unexpectedly, a dark figure stepped forward, blocking her path. She stopped in mid-stride, holding back a gasp of fright. The man's face was in shadow. Her already rapid heartbeat skipped. Then he spoke.

"Up late?"

The flutter in her stomach turned to a tight fist when she recognized the voice and her interrogator stepped into the light. It was Lawrence Bernard, the first officer.

Antoinette tensed. He couldn't have overheard her conversation with Jacques. Surely he was making idle conversation.

She softened her voice, maintaining her self-control.

"*Oui, Monsieur.*"

She moved to pass him. Without warning Bernard grabbed her arm.

Anger seethed within her at his forward behavior. She did not know this man. She had never spoken a full sentence to him and did not intend to do so now. She could read the disquieting intentions betrayed in his dark feral eyes. A shadowy sneer hovered about his thin mouth.

"You need not look to *old* men for companionship," he said. "My quarters are not as private as the captain's, but they would suffice for a—"

"—*Monsieur,* you are mistaken." A sudden thread of nausea ran through her. She shot him a disdainful glance then jerked her arm free.

"Am I, Étienne?" Bernard took a half-step forward. His eyes blazed like a man in trance, his gaze pulled her to him. "I see the way you look at him."

Antoinette swayed slightly as the implications of his words spun through her head. She knew she must manage to stand her ground without insulting a superior.

"I see the way he looks at you," Bernard continued. "You are with him—have been with him—for hours on end, night after night." He raised his hand as if to grab for her again, then slowly lowered it back to his side. "Give me a try. You will be better off with me in the long run than with that—Frenchman."

Bernard's loathing of the French was undeniable and Antoinette wondered briefly why a Burgundian served aboard a French king's ship. But she had no time to question his reasons. Bernard took another menacing step toward her.

For once in her life words failed her. She had no retort for his accusations or his suggestive remarks. Nothing that would not land her in chains for insubordination or get her tossed overboard for witchcraft.

She felt for the stairs behind her and slowly backed away, keeping him locked in her gaze. One by one, she backed up the stairs. Once at the top, she turned and swiftly ran out onto the open deck.

"Bastard!" Bernard's scorching whisper followed her through the hatchway, but she was unsure if it was meant for her or for Jacques.

Antoinette raced to the foredeck. Surely Bernard would not be bold enough to parade his offensive behavior above deck. There were too many chances of being seen. To her relief, the helmsman manned the quarter deck, standing his post at the rudder. A few men dozed in the center of the main deck, near the mainmast, waiting to make a sail change if necessary.

The helmsman gave her a nod of acknowledgment, a small signal of civility to his familiar nightly companion, then he continued his duty.

Antoinette took a long breath of relief as she walked to the railing. Let Bernard think what he would, she mused. Perhaps if the whole crew believed she was Jacques' lover, they would leave her alone. Then in a sudden panic, she wondered if the men already thought her, as Étienne, to be Jacques' consort.

She knew of these things, of men loving other men, of women loving other women; indeed, it was not a rare occurrence. But she had never been faced with the reality of it, until now.

To each his own, she reaffirmed, shaking the last of the strange images from her mind. This time she had escaped a precarious situation unharmed and with her disguise intact. But she must remain alert.

Antoinette's heart regained its normal rhythm as she climbed up to the quarter-deck and her mizzenmast refuge. The night's mist had disappeared with the sharp, strong wind and the early morning star of summer crested the eastern horizon.

Secure in her safety, Antoinette closed her eyes.

Beloved Brighid. I know you must have a great reason for my trials. You would not place me where I cannot serve you, but please—please don't test me beyond my abilities.

Alone, with the men sleeping and the helmsman intent on his duty, Antoinette looked out past the white wake spreading from the stern of the ship—the only evidence of their passage on the vast open sea. She turned to see the waning moon, still visible just beyond the bow of the ship.

She raised her arms up to the heavens in supplication, evoking the energy of the stars. She tried to draw down a spark from their radiance, but she was too exhausted to work her magic. Food and a deep sleep would renew her before sunrise.

Cautiously, Antoinette returned below deck, this time

aware of hidden dangers in the shadows. She tip-toed through the sleeping men to her bedroll nestled behind the folded sailcloth and line. Stopping for a moment, she mentally placed a protective halo around her. She envisioned a great red dragon guarding his lair. She would wake if this psychic barrier was penetrated.

As she made herself ready for bed, Antoinette thought of the dark-eyed man, wondering if he would come to her in her dreams again tonight. His image had been stronger over the last few nights and she wondered if he were somehow coming closer to her in reality.

The high pitch of the wind whistling through the rigging and the soft lament of the ship lulled Antoinette toward sleep. Exhausted, she burrowed into the thin straw stuffed mattress. She drifted into dreams of tree-dappled hillsides and vast green valleys where untethered hawks circled in the high uplifting currents, safe from hunter's arrows and captive cages.

Chapter 8

The Forests of Amboise, France

The king's falcon circled in the updraft of currents flowing across the valley. Its wings sliced through the warm air, sending the splendid bird soaring past verdant fields full with late summer bounty. Ripening grain and fruits spread beneath the falcon's gaze as it hunted for its master's pleasure.

King Charles stood in the clearing admiring the magnificent killer gliding over his land, his people, his domain. He took a deep breath of the honey and dust laden air and his thoughts drifted to his pending marriage.

"Ah— to be as victorious as the bird of prey," he whispered to the falcon master, not expecting a reply.

The falcon master glanced at his regent, noting his resemblance to the falcon. King Charles' profile was sharp, his legs stocky, his body short and compact. He was a fitting man for the sport. More fitted, the falcon master thought, for hunting than for leading an army into battle.

The falcon screamed and dived toward the treetops. The falcon master pointed at the bird. "Your Highness, he has sighted his prey."

Both men stood motionless, waiting for the moment when the bird would grasp the prey in its sharp and inescapable talons. It swooped once – twice, but the small dove slipped beyond the falcon's reach, disappearing into a thick growth of underbrush. The falcon soared to begin the hunt again.

"Good try!" Charles' eyes glittered with the excitement of the hunt. This was his prized bird, trained from the nest. A small mistake in its judgment was not critical.

Clanging chains and pounding hooves shattered Charles' reverie. He turned, remembering the invitation he had extended to Cardinal Visconti.

Charles looked at the falcon master and chuckled. "We did not realize he would bring a retinue of armed guards when we suggested he join us. Perhaps he fears my talons."

"Yes, Mi'lord," the falcon master replied, suppressing a smile as he walked away from the king to begin to call the falcon from his hunt.

The gilded coach creaked to a halt at the edge of the clearing and a handsome footman dressed in gray velvet descended to open the carriage door.

Charles watched Visconti disembark from the carriage, obviously out of place near the forests of Amboise, his red and black robes contrasted with the deep greens and blues of the forest. He was an animal of the Court, unaccustomed to the wildness of nature.

King Charles waited motionless as the Cardinal climbed the hill toward him. There was no need to hurry. He would show Visconti that he would only go so far to oblige the Church.

Visconti climbed the low incline, sweat glistening on his brow. Even at mid-morning it was hot. Breathless, he stood before Charles, and extended a gloved hand.

Obligingly, Charles bent to kiss his ring.

"Your Grace." Charles held back a smile at the older man's obvious discomfort. "We are honored by your presence."

He motioned to the falcon master and the bird was called from his flight. Everyone watched in silence as the bird flew toward them, its wings beating effortlessly toward the King's upraised arm.

With quiet grace, it landed sure-footed on Charles' glove and he gently stroked its perfect gray plumage.

"My Lord," Cardinal Visconti said impatiently. "I see you have invited me to experience the natural splendor of God's earth."

"Yes, Your Grace." Charles covered the falcon's head with a leather hood, then transferred it to the falcon master's care and turned to face his visitor. "Sometimes we feel God speaks to us when we are standing within His creation."

Charles watched the Cardinal's jaw tense at the suggestion of his direct communication with the Deity. It was an emotion Charles found amusing and he stored the reaction in his memory for later use.

Taking off his glove, Charles dismissed the attendants and motioned Visconti toward the shaded pavilion across the field. The King's colors of red and blue flew high above the small tent. There was no welcoming banner acknowledging the Church, yet the shade of the pavilion beckoned the Cardinal like a welcomed oasis.

"Let us walk together, my friend. We have much to discuss." Charles slowed his stride to accommodate the Cardinal's short legs, then stopped before the pavilion and turned toward his guest. "I wish to dispense with amenities and get to the heart of the matter. It is obvious I have not asked you here to falcon, but to discuss the disappearance of Antoinette Charboneau."

Short of breath, the cardinal nodded his acknowledgment as they walked into the shade of the open pavilion. It was decorously arranged with a long table of ripened fruit and cold meats. Visconti accepted a proffered chair and arranged his robes.

"Did you not ask me to handle the matter, Your Lordship?"

Charles winced at such an overt expression of the Church's authority over him. "Yes, Your Eminence. I did convey a desire to have her leave Brittany. But it seems we have a bigger problem. The girl has not yet sent word of her safety to Anne and M'lady is sorely distressed. She is calling the adventure foul play."

Visconti's pale eyes became flat and unreadable as both men waited for an attendant to fill the silver goblets with wine and leave their company.

"I assure you the maid has come to no harm by my hand. My agents attempted to escort her from Brittany, but she eluded them. They later informed me that she had disappeared," he waved his arm into the air. "Gone into the mists with her heathen friends, no doubt. She did not leave by any port of call north of Portugal."

Charles noted the breadth of Visconti's influence with chagrin. Could the range of his spies be so broad that he knew of *La Réale* and her mission?

"Do you have so much authority as to examine every ship that leaves these harbors? Surely one girl can be easily found."

Visconti waved his hand in a gesture of dismissal.

"Ah—Your Majesty, the Church is not omniscient."

"It would not bode well for us to hear Antoinette came to harm by the Church's hand or to have it blamed on the Crown. We do not wish to be remembered by our mistakes. Brittany does not need a martyr to fuel her complaints against us."

The Cardinal tented his jeweled gloves beneath his chin in a prayerful manner, his voice was cold and exact.

"Your Highness, you have my assurance that if she is alive, she will be found," he sighed, "and returned."

The men stared unwaveringly at one another for a long heartbeat. Charles had made his point.

"We will expect you to make it so," he said with a commanding nod of his head. "and she will be unharmed."

Visconti lifted his neglected goblet and sipped at the contents. After a moment of contemplation he set it back on the food laden table.

"Let us discuss larger issues, Your Highness. What of your crusade against the infidel Turks? Have you secured the funds of the duchy as well as the heart of the Duchess?"

"We do not have either yet. M'lady has delayed the wedding until Yuletide, claiming that she must know of her friend's well being. It would be a shame to have both events stalled until Antoinette can be found."

He looked at Visconti, hoping for signs of misconduct in his face. Cardinal Visconti shifted his weight in the chair.

"Your Highness," he began. "The Throne of Naples and the Crown of the Holy Roman Empire await you. The sovereigns of Europe—Savoy, Saluzzo and Montferrat—they expect your entourage by late Spring. You must not be delayed by the whims of a woman. You have the army of King Louis at your disposal. Your marriage will bring you Brittany's funds and her navy to command."

Charles sensed Visconti's attempt at manipulation. "What of Maximilian? Will he also welcome us? We have already challenged his claim to Anne and Brittany and angered him by rejecting his daughter Margaret. He will not simply allow me to take the Empire from him."

"You should not concern your thoughts with Maximilian. The Princes of Italy and the Church are behind you. The Duke of Milan, Ludovicio Sforza, will personally extend his hand in tribute as you pass through his duchy on your way to Naples. Do you think that Maximilian will cross his country so easily? Your Highness need not bother yourself with petty monarchs such as he."

Yes, Charles thought. The Hapsburgs were petty monarchs, unfit to wear the Crown of Charlemagne, unworthy to continue their charade at playing guardians of the Holy Roman Empire. Charles owned the sword of Charlemagne and he would rule the Empire, wearing the sword proudly on his side as he claimed the throne.

Visions of glory and grandeur flooded his thoughts as he looked over the rim of his glass at the Cardinal. To him Visconti was merely an insignificant pawn.

"Find the girl, Your Grace." Charles set his glass down hard on the table. "Find Antoinette Charboneau and our crusade will begin."

Château de Langeais - France

Anne dripped wax onto the folded parchment and pressed her seal against the molten tallow. She looked up from her desk to the young bard, Alain, as she handed him the letter.

"This letter of introduction will allow you entrance onto the Île du Sein. Once there, Mère Deirdre, the High Priestess, will permit you to enter the House."

"*Bien sûr, Mademoiselle.*" Alain took the parchment and placed it in the hidden pocket of his overcoat, all the while struggling to restrain his excitement at the opportunity Anne was giving him. To make a voyage to Île du Sein, the mythical island of the ancient Druids, was an honor. This was something that a bard could wait a lifetime to experience and Alain was still very young.

The Île du Sein was at the edge of the earth and the refuge of the Sisterhood of the Moon, the beautiful priestesses of the Goddess. Just the trip to the island would give Alain countless stories to turn into song, not to mention having an audience with Mère Deirdre.

"I will bring you the return message as soon as my humble feet allow."

Anne gave him a hesitant smile. "The mission is not as easy as it appears. It can be dangerous. Near Pointe du Raz, on the North coastline of Audierne Bay, you will pass a large menhir on the roadway. There is a fisherman's house of whitewashed stone not far." Anne reached into her pocket then handed Alain a small carved figurine of a woman with large rounded breasts and overly full hips. "Give this to the fisherman's wife and she will see that her husband gives you safe passage from the treacherous Pointe du Ruz to the island. Once there, make no mistakes, or the sisters will turn you away. They do not welcome strangers within their stone walls. Present my letter and then ask specifically to see the prioress. They will take you to her with haste."

An amused look crossed Alain's face as he placed the sculpture deep into his pocket

"I have heard that only the most lovely of women are allowed on Île du Sein."

"It is true, Alain. All the women are beautiful. But it is not only an outward beauty. The sisters must be beautiful in their hearts and carry the love of the Goddess within them. This is the beauty of which you sing in your ballads."

He lowered his eyes with embarrassment. Of course. They would all be beautiful when he sang of them. No one wanted to hear love songs about unattractive women.

Anne took the young man's hand and looked into his eyes. "Speak my words to no other than Mère Deirdre. She alone will know what to do."

The bard pressed his lips lightly to Anne's hand then gracefully backed away. "As you wish. I will speak your words clear and true. And with your permission, I will return this time by foot instead of fish cart." Alain smiled, and with a light bow he slipped though the doorway.

Anne leaned back into her chair and closed her eyes. There was more happening to Antoinette than she had feared. Much more than Charles or even Cardinal Visconti could account for. And they were obviously doing nothing to find Antoinette. It was almost as though she had never existed.

In the past few weeks, Anne's network of loyal Bretons had uncovered much more than Alain had first told her. Sebastian discovered that the boy, Étienne, had not been placed aboard *La Réale* by King Charles, as they first thought. He had been chosen specifically for his post as apprentice to Jacques DuPrey by the Navigators Guild and the Knights of Christ.

Even though Sebastian's father was a navigator and a Master of the Guild, Sebastian could find out nothing more. The King of France's business, the Guild told him, was none of their concern. If his majesty had hired one of their trained navigators to captain his ship, then it simply showed the regent's good judgment in men.

Sebastian believed that the Knights of Christ had other intentions for the King's ship. It would not be an unusual occurrence. When they were openly known as the Knights

Templar, they frequently interfered with many a monarch's plans.

Anne knew Charles was reluctant to share his plans with her and it pained her that she had not yet won his trust. Her last hope was that the Sisterhood could find Antoinette. Perhaps they would be able to uncover the new information. Surely, with all their powers they would know if Antoinette still lived. If nothing else, Mère Deirdre would know who Anne could trust to find Antoinette and bring her home.

A light knock on the door roused Anne from her weariness. It would be Miriam, come to dress her for dinner with the King. He had just returned to the château from Amboise, accompanied by Cardinal Visconti. She was not at all sure she was up to dealing with both men tonight. Separately she could handle them, but together, they were almost overwhelming. But it would have to be done. Better now than later. Anne placed her writing instruments into the drawer of her desk.

It was not Miriam who entered her room, but Charles, preceded by two large hunting dogs that bounded past him in two streaks of golden fur. Anne rose from her writing table and bowed low.

Charles beckoned her to rise and with a single command, ordered the dogs to sit by the hearth. He was still covered with dust and smelled of horse and sweat. But he needed to speak with her before she had notice of any changes in his plans, before her spies could carry any news of his meeting with Visconti.

His manner was brusque. "M'lady. We must talk in earnest." Charles took off his riding gloves and reached for her hand. "Am I really so terrible you would not have me as your husband?"

Anne pulled her hand away. "It is not your disposition that annoys me, nor your person. I have expressed my wishes to you and I am not at present willing to change them."

"I have spoken to Cardinal Visconti and he assures me Antoinette has come to no harm. He has agreed to use the powers of the Church to help us find her."

"*That* is the worst thing that could happen. If Visconti finds her before you do, he will surely bring her before his Inquisitors. You must have him call off his search at once."

Charles looked at his future bride and shook his head. Would there be no pleasing this woman?

Pouring himself a goblet of wine, he settled into a large chair across from the glowing fire. This meeting was not proceeding as he had hoped, but the sudden turn of events might well be what he had been waiting for. If Anne was desperate enough to have him call off the Church's hunt for Antoinette, perhaps he could dangle her own freedom before her and get her to commit to a date for the wedding.

"Very well, I will speak with the Cardinal before we dine and tell him that you have the situation under control."

Irritated by his mocking tone, Anne turned away.

Charles was persistent but courteous. "May I ask how you intend to find your friend when you are here at Château Amboise?"

Anne hesitated as she moved across the room to face Charles.

"You know how much power I have in Brittany, even in my absence," she said. "I will send word to my court to have the search area expanded."

Her retort was biting but the sting was not enough to waver Charles' defenses. He sat motionless, his leg thrown across the arm of the chair. One of his hands stroked a dog's head; the other held the goblet. "I know you have done this already. And I know you have turned up very little. Do you think that you would have better results if you were back in Nantes, heading the search yourself?"

Would he really let her have her freedom? she wondered. Would he trust her not to leave France and rally her people against him? "What do you mean?"

"I mean that if you are willing to set a date for our wedding and pledge your sincerity, then I will release you and you can go home to Nantes." Charles raised his hand to stay her words. "Of course, I will have to send someone with you to provide for your safety."

"Not Visconti!"

"No, my dear. I will find someone more suitable, someone who will not send you into a rage at hearing their name."

Anne turned away from Charles and walked the length of the hearth, walked past the dog that lay at her feet, stopping as she neared the edge of the mantle. She turned, her long gown flowing across her shoes with the whispering sound of velvet against lace.

"If you will allow me to return to Nantes and conduct the business of my court in person, then I will pledge my loyalty to you. *And*, if you will allow me the freedom to search for Antoinette, unhindered by the Church, Visconti or by your Crown, then I will agree to marry you, in Langeais in December."

"*Très bien*!" Charles could hardly contain the happiness in his voice. He rose from his chair and the dogs rose with him. They all crossed the short distance to stand by Anne. Charles took her small hand in his, and was pleased when she did not withdraw it. He could not hide his growing love for the young woman and he would have her know his true feelings.

"Ah—*ma petite Brette.* You may leave as soon as I can secure a proper escort. It gives me great pleasure to know I will be welcome at your court. Perhaps if I leave Visconti behind?"

Anne smiled at her king. For all his boisterous efforts at being a hard monarch, he was truly a kind and generous man. It just might be possible, she thought, that she could come to love him. But he would first have to mend his ways and leave the dogs outside her chambers.

She curtsied and raised her gaze to his. "We will be most honored to have you attend our court, Your Highness."

Chapter 9

La Réale - At Sea

Antoinette planned her escape.

If she got within a hair's breadth of land, she was going to get off *La Réale.* She'd investigated the small dinghy tied to the starboard side of the ship, determining which lines held it in place and asking innocent questions about its seaworthiness. She had yet to determine how to lower the boat without assistance. It would be a reckless venture to set out alone, but she could not imagine a return trip to France aboard *La Réale.* Time was running out on her good fortune.

By now Anne surely believed her to be dead or at the least imprisoned by Visconti. No one from the Sisterhood, not even Ursule, had come to comfort her in her dreams. Perhaps she was too far away for their magic to work or perhaps no one was looking for her anymore. It hardly mattered. She would still escape. Until then, she would make no trouble.

Over the last few days, since her visit with Jacques and her encounter with *Monsieur* Bernard, she had seldom spoken to anyone. Even though she had entrusted Jacques with her secret, she felt worse than before. If she was discovered now, Jacques would be in danger as well. Who would believe him if he pleaded ignorance of her femininity? It would be below his dignity to lie.

Several times a day she passed his quarters, but she would not disturb him. When they were together, they spoke little and looked at each other even less. Their visits, both above and below deck, had ceased. She had succeeded in making herself nearly invisible to the men, but the alienation was taking its toll on her light spirit. Even with the cooling breezes at night, she stayed below deck, listening to the strain of the ship's rigging and the waves slapping against the hull. And when she slept, she had no visions of her future. Not even the man with the dark fathomless eyes had come to visit her in her dreams.

Tonight, as she listened to the incessant rush of water pass the keel of the ship, she felt a distant, familiar void lingering just beyond her consciousness. The sorrow from her childhood that she had never taken the time to fully examine surfaced in her thoughts and she found herself thinking of her family, remembering her mother Marguerite.

At the age of ten, Antoinette had been too young to begin her training with the Sisterhood, but Ursule had insisted and Marguerite did not protest. At the time she had no choice. She later learned that the High Priestess of the Sisterhood, Mère Deirdre, had declared it long past time for her to leave Rennes and Marguerite.

She could barely remember her father, Guillaume. She wished she had known him by more than the stories of gallant knighthood that her mother had shared with her. She knew he had served Louis XI, King of France, that he had been decorated with the King's highest honors then had died in battle. She learned from Ursule, of his ill temper and the shameful neglect and mistreatment of her mother and brother.

"Men!" Ursule had once exclaimed. "Why the Goddess lets them rule the world, I'll never know. They're only good for two things: throwing out the slop and keeping your feet warm at night."

Antoinette's relationship with her brother Gaston, had only proved Ursule's assessment of men to be true. Gaston had troubled her childhood.

It was only after she'd met Jacques that she'd begun to question Ursule's opinion. She knew now that men could be as different as the phases of the moon and their temperament as varied as the number of stars in the heavens. Jacques seemed to be one of the better ones; a man with a kind nature.

Since she had confided in Jacques the navigational lessons had ceased, and so had his frequent companionship.

Antoinette admitted to herself that she had become accustomed to his company, to the confidence hidden in the deep tones of his voice and—Goddess help her—she enjoyed simply watching him. She longed for his approval when the night's charting proved accurate and the artful wave of his hand as he expounded on the mystery of the heavens. She longed to hear the soft sound of his voice explaining an intricate detail on a map. Most of all she missed their lively discussions and the long quiet silences they spent together as they experienced the ever-changing skies.

She wondered briefly if she was falling in love with Jacques, but pushed the idea from her mind. Love was an emotion she had yet to put much faith in.

The bad weather of the last few days had not helped to clear her thoughts. The elements were as unpredictable and as dismal as her feelings. The stifling heat below deck was often unbearable and the rain-drenched decks topside were always dangerous. Anyone in the crew could be swept overboard in the space of a breath and never found again. Mother Ocean had already claimed two crewmen, embracing them in her dark blue bosom like new born babes.

It was impossible to predict the weather. The wind would be blowing steady, then suddenly it would cease, leaving the sails slack, the air breathless and the ship floating slowly without direction or speed. *La Réale* was either tossed on turbulent seas or sliding down endless rolling waves. Seasickness and ill humor plagued the crew and the cook gave Antoinette permission to brew herbal teas and tonics to treat the *mal de mer.*

It surprised her that no one asked where Étienne, a navigator's apprentice, had learned his craft with herbs, but no one questioned her skill at healing.

As much as she wanted, Antoinette resisted the urge to visit Jacques. He evidently had no need for her tonics or teas and she did not inquire about his health. Not wanting to face him for fear she would betray her confused feelings, she began leaving his meals outside his cabin door. She had overcome her own seasickness, but her heart-sickness remained.

To escape the heat in the confined space of the sleeping galley, she had moved her sleeping pallet deep within the storage hold of the ship. Though there was little fresh air, the cool depth of the water around the hull tempered the heat.

High atop a row of barrels and a layer of sailcloth, she stowed her possessions and laid out her sleeping pallet. Here she felt safe, but topside, she could not shake the foreboding feeling that someone was still watching her. Not with simply curious eyes, but with eyes that mirrored sinister thoughts and corrupt desires. Only when she was deep within the bowels of the ship could she relax.

As though the gods finally answered her prayers, the sea turned calm. The ship sailed onward with a constant wind from the east.

Antoinette lay on her pallet drifting in and out of a light sleep.

"Étienne." A weak voice whispered in the darkness, tugging at her dreams."—Étienne, *mon ami.* I need your help."

Antoinette woke with her heart pounding. Who had found her? Who had passed through the invisible barrier she'd made to protect herself? Her magic was slipping. She could feel panic in the motionless air. Someone was desperate and needed help.

Without hesitating, she lit a small candle and held the light out in front of her. Her eyes adjusted to the stark light in the darkness and she recognized her visitor. Paul, the young steward, knelt at the foot of her pallet. His head rested on his folded arms.

Although they were similar in rank, she knew little about him. He was a slight youth. His delicate features seemed out of place in this rough environment, yet he had way about him that told of a hard life. His straight blond hair, not being long enough to pull back, always fell forward to circle his face. Now, it shimmered over his arms like flickering sheets of gold.

His clothing, like hers, was simple and threadbare, but made of better cloth. She remembered he had been a tailor's son. His short, raspy breathing brought her back to the question. Why was he here? What did he want?

"Étienne, I am ill." Paul lifted his head.

Antoinette sat up and placed the candle in a small niche beside her. The flame brightened her burrow and a soft gasp escaped her lips before she could suppress it. A strong wave of sympathy overcame her first instinct of anger as she saw Paul's disheveled appearance. His once glittering blue eyes were now small slits, shut tight with a fierce swelling. His cherub-like lips were cut and bleeding. Dried tears streaked the light layer of dirt on his tanned cheeks.

Antoinette raised her hand to place a compassionate touch on his shoulder. He flinched, then began to weep.

"Who did this to you?" She could hardly hold in her anger. But it would do no good to let the boy see her rage.

"I—I can't tell you." Paul whispered, his voice breaking as

he struggled to speak. "He said I mustn't tell, or—he'd kill me for sure. Please—help me."

She reached out to touch his thoughts, trying to find the answer to his unspoken words, but the images were clouded with his pain. The knowing could wait. She needed to treat his wounds first, then find the rogue who had treated him so. "*Bien sûr, mon ami*," she said comfortingly. "Of course."

This time Paul did not flinch as she reached out to touch him and she pulled him up into her makeshift bunk. He wept silently as she held him to her shoulder.

"Let me tend your wounds. I have salves, ointments—"

"*Merci*." Paul sighed, sinking down onto Antoinette's cool coverlet. "But I must ask for more than your herbs and medicines." It seemed as though he had relaxed at her touch. His words were clearer to her ears, but his mind was still blurred with erratic images.

"What can I do, Paul? If one of the crew has mistreated you, I will seek out the captain for their punishment."

"*Non*!" Paul leaned up on his arm, his eyes blazing with terror. "You can't let anyone know I'm here, or that I've come to you for help."

"Then what do you want from me?" Antoinette asked.

Exhausted from his efforts, Paul laid back down on the pallet and closed his eyes. "I need you to—to take my place. Please. Tell them I have the sea sickness or the fever."

He was not far from wrong. When Antoinette touched his forehead, it burned like the coals of the cook's fire. She knew without a good rest the young boy would slip into the arms of despair and possibly death. But there was little she could do but offer him comfort and salves.

"Don't talk now," she said reassuringly. She took a vial of liquid from her bag and held it to his mouth, coaxing him to drink the bitter tonic. "We'll think of something."

While Paul's consciousness yielded to the strong sleeping potion, she made a poultice of dried comfrey leaves to take the swelling from his face. Silently, and with skillful hands, she examined his injuries.

This was not his first encounter with violence. Many of his bruises were old and had turned dark and yellow. The cuts on his face were matched with newly healed lash marks on his shoulders and arms. She guessed he had become a silent victim of someone's temper shortly after the voyage began. Someone like Lawrence Bernard.

The time passed slowly as she held him, comforted him, and kept him from crying out in his fevered dreams. She tried desperately to decide what she should do come morning.

If Paul did not show up for his chores without a suitable excuse, there would surely be trouble. Neither could she let him be found in her bunk, especially with such disgraceful injuries.

Jacques would understand the situation, but there was nothing he could do. Without a witness to Paul's beating, there was no evidence to charge anyone with the assault.

Feeling the dawn approach, she lay down next to the boy. She would have to take Paul's place come morning. She would conceal his illness with a story of sea sickness and try to find out who had hurt her friend.

A warm hand on Antoinette's leg woke her with a start. Antoinette peered out over the edge of her precipice of rope. The cook stood below the coils of line, his look grim and stern. He held a long spoon in one hand and a small candle in his other.

"Here, boy—you'd best be tending to your chores. It's getting well on to sunrise and you've not set the cook-fire. Men will be fierce all day if they have to eat dry cold porridge." Cook's voice faded as she heard him climb up the hatchway toward the galley.

Antoinette lay back on the pallet trying to still her pounding heart. Slowly her head began to clear and she remembered the earlier problem. Thank the Goddess Cook had not seen Paul among the folds of sail and line. She wondered how he too had found her sleeping place and who else knew where it was.

She said a quick prayer to her protectress, Brighid, and pulled on her light leather deck shoes. She would need all the grace that The Mother could spare her and from the way Paul looked, she would be running fast all day.

She placed her hand on Paul's forehead. He was still sleeping soundly. His fever had subsided and a light rosy color was returning to his cheeks. But, she reaffirmed, he should not leave bed without further rest. And not at all today.

Antoinette had no appetite as she rushed through her galley duties laying out the meals for the crew and officers. She visualized each man aboard and briefly wondered which one was responsible for Paul's injuries. No one's thoughts betrayed them. Paul had been opposed to her telling anyone of his injuries. Obviously he did not want to risk another beating.

As usual, Antoinette fixed Jacques' morning meal of cold porridge and took it to his cabin. It would be the perfect opportunity to talk to him about Paul and about her encounter with the first officer.

When he did not respond to her knock, she reached down to unlatch the door. It pushed open easily. The morning light shone through the portholes and she saw the room clearly. Jacques' books and clothing were scattered in great heaps across the floor. An empty wine bottle sat on the table; a goblet lay on its side. Droplets of wine spilled from its gaping mouth as it rolled from side to side with the movement of the ship. His books and charts were scattered like discarded toys. Someone had thoroughly searched his quarters.

Antoinette's heart skipped and her thoughts raced in panic as she remembered that she had not seen Jacques during his midnight sighting.

The hard tug of the halyards and braces as the sails were hoisted to catch the morning wind filled the silence and she stepped back from the chaos to gather her wits. Had Jacques come to harm?

She turned to begin her search for him, then heard his commanding voice shouting orders topside.

Relieved that he was safe, she headed toward the door intending to tell him of the condition of his room. As she passed the writing desk, something flashed her a silent beacon. She turned.

A single ray of mote-dusted light bathed the desk. Antoinette blinked her eyes and focus on the jumble of papers and books. Did she dare take a closer look?

Curiosity won the battle in her mind. She set the food tray on the dining table under the port side window, then entered full into the confusion of the room. Stepping cautiously over Jacques' belongings, she headed toward the desk.

Letting out a long held-in breath, she leaned closer and within a few seconds found the object that gleamed in a stray beam of sunlight. A gold key on a small chain stuck out from under a heavy silver inkwell.

Boldness replaced her anxiety and she looked surreptitiously around the room. What did the key fit? Within a hand's width of her wishes, she saw a lock built into the desk drawer.

Antoinette slid the key soundlessly into the lock. It disconnected the latch in one silent turn. Slowly, she opened the drawer and the sun illuminated its contents: A feather pen, a small knife, a tin of snuff, a large black key, a small pistol—a leather bound book.

Antoinette smiled. She glanced at the door before she withdrew the book from the depths of the shallow drawer and opened to the place marked with a gilded leather bookmark. The text was eloquently scribed.

20 July 1491.

Winds steady from the east till noon. Today, as usual, it rained preventing me from taking my readings. By nightfall we were sweltering from the incessant heat and humidity. Of late there is no constant wind to fill our sails. The first mate is wary of a squall by week's end. The crew's behavior is tense and many have taken ill with the heat. We are well past midway and should rendezvous with the fleet in less than five days time. But I cannot find the area on my chart.

I am disturbed by —

The entry ended with a light ink blot, mirrored on the opposite page. Had Jacques been interrupted, closed the book and locked it away before he could finish his entry? She cursed under her breath. She had come so close to unraveling the mystery and she knew the information she needed lay somewhere written inside. If only there was time to look.

Turning the pages quietly and carefully, she flipped farther back into the book. Jacque wrote of food counts, wind directions, time, speed and weather conditions, various shipboard problems, but there was no mention of their destination.

"Damn!" She gritted her teeth in frustration. Her search was futile. There was no explanation of the voyage's purpose within the bounds of the book. Was *La Réale* on a secret mission? Did Jacques even know where they were going?

Angry and frustrated, Antoinette closed the book, replaced it inside the desk and slid the key back under the inkwell. Glancing once more at the room, she retrieved the food tray then closed and locked the door behind her. She would find Jacques as soon as possible and convince him, by whatever means she must, to tell her their exact destination.

ଔ

Antoinette sat next to Paul, feeding him a hard biscuit softened in willow bark tea.

"I'm risking a lot to take your place." This time she was more forceful in her approach. "Don't you think you should tell me what happened? I need to know what dangers I might face aboard this ship."

Paul showed no emotion. He looked past Antoinette in a distracted silence. Small tears swelled in the corner of his eyes, slowly trickling down the curve of his rounded cheek.

She knew she would learn nothing from him in his present condition and she was not in a good enough frame of mind to handle his kind of sickness, a sickness of the spirit.

"Blessed be." She tucked a blanket around Paul's shoulders and shook her head in bewilderment.

Paul stared up toward the rafters. His thoughts had disappeared into the void, blessedly distancing him from his physical pain.

ଔ

"*Mon Dieu*!"

Jacques paced his room in anger. The mid-morning sun cast shortened rays of light through the porthole window and Antoinette watched the tiny dust motes swirl and dive as Jacques crisscrossed in their pathway. "You should have told me sooner about the boy. And about Bernard."

"I did not see him as a real threat until Paul came to me. It might not even be Bernard, though he has had opportunity enough." Antoinette took a step closer to him. "Paul is unfit to work. He is scared, ill."

"And he will not tell you who is responsible for his condition?"

Antoinette shook her head.

"There is a chance Bernard will try to bother you again."

"*Mais non!* He believes—" Antoinette suppressed a blush.

Jacques turned toward her. "Believes what?"

"He believes that we are lovers."

Jacques face flushed with anger. He walked to his closet and slammed his hand onto on its surface. "The bastard," he said through clenched teeth. "He thinks me so desperate as to take a child to my bed? And you—," he turned to face her, his eyes filled with regret. "—he believes you are my *mignon*."

Antoinette firmed her lips, turning her eyes away from his gaze. It was true. Bernard thought her to be the Captain's favorite.

"I do not blame you, Antoinette," he said as he walked to her. He took her chin in his hands and lifted her face to look into her eyes. "You are innocent. I am sorry you have learned that men can be such fools."

Jacques' assessment of her knowledge was partly correct. She had lived her early life in near seclusion, surrounded by the walls of Anne's private gardens and the mantle of her vocation. She was inexperienced with the desires of men. She knew only how to unnerve them and keep them at arms length. But she had come this far using her common sense and she was determined to survive. It was time Jacques knew she was no weakling.

"And so deceptive." She stated flatly. "What happened to your quarters? And whose fleet will we be meeting, Jacques? I know we have five days until we reach the fleet."

"I have underestimated your guile, *ma petite espionne.*" He stepped back. "Does this—goddess you worship give you unnatural powers?"

"Hardly. When I brought your morning meal, I saw your room in disarray. I saw a key under the ink well, opened your desk and looked at your log book. There is nothing unnatural about feminine curiosity."

Jacques' lifted his hand to his shirt and touched the small key he tried to remember to keep with him. "About the room...I had an intruder who lacked your keen eye and inquisitiveness. How much more do you know?"

"I know we are past midway. Nothing more."

He paced across the room. "The less you know, the better."

"Please." She moved toward him, touching his arm. How easy it would be to cling to him, to let him absorb all her fears, she thought. "If my life is truly in danger, I deserve to know the truth? I promise I will leave when we make landfall. Then I will no longer burden you or your conscience."

There was a long pause as Jacques gazed down into her eyes. "The *fleet* is His Majesty's fishing fleet," he sighed. Did you not wonder why we carry so much rope and sail, so much wine and salt? We are will supply the fleet with goods so they may continue their fishing throughout the remainder of the year. They do not have an established colony to provide for their needs. They live and die at sea, with little support from a meager repair yard on land."

"But surely there are towns to which I can escape."

Jacques walked toward his charts and brushed his hand over the surface of the exposed parchment. "You have seen my charts, and I believe you ventured a guess that we were headed for new lands." He ran his hand nervously through his hair.

"We are not only the King's supply ship, we are an unofficial exploration vessel for the Navigator's Guild. My purpose here is to confirm a safe route for their future explorers." He paused briefly, then turned toward her.

A sudden bitterness she did not expect filled his words. "To confirm the route, but not to have the glory of discovery. *Non, ma petite*, we will not make landfall with *this* vessel."

The finality of his words shattered her hopes. She could feel the strength draining from her. He was telling her there was no hope of her escape. She sank slowly into the chair by her side and buried her face in her hands trying to block out the inevitable destiny that lay before her.

"What will I do?" she asked. "I don't think I can keep up this charade much longer. I am tired and someone will eventually catch me off guard."

Jacques crossed to her and placed his hand on her shoulder. Suddenly, she felt grounded in her spinning, shifting world.

"My friend, your future is in the hands of your beloved Brighid," he said. "You are at the mercy of your goddess."

In her heart she knew the truth in Jacques' words. Her life was—and had always been—in the Mother's hands. And it would be by Her grace if she made it through this nightmare.

Antoinette summoned her last bit of energy. She had to appeal to Jacques' sense of spirituality. It was the only way to penetrate his hard barriers. She turned her face to meet his gaze.

"In the name of the Holy Mother Mary, I beg you to tell me what to expect from this unknown land."

He looked at her in amazement, reached for his crucifix and looked away for a long moment, gazing into the distance. She knew he felt the respect in her voice as she called upon his own guardian for help.

"For the Holy Mother's sake—and for the love and respect that I hold for your family, I will tell you what I can," he said. "But—you will be responsible for holding this knowledge in secrecy."

"Is it not evident that such skills are at my command, *Monsieur*?"

The tension between them disappeared as a smile crossed Jacques' face.

"*Ah, mais oui.*" He turned toward the charts and beckoned her to his side.

He gave her detailed descriptions of their destination. The shaded area to the north of Ireland was called Iceland. A bleak country filled with volcanoes and ice and ruled by the Danes, a new ally to the French.

Further west was the vast uninhabited continent of Altima Thule, the land of the Vikings and the mythical home of the ancient Nordic Gods.

The coastlines he would chart were yet unclaimed by the Europeans, though the French and Portuguese fleets had fished the nearby coastal banks for many years. These were rugged lands inhabited by fierce savages; wild lands, ripe with bounty and gold for whichever ruler staked the first claim.

"If this country is known to the French," she asked, "why hasn't someone established a colony before now?"

Jacques hesitated, then gathered up the charts, rolled them tightly and tied them together as if to seal their secrets from further escaping.

"Only the fishermen have seen these lands. The transfer of cargo takes place at sea. The ships raft together, transfer goods, then depart to their fishing grounds. The supply ships always return to France. But on this trip, we will follow them back to their harbors and I am going to map their coastline. My employer is eager to send an expedition to the New World."

"But won't the fishermen resist revealing the location of their fishing grounds?" she asked.

"*Ah— certainement*! But these men are the King's subjects and we are here at his command. I have a sealed document demanding their cooperation."

Jacques walked to his bed and withdrew the pistol from beneath his pillow. He waved it in the air to emphasize his words.

"If all else fails, *mon amie*, King Charles has given us the weapons to persuade them."

Chapter 10

Antoinette wondered why she was so attracted to Jacques. He was nearly twice her age and not at all inclined to believe in her philosophy of life. In Jacques' presence, she felt safe. But there was something more. She felt a strange and powerful force when she was around him, a feeling that spoke of love and of trust mixed with a hint of danger. She could not understand the fragmented words her heart spoke, no matter how desperately she tried to arrange the pieces.

With this new understanding of her situation she was anxious, but still confident of her survival, at least until she reached the new lands. After landfall—well, she would face those days as they came.

All of her questions needed to be answered. Paul held the key to unlock part of the mystery and it was time she knew the truth.

"Paul," she called softly as she entered the storage hold. She called again, but there was no answer. Her heart skipped. Was he dead?

Hastily, she climbed to her hiding place. Paul was not there. The pallet was still warm to her touch. He had not been gone long. She turned toward the tumble of lines and canvas.

"Paul," she called. "It's Étienne."

When she found him, he was beneath an open ventilator shaft on the lower deck. Dust motes danced in the bright ray of evening light and the fresh air from the vent seemed to be slowly reviving his spirit.

He'd washed himself and seemed better, but his eyes still held a look of pain and detachment.

Antoinette sat down beside him. She lit a candle and it flickered, filling the dark compartment with an eerie glow.

"We have to talk."

"Talk, Étienne?—no. I cannot talk about it." He pushed a straying lock of hair behind his ear and looked directly into Antoinette's eyes. "I want to thank you for all you've done, for your friendship and your kindness."

Antoinette was tired of his avoidance. She needed answers. She threaded authority into her voice as she spoke, using the same tone of command Ursule often used on her.

"You can thank me by telling me who did such horrible things to you."

Paul's voice cracked as he struggled to keep his composure. A thin line of sweat beaded on his brow and Antoinette could tell he was resisting the desire to tell her everything.

"All I can tell you is...trust no one!" He sighed deeply resolving himself to his fate. "Has anyone asked about me?"

Antoinette knew she would get no more information from Paul if she let her irritation show. He needed comfort, assurance that his secrets, however bad they were, could be shared. He did not need to be bullied anymore.

"Ah, *oui. Monsieur* DuPrey and Cook wondered where you were. I told them you were ill." She placed her hand on his arm and rubbed it, warming his cold skin. "Paul, you can't hide here forever."

"Another few hours...I'll be better. Tell them I'll be fit to work tonight." He shrugged and pulled his knees up to his chest, burying his face in his arms. "I can't face anyone right now."

He looked so innocent with his fair hair streaming over his folded arms like golden armor. She knew he had shut her out and no amount of persuasion, gentle or otherwise, would make him reveal his assailant now. She also knew that the treatment for his pain was beyond the realm of her simple herbs and salves. There was nothing left for her to do except to be his friend. Paul's healing would have to come from deep inside his soul.

"Are you sure, Paul? I'm managing. Another day of rest will restore your health."

After a few moments, Paul reached out and laid his hand on her shoulder. "Étienne, I know I must face my fears and do my own job. I can't let the captain or—anyone think I'm weak. I don't want to be a steward forever."

Paul was right. If he involved himself in his duties, he would probably heal faster. Antoinette hoped that whoever mistreated him would be warned off.

"*Très bien,* I'll tell the captain." She hesitated for a moment to make sure Paul's decision was final.

Paul sighed. "Why have you been so kind to me?"

"*Je vous en prie, mon ami.*" She put a hand out to him. "You would have done the same for me."

☙

Determined to stay out of the way, Antoinette took advantage of Jacques' evening sighting to linger in his quarters. She opened the large rear windows and the side portholes and the fresh sea air streamed in. The wake streamed out in white foam from the rudder just below Jacques' cabin. Long slow waves rose and fell behind the stern and the ship seemed to slide from the crests to the troughs with grace and simplicity. The clouds high above the horizon, far in the distance like tufts of wool floating on a clear lake.

The vastness of the clouds and the open expanse of the sea made her trials seem trivial. Why should the Great Goddess even bother with the mundane problems of people? Humans were so involved with petty desires and beliefs. Nature simply *was*. Clouds, sea, flowers, trees. They could exist without people. Nature could give the gods pleasure without the asking for anything. But then, Antoinette wondered if the gods might need the people. Did the gods needed to feel loved, like their mortal children? Such thoughts deserved further pondering at a later time. Right now she needed answers to her earthly problems.

Antoinette walked to the desk and carefully lifted the silver ink well. As she suspected, the key was not there. Briefly, she thought about prying the latch open to look at the rutter, but walked quickly away. There was no sense in testing Jacques patience.

Instead she fluffed the straw of his mattress and spread the heavy blanket smoothly across the top. A tinkle of metal against metal caught her attention and she pulled up the edge of the mattress. An armory of muskets and swords were hidden in a compartment beneath his bedding. A chain was threaded through the hilts and handles and all were held together with a large metal lock. The key which she remembered lay in the locked drawer with the log book. It seemed an odd place to hide the weapons, she thought.

She replaced Jacques' empty wine bottle with a full one and wiped his goblet dry. A small shiver crept up her spine and she turned swiftly toward the door.

Lawrence Bernard stood behind her. A few seconds of uncertainty passed between them then Antoinette stepped behind the table. Bernard's glance quickly ran down the length of her body, then stopped at the table and the new bottle of wine. Slowly he walked toward it, uncorked the bottle and poured a drink. He consumed it in several large gulps, staring at her over the rim of the goblet.

"Where is Paul?" he asked.

"Paul has the fever." Her hand fell to her pocket and the small knife hidden inside. Confident that she had a barrier between them, she looked defiantly into his eyes. They were hooded with too much drink, and they seemed to hold a hint of amusement at her attempt to remain calm.

"I trust Paul will be back to health soon?"

"*Oui,*" she said. "He is...recovering."

Bernard turned and walked to Jacques' chart table, lifted the edge of a chart then let it fall back into place. "Tell him that I await his return; we have unfinished business."

Brute! How heartless to send a veiled threat to the boy. Antoinette took a quick breath as though she were about to jump into icy water. "Is there anything you require, *Monsieur*?"

Bernard returned to the table and poured himself a second goblet of wine. Its contents overflowed and the red liquor threatened to run off the edge of the table. Antoinette stifled an impulse to stop it.

"*Oui*!" he whispered, raising the cup to his lips and licking the wine off the rim with his tongue. "I would like your company tonight."

Antoinette gritted her teeth yet maintained her composure. "You have the wrong man, *Monsieur*."

"Ah—I had hoped you would be taking over all Paul's duties."

"*Non, Monsieur*. The captain has requested I attend him at his midnight sighting."

"Oh, I see." Bernard said with contempt. "How unfortunate. I do hope DuPrey is worth your efforts, though I believe it may not be in your best interest to be too friendly with the captain."

"Are you speaking about me?" Jacques stepped through the opened doorway. With the possibility of sighting the fleet, he had taken care to dress his rank and the effect was more than impressive. His full-length velvet cloak was a deep green and contrasted against his pristine white shirt, it gave him an air of stunning aristocracy. His log book and charts were held securely under his arm.

Bernard turned to face him. "I was merely expressing my concern that our little friend, Paul, is ill and that it is an inconvenience to all of us."

Jacques gave him a sideways glance as he walked toward his desk. "I appreciate your concern for the ship's affairs, but my inconvenience is none of your business."

"*Pardon, Monsieur*." Bernard nodded and gave Antoinette a half-lidded glance, sealing his unspoken promise of malice.

The tension was broken when two midshipmen walked past and called Bernard to join them in the galley. Without excusing himself, he handed the empty goblet to Antoinette and left the room.

"Thank you for interrupting us," Antoinette whispered. Her hands shook as she placed the goblet on the table.

"You still have a lot to learn, *mon amie*." Jacques said calmly. He slipped the chain and key from around his neck and sat down at his desk. "Stay well away from him. He has more on his mind than the ship's well being."

"You can be sure I will avoid him like the plague."

Annoyed at Jacques' indifferent attitude, she left the room and went topside. The growing moon had risen high above the horizon. Dark clouds towered against the western sky, reflecting the storm brewing aboard the ship.

Antoinette thought of the Île du Sein and of the Sisterhood, of Mère Deirdre and of her oath to serve the Goddess. It was strange how no one had come to her in her dreams. Not even Anne cried out for her to return. It was almost as though she had been forgotten, that her connection with her friends in Brittany had been severed by the growing distance. Surely someone could feel she was in danger. Someone must know she needed assistance.

The damp night air crept into Antoinette's clothing, and droplets of rain pulled her from her thoughts. The sky was turning black, hiding the moon as well as the sea.

Chapter II

Tension filled the afternoon air. An extra watch had been set to sight the fleet and all hands were busy with work. The decks had been cleaned, the supplies inventoried for transfer, and made ready .

Jacques worked on the quarter-deck, away from the hustle of men and lines. He watched Antoinette working with the men and pondered the fragile bonds of friendships. But his thoughts did not concern Antoinette, they revolved around her brother, Gaston.

Gaston had once been the other half of Jacques' existence, From the first time they met at school in Navarre they had been inseparable. Both too young to serve King Louis in his battle with either the English or the Burgundians, they dreamed of far off quests and exploration. Then in the summer of Jacques' sixteenth year he had stayed at the Charboneau home in Rennes. It was a summer he would never forget. The summer that ended his friendship with Gaston.

Jacques shook his head to dispel his thoughts and turned away from the scene below him to look out at the sea. So much weighed on the events of the next few days—finding the fleet, sighting land—he could not risk a fit of melancholia.

Noticing Jacques' movement, Antoinette started to move toward him, but someone grabbed her shoulder. She turned abruptly, and stepped back. Lawrence Bernard glared down at her.

"Chores finished so soon, my boy?" he asked.

"*Oui, Monsieur,*" she managed to say.

"If you are idle I will find something else for you to do." His eyes searched her face and his lip curled into a small smile. "Go below."

He gripped her arm and guided her roughly toward the hatchway.

She was determined that she'd never end up like Paul, beaten and helpless. She opened her mouth to protest, but Bernard shoved her down the hatchway before she could speak. Someone called out his name and when he turned she took the opportunity to run.

She needed time to think. Could she get to the firearms? Would she use a gun to defend herself?

Antoinette raced below deck, unlocked the door to Jacques' quarters and ran to the desk. Hopefully he'd forgotten to take the key as he often did. Yes, she would find the key and get the pistol out of the desk. She looked frantically under the inkwell, under the papers, then rushed to the side locker to get Jacques' sword. She would defend herself as best she could. As she reached for the locker she heard the snap of the latch bolt shut against the heavy oak door.

"Is this what you are looking for?" Bernard's back was against the closed and bolted door. A gold key dangled from a chain held between his fingers. He held a pistol his other hand. Its silver barrel pointed at Antoinette's belly. "It appears that the Captain forgot to complete his dress this morning. He has been overly distracted lately."

Antoinette fought panic as the realization of his intentions hit her. She wondered if he knew where the arms were hidden.

Antoinette backed up, her heart pounding an irregular cacophony in her chest. Jacques had been right about the man. He was evil and not above killing for what he wanted. His eyes were heavy with what she assumed was drunkenness. It was no wonder he chose the night to hide his face.

He waved the gun at the debris scattered around the room. "Did you do this?" he asked, cold and mocking.

For the first time, Antoinette noticed that the room was once more in total disarray. Bernard had surely been Jacques' previous uninvited guest.

"You must be a spy," he said. "Yes. That is what I will tell the captain. I heard someone in his quarters, opened the door and found you searching through his belongings." He made a light chuckle, slowly crossing the room. "But, just now, I want to see why DuPrey is so interested in you."

She glanced quickly around the room. There was no avenue of escape, save for the bolted door and the large windows behind the berth.

"*You* are mistaken, he will never believe you," she said, stalling for time. Surely Jacques would be just behind them, following them below deck. "You won't get away with this."

Bernard advanced. Instinctively, she backed away from the locker, toward the window, ready to jump if she had to.

"*Tais-toi!* That's enough!" He waved his pistol. "You are as insolent as Paul."

"Paul?"

Bernard shook his head. "I know he told you about me. He hides in your bed licking his wounds like a lost puppy."

"So it *was* you." Antoinette's anger soared at the thought of Paul submitting to this man's torture. "You're despicable."

Bernard laughed. "Despicable? I've been called far worse things before, but never that. Paul called me quite a few names, I remember. But he still refused to tell me where DuPrey hides his chart or the guns."

"And you think I will?"

His voice lowered to a whisper and he nodded. "You saw what happened to Paul. You saw his face, his body. Did he tell you what else I did to him?" He chuckled. "No, he wouldn't. He fears me too much."

He made a threatening step and Antoinette stepped back, reaching out behind her. As she backed up to the table, the heavy silver ink well fell within her grasp and she wrapped her hands around it. Quickly judging the distance between them she threw it at Bernard. The sharp edge grazed his cheek, then the ink well fell to his feet and hit the floor. Black ink splattered on his shoes and across the floor.

He stopped momentarily and wiped the blood trickling from the jagged wound with the back of his sleeve.

"A fighter." His eyes flickered unnaturally, like a candle flame starving for air. He laid the pistol on the table, withdrew a small silver dirk from his waistband. "I like to tame a hell cat once in a while." He smiled again, demonically. "You'll purr beneath my petting when all is done. Then *mon joli*, you will slink back to me for more."

His eyes narrowed to match his thin tight lips.

"Do you fight with DuPrey? Or have you been his willing lover for a long time?"

Antoinette could back up no further; the lockers and the hull stopped her flight. The window was now too far away.

"Our friendship is none of your business," she said,

wishing she could find harsh words to fling back at him. Better yet, another inkwell or a knife. No one had ever spoken to her this way. Not even Visconti. But it would be no use defending her virtue to this man, he would not hear or believe her.

Bravely, she stood her ground. "What are you doing in the captain's cabin? You have no right to be here."

Undaunted, Bernard moved closer.

"Let's just say DuPrey has something my employer will pay dearly for. He has led us to the New World and I intend to claim it for the Church. Only one thing stands in my way. I need those charts. Before we meet the fleet, my men will take charge of this vessel and I will command them." He smiled again, this time reminding her of a ferret about to dine. "Then—*Mademoiselle* Charboneau, *you* will be *my* consort."

Antoinette stifled a gasp. Had he known since the beginning of the voyage who she was? Was he in league with Cardinal Visconti or acting for someone else?

The politics of the Church did not matter now; there were mutineers aboard *La Réale* awaiting this man's command and her honor was perilously dangling from his hands like the cold metal key. She took a calming breath and boldly lifted her chin.

"You know my name. You must also know my status."

"Oh, I know what you claim to be. A sorceress, a pagan." He took a challenging step forward. "But I do not believe in superstitions. I have traveled far and seen too much. I believe you are a woman, nothing more."

Her breath nearly left her. If she could not control the situation, her fear would kill her before Bernard had the chance.

Before she could react, he closed the space between them. He forced her into the small alcove between the locker and berth and waved the dirk menacingly back and forth in front of her.

He was twice her size, but she was determined to fight. She had to out-maneuver him, she thought. She must use her small figure to her advantage. She feigned a move to the right, but Bernard's well honed reflexes were quick. He caught her waist with his outstretched arm and slammed her against the door of the storage locker.

The impact stole what was left of her breath. Momentarily stunned, Antoinette closed her eyes and waited for the knife to swiftly slit her throat.

A long heartbeat later, she was still alive.

When she opened her eyes, Bernard's face hovered a hand

span away from her own. His breath was shallow, sour and nearly as rapid as her own.

"Don't move," he whispered, pressing his full weight against her. The locker's brass knobs dug into her back as she yielded from the pressure of his hard body.

His knife moved swiftly to her neck and with stunning precision slid along her fear-glistened skin. Indelicately, he lifted her chin with its sharp point.

A warm trickle of blood seeped past the dirk's shallow incision as the hard steel pierced her flesh.

She looked into Bernard's eyes with cold defiance. The night they'd met in the dark recess of the lower deck, his eyes had been dark and unmoving. Now they burned with an inhuman desire, searing her skin worse than the sharpness of his knife.

Unexpectedly, the pressure lightened, then his eyes and the dirk traced a path down her shirt. Both stopped above her breastbone. The point of the knife parted her shirt with calculated precision. The tip barely touched her skin.

Her head pounded. She dared not move. She held her breath, firmed her jaw. "Get it over with. Kill me now, for you'll have no cooperation from me while I live."

With a flick of his wrist the knife ripped through the linen, exposing one soft rounded breast.

Bernard leaned back. A wicked smile crossed his lips. "*Bon Dieu*! You are quite a woman! I have waited too long."

She pulled the torn garment around her, but Bernard's quick hand reached out and grabbed her wrist.

"I have you now." He pinned her arm behind her. "I was tiring of the lad."

Pain shot through her limbs and down her back. She looked up, searching his eyes. Without looking down, he traced the outline of her breast, stopping the gleaming tip just above her heart. He pulled her wrist up behind her, forcing her to lean against him. He slid his mouth close to her ear.

"I wondered if you would be indifferent to my advances," he whispered sharing his intimate secret. "Now I know you will satisfy my desires." He sniffed at her hair. His hot breath sent shivers across her body. "Even Paul was unwilling...at first."

Antoinette's stomach lurched and she turned her face away from his gaze. She would die before she became victim to his sadistic seduction. If not by his hand, then by her own.

"Have you forgotten?" He wrenched her arm up again to regain her attention. "You are a spy, and a woman. The crew will not allow DuPrey to save you. You've betrayed them as well with your disguise."

She closed her eyes in defiance, trying desperately to concentrate, to call on the Goddess for help. But with the knife held so close to her heart, she dared not move unless she was really willing to die. All she had to do was press against him and in one quick move it would be all over. No more pain. No more fear. No more.

"Death? So close," he whispered, echoing her thoughts. He pressed the knife into her skin. "Tell me what I need to know. I would hate to kill you before you really get to know me."

Brighid protect me, she prayed, knowing full well it might be her last invocation. *Guide me into the arms of death.* She took a deep breath and prepared to move toward him, to welcome the knife.

"No!" Bernard moved back and threw the knife aside. It slid across the floor. The point lodged in the soft wood at the base of the captain's berth. "To waste the pleasure of your body would be a tragedy."

In one brief instant the feeble stitches of her shirt gave way to his defiling hands. He ripped the remainder of the fabric and pushed it over her shoulder using it as a tether to bind back her arms then shoved her back into the alcove.

She struggled against her bonds, kicking wildly at his legs.

Bernard wound his hands into her hair and jerked her head back. His lips pressed violently against hers and he thrust his tongue deep within her mouth. His leg pressed hard between her thighs. The locker knob bit into her back.

A hard rage rose within her. The bastard had robbed her of her dignity. By the Goddess! He would have nothing else.

"*Non*!" She twisted her head away. "Jacques will kill you."

"Yes, call your lover's name." Bernard hissed. "It excites me. I want him to witness what I've done with his whore. Then, I will hang him for his heresy. But, I think before he dies, I will have him as well."

Lacking words for combat, Antoinette spat in his face. Bernard retorted with the back of his hand across her cheek. Dazed, and freed from his grip, she fell against the desk, fighting a sudden uncontrollable weakness. Memories of her childhood flashed before her. Memories of her brother, Gaston, pushing her aside when she tried to be close to him, hitting her to make her cry, locking her away so he could spend time alone with their mother. But that was before she knew of the Goddess, before she could call on the power of the Ancient Ones to make her strong.

"Give me strength to fight. Great Goddess, infuse me with your spirit," she said.

Bernard lunged at her again. The heat of his hands scorched her skin. She must forget her body, she remembered. Remove herself from the violence. Concentrate and summon the Goddess to assist her.

Fabric ripped. Antoinette detached herself from the sound and from the demanding hands exploring her body.

Forgive my doubts, Great Mother. Forgive my faults. Cleanse me with your power.

Her silent litany continued, then in a sudden breathless moment she was free, lifting her consciousness outward, upward, leaving her weighted earth-bound struggle behind.

She watched as the unreal vision unfolded beneath her. Two figures locked in mortal struggle, their bodies barely visible in the waves of vibrant color surrounding them, like actors in timeless motion. She could leave now. Drift into the darkness and be one with the Goddess. But something would not release her spirit.

A low moan forced her attention back to the play of energy dancing below her and she remembered that for some reason, time was important. These people were important. The poor girl struggling below her was not destined to die like this.

Antoinette stretched out her ethereal arms.

Make me yours Blessed Mother! Come to me! Give me your power, Great Goddess of Justice!

A sudden sharpness filled the room and Antoinette's earthly body flared with light. Bernard let her go and took a half-step back. His face convulsed with fear as he witnessed Antoinette's body blaze with a red flickering flame. Tenuous fingers of fire licked toward him, stinging his skin.

Bernard instinctively drew the sign of the cross over his chest. "Mother of God!"

A quick snap distracted him and he turned his head toward the door as an explosion echoed throughout the room.

Antoinette's awareness jerked back into her fragile earthly body and looked with her mortal eyes toward the source of the sound. She watched with bemused detachment as her assailant sank to the floor. Then she looked up to the opened doorway. A plume of smoke hovered above a pistol in Jacques' steady hand. Antoinette heard her name and reached out. Her legs went limp. The room went black.

Chapter 12

A loud pop wrenched Antoinette from a dreamless sleep. She bolted upright and took several gasping breaths, attempting to recover her body's normal rhythms.

It was dark and she could barely make out the shapes of a table and a chair, a covered porthole. As her eyes adjusted, she realized she was viewing the room from within a ship's berth. From Jacques' berth. She was safe in Jacques' bed.

Antoinette shivered, remembering the bewildered look on Bernard's face, the icy glare of Jacques' eyes and the emptiness she felt as the Goddess withdrew from her. For one brief instant, she'd burned with the power of the gods, with the all consuming passion of the Goddess.

Had it all been a dream? No, not a dream, a nightmare. A nightmare beyond anything she could have ever imagined.

Bernard had bruised more than her pride and her courage. Her skin crawled as she remembered the feel of his defiling hands. She felt unclean and befouled by the violent energy still lingering around her. She stifled a wave of nausea, slipped back into the security of Jacques' bed and thanked the gods Lawrence Bernard was dead.

The popping sound of the topgallant sail filling with gusts of the late evening wind echoed in the room, snapping back and forth like her thoughts. The wind beckoned her topside but she was too tired and too much in disgrace.

She pulled up the light blanket covering her and thought of Jacques. He had seen her naked through her ripped clothing and at the mercy of a madman's lust. How would she ever face him again?

In that instant, she wished Bernard had killed her. Then she would not have to face Jacques or see the pity in his eyes every time he looked at her. Instinctively, she touched her left forearm, and her birthmark. What if Jacques had seen the crescent mark? What if everyone knew she was a woman? They were probably waiting to dispatch her as soon as they dealt with Lawrence Bernard's remains.

If she had trusted Jacques' intuition and watched Bernard more closely, she would have been prepared to defend herself. Paul had even tried to warn her of danger. Now she understood the fear she'd seen in his eyes, the loss of his dignity, the loss of his honor. It was a pity Paul did not have the fire of the Goddess to protect him.

Closing her eyes, Antoinette could feel a spark of the Great Mother's energy lingering within her. A small part of the rapture of Her white light of Power still remained. If she could only touch the Goddess once more. Could she smell wild lavender? Roses? Mint? The perfumes of the Goddess?

Her skin tingled and a feeling of well-being surrounded her. Yes, the Goddess was near.

"Beloved Mother," she prayed in a low whisper. "How can I thank you for my life?"

"You can thank me." Jacques answered from the shadows. He had been waiting for her to wake.

Antoinette snatched at the coverlet, drawing it high up under her chin. The sound of a flint striking a tinderbox hissed and a candle flame chased away the darkness.

"I did not know you were here." She felt a flush of crimson invade her cheeks. "I most humbly thank you as well."

Jacques wasted no time coming to her side. He reached for her hand and gently lifted it to his lips.

A faint thread of confusion swept over her. For an instant, she wanted to recoil from his touch, but her heart and his kind words urged her to be still. His touch was not like Bernard's. His voice was hypnotic, quickly silencing her fears.

"Antoinette. *Ma petite chère. Je suis désolé de votre mésaventure.* I should have been here to aid you sooner."

His eyes were compelling as they searched her face. How could she deny his sincerity? She turned her face away, trying to control her emotions.

Jacques recognized the anguished expression on her face and his tone turned serious. He needed to know the extent of her injuries. "Did he—"

"No!" Antoinette pulled her shredded honor together and the blanket higher around her neck. "It is my pride and my dignity that are spoiled."

Jacques kissed her hand lightly, holding it tenderly between his own.

"Oh, *mon amie.* I thought I'd lost you."

A comforting glow surrounded her, a glow that deepened when she looked into his eyes. She could not help, but welcome the feelings of protection and tenderness he offered. Wrapped in the love of the Goddess she had felt the same calmness. Had he too been touched by the Goddess?

"Did you see what happened?" she asked.

"I wish I had been able to leave the deck sooner, but I did not see him with you."

Jacques paused, reading the unspoken query in her eyes. "I came below, not knowing why. Then I heard your cries from outside my quarters and I realized you were in danger." He shook his head in disgust. "I can't tell you what I feared I would find when the bolt finally gave way. "

Did he see Her? Did the Goddess appear to him? Antoinette wanted to ask, but she knew the flames of Justice were only for Bernard's eyes. Jacques' pure heart would never let him see the vengeance of the Goddess.

Her mouth was dry as she tried to speak. "Is he dead?" She watched Jacques' jaw tighten.

He shook his head. "*Non!* But I'm sure by now that he wishes he were." Jacques threw her a questioning glance. "I suspected a spy aboard ship and was nearly sure I had found him out. I intended to question Bernard but had no real evidence to accuse him of anything."

She shook her head. "Yesterday morning, your cabin was in disarray."

"It was Bernard's handiwork."

"Ah," she said. "It all fits into place. Paul was on duty, he must have seen him in here. But his bruises were not all new. He had been beaten before."

"*C'est vrai!* I tried to tell you about Bernard. I heard rumors about Bernard's attachment to Paul. He has been Bernard's silent victim since we first set sail."

"You suspected something was wrong. Why didn't you tell me about Paul?"

"I tried." He ran his hands through his hair. "I had no words to explain these things to you—these harsh facts of life. It is hard to confess the sins of my fellowmen."

She silently agreed. He'd tried to warn her, but she would not listen. Until today she would not have believed him.

Shadows from the candlelight played on Antoinette's brow and Jacques brushed away a stray lock of dark hair from her forehead.

"I am sorry I suspected you and most distressed you found the true spy before I did."

"Ah, *oui.*" She reached up to touch her bruised face. "I am too."

At that moment she knew Jacques to be more than her friend. He had saved her life and her honor and she owed him a great debt.

For a long moment they sat in silence, then Jacques laid

her hand down on the coverlet and rose to leave. He steadied his hand on the desk beside him.

Did he feel it too? Antoinette wondered. Did he feel the bond strengthening between them?

Jacques cleared his throat and turned away.

"I'd better take a look at that blackguard and see if we can keep him alive for the balance of the voyage. I'd like you to have the pleasure of seeing him hang."

The thought of Bernard swinging helplessly in the King's gallows absurdly appealed to her.

"Jacques, Lawrence had the key to your desk. He was looking for some kind of map. He said there are mutineers on board waiting for his signal. He is—"

"Rest easy!" Jacques' command stopped her words. "You needn't worry about these things now."

"But—he knows who I am, what I am—"

"Antoinette." His voice soothing and comforting. "If he lives, I will make sure he tells no one that you are a most *lovely* woman."

She pulled the coverlet closer to her neck. It was not her gender she was concerned with now. Lawrence Bernard had heard her call upon the Goddess and he had felt Her fire. He knew Antoinette was more than *just* a woman.

Jacques turned to go, but there was one more thing she needed to know before she could rest easy.

"Jacques, if you did not see me with Bernard, why *did* you come below?"

"I—I don't know." He reached for the door. "I thought I heard you calling me. I felt—" He stopped and turned to her, wrinkling his brow. "Rest now. I'll return later."

Antoinette smiled and closed her eyes as Jacques left the room. He locked the door behind him and she heard him remove the key from the latch.

The Goddess worked in mystifying ways. In her time of need Antoinette had not called on her mortal friends for help. Instead, she called upon the Goddess and the Goddess in turn reached out to Jacques.

Yes. The Goddess had touched him, but only with Her gentle whisper.

ଓ

Antoinette resisted Jacques' tugging as he led her toward the dark prison hold and closer to Lawrence Bernard. She stopped some few feet from the locked doorway, unsure if she could look at him without despising him.

She was not pleased to find he had not died from his wounds and she was not at all sure she would not be tempted to finish the job. She shook her head at her unethical thoughts. She could never take someone's life, especially if they could not defend themselves. Even if it was someone as evil as Lawrence Bernard.

It was evident that Jacques' patience was waning.

"Come. You must keep him alive and for God's sake give him something to quiet him. We don't want him telling the crew about you." He held the oil light high enough to look at her face. "Antoinette, you are a healer. If Bernard dies we will never know who actually placed him aboard *La Réale*, or if we can trust anyone aboard ship."

She knew Jacques was right. If Bernard died without exposing his colleagues, they would never know who might surface to fulfill his mission. Antoinette nodded and she slid the lock back on its rusted track. Jacques pulled out his pistol and they stepped into the small cell together.

The light fell across Lawrence Bernard and Antoinette cringed as she walked the few steps toward him. He was pale, his face slack. Someone had made a crude attempt to stop his bleeding but the spreading red stain on the matted straw assured her that his injuries were severe.

If there was a pistol ball still lodged somewhere in his body, it would have to be removed or he would die. Even with her limited surgery skills, Bernard's chances were poor.

The stifling heat and the decaying smell of the prison hold made it hard to breathe. She turned her face up to Jacques, trying to focus on his eyes and not the swaying of the ship.

"I'm afraid his injuries may be beyond my skills. I don't think I can do anything for him."

Jacques waved the pistol in Bernard's direction.

"Either you heal him or I'll speed his departure. We can't leave him to suffer."

Antoinette's oath of healing vibrated in her head.

'I swear to heal all those in need.' The words echoed in her mind until she reluctantly acquiesced.

"I'll try. But I can't promise he will survive. I have not tended bullet wounds before. They require the skill of a surgeon, not a seamstress."

A moan escaped from the wounded man's lips and her healer's instinct ignited.

"I will need my pack with my bags of herbs and salves, hot water and a wash basin."

Jacques rose to leave, then stopped and cast her a concerned look. He pressed the pistol into her hand.

"Will you be all right? Alone with him?"

"*Mais oui.*" Antoinette replied as she began to cut away Bernard's bloodied shirt. Yes, she would be all right. She was protected by the Goddess. She would never be truly alone again.

Jacques turned as he reached the door and looked back. He was proud of Antoinette's strength. She was a formidable woman, capable of overcoming her misfortunes. Most definitely Marguerite's child. A touch of Guillaume's bravery shone through. Yes, she was brave, sensitive and beautiful. He felt a small twinge of longing as he thought of the artful grace of Antoinette's mother.

Marguerite. How he had worshiped her. She had been kind to him when he was not much older than Antoinette. Marguerite had been the first woman he had fallen in love with and the first to break his heart.

She was unattainable, the mother of his best friend and another man's wife. Chivalry demanded his discretion. He remembered the endless confessions he attended and the countless hours spent atoning for his sinful thoughts. The priests had been strict with his penance, but not strict enough for him to give up his longing for the beautiful woman.

Now much older, and hopefully wiser, Jacques knew it was normal for a virile young man to fall in love with such a beautiful woman—a woman whose compassion he saw reflected in her daughter's eyes.

Jacques wound his way through the lower decks, past the storage rooms and the crew's quarters. He was shocked to see the unhealthy surroundings Antoinette had endured without complaint.

Witnessing the half dressed men, gambling and sleeping in the near darkness, he understood why she had moved her pallet to a more secure location. As she had instructed, he passed the galley and slipped through a small doorway leading to the forward supply hold where she'd hidden her bed. It took him great effort to navigate her obstacle course even though she had been explicit in her directions.

Remembering Bernard's threat of mutineers, he gathered her shoulder pack and pallet in his arms. He would take her belongings to his quarters. The men would talk among themselves, but no one would dare to complain.

Antoinette removed the remainder of Bernard's shirt with a knife. It seemed absurd that she should save his life now, only to have him hanged later. It was even possible the courts would let him go without punishment. After all it would be her word against his. And she was, in essence, a stowaway. She shook her head in disgust. Men's logic was never sensible.

Jacques returned with her shoulder pack and placed it by her side. "Antoinette, I've moved your bedroll to my quarters."

She made no reply but looked up with questioning eyes that shimmered in the pale lamplight. Her hair strayed from its bounds and streamed down over her shoulders, barely touching her breasts.

"I felt, under the circumstances, you should not remain there. Quite honestly, I had no idea you were living in such horrid conditions."

"And the men, Jacques? Doesn't it bother you what they will say?"

"Antoinette, you are in danger." He shook his head, kneeling beside her. "We are all in danger and I cannot allow you to be placed in jeopardy again. These men have been at sea, away too long from their wives and lovers." He motioned to Bernard. "Next time I might not be around."

.His implication sent a cold shiver down her spine.

"What are the men saying about Bernard? About me?"

"They know I interrupted Bernard as he searched my quarters. They know he hurt you, but not that he attacked you." Jacques touched her shoulder. "They are suspicious. Evidently, you have been on his mind for quite some time. He made boast of his preference for your company. Though there is no evidence he told them you were a woman."

A crimson blush slowly crept up her face and she looked at Bernard, yet she steadied her hand as she thoroughly probed his side wound for a bullet.

Antoinette sighed in resignation. There was sound reasoning behind Jacques' actions. She had no way of knowing if summoning the Goddess was a one-time blessing or even if she could bring herself to kill for self-defense. But now she carried a small knife in her pocket. She would not be caught unarmed again and she would get off the ship as soon as land was near.

Antoinette pushed the thoughts of freedom aside and

turned her attention to Bernard's wound. The bullet was not deep, but was lodged in his side, very near his stomach. The bullet had to be removed and the bleeding stopped. She would have to make do with her crude surgical implements, a limited supply of herbs and ointments and Jacques' assistance. If properly tended, Bernard might have a chance of surviving.

Antoinette rummaged through her pack. Her supplies were dwindling. Nearly every bundle of mint and chamomile had been used for sea sickness. Almost every pot of healing balm for sun blisters. She withdrew a packet of powdered garlic, a crude cleanser at best but effective.

Working in silence, she prayed to Brighid to guide her knife to the object of her search as she recited her oath of patience and compassion.

"To heal all, wound none."

Jacques watched her skillfully administer her craft to Bernard's wound. He noticed her eyes and how intensely they focused when she found the bullet and removed it from Bernard's listless body. It seemed as though she felt the pain of her patient and he was amazed that she could express so much empathy for a man who had just tried to rape her. She was so delicate, yet so intense.

Holy Mother! Jacques turned his gaze from the loose curl stuck tight to Antoinette's damp neck. He could not be falling in love with her—not here, not now.

It would not do. He could not let it happen. But he knew he was powerless to stop his feelings.

When she washed the blood from her hands, he laid his hand on her shoulder. The unnatural coolness of her skin shocked him, yet he resisted the urge to pull her close to share his warmth.

It was evident she had depleted her energy with her efforts to heal her patient.

"Are you all right?" he asked.

"Yes. It's just so hot and I have been through so much today."

Jacques sat down next to her. "I am relieved to know I will not have to explain your death to the duchess."

Antoinette stretched out on the straw and leaned back against the cool wooden hull of the ship. Her head ached. She was exhausted. Her borrowed shirt and britches stuck to her like glue from Bernard's blood. What more could happen to her today?

Closing her eyes she gathered her remaining strength. She must tell Jacques everything before she lost her courage.

"Don't count yourself lucky yet," she said with a heavy sign. "There is much that you do not know of this evening's events. Before you shot him, I—"

"No!" Jacques interrupted her, shaking his head. "You don't have to tell me anything."

"Wait." Antoinette searched for a way to explain the power she'd shared with her protectress. The terrible power she had held over life and death. "Something happened—I can't explain it, but he must not regain consciousness until I am off this ship. He knows me. He has seen me. No, not just my body. He has seen—a manifestation of the Goddess."

Jacques looked at her with confusion, his eyes straining to focus on her dimly lit face.

"The Goddess came to me—shielded me—until you appeared," she said. "If Bernard recovers, he can stand witness to my powers. He might accuse me of witchcraft."

She waited for Jacques' expression to turn from sympathy to disgust, but his face was serious.

"That does pose a problem," he said calmly.

She could hardly believe Jacques' casual response. By aiding her, he was placing himself in even greater danger. He could be court-martialed, imprisoned or hanged.

"Treat his wounds and keep him drugged," Jacques said reassuringly. "Keep him secured and quiet. I'll deal with the crew."

Antoinette looked toward Bernard and hesitated, not wanting to foretell the man's future.

"I don't think he will make it back to France alive. His wound is too serious."

"Perhaps not." Jacques stood and offered his outstretched hand to her. "If he dies, we will have nothing to worry about. *N'est- ce pas?*"

"It is so," she said, rising wearily against his arm.

Though her hands were cool, her touch ignited a spark in his heart. It took determined effort not to pull her close. How easy it would be to hold her and seek out the comfort of her body. To touch her small, perfect lips and linger in their sweetness. But it was too soon and not the proper place to show her his affection.

"Antoinette. I've missed you."

"Ah—Jacques," she said boldly leaning against him. "It is long past time to heal our friendship."

Antoinette lay in Jacques' bed. The bright morning sunlight streamed through the open porthole. Jacques was still asleep on her pallet, his back turned away from her. The stray sunbeams played upon his bare shoulders, glittered among the fine silver threads of his hair then trailed down his back to his britches.

The past evening as he worked at his desk, copying his notes from his rutter to his chart, she'd watched him with mild amusement and pleasure. His white linen shirt had clung to his shoulders in the night's quiescent heat and he'd pulled his hair up from his neck in a tight queue to cool himself. But he'd refused to take off his shirt in her presence.

She watched the muscles of his arms tighten as he traced the outlined drawings with a gentle slide of his fingers before he lay pen to paper and made his mark, and she imagined the pressure of his finger sliding across her skin, gentle and caressing.

To think that he had once been a part of her family's life and she had never known of him. He was unpretentious, yet mysterious. She wondered why he spoke fondly of Ursule and Marguerite, but would not speak of his friendship with Gaston.

It pleased her to think Jacques was a part of her life now and the thought of leaving him filled her with melancholy. He'd been so kind to her, she found herself wanting to repay his kindness. His friendship gave her a sense of warmth and a comfort she had never known from a man.

She wondered if she'd met him in Brittany, if they would have become so close? Perhaps even become lovers? But they would never have met, she assured herself. The court and the sea were worlds apart.

The morning bells sounded the change of watch as Antoinette was falling asleep. She jumped hastily to her feet, regretting she must leave the security of Jacques' cabin and return to her shipboard duties. But things had to appear normal. Even if her sides still ached with bruises and her nerves were still on edge.

Jacques had given her new clothing. The britches were big for her slender figure, but cinched up and the length cut off, they fit and the cleanliness was welcome. They smelled of Jacques' locker, like cinnamon and sandalwood. A heady scent that stirred a strange feeling inside her. A feeling that would have to wait.

Jacques lay awake, staring at the wall, watching a small spider entwine its captured treasure in a fine crystalline thread. He had not slept—could not sleep. Not with Antoinette sleeping so near him. He admonished himself all night for bringing her to his quarters. But the idea of her falling to the lust of the crew made his stomach turn.

The men were anxious enough with the bad weather and the pending rendezvous with the fleet. Even the rumor that an officer might be sharing forbidden pleasures would probably be enough to cause a mutiny in itself. *La Réale* had to turn around soon, for everyone's sake. Especially for his peace of mind. Being near Antoinette was too tempting, too perilous for them both.

Jacques took a deep breath as her heard the door close when Antoinette left the cabin. All night his thoughts had been chaotic. Lovely Antoinette, sleeping peacefully on his bed. Desirable Antoinette, laying just within his reach. Dangerous Antoinette, a precarious piece of the puzzle of his life.

He had known many women, even loved a few, but Antoinette's innocence and strength pulled at his heart and mesmerized his soul. Even as he thought of her now, he ached to know more about her, to simply be with her. To hold her against him, feel her heart beat alongside his own. To comfort her and show her how much he cared for her, with tenderness and soft words.

Vagrant images floated through his mind and he struggled to push them away. He tried to concentrate on the creaking of the rigging as the sails were changed to catch the morning winds. Anything. Anything to shift his thoughts from Antoinette . But his mind returned hopelessly to her.

Chapter 13

Jacques' decision to move Antoinette's pallet was well-timed. It was evident Bernard had boasted about his desire for the young Étienne, and although no one knew exactly what happened between them, many of the crew believed Bernard had been shot in a lovers' quarrel.

Some of the men looked suspiciously at Antoinette, but none dared say a word. She watched them carefully, remembering no one could be trusted, except perhaps for Paul and maybe Cook.

Paul and Antoinette had sealed their shared secret with the promise that Paul would have the pleasure of testifying against Bernard at the King's High Court.

Now that he possessed power over the man who had humiliated him and so mortally wounded his spirit, Paul's self image flourished. He no longer looked like an abused child. He even sat watch over Bernard, but from the other side of the barred and bolted door.

"*Monsieur* Bernard is rousing," he whispered to Antoinette when she came to check on her patient. "He raves like a mad man. Talks of witches and curses."

"It's the fever. He'll be delirious for a while." She placed her hand on Paul's arm. "Thank you, *mon ami*, you are brave to face your adversary so calmly."

"No task is beyond your asking. You pulled me from the black depths of hell. I will always be indebted."

A soft down of a beard was beginning to show and Antoinette knew this lovely boy was quickly becoming a handsome man. Yet a worried look passed over his face.

"Is something wrong Paul?"

"It's just that—"

"Oui? You must know by now that you can speak freely with me."

He hesitated, then blurted out, "I know that you are not Étienne Clement." Paul's breathing quickened as they stood close in the small room.

"So—who do you think I am?"

"I don't know your true name, but I know you are someone important, someone who does not belong on a ship with men like us."

"Ah. What makes you so sure?"

Paul lowered his head lightly and she could tell he was blushing. "The other night, as you slept beside me... I woke and thought I had died. Then, I saw an angel behind you. A glow of light hovered about us, almost as if it guarded us as we slept. I woke again during the night and you were holding me. I felt as though I was in my mother's arms again. I knew then that you were not Étienne. No man could be so compassionate, or hold a friend so tenderly and fight for his life as desperately as you did for mine. I knew then that you were a woman."

He took a long deep breath as if a weight had been lifted from his shoulders. "I thought I dreamed my vision. I was embarrassed. But when I sat in the sunlight and you touched me, I felt that spark of light again, like a healing fire coursing through my body. I saw the angel around you again and your face softened. I knew you were more than you appeared to be; you are God's angel sent to save me."

Antoinette stood in silence. She hoped Paul would not betray her. The tone of his voice was without menace. But she was unsure how to respond. She placed her hand on his arm, to reassure him she was not upset at his confession.

"It's true, Paul. I am not Étienne, but neither am I God's angel." She could feel him relax under her touch as his convictions were confirmed.

"Then what are you doing here aboard this ship?"

"It is too long a story to tell you now. But until I can, you must not reveal my secret to anyone. *Monsieur* DuPrey knows my true identity. *Monsieur* Bernard has also seen the angel that protects me, but his mind has twisted it into a demon. That is why we must keep him quiet. No one else must know or I will not make it off this ship alive."

Paul nodded his understanding but Antoinette could tell that the man within the child needed a better explanation.

"I promise you will know the reasons behind my secrecy when it is safe to tell you. Until then, please keep our secret."

Paul smiled and as they parted Antoinette knew she could count on his silence and his friendship.

Antoinette climbed down the steep ladder to the dark hold. There was no light, save for the oil lamp she carried in her free hand, yet she felt no guilt at leaving Bernard alone in the dark. It was too dangerous to have fire so close to the tightly packed cargo. In fact she was bending the rules to even bring the oil lamp below deck.

He was awake when she unlocked the door and as the stark light hit Bernard's face, he turned his head toward the wall to protect his eyes. The light between them blinded his vision.

"Who's there?" His voice was weak. He struggled against his bonds. "Where am I?"

She had not anticipated his waking so soon. Approaching his side, she lowered her voice imitating Cook's provincial accent and placed the light near his head. "You are in the prison hold, *Monsieur.* Capn's orders."

"The captain? The bastard. I must tell someone he is bewitched. We have a witch, a demon, on this ship."

"Drink this."

She placed the cup in his lips, tilting it back so the thick bitter liquid slid down his throat. He coughed as the potion stung his gullet and when she lifted his head to offer him water he saw her face.

Antoinette returned his gaze, watching his eyes glaze and his face slacken from terror to helplessness as the potion took hold of him.

"I'll take you to hell with me," he whispered. "You won't get away with this."

Antoinette backed into the shadows and watched as the drug took affect, then she bolted the door behind her and raced up the steps. She prayed she had not killed him with her potion. There was nothing she could do but wait.

☙

Jacques spun on his heels. The wind whipped his cloak around his knees. "They're not here." He waved his hand toward the vacant horizon. "I couldn't have made an error. We should have met the fleet by sunrise."

Paul raised his hands to the billowing clouds. "I would not send men into weather like this," he said. Since his recovery he had never been far from Antoinette or Jacques' side. "I would wait until the seas were calm. Surely the fishermen are waiting out the coming storm."

Jacques stepped toward Antoinette who had come to join him and Paul on deck. He spoke to them in a low whisper, nodding over his shoulder at the men gathered around the lower deck. "You must both get about your work. We cannot afford for the crew to become alarmed."

"*Oui*, Captain." Paul smiled at Antoinette before he raced down the ladder. "He will not get us lost. He is the navigator."

Jacques turned to face Antoinette. He could read the disappointment on her face and he stepped to her side.

"Lost?" she asked.

This couldn't have come at a worse time, he thought. The men were already anxious, the weather was definitely changing and by the next evening they would probably be in the midst of a great storm.

"Be still, *mon amie*." He pulled her into the lee of the sails. "I know where we are."

"I have faith in you, Jacques. But where is the fleet?"

"Paul is right. The fishermen are wise, they read the signs of the sky. They won't risk the building seas and the storm that approaches. It is still far away. It may not even hit until tomorrow." He looked up at the sky. "Feel how the winds pull into the clouds. They will gather strength then lash out with fury as they come across the sea."

He turned back to face her. Seeing the worry on her face,

he placed his hand on her arm. He had to hide his concern at the signs of the approaching storm.

"Don't be afraid. I have been through many storms. It comes with the trade. But it's wise to be concerned and prepared. By the way, how is our captive?"

"I've tied him up and given him a strong draught, he'll sleep the day out." She did not tell him of the terror she saw in Bernard's face. "If I he lives through the soporific I gave him."

Jacques looked into her bright eyes and the storm seemed suddenly unimportant. He could feel the softness of her flesh through the shirt's thin fabric and quickly removed his hand.

"Remind me to stay on your good side," he whispered as he returned to his sightings.

Strong winds pulled *La Réale* on a broad reach to the west. Jacques kept his course, hoping the fleet would appear, but his instincts told him they would not venture into the building seas unless they were desperate for supplies.

The crewmen waited restlessly, watching, dreading the certainty of the pending squall as *La Réale* continued to sail on slow rolling waves.

It was long into evening before Antoinette returned to check on Bernard. As she descended into the dark hold, she prepared herself for the possibility he might be dead from his wound or that she may have killed him with too much of the opiate.

When she entered the cell, he lay quiet on the pallet. She could tell he was awake. He had tried to loosen his bonds, but had only succeeded in tearing open his wound. His dark hair matted against his head in fever, his face as pale as the straw he lay upon. The energy surrounding him glowed red with hatred.

He glared at her, his face pained with fatigue. There was no doubt that he knew his perilous position.

Antoinette stepped toward him, holding the light so she could inspect his injuries.

"My men will have you stripped and beaten and your lifeless body hauled to the top of the mast when they learn who you really are," he said coldly.

"Silence!" She tugged at his blood soaked bandage and he winced in pain. "What makes you think anyone will listen to the ravings of a traitor?"

She cleaned the wound, this time without the aid of numbing drugs, and winced as she watched the pain shoot through him.

Still, malice seethed through his words. "Jacques will pay for this as well, you know. I will question him first and finish with him what I started with you."

Antoinette looked into his eyes. Her glance was hard and pitiless, yet she refused to take the bait he dangled in front of her.

"Don't worry. I will keep him alive," Bernard continued. "I will need him to keep me company and to guide us safely back to France."

Unflustered by his threats, she finished her work and turned away from the fear he tried to plant in her mind. She could not let him think he might win this battle. A sudden flash of defensive spirit rallied inside her.

"This is between the two of us. I hold the power now," she said, remembering his threat as he had held his knife to her heart. "I can *heal* you or *kill* you. Leave Jacques out of this or I swear by the Goddess I will leave you here to die and your flesh to rot."

"Begone from me, whore of Satan!" Bernard shouted, pulling against his restraining ropes. His words were followed by a groan of pain.

His vile threat stung her courage, the volume of his fear threatened to steal her strength. Yet she said nothing knowing a retort would give him too much pleasure. Instead, she bolted the door behind her, leaving him in darkness.

Chapter 14

Jacques scanned his cabin, checking the details. Everything had to be perfect. He'd arranged for Antoinette to enjoy a bath in the seclusion of his cabin and a few minutes of solitude to pray to her goddess. Praying—if it was proper to call it praying—was something he noticed she did with discretion. Now that he knew her philosophy, he realized the words she spoke in low whispers and the small subtle gestures she made to the sea and the heavens were her way of honoring her gods.

If tomorrow's gale was as strong as he feared, everyone aboard *La Réale* should pray to whatever gods they revered. He had already made his act of contrition and felt certain Antoinette would appreciate the time alone.

Afterward, they would share a meal and if he could form his desire into the right words, he would tell her how much he cared for her. It had to be tonight. He could wait no longer. He would pledge his love and in the morning they would face the storm and possibly death at sea together.

The small oil lamp glowed on the edge of his chart table, and the light from several candles bathed the small room with an intimate ambiance. He wished he could watch her wash, watch her pour the water through her long dark hair and see the water bead on her body like fresh pearls plucked from their shells. He remembered the graceful swell of her breasts beneath the blankets as she lay unconscious in his bed. He'd removed her torn shirt, bloodied by Bernard's wound, but he'd been too concerned for her safety to feel anything but compassion. No desire crossed his mind until he watched her sleeping, listened to her soft rhythmic breathing. When she opened her eyes and thanked him for saving her life, whatever small glimmer of love that was secreted in his heart had burst into full flame.

Jacques sighed, knowing only his charts and books would be witnesses to her privacy.

He fingered the lace on the white tunic laying across his bed. He'd purchased it in Paris, intended to wear it on his return interview with King Charles, but now he would give it to Antoinette. With a few decorative additions he'd gathered together, the tunic made an excellent gown. It would allow her to feel like the lovely young woman she was.

He took a dark green scarf decorated with silver embroidery from the depths of his locker and laid it across the tunic. It was the same deep green as Antoinette's eyes.

"Antoinette." He whispered to the empty room. "My beautiful Antoinette."

There was no denying that he was hopelessly, helplessly in love. He wished he could give her more than a meager offering of a bath and a meal.

A short rap on the door vanished the bold thoughts from Jacques' mind. He jumped up, crossed the small room and opened the latch with one fluid motion.

Antoinette stood in the doorway. She did not look at all like the beautiful woman he had just imagined, more like a small boy with a smudged and dirty face, clothes dusty and smelly from a long day's work.

As she stepped into the room, her eyes widened with curiosity. Her gaze traveled from the buckets of water to the empty wash tub.

"What's this?"

Jacques quickly closed the door. "I thought you would enjoy a bath. In private, of course," he added quickly. "It will take me an hour or so to take the readings I need. You will have plenty of time and you may want to do... whatever it is you do, to ask for your Goddess' blessings. The approaching storm may be worse than we all fear. The seas are calm now, but they will build through the night."

Antoinette walked past him to the center of the room and dipped her hand into the water.

"It has been so long since I really washed my hair." She turned back to Jacques, her green eyes dancing. "Yes, if you do not mind, afterward I would like some time. I would like to pay homage to the Goddess, to the Ancient Ones. Her look was innocent, uncompromising.

"If you wish, you may participate in my ritual. I promise you would not be offended. I could include the Blessed Virgin in my ceremony."

Jacques was surprised at her offer and checked his impulse to reach for the crucifix against his chest.

"Thank you, but I must take my readings before the clouds completely obscure the sky."

Antoinette nodded. "I understand. Perhaps next time I can persuade you."

Jacques took her hand and held it for a long moment.

"I would be proud to witness the love you have for your Goddess. She must be very special to warrant your prayers."

"The Goddess deserves all our prayers."

Antoinette was glad to have a friend who accepted her, who did not reproach her for her beliefs. Jacques, a devoted Christian, had set aside his personal convictions to allow her the freedom to be herself. She could see the sincerity in his face, read it in his eyes.

"After your ceremony," he said, releasing her hand. "I hope you will share a meal with me." He motioned to the tins of food and bottle on the table. "It's not much, some fruit, nuts, cider from Rouen."

Antoinette lowered her gaze and her dark lashes brushed lightly against her cheeks.

"*Mon plaisir.*"

Jacques swung his green cloak about his shoulders then

left her with a strict command to bolt the door. He would not return until the change of watch at least an hour away.

Alone, Antoinette looked at the lavish amount of fresh water he'd procured for her bath. Fresh water was precious, the sustenance of life aboard ship and the two buckets of water in the middle of the room were an extravagance.

Antoinette bolted the door and cast aside her clothing. She took four candles from the table and placed them around the room, marking the four directions, then placed the buckets of water and the empty washbasin in the center.

From her shoulder pack she withdrew an athame, the silver ritual dagger and a ceramic chalice which she placed at her feet. She unstopped a vial of lavender oil and allowed one drop to touch her finger, then anointed her forehead, tracing the shape of an upturned crescent with the sweet scented essence.

"Great Mother. Bless me. Grant me your wisdom and your love."

The chalice filled with water she held in one hand, her athame in the other. She lifted her arms to the East, casting the sacred circle to open the veil between the worlds.

"Ancient Ones, welcome! May I always listen to the spirit winds that bring me your voices." She turned southward. "May I always honor the sacred fires that live in all creation." She turned westward toward the setting sun. "May the waters that give life to all the Mother's children be revered."

Finally she turned to the North. "May the powers of earth guard this circle with their strength."

She moved back to the center of her circle and faced East once more, the direction of her power.

"The circle is bound, with love around.
Between the worlds I stand,
at the Ancient Ones' command."

With the circle completed, the magic would protect her. If there were intruders threatening her ancient ritual of cleansing, the energy surrounding the circle would shimmer and darken, warning her of danger. The chalice and dagger resting at her feet, she raised her hands and palms toward the sky. Her voice was soft and reverent.

"Lady of Light, eternal circle, hear the call of your priestess, hear the voice of your daughter, touch me with your magic."

She crossed her hands above her heart and listened to the rhythm of her breathing. Soon it matched the beat of her pulse and she stretched her hands over the bucket of water.

"Anoint my soul with your holy fire."

Instantly, Antoinette's hands tingled and the water charged with the power of the Ancient Ones. She opened her eyes. Brighid's holy flame reflected in the water.

Antoinette was always amazed at the immense power such simple chants invoked. Yet she knew they were not just simple chants. The true meaning of the words were ancient, powerful and magical.

She scooped the magically warmed water into her hands and washed her face. As she worked the hard soap into her tangled hair, she thought of all the fear and anger she had witnessed—in Brittany, on the ship—and as she rinsed her hair she visualized all that hate and sorrow washing from her mind.

She soaped herself from head to toe then stepped into the washtub and slid down into the water, letting the soapy bubbles seek out long neglected places.

Cup by cup, the cleansing water washed the vexing problems away. She settled into the moment and relaxed until the water began to chill. Then she stood and poured the remaining clear water over her body. The water glistened on her skin like shining raindrops. A rough linen towel scrubbed away the remaining smudges of dirt.

She slipped the white tunic over her head, delighting in the crisp feel of newness and the smell of sandalwood incense from Jacques' locker. It was surely his finest and quite expensive, for it felt exquisite against her clean naked skin. She held the delicate green silk scarf up to the candlelight and looked through the gossamer fabric at the outline of her hand. On either end of the scarf faint outlines of flying birds were embroidered into the fabric with tiny silver threads.

Respectfully, she kissed the scarf as though it were a sacrament and tied it around her waist. She pinned the silver brooch Anne had given her to the sash. She wished for a mirror to groom her hair, to look her best for Jacques, but was satisfied with her reflection in the wash basin. She was pleased he would want to spend time with her, not as his apprentice but as a woman.

A blush crept across her face as she remembered the few times he had touched her, of the fire, no, the *flame* that kissed her skin and spread its fingers through her body. The feeling was akin to an empty longing in the center of her heart. Was this love? she wondered.

Jacques' voice turned soft when he spoke to her alone. Did

he desire to be more than just her friend? Did his feelings mirror her own?

Antoinette wondered with an anxious heart what she could expect from an intimate evening with him. She owed her life to him and she would gladly welcome him as her first lover. Although this was hardly the place to begin such an affair, hardly the time to start something so precious.

As she combed her hair she sat in the glow of the soft candlelight, listening to the waves glide past the sides of the ship. A cooling breeze blew through the open porthole.

Ah—Sister Wind.

The rhythm of the wind mimicked her heartbeat, then as her mind quieted, she watched the flickering candlelight.

"Guardians of water, giver of life. Bright lady of air—star seeker," she chanted softly. "Goddess of fire, spark of life. Powers of earth, center of all. Guide me tonight, fill me with your love and light. Reveal to me my destiny."

Antoinette closed her eyes and leaned back against the berth. She drifted and dreamed of soft kisses and caresses, of lying in her lover's arms, strong and safe. She could smell the faint scent of lavender amidst the sharp sea air, the crisp smell of evergreens and the raw freshness of earth. She saw herself running across fields brushed with flowers, running playfully away from her lover. He called her name in a slow, deep rhythm. She turned.

The ring of the night watch broke her spell, jarring her back to the cabin. She tried in vain to pull the memory back, to calm her heartbeat. She had seen her lover's face, fine boned and bronzed and the same dark eyes that disrupted her dreams. Eyes that shimmered beneath finely shaped brows like polished ebony set in a golden broach.

Her heart felt suddenly heavy. The eyes were dark, entrancing; not light and silver, like Jacques'.

Whose eyes then? What man invaded her visions? She rubbed her hands across her face as though she could wipe away the foolishness of her request. She had asked to see her destiny and her visions seldom lied. Someone waited for her. But where?

Heavy footfalls of the crew moving to their stations urged her to regain her composure. She must lift the veil of magic before Jacques returned.

Walking counter clockwise to close the circle she chanted. "Depart in peace all powers of the visible and invisible."

Her words felt hollow, her heart and senses confused.

"Blessed Mother, you are always with me, in me—may I go

forth with your blessings in my heart."

A soft knock pulled her from her prayers. Quickly she replaced the candles on the table and put away her ceremonial tools. The magic would dissipate once she opened the door.

Antoinette emptied the washtub out the rear cabin window, moved the buckets to the opposite side of the room and threw back the bolt on the door. Jacques slipped inside, closing the door behind him.

The faint intermingling scent of lavender and sandalwood filled his senses. He looked in awe at the beautiful woman standing before him. She was more exquisite than he had ever imagined, the most beautiful woman he had ever known and she stood there, before him, waiting for him.

He strained against the growing passion that threatened to betray him. He'd promised himself to go slowly, to make the moments last.

Soft brown hair floated over Antoinette's shoulders like gossamer, a few stray wisps of brown curls still clung damply against her forehead. The white tunic glowed against her tanned skin and the scarf tied around her waist accentuated the firmness of her breasts.

When she lifted her head to greet him, her trance-glazed eyes shone like iridescent emeralds. He took her hands in his, desperately searching for words to describe her.

"You are—magnificent."

Antoinette lowered her head in such innocent modesty that he almost shared her embarrassment at his compliment. The hot blush of her skin transferred to his hands and he quickly pushed her out to arm's length, spinning her around like a dancer.

"Let me look at you." He grinned as though he'd found a lost jewel. "Such elegance in simplicity. *Très bon*!" He unclasped his dark green cloak and laid it at the foot of his bed. "Come, let us dine together and begin our friendship anew."

Antoinette watched with anticipation as he took a fine linen cloth from his locker and spread it over the small writing table. He brought out more tins of fruit and two goblets, arranging the items so they made a dazzling display in the candlelight.

She wondered if she had misread his intentions. He was not acting at all like the lovesick suitors that clamored at Anne's door. He was a gentle man, an honorable man.

Jacques took her hand and led her to the table.

"Until I may better serve you, *Mademoiselle,* I can only offer you a wanderer's sup."

His cheerfulness slowly broke through her uncertainty. In spite of her disturbing vision, she would enjoy their evening , whatever came to pass.

Carefully arranged before her was no pauper's meal, but one fit for the Queen herself. Exquisite dried fruits and nuts and other exotic delicacies laid on a golden plate, waited her appetite.

She knew of Jacques' status. He traveled often as emissary for the king. He had traded with the merchants of the Far East and had sailed the length of the African coast and width of the Mediterranean Sea. But she had no idea of his wealth.

He handed her a goblet of cider and she raised it in a toast to their friendship.

"May your way be guided by light and love."

"And yours," he replied. He wondered if the love she spoke of was the love of God or a deep and abiding love between kindred souls.

"I can feel the ship strain to push through the waves." Antoinette remarked, breaking into his thoughts. The drink slipped over the rim of her goblet and drops of red cider spread onto the white linen cloth. "Is the sky still angry?"

"*Oui, chère,*" he sighed. "The men will be storm rigging the ship and preparing for a squall come morning."

He waved his hand, dismissing the outside world. "But let's not talk of that. I wish to think of other things tonight." He saw a faint blush ascend her cheeks as she turned her head in the candlelight. Was she so pure at heart that the mere suggestion of his companionship embarrassed her?

"Antoinette." He took her hand and kissed it lightly. "Has no one told you that you are beautiful or that they delight in your company?"

She lifted her gaze from her hand to Jacques' face. A light smile crossing her lips. So it comes, she thought. He did intend to seduce her.

"You forget, Jacques, I have not lived the normal life of a Breton maiden. I was schooled in the arts of healing and in the service to the Goddess. I have never known the love of a man." Her hand burned where Jacques had kissed it so tenderly and she quickly withdrew it from further capture.

"Ah, love." He leaned back against the hard wooden chair. "Many have known love, but have never truly been loved."

Jacques grew silent, remembering that he had loved only one woman in his life—Marguerite Charboneau. And he was falling in love with her all over again.

Antoinette was so much like her mother; they both

possessed a mystical love of life and a passionate, caring soul. Yes, he had loved Marguerite, with all his heart, but this time things would be right. He would not have to repent for his sin of coveting another man's wife or for his thoughts of impropriety.

Jacques suddenly realized he had been silent far too long for good manners. "*Pardon.* I was thinking about your mother. She was also a most beautiful woman."

"They say she is still beautiful. Do you know that she has lived with the Carmelites at their convent in Saint-Pol-de-Leon these past few years? I have not seen her, but I understand she has taken the vows of the sisters." Surely, as a Christian, Jacques would be happy that her mother had embraced the Blessed Virgin and had not joined the pagan sisterhood. "How well did you know my family?" she asked. "I have never heard Ursule speak of you." She bit into a piece of dried apricot.

"It's a long story." Gaston and I—we parted friendship under less than favorable circumstances. Reasons that would be better left to rest. Perhaps someday I will tell you, but not tonight."

Jacques rose from the table and walked to his charts. He busied himself rearranging them, hoping Antoinette would not notice his anxiety. But his memories would not let go. She had re-opened a wound in his soul that would never heal. A wound he would carry with him to the grave.

Marguerite was already a mature woman when Gaston took him to their home in Rennes. Like her daughter, Marguerite had a lust for life, a quick wit and a delicate enchanting laugh. Her husband, Guillaume, was a hired mercenary for King Louis. He preferred the treasures of the crusades and the riches of war to Marguerite's love and was seldom home. His infrequent visits yielded only sorrow and pain for Gaston's mother.

But Marguerite was a strong woman. She managed their estate at Rennes quite efficiently while her husband was away.

During the summer of Jacques' sixteenth year, while spending a few months at Rennes, he and Marguerite developed a close friendship. They shared their secrets and his dreams for the future.

One warm evening he and Marguerite were walking in her private garden. She had just placed a light kiss on Jacques' cheek when Gaston came upon them. Convinced that Jacques and his mother were lovers, he drew his sword and challenged Jacques.

Marguerite begged him to spare Jacques' life and swore

that they were chaste friends; that they were unjustly accused. After much persuasion and many harsh words, Gaston released Jacques from his challenge. Jacques, heartbroken, left Rennes forever.

Several years had passed when he learned of Guillaume's death in the war. Soon afterward Gaston dropped out of sight and Jacques lost all hope of ever reconciling with his friend.

Jacques brushed his hand over his face as if he could wipe away the memories. Pensively, he crossed the room and withdrew a small object from his locker, then knelt at Antoinette's side. He placed a locket in her palm.

She looked curiously at Jacques, then opened the delicate gold catch. Inside the locket were two miniature portraits, one of Gaston and one of her mother.

"You see," Jacques said, pointing to the portraits. "Gaston and I were once the very best of friends."

She held the locket up to the candle, admiring the detailed workmanship and the delicately painted images of long forgotten faces. Gaston, at sixteen, had a shock of golden hair, a delicate smile and a hard straight brow. His eyes were blue and shaped like their mother's. Marguerite's hair was dark. Her eyes were green like Antoinette's but her skin was translucent and pale, like the fine silky wings of a white butterfly.

Antoinette turned to Jacques, focusing her attention on his face, so different from Gaston's. "They are wonderful. Thank you for sharing them with me."

Gently, he took the locket from her, placed it on the small table. "I want you to have the locket," he said. "But I don't want to talk of family or friends or the past. I want to talk about you, learn who you are, what you desire. I want to know everything."

He took her hand and touched her fingers to his lips; they smelled of apricots and cinnamon. The softness of her skin made him anxious to hold her closer and when he looked into her trusting face he knew that, if unchecked, his passion for her would soon overwhelm him.

"*Par Dieu!*" He rose hastily and towered above her for a moment before turning toward the porthole window. He let out a breath of frustration with his words. "Can't you see I am at your mercy?"

Antoinette moved quickly to his side. "If I have misled you to think I have experience in matters of the heart, I beg pardon." She placed her hand on his shoulder. His muscles tightened at her touch. "I do not know how to react to such words of love."

The tension released in his body and he slowly turned to face her. For a moment they stood in silence, then she raised her hand from his shoulder to his neck. Trembling, as she untied the few laces down the front of his tunic and boldly pushed it back over his shoulders. She ran her palms across his warm smooth skin, allowing her fingers to choose their path, tracing the jagged scar traversing the taut muscles of his sword arm, where a well-aimed blade had nearly found its mark.

A small hiss escaped Jacques' lips and she glanced up to see a wave of pleasure cross his face. His breath quickened and she leaned forward to kiss him.

"No," Jacques said softly, clasping her arms and stepping back. "Not yet." His whispered words were barely audible in the deafening silence of the room. Then he stroked her hair, caught a curl in his fingers, and let the silken strands slide back to rest against her neck. He touched her cheek with the back of his hand then moved down her neck to the collar of her tunic.

Antoinette closed her eyes as the caressing vibrations filled her, waiting for his embrace to enfold her again. Yes, she thought. This is the feeling she had been waiting for.

Jacques pulled her to him, encircled her in his arms. They were firm, as she suspected, yet gently comforting. She buried her face into the folds of his shirt. Like her tunic, it smelled of incense, sandalwood and cedar, and the underlying scent of a man.

"*Mon cœur*, my heart." He kissed her hair. "I would introduce you to the wonders of love, of passion, but only when you are sure that it is time for you to experience these things."

She was silent for the space of a heartbeat before she answered. "I am sure."

He cupped her chin in his hand and placed a slow kiss on her lips. With the tender guidance of his hand, he urged her to sit on the edge of the berth. Slowly he unbuttoned the cuff at the end of her billowing sleeve. Antoinette closed her eyes and sighed, listening to her heart beat loudly, feeling the warmth of his body. He took her hand once more and raised it to his lips then turning it over, kissed her palm, her wrist.

Antoinette held her breath. She had forgotten the crescent symbol on her wrist and the superstitions of the Christians. Her birthmark was considered the marking of a witch. She began to pull her arm away but Jacques kissed the pink moon shape, looked up at her and smiled.

"It is the mark of my birth," she quickly explained.

"*Ma chère.*" The words took on new meaning in his heart even as he spoke them. "Remember? I have seen your wrist before. I know you are not an enchantress. But if you were, I would love you still."

She looked up at him, her gaze filled with pleasure.

"Really, Jacques? You are not afraid of me?"

"No. If what I feel for you is but a spell you have cast upon me, then so be it." He eased her into dark shadows of the berth. "Come lie beside me."

He leaned to kiss her lips and she looked deeply into his eyes. They were dark and rimmed in silver. They were not the eyes she had seen in her vision, she realized, but they held a deep love she wanted desperately to return.

Suddenly, the sound of ripping wood echoed against the walls of the small room. The hinges and bolt of the cabin door gave way with an exploding shatter.

Chapter 15

Jacques jumped to his feet, steadying himself against the rolling of the ship. He pulled his pistol from beneath his pillow. It was loaded and ready to fire.

Undaunted by Jacques' gun, three swarthy men rushed through the doorway, filling the cabin with their bulky form. They held small knives and pistols.

"What is the meaning of this?" he demanded.

There was a moment of silence, then from behind the men Lawrence Bernard sauntered forward, his face as pale as death. He moved unsteadily as the ship pitched beneath him. If it had not been for the bright stain of blood spreading through the bandage at his side, Jacques would have believed Bernard to be a walking wraith.

"Step aside." Bernard enforced his command with a wave of a pistol. His anger was wild and uncontrollable. "Hand over the witch. We will release you from her enchantment."

Instinctively, Jacques moved to shield Antoinette.

"Stand back! She is not a witch. Leave my cabin or I'll blow a hole *through* you this time!"

"You have no more authority. The ship now belongs to the Church." Bernard mocked. "I'll have that key to the armory locker as well."

Fearless of Jacques' weapon, Bernard stepped forward. Jacques blocked his way and aimed his pistol at Bernard. Just as quickly Bernard turned his weapon toward Antoinette.

For an instant Jacques' gaze shifted past his adversary to the men behind him. They were all deckhands with whom he'd shared a word or two.

"Where are my men?" Jacques asked.

Bernard's nostrils flared. His lips formed a thin smile beneath his mustache. "They are in the hold, where you will soon join them."

It was worse than Jacques feared. With no men to back him up, all was lost. Bernard would have the ship, and worst of all, he would have Antoinette.

Bernard seized Jacques' brief moment of indecision to act. With a silent nod from Bernard, a man rushed toward Antoinette. Jacques swirled, fired his pistol and the man fell to his knees. Then strong arms grabbed Jacques. He struggled as the men pulled Antoinette from his berth. One of the men cast the bedroll aside and the weapons beneath it were revealed.

"Take him below! We'll shoot the lock off." Bernard turned to Antoinette. "Take her topside."

Resisting, she lashed out at her assailants' knees and face. Strong arms encircled her, blocked her movements. She saw a somber expression cross Jacques' face and realized the hopelessness of their situation. Even if he lived, he would be powerless to help her.

She spun toward Bernard with rage. "You will regret this. You have no idea of the danger you are calling forth. Have you forgotten my power so quickly?"

Bernard's eyes blazed with a mixture of fear and apprehension. "Your threats will be useless when I'm done with you."

Jacques struggled against his captors as Antoinette was roughly ushered from the cabin. His world—their world—was tumbling in chaos.

Bernard turned to him. A muscle flicked slowly at the edge of his mouth. He raised his arm and stroked Jacques' cheek with the back of his hand.

"I will deal with you later, *mon ami.* We have things to discuss."

Jacques made no move to resist the man's caress, but his gray eyes narrowed and burned with his undeniable, unspoken response. Bernard turned coldly away and walked to the charts. Jacques stiffened and Bernard made a low laugh of triumph.

"We're near, aren't we?" he said, delicately fingering the parchment. "The New World is within our grasp. Where is the original chart?"

"You'll never see the New World, Bernard. Even if there was a chart, you would never be able to follow it. Your kind lack the courage to venture into the unknown."

Bernard crossed the distance of the room in two steps, drew back his hand and struck Jacques swiftly across the face.

"Throw him in the hold," he demanded. "But don't harm him. We'll need him for the return trip."

A heavy rain loomed in the west, hanging like a dark omen in the belly of the clouds. Ominous shapes built over the water, holding back their majestic fury. Rain fell atop the whitecaps in the distance.

La Réale tossed, waves breaking across her bow. Torrents of water streamed across the deck and drained into open hatchways.

Antoinette was silent as the men forced her topside. She knew that words of anger and outrage would diminish her power. The wind pushed her white gown tight against the swell of her breasts and whipped her long unbound hair across her face with each heavy gust. The deck fell beneath her feet as the ship dipped into the trough of a wave to rise up again as it crested the next, but she was not frightened. She would bide her time before she called on the Goddess to challenge her persecutors.

The sky shuddered with crash of thunder and suddenly Lawrence Bernard stood before her, his face reflecting the dark rage of the clouds behind him. He gripped the railing, resisting the pitch and roll of the ship.

Antoinette concentrated on Bernard's face. Whatever he intended to do, she would fight him till the end.

"Tie her to the mast!" Bernard said triumphantly.

The men turned her and secured her arms around the heavy beam. The side of her face pressed hard against the rough timber and the bitter smell of pitch stung her nostrils. She looked beyond the swaying rails, into the rolling sea, and her stomach spun with a sudden weakness. Closing her eyes, she swallowed the tightness that gripped her throat. There was so much motion, too much confusion to concentrate.

She felt Bernard standing beside her and she snapped

open her eyes. He leaned close to her ear.

"You should have finished me when you had the chance," he whispered.

Antoinette focused her defiant gaze on him and he stepped back. A visible desperate panic flowed over him.

"It is not *I* whom you should fear for your actions this day," she said calmly. "but the wrath of the Goddess and the Ancient Ones whom I serve. Their justice will follow you wherever you go from this day forward, and Their judgment will prevail upon your destiny."

Bernard grabbed a cloth from a nearby crewman, ripped it in half, and tied one piece firmly across Antoinette's mouth.

A short flicker of lightning hit the water in front of the ship and in that moment of brightness Antoinette saw Paul hiding behind a barrel at the end of the deck. She struggled to hold his gaze, sending him a warning and a plea for help. Then just as quickly Paul disappeared down the far hatchway. Had he understood her? Would he have enough courage?

Gusting wind tore violently at the unattended sails, sending ragged tears down the length of the storm jib. Lightning flashed, threatening to strike the tall mast.

Without warning Bernard bound the remainder of the foul smelling cloth across Antoinette eyes.

"Set weather sail," the quartermaster commanded from across the deck.

Hastily storm seasoned men left the deck and scrambled up the rigging to secure the sails. Then Antoinette heard the quartermaster step forward.

"*Monsieur* Bernard. End this soon and get the men below. The storm is full upon us. "

The truth in the old man's words was evident and Bernard hastened to heed them. Grabbing the back of Antoinette's tunic, he ripped the fabric to her waist. He snatched a whip from the boatswain's hand and cracked the tip against the fury of the wind.

"Now, you will suffer for your sins against God and your defiance toward me!"

The sky crackled with sparks of fire as the leather of the whip bit into Antoinette's skin, tracing ragged pink swells across her back. Her body flinched, reacting to the pain.

Beloved Mother come to me, she prayed. *Send me your power to overcome my human weakness.*

La Réale lurched across an angry wave, knocking Bernard back against the structure of the mizzendeck. He regained his footing, cringed at the pain spreading through his reopened wound. He raised the whip, struck again, and thin lines of blood trickled down Antoinette's back, staining the deep green silk still tied about her waist.

Bernard's actions echoed the building force of the wind. Fighting against the rolling of the ship, he staggered toward her, dagger in his hand.

A rogue wave slammed against *La Réale's* hull, pitched the ship sideways against the waves and slammed Bernard onto his already injured side. Torrents of water streamed across the deck, pulling him with apocalyptic force against the wooden railing. He struggled for a handhold as the water beat relentlessly against him, rolled him, tossed him, then spit him wet and breathless back onto the lurching deck.

His words were swallowed by the howling wind. "Die, witch! May God send you to the depths of Hell!"

Raising himself to his knees, he pulled against a dangling line and inched his way toward the open hatchway. With a slam of the hard wooden doors, he closed the hatch and disappeared.

Through the din of the storm, Antoinette heard the hatch close and realized she had been left to perish in the storm.

Blessed Mother, do *with me as you will. I am ready.*

ꝏ

How could I have been so blind? What a fool!

Jacques' mind raced in torment as he weathered the storm in the prison hold. He should have killed Lawrence Bernard, he thought. But he'd let the bastard live. Now his heart rent as fiercely as the sails he could hear ripping above him. He'd found Antoinette only to lose her by his inaction. Now their fate was in the hands of God.

"Holy Virgin, Mother of God," Jacques prayed. "Blessed is the fruit of Thy womb Jesus—"

"*Monsieur* DuPrey, *Monsieur* DuPrey."

Paul called to him in the darkness. A dim light shown through the cracks in the hold's door. It could mean his freedom.

"Here lad! Behind the door. Spring the latch."

Paul's hands shook as he fumbled awkwardly with the bolt. "*Monsieur, Monsieur*—Our friend is in great danger, Lawrence Bernard has tied her to the mast. He will kill her. We must help."

The door sprang open with a *thud* as Jacques pushed it outward. The ship's sudden roll nearly knocked them both to the floor. He clutched the boy by the shoulders.

"What did you say?"

Paul voice was shaky voice. "*Monsieur* Bernard has taken her topside. He will kill her, I know he will."

Jacques released his grip and leapt up the ladder, two steps at a time.

Paul tugged at his pant's leg. "Let me come with you *Monsieur*. You will need help. The first officer is a dangerous man."

Jacques looked down at Paul and saw the fear in the young lad's eyes. He knew if Paul did not have a chance to redeem his honor now, the boy would always carry the scars of Bernard's cruelty. "Very well. Come with me, but stay well behind."

They had no trouble navigating through the depths of the ship unnoticed. The men were too engrossed in their prayers for survival and worried at the relentless rage of the sea to notice the released captive.

Jacques and Paul passed through the galley and into the hold that Antoinette once called her home. Jacques could still smell the faint aroma of lavender from her sojourn among the sails and was tempted to stop, but they moved toward the forward hold where *La Réale's* loyal crewmen were imprisoned.

Paul quickly untied their bonds, but urged them to stay safely below until they were needed.

Jacques forged ahead and lifted the small passage door that led to the forward deck. He threw back the hatch then sprang onto the deck.

Only the helmsman, who was tied to the rudder below the mizzen deck, remained topside and he was struggling to keep the ship headed into the wind, forcing *La Réale* to ride the crests of the waves. He would be no trouble.

Rough waves broke across the bow, smashing against the hull in frenzy. Loosened barrels and debris washed from port to starboard like so many discarded toys. Shreds of the canvas sails dangled from halyards, entangling themselves within the rigging.

Jacques looked frantically for Antoinette. Finally he saw her, secured to the main mast, but fallen to her knees. The waves tugged at her bonds, pulling her toward the sea.

The clouds parted and the sun pierced through the thick veil of rain. In the distance Jacques saw the distinctive outline of land, mountains rising out of nowhere. Instantly he knew what he must do. He turned to the frightened boy behind him.

"Go to my cabin. Take the food tins, wine, candles, anything that can be used for survival and stuff it into the black shoulder pack at the foot of my chart table. Bring it to me quickly!." Paul turned to go, but Jacques grabbed his arm in afterthought. "Wait! There's a small chart hidden in the folded drape above my berth. Get that chart and tuck it far into the bottom of the pack. Bring it all topside. Back through this hatchway. Go!"

Paul ran toward the hatch and disappeared.

At once Jacques was at Antoinette's side, pulling at the lines that held her to the mast. He struggled with the wet knots until he finally freed her from her bonds.

Unconscious, she slipped limply into his arms. Her body was chilled, but she still held on to a thin thread of life. Her breath was shallow and faltering, slowing even as the waves quietly subsided. Jacques pulled the cloth from her mouth and uncovered her eyes, then touched her cheek.

"*Mère du Christ*! How could I have let this happen to you?" He brushed the wet and tangled hair from her face then held her close in his arms, hoping his warmth could somehow revive her.

Antoinette's eyes fluttered lightly and she looked at him with a distant gaze. "Jacques?" Her voice was low and soundless. She raised her hand to touch his face and smiled. "We will meet again— in the Otherworld."

She closed her eyes and her hand dropped to her chest.

"My love," he said, striving to reach her, to pull her back. "We have not finished with this world."

The ship lessened its roll and the waves began to settle. Time was running out. The momentary lull in the squall would soon pass and the seas would build again and with the calming of the seas, the mutineers would bombard the deck, desperate to be released from the sweltering hold.

"Where the devil is Paul?" he cursed.

Jacques laid Antoinette down, then rushed to lock the outside bolt on the main hatchway. He ran to the launch, loosened the lines holding it fast and swung it toward the railing. Paul appeared at his side with Antoinette's shoulder pack and Jacques' long green velvet cloak. Together they lowered the dinghy down the side of the ship.

Jacques gently wrapped the cloak around Antoinette's chilled body, then they lifted her and laid her in the bottom of the dinghy. Paul placed the black bag, now bulging with the contents of Jacques' table, into the deep swell of the boat. He touched her hand briefly then turned to Jacques.

"You will go with her, *Monsieur*?"

"Ah—no, Paul." He shook his head. "I must stay. My duty

is here aboard *La Réale*. Her destiny is not with me and she is no longer safe here."

Realizing that Jacques wanted to say his farewell alone, Paul stepped back a few paces and turned to guard the hatchway doors. The helmsman looked squarely at the boy and nodded his approval.

Tears swelled in Jacques' eyes. "I will be with you always, my love," he whispered softly. He removed his crucifix and placed the black corded medallion over Antoinette's head. He kissed her cheeks then traced her forehead with the sign of the cross. "I will send my savior to protect you, too. May your Beloved Brighid and the Blessed Holy Virgin keep you safe."

Paul returned and they lowered the dinghy over the side of the ship. With every slow roll of the ship it bumped hard against the sides until, at last, it reached the water. As they set free the lines, Jacques looked once again to the western horizon, straining to see the land, marking the spot firmly in his memory. He would seek her out if he could regain the ship.

The distant mountains were clearer now, and a faint mist seemed to rise from the darkened headlands. If Antoinette could make land, she would survive.

"*A brebis tondue Dieu mesure le vent*," he whispered. "God tempers the wind to the shorn lamb".

Antoinette's frail craft floated away from the ship on softly rolling waves. Jacques sighed with regret for all that might have been, for the life they could have shared.

Bracing himself against the wrenching pain in his heart, he turned away from Antoinette and the small dinghy and steadied his feet on the swaying deck. He placed his hand on Paul's shoulder and focused his gaze on the main hatchway.

"Paul, it is up to us. Together we must reclaim *La Réale* for the King of France. Go rally our men."

Lightning swept across the clouds as the main hatchway burst open.

Chapter 16

Finistère -Along the Western Coast of Brittany

Alain picked his way along the steep gravel road, careful to place his feet on solid ground. He could hear the breakers beating against the rocks below him. Hidden in the fog loomed the dark Bay of Audierne and beyond it Pointe du Raz, and beyond that the Île du Sein, the fortress of the Sisterhood of the Moon.

The fog rolled in like a widow's dark veil, covering the beautiful and rugged coastline with a soft haze. It was dense and dark Alain could see nothing before him, but his hands and feet. Stranded in the mists, and in such unfamiliar and unearthly terrain, he questioned his direction from the small town of Plogoff. He prayed that when he actually found the fisherman's home there would be a warm fire burning in the hearth and a comfortable place for him to sleep. Surely, he would have to wait until the mists lifted before he crossed the treacherous channel to the island.

The road edged closer to the cliff, the fog grew thicker and the night darker. A bone chilling cold pierced through Alain's clothing. He was unsure if he had passed the large stone menhir that Anne had described as the benchmark of the journey. Where was the standing stone? At the end of the road? The edge of the cliff?

Like a godsend for his weary legs, a large flat stone appeared at the edge of the mist. Alain sat and pulled his blue wool cloak tightly around his shoulders. The hard surface of the carved stone figurine grazed his thigh and he retrieved it from his pocket.

It was a curious statue. A caricature of a woman, round and voluptuous. Not at all his idea of perfection, but it had significance to Anne and obviously to the fisherman's wife. He wondered if it was a symbol of one of the Ancient Ones he sang so often about. Silently, he went over the many names of the Goddess, picturing each with a specific woman's figure in his mind.

Brighid would be small boned and fair skinned. Druantia, Queen of the Druids, dark and willowy. Hecate, old and withered. Morrigan...

The stone grew warm in his hands and he shoved the small figurine back into his pocket. He had been trained in the arts of magic, learned the songs and chants to summon the Gods. He should not be thinking of Morrigan, Queen of Phantoms and Demons. She was the last goddess he wanted to summon in this thick menacing fog.

As a Bard, a poet and keeper of the Ancient Wisdom, Alain had traveled far; to the hills of Ireland and coastlines of Wales and to the Southern shores of France, singing his stories to whomever was willing to provide his lodging. He knew the spells and incantations for love and health, but calling on the gods and goddesses, that was magic best left to the men and women who had dedicated their entire lives to serving the Ancient Ones.

Anne had kept him busy, searching and asking questions of Antoinette. Only the gods—and the Goddess—would know where Anne would send him next. But right now he was here. Somewhere on the peninsula between Audierne and Du Ruz. Somewhere lost in the fog and the mists. Somewhere Alain wished he were not.

Bells clanged in the distance and Alain jumped from his thoughts, straining to determine the direction of the sound. The unmistakable odor of fish mixed with wet horse flesh hit his nostrils long before a cart rolled out of the fog. A short, round man with a shock of long brown hair and a long square jaw sat atop a cart which pulled by a small horse.

"Ah!—Bonjour." The man smiled brightly as his face came into Alain's view.

"Bonjour." Alain nodded. "Have you any idea where we are?"

"Oh oui, *Monsieur.* We are in Finistère."

"No, no. I mean here." Alain pointed to the ground. "Where I am standing?"

"On the road to Plogoff." The man scratched his beard with long withered fingers. He looked at Alain with a slow questioning gaze. His brows arched. "What's a well dressed lad like you doing here in the fog? You're not one of them highwaymen are you?" He paused for a quick breath, not allowing time for Alain to defend his honor. "If you are, you're out of luck." The man tilted his head back over his shoulder to the empty fish cart. "Got nothing to steal, as you can see."

"No," Alain replied. "I'm on my way to see... I'm on my way to—" He couldn't tell a stranger he was on his way to the Île du Sein. "I need to get to the fisherman's house just past a large standing stone."

The old man chuckled. "Well lad, your luck is good. I'm on my way there."

"*Vraiment*?" Alain's light blue eyes lit up with delight. "Could I ride with you? I'm in a bit of a hurry."

"What for?" the old man asked with a shrug. "You can't set sail till the fog lifts and that could be tonight or tomorrow or next week."

"Next week?" Alain looked questioningly at the man. "What makes you think I need to sail somewhere?"

"I think you are not roaming around in the fog for your

health."

"That is true, *Monsieur.*" Alain smiled. "You are very perceptive."

"Not really. No one comes here except for fishing or for adventure." He glanced at the harp slung over Alain's shoulder. "You are not a fisherman." The old man waved his hand into the fog, scattering the mist near his face. "I would guess that you are from Paris or from Nantes and that you are going to serenade the mistress of the island."

Alain shrugged, then smiled and climbed up onto the cart. "Perhaps I'm here to entertain the fisherman's wife."

The old man laughed, but his voice was swallowed up by the mists. He clucked lightly to the horse.

"The old woman won't give you any spells to win your lover."

"I don't expect her to give me a charm," Alain answered politely.

"Ah, well then you must be on an errand."

"*Monsieur,* I have business with the fisherman's wife and I am not at liberty to discuss it."

The old man chuckled to himself. "Oh, then you needn't know that the Prioress is gone from the island, do you?"

Alain tensed. "Mère Deirdre is not there?"

The fisherman laughed, "You may sing a good song, son, but you'd not be a good spy. You give away too much."

The old man was right. Love-making, not espionage, was the intrigue Alain knew best.

"Then Mère Deirdre is on the island?"

"Oh, *oui.* She never leaves."

Alain shook his head. "You should not have tricked me."

The fisherman clicked the reins. "It's part of my job, lad." He turned to Alain with a warm smile. "I'll be taking you to the island. That is, if my wife gives you leave to go."

The old man began to whistle merrily as though none of this evening's events were serious or hurried. Alain rode in silence beside the fisherman wondering, as the wheels of the cart bumped their way across the rocky path, why all the trickery was necessary. He was making a simple channel crossing.

As they rounded a bend in the road, the fog suddenly stopped. It did not fade with a mysterious softness like the woodland fogs Alain knew so well, but stopped with a hard edge as though it were the end of a long passageway.

Lying before the travelers in the orange glow of a brilliant sunset gleamed the dark waters of the vast ocean-sea. From the small white stone cottage, from the rugged coastline to the edge of the southern horizon there was nothing but blue water. Nothing but adventure.

Alain had seen many sunsets along the western coastlines of Wales, of Scotland, and of Brittany, but never one so magical. Centered in the midst of the western horizon, lay a small irregular shaped island.

Alain stretched out his arm, pointing to the island. "Is that it? It seems so—insignificant."

The fisherman threw back his head in laughter. "Why do you think the fog is so thick? To keep young men from venturing down to the coastline. No, no! The Sisterhood keeps the veil thick and constant, to bar unwanted guests from coming to their island. You'll only get there from land if you pass my wife's inspection and if the seas give us permission to cross."

Alain felt for the figurine in his pocket, hoping Anne had not been mistaken about the power of the little stone statue. "What if she does not give me permission?"

The fisherman shook his head and sighed, "Who knows? Some leave. Some stay."

The small white-washed house seemed to dangle on the very edge of the cliffs, high above the harbor. The porch was covered with flower pots holding a variety of gaily blooming flowers and sweet smelling herbs. A cat stretched out asleep on the cool flagstones that made up a small patio. A woman in a black frock and a white lace bonnet rocked back and forth in an old wooden armchair. She hummed a tune Alain found oddly familiar yet somehow disquieting. It was almost as though her music was weaving a spell.

The fisherman turned the cart toward the road leading down to the water. He spoke to Alain over his shoulder in a whisper. "Did I forget to tell you that if you have the wrong answer, my wife's likely to be very angry? Make sure you take care with your words. I'd not like to be picking you up from below the cliff."

Alain glanced over the edge of the precipice at the craggy shoreline some distance below. As if answering his question, a wave threw up a spray of water, then towered above the rocks with a roar. He could almost see his limp body lying at the bottom of the precipice.

Swallowing his anxiety, Alain turned to greet his destiny. The fisherman's wife was small and frail, but as she rose from her chair and walked toward him, he could tell she was not a woman to be trifled with. He bowed low, then straightened tall summoning his best manners.

"*Bonjour*, M'lady."

She wiped her hands nonchalantly on her apron and smiled. She was obviously not a person to be placated with niceties and Alain wondered how he would proceed.

"I am Alain Bodrot, Bard of Brittany. I have come to cross to the Île du Sein."

"What is your purpose?" Her voice was calm, her gaze steady and without any undercurrent of malice, yet Alain remembered the fisherman's warning and eased away from the edge of the cliff.

There was no reason not to tell her the truth of his mission. "I have come at the request of Anne de Bretagne, to ask a favor of the Lady of the Isle."

"A favor?" The wife stepped back toward the house. For an instant Alain's heart stopped as she reached out toward a pitchfork lying against the wall. She hesitated, then picked a piece of mint from a pot beside it.

He gave a shallow sigh as she turned toward him, wrinkling the pungent leaf under her nose.

"How do I know you are telling me the truth?" she asked.

Alain wasted no time. He reached into his pocket for the small figurine. Surely it was meant to safeguard his passage to the island. He placed it solidly in the woman's hand and stepped between her and the pitchfork.

"I see." She raised her eyebrows. "Do you know what this is?"

Alain hesitated. If he gave the wrong answer, he'd surely find himself at the bottom of the cliff. Quickly and desperately he searched his mind for the name of the Goddess of fertility. For surely the little statue made of white moonstone was she.

"M'lady, it can be no other than Ceridwen, the Great Goddess of the Moon, for she rules travel by sea and tide."

The woman looked hard at Alain, from his blue cap to his dusty shoes. Suddenly her stern look turned to one of gentleness. "Someone has instructed you well, young Bard of Brittany. Only those men who are trustworthy, may carry the image of the Great Goddess in their pockets, so close to their treasures of manhood." The wife looked out at the island and tilted her head. "And only those who are brave at heart would risk passage across this channel."

She put the small statue in her apron then laid her hand gently on his arm. "Come inside and I will get you a bowl of soup. Poor boy, you must be wet to the bone."

Alain let out a deep sigh, not realizing he had been holding his breath. For all her diminutive form, the fisherman's wife was a formidable gatekeeper.

☙

At the turning of the morning tide they set out in a small fishing boat, pulling well away from the breakers at the rough and dangerous Pointe du Raz on a brisk northerly wind. The currents pulled hard against the little boat and the sails popped back and forth in the gusty wind. Alain was sure that much of the time they were sailing not forward but backward. The crossing was rough and Alain was glad when they finally landed on a makeshift dock at the edge of a cove.

"Where do I go from here?" Alain asked.

"Don't worry lad, someone will come to fetch you." The fisherman pushed his craft away from the dock with the end of a paddle. He tipped his hat. "Remember to be here at sunset; no man is allowed to remain on the Isle at night."

Alain watched the fisherman disappear behind the swells of the waves then suddenly, without a sound, a young girl was standing behind him.

"You are here to see Mère Deirdre?" she asked. Her voice was sweet and fair. Her face was small and precious, like a carved wooden doll.

"*Oui, Mademoiselle.* I am here at the request of the Duchess of Brittany."

She laughed and Alain knew, given the opportunity, he could fall madly in love with this beautiful woman. He checked his thoughts. These maidens of the Goddess were untouchable. They were priestesses dedicated to the Sisterhood of the Moon. He could be killed for even thinking such thoughts about them.

"It's all right, Alain."

He was startled that she knew his name. "How—"

"Your thoughts are easily read on your face. It is my task to know if those who come to our island have honorable intentions."

"I assure you that my thoughts—however impure they may appear—are always honorable."

She laughed and placed her hand up to her mouth, hiding her smile. She was enchanting in her innocence.

"Such steps for secrecy the Sisterhood takes for the island. Is there much problem with trespassers?"

"Oh, yes, Alain." She composed her features. A look of determination passed over her face. "There are many who would see us disbanded and the priory burned to the ground with the Sisterhood inside. We are always on our guard. That is why the fisherman's wife selects our visitors. There are many who do not make it past her cottage."

Alain remembered the pitchfork and nodded. He wondered momentarily if the fisherman's wife had really used it for things other than hay. He pulled the parchment from his pack, remembering his mission. "Anne de Bretagne has asked that I be allowed to see Mère Deirdre."

"Yes. We know." The girl waved her hand toward the pathway and led the way up a steep cliff. "Deirdre is waiting. She will see you within the hour."

They walked into a large stone paved courtyard where bowers of white and lavender wisteria bloomed among the shade trees and she ushered him to a long stone bench under the shade of a large oak. It was a courtyard made more for clandestine meetings than for prayers.

"Please wait here and Deirdre will send for you when she is ready."

The girl turned to walk away and Alain lightly touched her arm. He knew better than to ask her name before they were properly introduced, but he could not bear the thought of never seeing her again.

"Will you come to escort me to her chambers?"

She tilted her head and smiled. "We shall see."

"Alain?" There was a light touch on his shoulder along with the whisper of his name, like the song of a summer breeze waking him from a long deep sleep. The young guide had returned and now seemed lovelier than before. "Mère Deirdre will see you now."

Alain stood quickly and the young girl offered a disapproving glance. "You really must stop thinking such thoughts about me or I will ask another sister to accompany you during your visit with us."

"I apologize, *Mademoiselle,* but you are the most beautiful woman I have ever seen."

She smiled and Alain's heart fell to his feet.

"You have not met Deirdre yet. I am paled by her beauty."

"I know this is forward of me, but may I ask your name? I wish to sing of your loveliness once I am back on the mainland."

The young girl giggled. "You would do that?"

"Oh yes, I am a Bard, a troubadour, a poet." He motioned to the harp across his back. "I will sing your name to the Kings and Queens throughout the Empire."

"Shh—" The girl raised a finger to her lips and motioned to a set of wooden doors. "We are nearing Deirdre's quarters. I will come for you when your interview is completed."

Alain watched her walk across the garden, wondering if she would return as promised. Words and melodies praising her beauty and virtues rambled through his head. He must know her name to give the song its proper cadence.

He turned to greet yet another woman—older but just as lovely. She opened the door, gesturing with a low wave of her hand for him to enter

The room was not at all as he expected. It was not gloomy and dark, as legend would have it, but bright and airy. Large open windows overlooked the crystal blue bay. A tall woman with long silver-gray hair stood by one window, gazing toward the sea. She did not turn to face him, but looked to the horizon at a ship skirting the rugged coastline.

"They say, Alain Bodrot, that if one wishes hard enough for something, one's wishes will be granted. Do you believe this?"

Alain was stunned at the prioress' easy manner. "*C'est vrai*, M'lady. But one's wishes must be noble and unselfish."

Deirdre turned to face him with quiet elegance and grace. Like a dove in flight, Alain thought. Like a leaf dancing on the wind. She smiled and her eyes sparkled with the reflection from the sea. "You have much wisdom for one so young." Her long white gown slid across the polished floor as she walked toward him. "Please, tell me what you wish of the Sisterhood."

Alain pulled the parchment from his pack and handed it to Mère Deirdre. She held it for a moment, then laid it on the table before her, unopened. Her voice was but a whisper followed by a long sigh.

"So it begins. They have discovered that the small one has flown from our nest."

Alain struggled to understand the meaning behind her words. "M'lady?"

Deirdre waved her hand into the air, dismissing her thoughts. "What does Anne expect the Sisterhood to do?

"She wishes to know if you have heard from Antoinette. She boarded a ship in St. Malo and has not been heard of for over a fortnight."

"Ah yes, the ship." She closed her eyes as though searching for a vision. "Tell me about the ship."

"It was *La Réale*, the merchant ship of the King of France.

Anne wants to know if Antoinette still lives, if there is hope of bringing her back. The King says that he is powerless to find her. Anne does not believe him."

Deirdre gazed past him and she crossed the room to stand before a polished silver bowl. An eerie chill crossed Alain's spine as he watched her eyes glaze as if in trance. She was silent for some time, then looked up at Alain, her eyes still lost in the mists of Sight. Her voice was deep, yet crisp and clear.

"Charles has spoken the truth. The ship may be chartered by the Crown and the mission of his choosing, but I see the ship flies the red cross pateé, the sign of the Templars." She shook her head. "It is to them that you must go to find Antoinette. She is beyond our reach."

"The Knights Templar?" he questioned. "Surely they are no longer mounting campaigns. It has been over a hundred years since they fought the Turks."

Deirdre walked back to the window. "They are still quite active in France, in Scotland and especially in Sagres where the Templars have their Navigator's Guild. The Knights of Christ owe allegiance to no one."

"I am not versed in the politics of governments, M'lady. I am a simple bard, not a priest or a warrior."

"But you do the bidding of Anne de Bretagne. Did you not know that Antoinette's brother, Gaston is a Templar?"

"No M'lady. Do you think he will help us?"

Silence filled the air as though Deirdre were collecting her thoughts from some distant realm. "Perhaps. It has been many years since I have seen him. He is an expatriate of France, but he is still a Templar."

"How will I find him? What if he is not willing to help?"

Mère Deirdre's somber face broke into a light ironic smile. "If Antoinette has gotten herself involved in a Templar mission, they will be more than willing to help locate her."

She stopped and looked at Alain somberly. "Is Anne willing to risk Antoinette's life? If she knows more than she should, they may not be willing to let her live."

Alain swallowed hard. Was it his place to answer for Anne? "The Duchess told me that you, and you alone, would know what was the best action to take. I must leave Antoinette's fate in your hands."

Deirdre glanced toward the ocean and breathed deeply. Her thoughts centered on the small girl she had watched grow to womanhood, controlled by the wishes and desires of the Sisterhood. *Antoinette, ma petite enfant. How long must your fate be in the hands of others?*

In that moment of silence, as the prioress stood in profile against the dark blue water, Alain thought she looked old and tired. Did she long to be traveling on the ship she so diligently watched? When she turned toward him, he realized he had been mistaken. Her body was vibrant, her voice steady and full of authority.

"We will send word to the Order of Christ, indirectly of course, that Antoinette may be aboard the King's ship. And you must tell Anne to ready a ship to sail at her request."

"*Merci.* I am sure my regent will be most grateful." Alain bent his head in acknowledgment of the wide range of her influence. He knew Anne supplied the priory with lavish gifts and money from the treasury of Brittany. But he also knew that Deirdre was not the kind of woman to sell the powers of the Sisterhood to the highest bidder. What she did for Anne must come from her love for Antoinette. He took a half step back to await his dismissal.

Deirdre sat in a chair by the window and gazed once again out to the sea. "I believe your guide, Vatice, has planned a meal for you and a walk along the balustrade before you leave." She turned once more to face him and this time he was sure that he saw a remote sadness in her eyes. "Please enjoy the hospitality of our island. She has permission to take you wherever you desire."

Holding back his eagerness to see the young woman again, he bowed low and turned to leave.

"Alain?" Her words stopped his departure. "Sing kindly of the Sisterhood. I fear that it will not be long before we have need to be remembered."

Alain nodded. There was nothing he could say to console the prioress. He turned and swept through the door behind him, thankful to leave the gloom that was settling in the air.

Vatice waited for him in the courtyard. He had been given her name and permission to be with her. Now he could openly tell her of his love. It was not unheard of for a maiden to leave the island. If she had not been pledged to serve the Ancient Ones, there was still hope for him.

They walked hand in hand toward the portico overlooking the ocean, and the words began to form in Alain's mind of how he would sing of the beauty of the Women of Sein, of their graciousness and their hidden passion for life.

Oiseaux du Paradis

Birds of Paradise

Chapter 17

Land of the People

Antoinette heard the sound of the sidhe, the fairy spirits of the Otherworld. Their soft ethereal voices summoned her, though she wasn't sure that they sang to her from outside her mind. She drifted in a hazy, disorienting awareness. Had she been dreaming? Or was this the dream?

Her last few conscious memories melted together, fluttered past her like the wind kissing the water. Memories so vivid, yet so distant. The sting of the whip in Lawrence Bernard's vengeful hand, the musty smell of seasoned wood and pitch, a swirl of power, water, then blackness. She though of Jacques. His sad face floated above her. A kiss, then the darkness descended once more.

Time had no meaning, no reason. Fairy spirits sang to her as she floated on their magic mists and she slept in the gentle rocking arms of the Great Mother. It was blissful. Quiet. Yet a sadness passed over her; an empty, hollow ache that grabbed at the corners of her heart. She might never see her loved ones again.

"Blessed Brighid, please, let things be better for me in this world."

Ready to accept death, she opened her eyes, but she could see only a few inches into the haze. By the feel of cloth surrounding her she could tell she was wrapped in a shroud. Her precious seal-skin shoulder pack lay beside her. With a deep sigh of relief she closed her eyes again. It was comforting to know her belongings would follow her into the afterlife. Her mind traced back to ancient stories from her childhood of long sea crossings to the Otherworld; to the shores of *Tir-Na-Nog,* the ancient land of eternal youth.

Like the stories of *Tir-Na-Nog,* she was in a small boat without mast or sail, with no rudder for steering, nor oars for rowing. She was certainly crossing the sea of death and would soon arrive on the sandy shores of Paradise. She could feel the power of the waters of the ocean as they pushed her forward on the slow rolling waves. Even Rhiannon's birds sang to her, welcoming her ashore.

As the time slowly passed she reassured herself that some radiant spirit would eventually come to retrieve her and usher her to the dwelling of the Ancient Ones. More confident now, she peeked out over the edge of the boat. Through the mists, the Otherworld looked very much like the earthly beaches of Brittany, of Tréguier on the North Coast and of Roscoff. But it could not be home, for *La Réale* had sailed due westward for nearly a month, far past the islands off Scotland. Yet the land seemed to hold a great magic. Yes, the mists gathered and swirled at the gates of *Tir-Na-Nog,* beckoning her to enter.

Letting her senses awaken to her new spirit body, she breathed in the fresh smell of the sea and the tangy scent of evergreens drifting on the wind. She wondered briefly why her voyage to the Otherworld had left her wet and cold, why her mouth tasted dry and salty.

Suddenly, the need to quench her thirst was overwhelming. A sharp arrow of pain spread across her back like streaks of fire. A surge of panic rushed over her and she sat upright. Tossing the dark green cloak aside, she scrambled to her knees. The small boat pitched sideways with the shift of her weight and she grasped for a quick handhold on the gunwale.

By the Goddess! She was not dead, but cast away. Set adrift not by the gods, but by men. By Jacques?

"Blessed Mother!" she cried. "Why couldn't you just let me die?"

Antoinette sank back into the depth of the boat and wrapped the damp velvet cloak tightly around her, shivering. She wanted to crawl into her grand-mère's arms, to be comforted, but Ursule was not there. No one was there. She was alone and very, very much alive. Disheartened, Antoinette fell back into the security of the small drifting dinghy and wept.

ଔ

A peal of thunder startled Antoinette from a fitful sleep. The mists had lifted and the sparse sunlight streamed through turbulent clouds. A rocky beach was visible nearby, but each breaking wave pulled her from the refuge of shore and lured the small craft back out to sea.

Antoinette's heart beat hard against her ribcage and the sour taste of fear caught in the back of her throat. Without thinking, she leapt into the bracing water, wincing at the sting of the sea on her whip-lashed back. But there was no time to recognize the pain, no time to panic. With every ounce of her fading strength she willed herself to swim with the drifting boat, knowing that the flimsy craft was her only asylum.

She beseeched the Celtic God of the Sea to spare her life. "Dylan, hold me steadfast above your waves! Help my humble feet to reach the Mother's earth."

Grabbing for the bow, she caught a drifting line and pulled hard, struggling against the cresting waves that forced her downward toward oblivion. *Swim. Float. Relax.*

With determined strokes, she swam toward the quickly diminishing shoreline, her strength and reserve fading with every undulation of the sea.

"Come with us, Antoinette," the waves seemed to call. "Be one with us."

She turned a deaf ear to the water's bidding and held onto the bow line with all her strength as the relentless undertow pulled her downward, tumbling her against the hard rocky bottom of the coastline. An exploding force pushed from inside her chest, threatening to burst her lungs. She was almost willing to accept the elementals' invitation, to give into their rhythm and become one with their song, but a deep voice filled the widening void around her.

"It is not her time, little sisters. Let her go. You will not have the pleasure of her company this day. There is more work for her among the earthbound."

As though the Great Mother had resolved the declaration, Antoinette felt the solidity of earth and she pushed upward, rising above the water with a gasp. A spark of survival pushed her onward. She swam against the racing currents, against the forces that would claim her. Each jerk of the boat's line increased the pain in her strained shoulders. Her arms felt like lead as she swam and pulled the craft with her through the retreating waves. She knew she could not abandon the boat and with it all hope of survival even though she could easily swim the distance to shore.

Red and black topped seaweed waved to her like marching soldiers from beneath the water and she swam toward it. Soon her feet felt the slippery surface of the rocky outcroppings. The smell of salty decay filled the air as she pulled the boat across the layers of dried dulse and to the far edge of the beach.

Exhausted, she sank onto the dry sand. She was wet, cold and lost. "Blessed Mother," she cried with relieved laughter. "Must you teach me lessons so dramatically?"

The beach was uninhabited. Save for an occasional bird soaring overhead, there was no other life in sight. She laughed at the irony of her situation, remembering her last conversation with Anne as she prepared to meet Cardinal Visconti at Château Rennes.

"The austere life at a regent's court does not appeal to me," she had said. "I will always have to remain in the background, in the shadows. I long to feel life, to experience its passion and adventure, but my vows to the Sisterhood prevent me. They have kept me sequestered and protected and I know nothing of life outside your realm, or outside their reach. I am chained to my responsibilities like Hecate's hounds to her gates. I know I will die an old woman in a priory and never know what I have missed."

Anne's prophetic words echoed in her head. "Be careful what you ask for, *ma chère*."

Now, Antoinette rolled over and looked up at the sky. She had certainly received what she asked for, but it was not at all what she had envisioned. She was alone, alive and thankful—yes thankful—that she had not died at Lawrence Bernard's hand and set up another chain of events to work out with his spirit in the afterlife.

These past few weeks had wakened feelings hidden deep within her soul. Feelings that she knew existed, but never dared to explore. Long before she felt the deep affection for Jacques, she knew she would eventually find love. She loved Anne and Ursule, but that was a different kind love; a love that was expected. Now she knew she could love with all her heart, but also knew she could hate with equal passion.

Although she did not fully understand Cardinal Visconti's greed or Lawrence Bernard's lust and rage, their destructive emotions had affected her. These two men, in their quest for power, had effectively exiled her from her home and family and stolen her future.

She thought of Jacques. He had shown her kindness and friendship. She felt a catch in her throat, realizing that she might never see him again. Antoinette thought of Anne and reached instinctively for the comfort of the amulet still fastened to the green silk scarf tied around her waist. Releasing the catch, she held the circlet in her hands, turning the silver to catch the sunlight streaming through the patchwork of clouds.

The brooch was all that remained of the old Antoinette Charboneau. Like the intricate silver wire, woven by a craftsman into the fine Celtic circle, her life had also been re-arranged, reshaped. She was no longer cloistered behind the castle walls in Nantes, or living a life of lies within a court of fools. She had passed beyond the convoluted life of kings and pontiffs and ventured into unexplored realms.

She had broken through the barriers of earth and spirit during her union with the Goddess. In one moment of ecstasy she had been given the endowment of a High Priestess, the power to call upon the Goddess and receive Her protection. She, Antoinette Charboneau, had finally been liberated.

As she sat in silence on the beach, Antoinette took a solemn vow. As the Ancient Ones were her witnesses, she would never let anyone have so much power over her again. She would let no one, man or woman, take away her freedom. She would answer only to the Goddess. Not to the Sisterhood, nor to any regent.

Without hesitation she stood upright, her hands thrust into the air, her palms held high. It had to be done, now! Before she lost her will.

"Hear me, Rhiannon, Companion of the Spirit Steed!"

A roar of thunder answered her invocation.

"Hear me, Lugh, whose spear and sling bring those unjust to right!" A flash of lightning cracked from the ominous clouds overhead and the increasing wind whipped her loosened hair into wild dark waves behind her. She raised her hands high over her head and shouted to the roaring ocean before her.

"Great Mother, Brighid, Ancient Ones, witness my request.
Where prayers to the heavens are not answered
Where power and corruption are not welcomed,
Where justice and truth are the way of life,
Where no goal is reached without pain and strife,
let such be the destiny of Cardinal Visconti."

She paused and took in a deep breath, letting her energy build with the increasing wind and the power of the waves crashing at her feet.

"Where there is no caring hand to heal the wound,
Where there is no love to tempt the heart,
Where there is no rest on sleepless nights,
Nor friends to share the bonds of peace,
let Lawrence Bernard through these lessons learn."

In answer to her petition, a flash of lightning struck at the cliffs behind her. The power of the Goddess was within her, her body vibrated with Her energy. Now she would use the power to make her greatest petition.

"Blessed Mother! Protector—Defender. Watch over those

who cannot watch themselves. Defend my loved ones with your arrows of righteousness. Shield them with your strength. Let them dwell under your sweet wings of love and let them know they are always in my heart. So be it!"

Her words sang with the final proclamation.

The dark clouds rushed overhead, disappearing as though they were never there. Only small, puffy remnants remained.

Her anger scattered with the clouds, Antoinette collapsed onto the sand. Physically drained, yet feeling at peace, she looked up at the sky mindlessly watching the retreating clouds, blending and reshaping their forms as they danced. The waves broke calmly on the rugged shoreline.

As if to comfort her, a light rain began to fall and she opened her mouth to drink the cool life blood of the sky. She would think of food and shelter later. It was the Mother's cleansing water she needed now, to revive her spirit and renew her soul.

The sun peeked from behind the last lingering cloud in the western sky. The ensuing darkness would bring a chilling mist. She had made her pact with the spirits of the sea and air and knew she would not die at the hands of the elements, but she had no knowledge of what fierce animals or men might loom along this rugged shoreline by night.

The rock strewn beach seemed to run forever into the fading sunlight. Rocks of every color and size littered the rugged terrain as if a giant had hurled them hither and yon in a casting of runes, then left his playthings in disarray. The sea bordered on one side and, running the length of the cove, sandstone cliffs with wooded thickets towered behind her. There would be shelter among the trees, but that would be tomorrow's task. The wielding of strong magic had drained what remained of her strength. She was tired, hungry and sleep called to her.

Would the small dinghy shelter her one more night?

She gathered what little remained of her stamina and pulled the boat in from the shoreline, well past the seaweed and the driftwood that gathered at the tide's edge. With a piece of driftwood for a shovel, she made a shallow depression in the sand, filled it with dried seaweed and covered it with her velvet cloak. Gently she tipped the boat bottom side up and slid it over the makeshift bed to provide a canopy. Then she lifted the boat up onto one edge and wedged the driftwood deep into the sand. Standing back, she smiled as she admired her new home. She would be comfortable sleeping on the soft seaweed and she would lower the boat after she entered, sealing her safely from the weather and curious animals.

The sky grew dark as twilight descended. Antoinette dug into her shoulder pack for an unsalted morsel of food. She pulled out a box of dried fruit and a bottle of wine from Jacques' cache. His kindness once again filled her heart with warmth.

"Bless you, my friend." She wished he were there to share the beauty of the sunset, now streaked with lavender, gray and magenta. Leaning against the edge of the boat, she watched the growing moon already high in the eastern sky. Stars brightened overhead. Within a week, the moon would rise at sunset and be full. It would be the moon that brought the celebration of Lughnasad, the beginning of first harvest. The first celebration of Autumn. The first ceremony she would perform in her new home.

Antoinette snuggled into her makeshift hut and fell asleep in the fading light, listening to the sound of the waves' rhythmic beating against the rocky shoreline.

Chapter 18

The fog lifted its veil from the shoreline by mid morning and the wind no longer smelled of rain. The sea rolled in calmly, breaking gentle waves against the rocky outcroppings. These were good signs. Signs the weather would be mild. Signs of the Mother's blessings.

Antoinette lay under the upturned boat, watching the seaweed undulate against the ebb and flow of the water as it washed in and out with the waves.

Tiny sandpipers skittered across the beach, pecking at debris and nibbling amid the dried dulse. White gulls flew just above the shoreline, swooping down to capture a fish or a wayward crab. Larger cormorants dove from tremendous heights into the water, returning above the waves with their breakfast of fish.

Fish!

Antoinette grabbed for her pack. She could learn to fish. She dug inside the front flap of the pack and took out a sharpened sewing needle she kept handy for mending. She held it up and tried to bend its shape with her fingers, but the metal resisted. Conquered by the needle's inner strength, she stuck it back through the flap. It was useless for fishing. She'd have to find another way.

Digging through the sack, she produced a small packet of hard biscuits and a leather bag filled with dried berries. She softened the lumps of bread in the remaining wine and leaned against the outside of the hut while she ate.

Her gaze wandered across the beauty of the landscape spreading out before her, to the woodlands above the cliffs and the high promontory beyond. If someone lived just beyond the embankment she might be rescued by nightfall. On the other hand, she might be alone forever. Or at least until the first blast of winter froze her body into tiny shards of ice. Thank the gods she at least had shelter from the rain.

Her meager breakfast complete, she spread the green cloak out onto the sand. Turning the bag inside out to make sure nothing was left uncounted, Antoinette dumped out the rest of her belongings.

There was not much there to insure her survival.

She touched her possessions, one by one, contemplating each object's importance. Foremost was a bulging leather parfleche, her medicine bag. Like the shoulder pack it was watertight and made of seal-skin. Inside were what remained of the small pouches of herbs, seeds, salves and vials of liquid potions she used for healing. The pack had been given to her at her initiation into the healer's circle and she kept it always near her, constantly adding to its contents whenever she could. She wished she had brought more medicinals with her. She had used so many on the ship. But how could she have known she would be gone so long?

She thought of her stillroom in Nantes, full of dried herbs and potions. A lifetime of collecting and research, every herb pouch was meticulously labeled, every bottle tightly sealed against the elements. She sighed. Someone else surely would have taken over the role of Healer by now.

A second bundle, this one wrapped with a fine white silk scarf and tied with a long green ribbon, contained her athame, the ceremonial dagger used in ritual, and a fine silver chalice. The blade of the athame was no longer than the length of her hand. It was inscribed with magical runes of protection. The hilt, half as long as the blade, was fashioned from burlwood and stained a golden brown.

She remembered her apprehension when Ursule first handed her the dagger. She had been afraid to hold it, then realized it held no real power until she herself infused it. The chalice she had purchased from a dealer in Brest. Its filigreed silver stem opened to a wide mouthed bowl and fit into the palm of her hand. Both tools had only been used in ceremony and ritual. They would now have to serve her in everyday use. Many things would have to change.

As she lifted the silk bundle from her pack, the blade of another knife glinted in the sunlight. A cold shiver ran down her spine. It was Bernard's dirk. How had the blade gotten into her bag?

She fingered the sharp edge cautiously, picked it up and turned it in the light. With a quick thrust, Antoinette threw the knife down onto the green velvet. Memories of her torture flew at her like hot ashes in the wind and she put her hands to her face, rubbing her eyes as if to wipe away the images flashing before them. But they would not go away. Lawrence Bernard's face hovered near, distorted in his madness.

She could still hear the high pitched snap of Bernard's whip as its thin leather tip bit into her flesh. She winced, recalling the first strike and the smell of the tar and pitch of the mast as her nose burned with the acrid vapors. Torrents of salt water had choked her, stung her back, and knocked her legs from beneath her.

In desperation she had called upon the gods to protect her, to ease the pain. She did not intended to call the demons of the sky and sea to avenge her. She meant only to seek the aid of the benevolent gods of wind and water. But speechless, sightless and tied to the mast, her mind had not been able to focus. In the end, she had beseeched them all. Then she had been left to die at the hands of the elements she had summoned.

The splitting wood had whined as the mast overhead snapped from the strain of the wind. Lighting had flashed across the deck in an angry fury. Then Jacques' warm body pressed against her. He had called her back from the darkness.

She remembered the blessing he had given her before his last kiss and she reached to her breast. A small crucifix slid from beneath her shredded tunic. She touched the cool gold and put the tiny symbol to her lips. Although the Christ was not her God, she was grateful Jacques' prayer had sheltered her and that she was still alive.

"Blessed be," she said, sending a loving wish to her friend. She removed the cross and stowed it in a hidden fold of her shoulder pack, safely beside Anne's silver talisman. Someday she would return it to Jacques and thank him.

All that remained in the depths of her bag were several gold coins, a strange piece of folded parchment and a tiny metal box. Curious of the contents, she opened the lid.

It was the tinderbox. She remembered Jacques holding it in his hands, lighting the candles in his room. She closed her eyes and held the box tightly. This small gift would probably save her from freezing.

"Goddess bless him," she whispered, laying it aside.

She turned her attention to the parchment and gingerly lifted an edge of the browned document, then smoothed it out on the cloak. It was a chart, but not like any chart she had ever seen. It was similar to the one Jacques had been drawing, but it was older, faded. Words written in what she believed to be Latin bordered the ragged edges.

CARTA DA NAVEGAR DE. . .

The words were blurred with water stains and age. It was or had been, she assumed, a part of a navigational chart. The rugged outline of coastal lands defined the outer boundaries of the map. The interior was dotted with islands and symbols.

"Estotiland, Estland, Frisland, Scotia." She read aloud, touching each area in turn. Had these islands been their destination? Could *La Réale* still be close by? Her gaze traveled to the horizon. There was nothing. No sign of a ship. She was stranded. Stranded with so many things left undone in her life. But she had to survive. She *must* survive. There were too many threads unwound from the circle of her life for her to give up now.

Solemnly, she arranged the belongings in the bag and untied the silk scarf from her waist. Pulling the scarf up and under her thick hair, she tied it loosely on the top of her head. A cooling breeze tickled the nape of her neck and she winced at the pain from her wounds. She cursed Lawrence Bernard again.

She slipped her tunic up over her head. It was rent from neck to waist in the back and torn with jagged holes across the hem. This damage had surely happened as she struggled with the boat and scraped against the rocky bottom of the coastline. Cutting off the torn lengths of cloth, she donned the reconstructed garment and pressed out the wrinkles with her hands.

The tunic reached just above her knees and was immodestly short. But who was around to chastise her? For all she knew, she could be the only human for miles. She slung her pack across her shoulder in defiance. It was time to find fresh water and food.

Antoinette took a bearing on her campsite, noting the shape of the trees on the cliff side above it, then she headed southward along the shoreline.

She'd made a plan. She would walk toward the cliffs in the distance across the cove, until the sun was overhead. Then she would turn around and return to her camp before dark. If she found no water, then tomorrow she would explore the beach in the other direction, leaving the high cliffs until last.

Further down the shoreline, the rocky outcropping gave way to coarse sandy beaches littered with rocks that glittered in the sunlight. Dried dulse and driftwood gathered at the high tide marks, sheltering empty clam shells and the flotsam and jetsam of the sea.

From time to time she paused to turn over a shell or rock, or to watch a cormorant snatch his supper from the sea. At the sound of her footsteps, a small crab shuffled across the sand and dove into the safety of a sandy hole. Small birds took flight as she passed them, their short wings swiftly taking them high above the waves.

Isolated coves along the shoreline gave shelter against the Northerly wind. She discovered a tidal pool containing a captive fish and marked it for a possible dinner. A large white gull flew at a safe distance behind her, hovering near her when she stopped and flying above her as she walked. She paid it little mind, yet welcomed the company.

Rounding a bend in the cove, she climbed onto a large boulder and looked out to sea. Was anyone still out there? Had *La Réale* turned back or had she floundered in the storm? From that height, she could see in both directions and realized she had traveled quite far in just a few hours.

She could no longer see her little camp and to her dismay, the beach ahead looked just like the beach behind. A large mountain loomed in the distance. There was no sign of human life and no sign of fresh water.

She stood on top of the rock and held out her hands, inhaling the rich sea air, then she sat down in the warm sunlight. She felt the force of ancient energy beneath her. The stone seemed to vibrate, renewing her with the captured warmth of the sun.

As she climbed down from her perch, her gaze was captured by a shiny, slender object just beyond the boulder. The sun glistened off the sand-polished end of a length of driftwood wedged in the water between two large rocks. It was just out of reach.

Setting her pack on the boulder, she stepped over flat rocky outcroppings, mindful of her footing on the seaweed topped surfaces. Careful not to step on the living shells that clung to their parent rocks, she squeezed through the two large boulders and stood at last facing her prize. A head-high piece of driftwood, wind and sand polished, beckoned for its freedom.

A spark of energy seemed to leap from the inert wood to her fingers when she reaching out to touch it. Still, she grasped the stick in both hands to wiggle it free. But it was stuck as tight as though the god of the Underworld held onto the other end. She wondered for a moment if it were the only protruding part of an entire tree.

Antoinette braced her foot among the rocks. She pulled and shoved, then gave one last heroic tug and the stick dislodged, sending her splashing into the water. She heard a whisper of a sigh as the driftwood lifted away from its entrapment, and she could have sworn she heard a low chuckle from the enslaving rocks. The large white gull cawed with laughter from a nearby rocky perch.

"*Merci.*" She laughed, holding the stick above the water. "The bath was well worth the treasure."

Standing, she held the stick in front of her. The branch had grown straight and evenly, but odd twists and dark shapes stained the wood's surface. From the ground to the height of her knee, it was smooth and shiny, like it had been polished with fine nut oils. From her thigh to her shoulder, the branch swirled where a vine had molded its shape, sending spirals of wood spinning as it grew. Above this was a good place for a handhold—and at the end of the branch, where it grew from its mother tree, there was a great gnarled knob, shadowing a myriad of faces and curves.

Antoinette knew at once that she held a powerful work of nature, a prize too good to leave behind. Besides, it had called to her for rescue and offered itself as a gift from the sea. It was a gift she would mold into her staff, her wand of power. She felt blessed, for such wands were not often found, but were sought out and worked with, until they were shaped to suit their caretakers.

Once, this wood belonged to an oak or rowan. How long had it lay captured, waiting for her to retrieve it, to awaken its stored energy? Now it was in her keeping, it would be her companion and help-mate and in return she would care for it and be responsible for its safety. She would awaken the energy of the tree and call upon it to carry her power and to defend her. She had found her first companion.

The landscape changed from rock to sand, and blue water rippled gently toward the shoreline. The sun cast short shadows from a majestic promontory in the distance. It was time to return to her campsite.

As Antoinette began to retrace her steps, the white gull suddenly swooped down. Its great wide wings flapping wildly in the air, knocked her backward into the sand.

Antoinette swung her staff protectively above her head, but the gull swooped and cawed in a great fury.

Confused at the strange actions of the bird, Antoinette ran toward the cover of the cliff side and the thick brush that grew along the high banks. The bird stopped following and landed some distance away.

As she paused to catch her breath, feeling silly at her sudden fright, she heard the sound she had been searching for. The sound of rushing water.

She ran to the cliff side, her heart pounding faster as the sound became louder. Beyond the piles of driftwood, a tiny rivulet of clear water cascaded from the cliff side. It bubbled across the colored rocks as it meandered through a small eroded stream bed until it merged with the sea.

"Blessed be!"

Amazed and excited, Antoinette knelt down and touched the sweet water to her mouth.

"Blessed bird." She smiled at the gull as it settled silently across from her on the bank of the stream. The bird bobbed his head and opened his yellow beak. It looked as though he had a smile on his face.

"Thank you my friend," she said.

Antoinette waded into the cool stream and stripped off her tunic, splashed the water over her until she stood dripping wet, naked and glistening in the sunlight.

She refilled her empty wine bottle, giving thanks once more to the Great Mother Earth for Her bounty. Then she turned to the gull.

"Well my friend, now you need to teach me how to catch that fish."

It didn't seem strange to her when the gull took to the air and headed toward the tidal pool. Antoinette grabbed her staff and tunic and ran behind him.

Together they herded the fish to the edge of the pool and, using her tunic as a net, caught the fish in the makeshift weir.

"We make a good team my friend." She held up the fish. "But I'll not ask for more magic tonight. Only that you share my supper."

She rinsed her clothes and hair in the fresh water then headed back towards camp. The gull followed, closer now, hovering just ahead of her. Once he swooped out onto the water to touch the top of a wave. Then he flew ahead of her as if to stand guard.

Back at her camp, Antoinette gathered rocks to make a fire pit. She harvested dry grass from the hillside and driftwood for her fire. All the while, the gull watched with intent curiosity, tilting its head from side to side as he inspected her every move.

She withdrew the tinderbox from her knapsack and said a quick, silent prayer. She fed the gull bits of the raw fish, then speared the fish through the gills and set it to cook over the open fire.

Leaning back against the sand, Antoinette relaxed as she watched the thin clouds paint their images against the pale twilight sky.

With a companion, a human companion, this would almost be ideal, she thought. But with a little less sand in her food and clothing.

She decided then, as she inhaled the cool evening breeze, that this might be the Otherworld after all. And, if it was not the Otherworld, it certainly bordered close to paradise.

When the first stars appeared Antoinette ate the last of her fish. Then a sudden deep loneliness crept over her as the night grew darker and the waves rolled silently ashore.

How could she have let Anne talk her into leaving so easily? she wondered. She should have stayed in Brittany, fought for the Sisterhood, fought for the freedom of the Bretons and their rights to worship the gods or goddesses of their choosing. She should have stayed—just one more day—and dared Cardinal Visconti to test his Inquisition against the forces of the Ancient Ones.

"Should have, could have, would have," she heard Ursule's reprimanding voice in her head. "Doesn't make the stars shine at night—doesn't make the sun rise in the morning."

Was Ursule's spirit hovering near? Protecting her?

Antoinette looked into the embers. Small flames flickered from coal to coal then settled within the burning wood to a hot radiant glow. A familiar tingle surrounded her body as the veil slowly lifted between the worlds. She slipped into a dreamlike vision.

A great ship poised on the edge of the ocean-sea, rows of armored soldiers lined up along her bow ready for battle. A dragon blew its flaming crimson breath towards the east, scorching the forests into wastelands. A white king with a ruby crested crown called down the powerful snows from the North, encompassing the red dragon in a frozen storm of ice. The dragon survived, but his wings were broken. He limped home to his lair with its painted walls and stained glass windows.

A queen held a harp in her arms, but she could not play the dance for the king. A pale man, mounted a white horse and a woman knelt before the Blessed Virgin Mary. Tears stained the woman's her face.

Suddenly, the stench of the smoldering forests surrounded her. A woman, fiery red from head to toe, loomed before her, the woman's silver eyes blazing like diamonds. The woman raised her arms and lifted into the air, then swooped like a seagull into the depths of the ocean.

A sea bird cried in the distance and Antoinette's consciousness snapped back to the fire. She wiped the wetness of tears from her cheeks. It had only been a moment. A fragment of time. But it had been vision enough. Dragons, painted men and soldiers. It was too much to think about tonight.

Exhausted, Antoinette stretched out her arms and yawned. She looked over at the gull sleeping quietly in the shadow of the firelight then crawled under her boat canopy.

"Tomorrow, we'll find you a name," she said to the bird.

☙

Antoinette spent the next few days exploring her tiny inlet, collecting birds' eggs, shells and feathers. Her skin began to glow with the healthy radiance of sunshine and fresh food. She learned to catch the little crabs by moonlight and to fish in the early morning's tidal pools. The salty flavor of the seaweed added spice to her food and driftwood made her fires. Every morning and evening she prayed for Brighid to place her feet upon the proper path and to let her forgive those who sent her into exile.

Today the morning sun glistened on the calm shores as the white gull hovered above her.

"*Mon petit ami*—" She threw a piece of fish to her feathered friend. "I've decided to call you Finder and I wish you to help me in my quest for the source of the fresh water. In return, you shall have my friendship and gratitude, a place by my fire and a share of my meals."

The gull flapped his wings, cawed once, flew swiftly down the beach then back to hover over her campsite.

Antoinette nodded to Finder. "I'll take that as an agreement."

She packed her belongings, pulled the boat close to the cliff then tied the bowline to a rocky outcropping. She scattered the rocks from her fire pit then headed down the beach. It was time to find the headwater that fed the stream and to prepare for the coming of cooler weather. The thought made her shiver. The nights were already chilly and the velvet cloak barely kept her warm. If she did not find humans, or a better shelter, she knew she would die.

Within an hour, she had reached the cliff where the spring swelled from a tiny trickle. Images of a clear lake and a warm shelter took shape in her mind and spurred her onward. Not a natural climber, she had never wanted to follow her brother as he climbed apple trees or played among the parapets of the castle. In truth, heights frightened her. Now, as she looked at the cliffs, she knew she had to climb; her survival lay beyond the top.

She wedged her staff between the pack and her back, found her first foothold and handhold and eased herself up onto the cliff side.

Her heart beat faster with the increasing height, as every movement pulled her farther upward and her weight pulled her downward. Her feet searched for secure footholds, but often found only loose dirt. She could hear Finder calling her from above the cliff, urging her onward.

"Come on," she said, commanding herself. Pushing her strength to its limits, she climbed higher despite her fear and the sound of blood pounding in her temples. "This cliff isn't as tall as the rubbish heap behind the kitchen, nor as high as Anne's featherbed." She inched up a bit further. "This mound isn't as high as the step-stool in my stillroom."

Pausing, she groped for a handhold, but the earth provided none. Her grip had crumbled into dust. She looked down and her heart leapt into her throat. She was at least forty feet above the beach. Instinctively, she flattened herself closer to the embankment.

"Mother Earth," she prayed in panic. "Hold me to your bosom."

Let your spirit soar, her mind said. *Be like Finder, his wings would lift you high. They would be sure and strong.*

Slowly Antoinette relaxed, felt the coolness of the earth beneath her fingertips and the musty fragrance of dirt and stone.

"Be like Finder," she repeated. If he could defy the power of the earth, so could she. Reaching outward, this time without panic, she found a rock wedged tightly into the cliff and without effort she pulled herself up to its height.

A downwind off the highlands carried the scent of greenery over the edge of the cliff. Surely the crest was a few more handholds away.

As though in answer, Finder urged her on with excited screeches.

Antoinette struggled to pull herself to the top of the cliff, threw her belongings onto the ledge then pulled herself over the top. She rolled onto the lush green grass covering the high ground and let out a long-held breath.

A warm breeze tinged with the scent of evergreen and heather blew from the woodlands and she let herself drift with the breeze as she stilled her rapid heartbeat. She looked at the white wisps of clouds and birds gliding effortlessly in the wind currents and thanked the Goddess for a successful climb.

But the day was not over. She could not rest until she found some type of shelter. Sitting, she looked beyond the cliff at the vast panorama that spread before her. Somewhere beyond the horizon lay her homeland and family. Could she really have crossed that vast ocean-sea? Could she really be in the new lands Jacques spoke of? Or was she simply a few miles from civilization?

"It will do me no good to dwell on the past," she said to Finder as she turned toward the woodlands. "I'll make a new home and I'll find a place to live in the forest and swim in the clear, sweet waters of a moonlit lake."

Fields of purple lupine, yarrow and yellow daisies waved in the open expanse of a meadow. As she walked, lush vegetation crushed beneath her feet and the fragrant smells guided her toward the verdant forests. As a child she had wandered the hills and forests near Nantes, studying with Ursule—gathering herbs and roots for healing. The secluded forests were her school room and play yard. There she knew she would be able to feast on the bounty of the magnificent woodlands.

As she walked into a sheltered glade she could no longer hear the sound of the ocean. It was a more familiar world, the world of the sidhe, of the fairies, where almost anything could happen. Finder's high pitched song echoed through the silence as he flew high above the treetops, directing her onward.

Antoinette plunged through the dense forest, ducking under limbs of majestic firs and birches, following Finder's call. She picked her way through the thick berry bushes ripe with their summer fruit, stuffing the plump red berries in her mouth as she passed. Chipmunks scurried away with their acorns and the sweet sound of yellow throated warblers and chickadees serenaded her passage.

She walked for several hours following Finder's call, winding downward, deeper and deeper into the forest. A quiver of aspen leaves stirred the silence of the forest and Antoinette stopped to listen.

Only once before, in the dark and ominous forests of Brittany at the time of her initiation, had she heard such silence or seen such pristine woods. But then she had been too excited to enjoy the solitude. Now, she could feel the energy from the ancient trees and the power of the woodland spirits around her.

Thick bracken ferns, moss and plantain grew at her feet, waiting for her to gather them for her medicine cache. But she could not stop. The sun was setting and a chilling dampness began to surround her.

Finder hovered overhead. Just a little farther, she told herself, still following his flight. She had to find shelter, water, and food before nightfall.

She had all but given up the quest for the headwaters of the stream when she found the sandy banks of a briskly running brook. Resolutely, she followed the creek bed, walking sometimes in the icy ankle high water or jumping across rocks and small waterfalls. All the while she watched as Finder flew deeper into the valley.

Exhausted, Antoinette sat on a flat rock to rest. Finder reappeared, settling by her side with a silent swish of his wings. For a long moment he looked at her with one eye, then tilted his head to look at her with the other. Suddenly he took flight. This was not their destination.

Patiently following the bird, Antoinette navigated the stream's edge, winding deeper and deeper into the darkness of the forest. When she heard a rush of water, she raced ahead. Around the bend a cascade of rainbow colors fell down the face of the cliff side. Finder flew upward, disappearing above the waterfall.

"Not another climb." She sighed, but hefted her pack onto her shoulder.

This time a well-worn path slowly inclined up the ravine. Whether it was made by animal or by human she could not tell. Her heart beat rapidly with a fear of the unknown. Who or what might she find at the other end of the path?

She stopped for a moment to listen to the sounds of the waterfall and to reassure herself that she would be all right. From the majestic birches and oaks to the tiny lichen underfoot, they were all part of the Mother, all part of the spiral of life. Everything had a purpose and a destiny to fulfill. At this moment, her destiny led to the top of the hill and to whatever awaited her there.

When the ground began to level out beyond the last rapids of the waterfall she saw the destination of her quest.

A placid lake with crystal clear water lay before her. Surrounded by a protective barrier of hearty woodlands, it was sure to be filled with food and harboring some type of shelter.

Antoinette rushed across the clearing. "This is perfect," she called to Finder. "I never doubted you for a minute."

He cawed and took wing into the twilight sky, flying in great circles and skimming the still water of the lake with his beak. She walked down to the water's edge just as the sun slipped beyond the treetops.

Chapter 19

The shaman, Muin, called Bear World-Walker by his people, heard the sound of wings beating above him. Even with his eyes closed he knew it was the white swan that flew past him on soft downy wings. He could see it as clearly in his mind as he had seen her at dawn, when it swam before him in the Lake of the Swans.

On the first night of his sojourn at the lake, while on a dream journey, the white swan had appeared in human shape, as Wapi'skw, Swan Woman. Rising from the shimmering lake, she came to him, pledged her friendship with a gentle whisper of a kiss, then together they traveled to the World Above the Earth.

Resting on wispy clouds, she told him many ancient

secrets. Bear's desire for her grew and Wapi'skw shared her love gift with Bear, promising to come to him whenever he needed her. Then they returned to the Earth, the shaman to his dreaming human body and Wapi'skw to her swan shape.

Bear had awakened the next morning to the songs of ground sparrows and mockingbirds, remembering the passion and the sweet voice of Wapi'skw, the Swan Woman. But as the mists of sleep floated from his thoughts, he could not recall the words of wisdom she had shared with him. All he could remember of the magical visitation was the pleasure.

On his second morning of isolation, he sought out the white swan, for he knew his dream was a sign from Great Power, Kji-kinap, creator of all life. There was a lesson he needed to learn from the swan, if nothing more than her graceful acceptance of life.

Now on the third day of his retreat, he sat on the banks of her lake. He willed his spirit body to drift silently beside the white bird like delicate leaves floating on still water. But still no vision came to him. He was growing weary of waiting.

Determined to remain in the realm of the Spirit, Bear listened and watched for the path to the Other World to appear. In truth, he had no other choice. He had to speak with Great Power, not only for himself, but for his people, the *El'nu*, the Micmac.

There was an uneasiness among the tribes. There had been needless deaths and unwarranted fighting. He could feel a strange vibration that rippled through all the Worlds—a vibration that began in the East with the rising of the sun.

Bear knew this was the cause of the People's problems. A new enemy was taking shape among them: an enemy named Greed. Before Greed appeared, all People shared the land and the food. They lived together in peace and in trust. Now, Greed lived among the chiefs and even sought the companionship of many shamans.

Greed took over the lives and minds of both men and women. It made them selfish, turned their hearts dark and their actions malevolent. The village raids by young men hunting a wife often resulted in bloodshed. Generous men no longer shared their hunting bounty with their neighbors and women were losing their honor and their wisdom.

Even Bear himself was not untouched by Greed. It had thrown his life into chaos. He could no longer Walk between the Worlds or see ten Worlds into the Future. Without his power he could not protect his people or find the best food for his tribe.

The paths that had always been so easy to follow were closed. Bear worried that his powers might be lost forever. But deep in his heart he knew this was not true, for he had lived his life as a man should, with honor and integrity. All the People respected him and followed his advice.

Why would Great Power refuse to speak to him? Why was Power hiding?

Seeking answers, Bear had traveled through the thick forests of birch and fir, always walking eastward past the smoking mountains, past the village of his brother and northward along the great water to the Lake of the Swans, the sacred place of Great Power.

After four days and four nights of fasting and contemplation, he would make a long and uninterrupted voyage into the Otherworld, a journey to regain his Power. Here he would cleanse his heart and hear Great Power's voice once more—the voice that spoke to men and women of great virtue. Now, Bear sat on the banks of the secluded lake, waiting in silence and reverence for the sun to fall beneath the earth, to end the third day of his quest.

He wore his hair unbraided and unadorned and it fell down his back like the sleek black feathers of a raven. He was naked, with only the sacred medicine bag hanging around his neck. He did not hide his body beneath the heavy quilled vest and leather robes of ceremony. He did not paint his high cheekbones with *weukuju*, the red ochre marks of Power, or take the sacred visionary herbs. These things he would do only if he could not make the vision quest unaided. To appear to Great Power in his true form showed the greatest honor.

The sunlight glistened off the curves of Bear's golden body, accentuating broad shoulders that were as familiar to hard work and hunting as to holding a newborn for first naming. Yet he was a warrior, trained by the best archers, and among the finest of the young men when it came to fishing.

Bear's eyes were keen and he could call forth great fish simply with his hunting songs. With a steady strong arm he would glide through the vast water with his companions, their birch bark canoes breaking the waves as they looked for sign of the great whale, *Putup* or *ko'ukadamp*, the sturgeon.

Once sighted, Bear would throw a swift and sure harpoon and the hunters would ride the fleeing wake of the beast until it gave up its life for the tribe's survival.

Bear's long legs were also strong and powerful. He could run great distances with little effort. Yet in dance, he was as graceful as an elk. Indeed, it was his strength, height and hunting skills that had earned him the honored name of *Muin*, Bear. When he found his calling as a healer, his teacher, Laughing Elk, gave him the title of World Walker. So he became known as Muin, Bear World-Walker.

No one knew that beneath Bear's courageous disguise beat a fragile, broken heart and an unrequited love for a young maiden of extraordinary beauty named Sparrowhawk.

Her people were the Kwetejk, the people from across the great waters to the North who came to his tribe with the last mid-summer gathering. A long winter without many caribou had driven them southward into the Micmac lands. By tribal agreement, they were allowed to share the summer hunting territory with the Micmac then return to their homes across the waters before the winter season.

Sparrowhawk was the daughter of a *puion*, a shamaness of the Kwetejk, and she had come to Bear's tribe to learn the Micmac way of healing. She was a delightful girl, full of joy and dance, and Bear knew from her first smile that he had fallen in love with her.

He was intrigued by her red hair and by the fine features that marked her as a child of the North men, who had long ago visited the lands of the People. He enjoyed teaching her the customs of the Micmac and the magic of the shamans.

Sparrowhawk was a quick student who devoured each lesson with enthusiasm. But Bear soon discovered she was more interested in learning the secrets of love. She teased him with her innocence and with her unending curiosity and Bear tried his best to appease her.

As a shaman, he was not considered to be like other men. He could openly speak to a young woman without damaging her honor or binding her to marriage.

Before Sparrowhawk came to the tribe, no woman had ever tried to claim him. They all knew he would share his blanket with a woman of Power, for his Power Spirit, Muin Wap'skw, White Bear, was too strong to be tamed.

Sparrowhawk and Bear shared many days together, wandering through the woodlands and shorelines. He taught her the names of the plants used for medicines, and how to prepare salves and potions. He taught her Power words and sacred dances and shared many of the shaman's deepest secrets with her. In return she taught him that passionate kisses and ardent caresses were harder to control than a basket full of eels. And twice as dangerous.

It was not unusual for her to leave him with his emotions in turmoil and his body aching for a release of his desire. He had always been able to control himself, to guard his emotions and his Power. Before he met Sparrowhawk, he had never truly been in love.

Sparrowhawk finally persuaded him to meet her in a secret place where they would share a night of passion and pledge their hearts to one another.

The hour came when they were to meet and Bear waited in anticipation, watching for his lover. He waited until the newly full moon was high into the sky, then until it faded into the dawn. When the sun rose into the morning sky, he knew Sparrowhawk had played him for a fool.

For the next few days, Old Woman, his foster mother, patiently tended his hearth. Without a word she placed a cupful of red clover tea before him and covered him with his Bear skin robe.

"She's gone," Old Woman told him. She had returned to her people. She never meant to be his woman, to share his hearth, his love or his bed. Old Woman had learned that Sparrowhawk came to Bear's tribe to distract him and to steal his magic. She was promised to Black Otter, the great Kwetejk warrior, and would never have been a true wife to Bear.

It did not take him long to realize that Sparrowhawk had accomplished her mission. She had stolen his heart, taken his love and with it, his Power.

Now Bear sat on the bank of the Lake of the Swans and searched for answers. Before it was too late, before anyone could discover his weakness, he would reclaim the shaman's right; to walk between the worlds and be one with the Great Power.

His body began to tease him out of his meditation as his legs began to prickle with the return of his wandering spirit. Images of Sparrowhawk's face floated through his thoughts.

"Thunder Brothers!" He whispered in exasperation. Sparrowhawk had conquered him again. If only he could open up his heart and seal the wound she had made, he knew his spirit would heal. But the path to that magic eluded him.

Bear stretched out his long legs and opened his eyes. Little had changed in the landscape since the dawning of the day, save for the darkening sky and the sound of the owls and whippoorwill beginning their evening songs. He wondered if the full moon tomorrow would bring the visions he sought.

The Keeping Moon was a special moon; its rays led to the pathways above the earth and he knew his spirit could easily fly to the heavens on Mother Moon's bright beams of light.

Stiff and still in the throes of a light trance, Bear made his way to the edge of the lake. He could see the white swan across the water, flapping her great wings and sending rippling waves toward him in greeting.

Come brother, swim with me.

Bear smiled and raised his head in acknowledgment.

Thank you my friend. He motioned to the bird with graceful movements of his hands. *When my task is through, we will fly to the heavens together.*

He lowered his sweat glistened body into the cool water, tempted to spend the rest of the evening swimming with the swan. But he could not spare the time for relaxation, he had to prepare for the rising of the moon.

Tonight he would meditate again and seek Kji-kinap once more. If Great Power did not answer him, then tomorrow night he would apply the colorful paints and wear the ceremonial power robes. He would fill his pipe with the sweet and pungent mixture of herbs and tobacco, smoke and travel to the Otherworld. He would meet Kji-kinap at any cost.

Antoinette stowed her shoulder pack among the trees and walked down to the lake. She pushed the end of her staff in the sand to stand guard for her safety and slipped into the lake.

"Blessed Mother of Waters, I thank Thee," she whispered, submerging herself fully clothed under the cool liquid. "Refresh my spirit, for I am weary; renew my soul, for I am spent. Cover me with your bounty and float away my fears."

She swam under the water, letting the cleansing liquid flow around her body and through her loosened hair, then she bobbed to the top and floated on her back, looking at the sky. Finder circled high overhead.

Swimming silently and quietly, Antoinette looked around the lake. Behind her, a majestic stand of trees led to the ocean. To her right, water reeds and cattails grew in abundance along the bank, promising a bounty of fish underneath. An occasional sandy beach dotted the irregular shoreline like patches of newly fallen snow. Across the water lofty birch trees fringed the banks, their hungry brown fingers intruding upon the secrecy of the water. It would be to the east, beyond the waterfall, that the moon would rise.

She could detect the life energy of the animals and birds of the forest lurking beyond the tree covered banks, but there were no signs of humans. A white swan swam near the water reeds.

Finder cawed from overhead, reminding her that the sun was beginning to pass behind the stand of trees in the west and that she should find a shelter before nightfall.

From her count of days, the moon would be full tomorrow, it would be Lughnasad and she would honor the Ancient Ones in ceremony. She had attended many similar feasts and rituals throughout the years. The full moon was always a time when the portals were open to the Otherworlds, but the high hallowed days and the turnings of the seasons were reserved to honor the Ancient Ones. She had been initiated many years ago at Candlemas. Held in the deepest part of winter, it was a time for cleansing and renewal, a time for the preparation of Spring. In that ceremony dedicated to the Maiden and to her protectress Brighid, Antoinette had spoken the words that bound her to the Sisterhood and set her path as a healer.

Now, on Lughnasad, the mid-point between the summer solstice and the fall equinox, it was the time to honor Lugh, the Celtic God of Light. It was the time to begin the laying away of foodstuffs for winter, to gather the last herbs of summer and to pledge bonds for spring marriages.

With the rising of this full moon, she would also give thanks to the Ancient Ones for her survival and share the high ceremony with her Sisters in Brittany. Together—though miles apart—they would recognize the waning of the Summer and the rising power of the Goddess.

Antoinette swam the long distance back to the edge of the lake. A bit light-headed and giddy, she cast off her cold, wet tunic as she walked up the sandy embankment. The damp evening air caressed her and a chill crept over her. She shivered uncontrollably and a sudden weakness overpowered her. Her head buzzed. Her eyes began to lose focus. She reached out to her staff for support, but instead she sank down to her knees in the sand.

☙

Bear rose from beneath the refreshing water. Something was wrong. A flash of light pierced the edge of his vision and he slipped behind the tall stand of reeds. Although he'd placed an invisible barrier around his campsite and he wore his protective medicine pouch, he couldn't be too cautious.

He parted the reeds just enough to see a strange figure emerge from the lake. He watched in awe as the white swan shed her wings and changed once again into the shape of a woman, with long dark hair and fair white skin.

Great magic always astonished him, even when it was magic he himself called forth. And this was surely great magic. His meeting with Wapi'skw, Swan Woman, had been in the Dreamworld, but she was shape changing now—in this world—and he was very much awake.

As a shaman, he told the ancient stories about animals and birds shape-shifting into humans, but it was actually happening before his eyes. He watched with excitement as the pale swan woman walked up the beach. He took in a silent, quick breath as she turned toward him. The swan was once again the graceful woman of his dreams, but this time she held an uncommon, otherworldly beauty.

The fragrant smell of wild lavender filled his senses. He shivered from a cool wind that brushed against his wet body, but he could not move. This time, he told himself, he would restrain his desires and ask Swan Woman for her wisdom.

From his hiding place across the lake he saw Swan Woman lean on a branch, then suddenly collapse on the sand. With the swiftness of a great buck he ran around the shoreline, dodging tree roots and rocks, coming to a halt a few feet away from her. His heart pounded with apprehension. She was a Power being, he reminded himself. He must be careful.

He reached for the medicine bag hanging around his neck and called on the protective energy within it, then he walked in a circle around the fallen woman. She was breathing and still alive, but her breathing was shallow and the color shimmering around her body was pale and lifeless. She lay on her side, hair partly covering her face. She did not move.

Bear stepped closer, noticing the wounds on her back. She wore no magical amulets. He moved closer, gently touching her arm to prove to himself she was real and not his imagination. Her body was cold. She needed help.

Instantly his instincts took the place of fear and he knelt by her side. His fingers trembled slightly as he passed them above the red lash marks on the pale skin of her back.

"Ah—Wapi'skw," he sighed. "You have shed your wings. Now you cannot fly back to the Otherworld."

Carefully turning her over, he took in a quick breath as he gazed upon her. She was indeed his Swan Woman. She was real. Surely she had crossed the worlds to come back to show him the path to Great Power. But the warmth of her body was fading. Something was stealing her life energy.

Bear placed his ear below her breast to listen for a heartbeat. It was slow but strong.

Taking her light body into his arms, he carried her toward

the shelter of the woods and laid her on the soft matted grass. "Stay alive, my friend." He moved his hands over her arms to warm her. "I need your wisdom." His gaze crossed the length of her body, pale and soft and just as desirable as in his vision. "Wapi'skw."

Ever so gently he brushed the hair from her face, lingering his fingers for an instant on her lips before he rose from her side.

Bear rushed the distance to his camp, his mind turning over the events in random confusion. In all the stories he'd heard or told, he did not remember an animal or bird having difficulty passing into human form.

Perhaps it was his fault, he worried. Perhaps he had desired her too much and his desire had trapped her animal spirit before it could properly change shape.

Bear gathered his thick fur blanket and his deerskin robe, suddenly wishing they were of better quality. He picked up his large medicine bundle and pulled his deerskin jacket over his head. It would not be proper for Swan Woman to see his nakedness, nor his desire; for when he thought of holding her close he was very much aroused.

He shook off the vagrant images. He must be a healer now, he said to himself. Not her lover.

With the great strides of a hunter, Bear returned to Antoinette's side. He placed his hand on her forehead, knelt beside her, then taking his medicine bag from around his neck, he held it tightly in his other hand.

"Kji-kinap, Great Power," he prayed. "Let my healing powers be rekindled, just once more. She should not die for my sake. She must live. I will care for her and listen to her words. I need her to live. Do not take her back."

Bear lifted Antoinette's light body onto the soft deer skin pallet and began his examination for the cause of her weakness. She was pale, much lighter than the women of his people and her skin was as soft as a new born fawn. He held her hand, examining the delicate shape of her fingers. Then he saw the small crescent moon shape on her wrist. He took in a quick breath. Swan Woman had been to the World Above the Sky. She had been kissed by Mother Moon.

Bear ran his hands down the length of her arms, feeling her muscles. They lacked the tone and strength of one accustomed to hard work, though they were firm and well formed. Her breasts were ample and round, the nipples small and faint, showing the signs of a maiden growing to womanhood. He guessed her human age to be not more than two or three summers younger than himself.

"I am a healer," he reminded himself as he touched her cool skin. "I must determine the cause of her sickness."

With caring hands he felt her stomach, feeling her hip bones too near to the skin. She would need much food before winter.

Covering Antoinette with the bearskin blanket, he examined her head, carefully lifting her eyelids to look into the depths of her eyes. Although they were green, an odd color, they were still clear and showed no signs of deep sickness, only the absence of her conscious spirit.

He felt her neck, then parted her lips with his fingers. There, red stains revealed the answer to his questions. Bear smiled with relief and tucked the blanket close around her body. Her condition was not serious, not deadly. She had eaten wild chokecherries. She was on a spirit journey, traveling to the Spirit World.

Bear made a fire and sat near Antoinette, guarding her body while her spirit traveled. He had attended his teacher, Laughing Elk, during his last and final spirit journey and knew from experience that a wandering spirit could get lost and never return. Laughing Elk's spirit now traveled the worlds unhindered by a physical body.

This would not happen to Swan. If her spirit did not return by morning, he would call upon Power and search all the worlds to bring her back.

He reached into the large parfleche that held his medicinals and withdrew a wooden box filled with red ochre powder. He mixed drops of water with a few pinches of powder on a piece of birch bark, to make a thick paste of red paint. Touching her gently, Bear painted a band of red around her wrists, ankles and neck. These lines of paint would seal her spirit to her body. They would help guide her back to him.

Finder, curious about his mistress, circled high in the air, then cautiously landed near the edge of the lake. He stood a few feet away from Antoinette, calling to her, flapping his wings in a great fury.

Bear stood up and Finder took flight. *I'll care for your bird sister,* he motioned to Finder with silent hand signals. *She lives in my world now.*

A sea bird cawed from the treetops in response and the forest awoke with the returning sounds of twilight. Then, having made his point, he flew to the ground.

Bear knew much magic was around and he half expected the gull to change into human form as well, but the bird set to preening his feathers. Bear watched in silence as the nearly full moon rose high above the tree line and the sun set with a tremendous flare of color.

He stared across the lake at the moon's bright reflection and wondered if Great Power was testing him.

To send him a woman to deal with when his heart was just mending was not a light burden to bear. And one so lovely and enchanting in her human form was too tempting to his honor.

Looking over the embers of the dying fire, he watched the sleeping shape of his Swan Woman, wishing he could watch her lithe body walk toward him and hear her voice as she spoke his name. He wanted to see the fire glow in her eyes when he touched her and feel her warm breasts against his cool bare skin.

Bear shook the fantasy from his head and laid another log on the fire. *She knows the path to Power. I must be patient—I must listen.*

Not wanting to move her, he had moved his camp, leaving the shelter of his birch bark lean-to and the protective forest windbreak.

The brisk breezes of summer's end raced across the lake and the thickening fog chilled him through his leather leggings and jacket. Bear shivered. He had not eaten for three days and had moved little in the past few hours. He knew he must either tend the fire all night or seek the warmth of his blankets. The idea of lying next to Swan Woman stirred his imagination, but he assured himself his thoughts were purely for survival. He knew he must set aside his physical desires, at least until they had properly met each other in this world.

Bear banked the fire and covered the dry twigs and touchwood with his clothing to hide them from the night's dew, then he slid into the envelope of warmth beside Antoinette. He was careful not to touch her, not to disturb her spirit's travel. But the soft musky scent of her body and the lingering herbal fragrance of her hair embraced him as he moved closer.

Great Power, you test me too strongly. I am but a man. Bear looked up at the cloud covered moon and the bright stars that peeked through the descending mists and smiled.

Ah, but I am a happy man.

He closed his eyes and listened to the soothing sound of a distant waterfall, welcoming the distraction of sleep.

Chapter 20

Bear awoke before dawn, looked over at his companion and smiled. She lay on her side turned toward him, deep in sleep. She had returned from her journey.

He longed to feel the softness of her skin once more, just to assure himself she was real. But instead he touched her with his eyes, taking in every curve and shadow of her face. Her long lashes curled up against her tightly closed eyes and her brow ached gracefully upward. Her lips, parted slightly in sleep, invited a kiss.

Bear moved his hand to touch her face, then stopped. He would not wake her from her rest.

I long to hear your voice, my Swan. And to touch you as a woman.

Now that her spirit had returned, her skin had a healthy glow even though it was quite pale. If she stayed in her earthly body she would survive.

Bear pushed aside any thought of her leaving. His stomach rumbled, reminding him he had not eaten for four days and he would fast again today. But Swan Woman would wake with a great hunger. A spirit journey depleted the body.

Reluctantly, he moved from her side, donned his clothing and rekindled the fire. With the rising of the sun he slipped quietly into the mist shrouded woods.

☙

Finder had not bothered Antoinette's sleep, but now with the intruder gone, he found his chance to check on his companion. He swooped down from the tall fir tree, circling above Antoinette. He cawed in his softest voice.

Wake! Wake!

Antoinette smiled in her dreaming as the familiar sound tugged at her mind. She took in a long deep breath and stretched. The smell of tanned leather surrounded her and the soft fur of the bear skin blanket on top of her naked body rubbed lightly against her skin. She opened her eyes, then bolted upright and stared at the blazing fire before her. Her heart raced. She could not recall anything since she emerged from the lake. How long had she been asleep?

Anxiously she looked around. A thick fog hovered above the lake obscuring the early morning sun and the forests beyond. She was in a well defined camp, but there were no people. There were no signs of life, no belongings except for the fur blanket covering her and leather sleeping pallet beneath her.

She threw back the coverlet and gasped. Red bands of paint striped her wrists and ankles and though she could not see her neck, she could feel the dried paint creeping around her throat. She stood up in panic, realizing someone had painted her body as she slept, looked at her, touched her.

A knot of fear tugged at her senses. Who would be so bold as to take such liberties?

There were footprints near the fire and along the beach and her apprehension grew as she realized they were not hers but the footprints of men. She looked at her ankles and wrists again. Had she fallen into a group of painted Moors like the slaves of the rich Portuguese noblemen she had seen at Anne's court? They were dark and tall and their faces were decorated with chalk and paint. Her fear accelerated as she thought of those strong and barbarous people being her captors. All her instincts told her to leave before she faced further danger.

Wrapping the blanket tightly around her and trying to keep her balance, she steadied herself. Her head spun in dizziness, her legs could barely support her weight, yet she rushed to the lakeside and retrieved her wet tunic, pulling it quickly over her head. She had to get away.

Glancing toward the woods she saw her shoulder pack hidden by the low branches of a fir tree. Without further thought Antoinette grabbed her staff and scrambled into the woods, reaching the cover of a wide cedar tree just as Bear reappeared near the campsite.

She leaned close against the tree, looking with frustration at her shoulder pack, lying only a few feet away. But she dared not move and risk discovery. Not until she saw who her captor was.

Bear looked at the vacant pallet in surprise, then at the footprints leading into the woods. He glanced toward the trees and his hunting eyes saw Antoinette's small white figure through the green brush. She stood silent and still. He smiled to himself. When she was ready, he would meet her properly. They would talk and he would listen.

Then he turned his attention to the rabbit he had killed for her meal and began to prepare it for cooking.

Antoinette watched, peering cautiously around the tree. She made an involuntary gasp when she saw the fierce looking man, painted with black and red stripes across his face and arms, slit the rabbit from neck to tail and strip its pelt with one clean pull. She knew in an instant this man could kill her as easily as he had skinned the rabbit. She reached for her pack.

Bear looked toward the sound and their gaze met.

She froze.

He was not a Moor. His skin was too light, his hair straight and long. No. He was surely one of the savages Jacques spoke of. A wild and fierce man like the ancient Picts of the Scottish Isles. Afraid of nothing.

Antoinette spun in panic and rushed into the woods. She had to escape, seek the safety of the ocean and the distance of the beach.

Finder, where are you?

She looked anxiously at the sky overhead. Finder could lead her back to the cliffs and somehow, some way, she would get back down to the beach and her boat. She heard Finder's distant reply and ran towards his call, ran without thought. Every bramble and thorn in the dense woods seemed to scratch her legs and arms.

Bear heard the loud rustle from the tree line and watched Antoinette's flight into the trees. Had he somehow offended her? he wondered. He must find out why she ran.

Stuffing the rabbit into his hunting pouch, Bear slung the quiver of arrows across his back and with his long bow in hand took to the trees behind her.

I can't let her go without telling her I will listen to her this time. That I mean her no harm.

Bear slowed his tracking to leisurely pace, knowing she could not go far. She ran where the woodlands were thick, up towards the cliff side and the great waters. Perhaps Swan was leading him to her special place of Power since she was leaving such a easy path for him to follow.

Suddenly, Antoinette broke through the thick brush and into a clearing of tall birch and poplar. She looked around the opening for Finder. He called from somewhere overhead, his voice echoed around her, but the tree tops and sky were still hidden in the hovering fog.

Lost!

Her mind screamed as she turned around and around in the clearing, losing her direction in the mists. A sudden movement in the brush startled her, then two chipmunks chased each other up a tree, winding around it like streamers on a May pole. Another sound came from behind her and she paced anxiously in the center of the glade, her senses alert to a danger she could not see.

The daze of sleep was gone from her mind and she could hear everything. Yet there was no sound, save for the heavy pulse of her blood beating loudly in her ears. Not even the birds had ventured into the damp sunless morning.

Antoinette knelt on the ground, her breathing heavy and labored. She steadied her thoughts, looking around cautiously. She must summon the sun and swiftly dispel the mists then find her way out of the dense forest and back to the shore. She must let Finder see her below the trees.

She stood, raising her arms towards the sky, a handful of earth in one hand and her staff in the other.

"Mother Sky." She waved the staff high in the air with a great swirling motion. "Your daughter of Earth would see the sun shine upon her."

Bear stood in the cover of the tree line, hidden by the thick underbrush. He could barely hear Swan's soft chanting, but he witnessed the mists part above her at the waving of her staff. Within a heartbeat the gull swooped through the parting haze and landed at Swan's feet with a great fluttering of its wings.

Bear watched as Swan talked to the bird. Her voice was soft and comforting, like a mother to her babe. It was the same voice he had heard in his dreams. She did not speak the words of his people.

Perhaps Swan was speaking one bird to another.

"Have we lost him, then?" Antoinette's voice was calm and controlled. "Perhaps I wasn't as good a catch as his rabbit. You have to lead me out of this clearing, back to the beach, back to safety." Antoinette rubbed her hands up and down her arms, trying to chase away the lingering chill of the fog.

Finder looked at her and turned his head from side to side, then hopped to the edge of the clearing near Bear's hiding place. Bear held his breath as the bird looked at him with a quick sideways glance. Strangely, it did not betray his hideout, but moved to the center of the clearing and took flight to the treetops with a loud, "*Caw! Caw!*"

The other birds took their cue from Finder's call and began their morning songs. The wind began to move the poplar leaves in a gentle hypnotic sway, lifting the last remnants of fog from the clearing.

Antoinette turned and raised her staff above her head to

thank the Ancient Ones for their help.

Afraid she would take flight like the gull, Bear suddenly emerged from the clearing and stood directly behind her.

Antoinette spun around at the sound and took in a startled breath. Their gaze locked on one another, but this time in a mutually quick assessment.

Bear saw Antoinette's jewel-like eyes glisten with the morning sun that streamed through the lifting fog. To him, her eyes expressed more challenge than fear. She has a brave heart, he thought. One he would like to know better.

Antoinette saw a youthful, powerful man, a head taller than herself, full with muscle and strength, dressed in tanned and painted leather leggings. She saw the face of a warrior, painted black and red, a quiver of arrows slung across his broad back and a long bow, held firmly in one hand. Beneath the paint, she saw dark eyes—eyes looking at her with anticipation.

Slowly she calmed her heartbeat and lowered her arms, heeling her staff on the ground before her. She could not let him see the fear swirling inside her.

Bear breathed a deep sigh of relief. He had stopped her flight, long enough he hoped, to explain his actions to her. He stepped forward.

"Stop." Antoinette lifted a quick outstretched hand. She threw her shoulders back and assumed her most commanding stance, ready to summon the Ancient Ones.

Bear felt a slap of power against his body, stopped in his stride and held his outstretched arms open in a gesture of friendship.

"Wapi'skw." Bear spoke in his language, "Swan Woman, I ask that you listen to me. Don't be afraid. Don't leave without hearing my words."

Antoinette was mesmerized: this man was no simple savage. Although strange, he could speak and his voice was low and soft.

"*Je ne comprend pas.*" Antoinette shook her head from side to side. "I don't understand."

Bear looked at the movement of her lips. Her voice was like the song of the white swan, lyrical and enchanting. Yet, he could not understand her. He thought for a brief moment, then slung his bow across his back. Somehow, he had to make her understand him. He began to speak to her with great fluid movements of his hands in the sign language of the People.

Please forgive my boldness. My heart is heavy for offending your spirit. I watched you fall—I came to help you while your spirit traveled and watched for your return. I meant no disrespect—I am a healer, a shaman to my People.

Antoinette watched the graceful motions of the man before her and wished she could understand. She realized he was trying to communicate through the talking of hands, an ancient language used by many people. She knew the very basic gestures of power that remained of the ancient Druids, the keepers of the mysteries of the Celts. They had used elaborate hand motions as a silent language in their secret ceremonies, often carrying on two levels of discourse at once, speaking words to the common people, while examining the deeper meanings with the initiates. Now, only the elders of Sisterhood knew the signals used in ritual.

Bear continued his explanation. *I know, White Swan Woman, that you have come to show me the path to* Kji-kinap. *I remember my dream vision. Forgive me if I was too hasty to satisfy my human desire.*

He stopped for a moment in thought, then continued. *If you will help me. I will be patient. When you are ready to speak—I will listen.* He cupped his hand below his mouth and raised his fingers as if to eat, then motioned with an extended arm toward the campsite. *I have food and fire for you. Come. I will not harm you.*

Antoinette remained silent as Bear looked at her with his questioning eyes. She knew he expected a response, but she could not give him one. When he turned and walked down the hillside, she sat down in the middle of the empty glade and watched as he disappeared.

She took a long slow breath to calm her nerves. How curious he was. He had not attacked her. Indeed, she sensed a kindness in him and an eagerness to help her. She understood the last of his lengthy address, that he had food and wanted her to come with him.

Antoinette rubbed her hand across her eyes and through her tangled hair in frustration, then turned her gaze upwards to follow the flight of the gull.

"Damn," she said. "My shoulder pack! I can't go without my things."

If she returned to the cliff without her pack she could not make a fire; without her cloak and warmth she would surely die. She would have to retrieve her belongings.

Bear walked back to camp in frustration. He had not been able to understand Swan's words and he was angry at himself for his obvious breach of conduct. Not only had he touched Swan without her permission, he had slept beside her and desired her. Why else would she be so frightened of him?

How should he act and how could he speak to her? he wondered. They had no common language.

He pulled the rabbit from his pouch and speared it with a spruce branch, then set it to spin over the fire on the makeshift rotisserie of newly cut wood. It would take some time to cook, but it would feed Swan, if she ever came out of the woods.

Surely she would, he thought. After all, *she* had come here to help him.

Bear took off his leggings and dove into the frigid water of the lake, hoping the rush of temperature would chase away the confusion in his mind. He washed off the hunting paint from his face and arms and he emerged from the water with a renewed determination to complete his last day's meditation. Either Swan would come down from the hills or she would not, he decided. It was beyond his power to make her choose.

ᘛ

The smell of the roasting rabbit drifted through the woods and Antoinette realized she was more hungry than afraid. She was hesitant to return to the lake, half dressed and unable to speak the man's language, but she needed her shoulder pack.

The gray morning sky turned to a bright blue. She had resolved to wait until dark to retrieve the rest of her belongings, but the aroma of the food filtered up the hillside and her stomach rumbled.

I can't go down now. What if there are other people with him? What if they aren't as civil?

But there had been no sign of other people near the lake, she remembered. No other belongings except the fur and skin covering. The footprints must have all been his. Perhaps he was not as fierce as he looked. Perhaps he wanted to help her.

Antoinette looked at her staff, her only tool, and knew she had no choice but to take the chance that the man meant her no harm.

Standing, she took a deep breath to steady her courage then slowly began her decent. This time she carefully avoided the coarse brush and brambles as she followed the path. She stopped at the edge of the woods and looked toward the campsite. The man was alone, tending the fire. He paid her no attention as she picked up her pack.

She withdrew her green cloak from inside her pack and slung it over her shoulders. She had her things now, she could go. She turned to walk toward the waterfall, but curiosity made her stop to take one last look at the man. He had not moved nor turned in her direction. The food smelled wonderful. The fire looked warm and inviting.

Could she risk leaving the invitation of a warm fire and a cooked meal? Could she stand the loneliness and isolation of the beach?

This stranger might be my only chance to reach civilization. I have to take the risk.

Antoinette took the dirk from her knapsack and placed it in the pocket of her cloak and with staff in hand, approached the campsite. She stopped a few feet away, watching as the man gave the roasting rabbit a spin above the fire.

The meat, suspended by a leather thong, hung from a spruce branch that was balanced between two 'Y' shaped poles shoved into the ground. It twisted from side to side as it slowly roasted above the fire.

Bear did not look up and made no move as she approached, and she took the opportunity to stare at him. He had washed the paint from his body and his wet hair gleamed in the sunlight. She could not see his face full-on, but his angular profile revealed high pronounced cheekbones and a sharp, well defined chin.

No. This man was not a Moor, she realized. But she had never seen anyone that looked like him. His arms were bare and his muscles tensed as he idly drew in the sand at his feet. His movements were graceful yet masculine and she could not take her eyes away from him. He had removed the brightly decorated deerskin leggings and now wore only his loincloth and moccasins. His thighs were solid and strong. The sight of his bronzed skin captivated her, yet somehow, in this natural environment, his near nakedness did not embarrass her. She had lived day and night with men aboard *La Réale* and stood sky-clad in ceremony with men who followed the religion of the Ancient Ones, but never had she beheld a man of such fine form.

Bear studied his companion with equal curiosity with the edges of his vision. He lowered his gaze as she approached, partly in respect and partly in awe. She was much more beautiful than he had realized. His heart raced as he watched her walk from the woods and come toward him. Her green robe flowed behind her like a pair of great wings. Her hair hung loose and free, surrounding her head like fine downy feathers of light. The outline of her body shimmered underneath the strange white clothing she wore and Bear knew, if he continued to watch her and think about her, his desire to hold her would consume him.

He shook his head to dispel his thoughts and turned his gaze toward the drawings he made in the sand. He must be patient. He must allow her to make the first move.

Antoinette cleared her throat. "Ah—*Pardon Monsieur.*"

Bear quit his drawing and slowly looked up. Their eyes locked. He smiled.

Antoinette took in a quick breath. It was him. She recognized his eyes from her visions. He was the one who beckoned her from the mists. A light blush crept up her neck.

"*Mon Dieu,*" she said in a hushed whisper. "You are the one. Your eyes are the eyes that fill my dreams."

Bear noticed her anxiety and looked away. With the skillful grace of a hunter he removed the rabbit from the cooking spit and withdrew his sharp stone knife to cut away a portion of the roasted meat. He offered it to her on the end of his knife.

Antoinette smiled in return. She was right, she realized. She was being welcomed as a guest. This man's actions were indications of friendship and the offer of food was a gesture that she did not wish to refuse.

Antoinette sat down in the sand. Cautiously, she lifted the meat from the end of Bear's knife. He handed her a cake of a white oily substance and motioned for her to eat it. She smelled the meat in her hand and took a small bite to test its heat. It was the best game she had ever eaten. The cake which the man insisted she eat, was on the other hand, thick and greasy and hard to swallow. It smelled rancid and tasted worse. She handed the rest of it back to him.

Bear shook his head, pushing the cake of fat back toward her. "*Moque.*" He accompanied his command by quick hand and arm movements. "No. You must eat this fat with your meat. It will renew the energy you used on your spirit journey."

Antoinette heard the insistence in his voice and forced herself to swallow the oily food.

Satisfied that he'd made his point, Bear returned to his drawings. He drew thanks to Rabbit for giving his life as food. He drew the story of his morning's hunt. The shape of the rabbit appeared as he drew, then his bow and a warrior.

Antoinette watched over his shoulder as he made a picture of simple marks and lines. Why was this man of her dreams so important? she wondered. Why had the Goddess taken her so far away from home to meet him?

She could feel the power in his drawings and saw a hunting scene unfolding on the sand before her.

"*Lapin?*" She pointed to the figure with long ears and bobbed tail.

Bear looked up at her and she held up her food then pointed once again to the drawing.

"Lapin."

"*Ablegamutc,*" Bear said in his language, pointing to the drawing then to the roasted meat with great excitement. "Laa-pin", he said, imitating Antoinette.

Antoinette chuckled at the gentle word spoken by the robust man before her. Bear smiled at her light giggle and threw his head back in a vibrant laugh that echoed across the quiet lake.

They had found the way to begin.

Chapter 21

Bear drew his magic in the sand and Antoinette watched with rapt attention. With his drawings he could call the moose and caribou to the nearest hunting ground. With his carving he could empower his harpoon to strike and hold the largest sturgeon. Now, Bear discovered, he could also capture Swan Woman's attention. His drawing had broken the barrier between them.

Bear pointed his spruce branch at the stick figure of the warrior and then to the outline of a bear and slowly said his name.

"Muin." Then he pointed to his chest. "Bear, World Walker, the shaman of many People."

Antoinette looked at him with a puzzled frown. His voice was gentle, but his words were so foreign. She spoke Latin, French, English and the secret language of magic. She had entertained royalty from many countries. But this man's language was unique, full of poetry, full of rhythm. It was almost like singing.

Bear repeated his name, placed his hand on his chest.

"Muin."

He pointed to the figure drawing of the great bear. "Moo-inn." She must have come from very far above the sky, not to understand his People's words.

"Ah!" Antoinette exclaimed. "Your name is Moo—inn."

"E'e." Bear smiled. "Yes. Muin. Bear."

He drew with the gentle slow stoke of a skilled artist and

Antoinette watched as a majestic bird flew above wavy lines of clouds. Bear was careful not to think of capturing her power with his magic as he drew. He wanted to show her flying to earth. He hoped Swan would understand. When she did not repeat his words he drew the form of a woman.

Perhaps, if I breathe understanding into my drawing, the magic will work again.

He pointed to the bird. "Wapi. Swan." Then he pointed to her "Wapi'skw, Swan Woman."

Bear smelled the lingering herbal fragrance in her hair as she leaned past him with a graceful extension of her hand and pointed toward the figure of the woman.

"Antoinette." She mimicked the same expressions and hand movements he initiated, placing one hand on her chest and another extended to the drawing. "Antoinette."

Bear turned the word over in his mind. It was such a strange sounding word. *An—towa-net.* It was not a name of his people. He shook his head, unsure his voice could even make such soft sounds. Yet he wanted to explore the language of the Otherworlds. He opened his mouth to try the name, then stopped in mid breath, remembering a story about Little Marten and his bad fortune.

Little Marten had captured a giant Whale woman in his salmon weir. Her smoked meat and fat would have fed his tribe for many months, but she escaped by tricking Little Marten into saying her power name.

Could Swan be giving him her power name? Would she disappear if he said this soft word? He looked into her eyes and at her face shining in the sunlight. He would not take the chance.

Bear pointed to the swan, then to Antoinette.

"Wapi'skw, Swan Woman."

Antoinette shook her head and plopped down in the sand beside him. "Antoinette," she repeated, pointing to her chest insistently. "My name is Antoinette."

Bear nodded in acknowledgment, but did not say her power name. "Wapi'skw."

Frustrated, Antoinette stood up and placed her hands on her hips. "Look, my name is Antoinette Charboneau. Not Wapi—whatever." She pointed her finger at her chest. "Antoinette, Antoinette Charboneau, and where I come from that name is very well respected."

Bear looked at her in amazement. Never had a woman spoken to him in such a curt manner. Even if she was Swan Woman, she had no right to show him disrespect and she would not use her power voice to make him say her secret name.

He sprang to his feet and scowled down at her, his arms folded in defiance. "Wapi," he said with a commanding voice. He wanted this woman, needed this woman, but she would know from the beginning he was not afraid of her. "Wapi'skw!"

Startled at his quick movements Antoinette took a half-step back from the towering man. He was magnificent, his body a sculpted work of nature, gleaming in the sunlight. His legs were strong and firm and she could not help but notice the obvious wealth of manhood his leather covering concealed. Her heart pounded rapidly and she lowered her head to hide the blush on her cheeks.

"All right." She was hardly in a position to argue with him. "Wapi'skw."

"*E'e*!" Bear nodded and motioned politely for her to sit near the fire.

Antoinette obliged him and sat.

Bear turned from his stance and walked toward the deerskin pallet in frustration. He could already see she was going to be a problem. What was he going to do with her? She was quickly becoming a real woman. Stubborn and headstrong. She no longer seemed the gentle swan. He smiled. But she was also very, very beautiful.

Bear squatted next to his pack and retrieved his leather jacket and medicine bundle. The thin fabric covering Swan would not last out the rugged trip. She would need better clothing if she were to travel with him. He brushed the dirt from his leather jacket and looked back at Swan. Her tongue had the bite of a snake, yet she looked so fragile against the background of the enormous trees. Would she really be strong enough to live in his world? If she stayed, would she be the one to make his robes and tend his hearth?

The next few days would show him, for he must travel back to his camp before the moon was gone from the night sky. His people would soon begin their biggest harvests of food for the winter season. But they would not begin until he returned, until he called the moose and caribou with his power.

He returned to Swan with his leather jacket in hand and offered it to her with a nod. She took it and ran her hands over the bold lines of red and black paint and over the sunbursts that decorated the sleeves. The dark outline of a bear was painted on the back.

The leather was tanned and soft and the unique artistry of the design quite skilled. The stitch work of his moccasins was not of the same quality as the jacket, but still showed the art of his people in its craftsmanship. She wondered if all the articles he owned were of such quality.

Bear carefully unrolled his medicine bundle on the sand. Apart from the magic medicine bag he kept tied to his waist, his medicine bundle was his most guarded possession. This object held his power. It had been given to him by Laughing Elk at his initiation and Bear could not remember a time in his adult life when it had not been his constant companion.

The outer covering was a well worn piece of thick moosehide, painted with bold geometric designs in black and red ochre. Several strips of rawhide laced through the cover served to pull the leather tight and make it water resistant. Sewn onto it were several small shells, a long shiny hollow bird bone, tubes of beaten metal that looked like copper and a small bear claw. All these ornaments warned others of the great power of the owner and discouraged intrusion by the uninvited.

He opened the covering, silently thanking the objects for their continued protection. Looking up from under his lashes, he saw the wonder in Swan's eyes and knew she understood the significance of his belongings.

Antoinette was amazed at the variety of articles in Bear's parfleche. She expected to see the normal things men carry in their personal satchels; shaving knives, flint boxes, kerchiefs and mementos. But she realized as Bear opened the bundle that this was no ordinary satchel, it was a well organized cache of medicinals. Its range of healing was much broader than her own.

Among the bunches of feathers, bones and dried birds' claws lay small leather packets, some stitched with embroidery of the same amazing artistry as his jacket. Others pouches were painted with bold black and red designs. All the packets were bound together by strips of thin sinew. One pouch was made from the head of a woodpecker, its neck and beak tied tight with strips of sinew. The fur pouches were the paws of animals, a mink and fox, with the claws still dangling on the ends.

She sat quietly, her hands folded in her lap, yet her eyes held a childlike curiosity about the contents. She watched patiently as Bear took out a small wooden bowl made of folded tree bark. Its concave shape was held tight by thin strips of white wood stitched at the seams and covered with resin. Stuffed inside the bowl was a small piece of chamois and a stone object about four inches long and rounded on one end.

Very similar, she thought, to an alchemist's pestle.

Bear unrolled a brightly colored pouch, removed a few dried dark blue flower petals and placed them in the bowl. With a few gentle strokes of the stone against the petals, he ground the flowers to a fine dark purple powder. He retrieved a black, sausage shaped object from the bundle and squeezed a drop of its oil onto a piece of leather, then he added the powder and mixed it all together with a small stick.

Antoinette watched with curiosity as he returned from the edge of the lake with a wet chamois. When he motioned to her arms and legs, she saw mud, scratches and dried blood on her legs. She had injured herself on her flight up the hill and she realized that Bear intended to apply his purple ointment to her wounds.

Springing to her feet, Antoinette took a hasty step back, suddenly afraid of his power. This man possessed great magic and she was still confused about her feelings toward him. If she let him heal her, she would be further in his debt. If he touched her, she knew she would never want to leave.

"No." She turned to go. "No, *Merci.*"

Bear's brows furrowed. He held the wet chamois out and motioned for her to take it from him.

I should leave now, she thought. But she could not make her legs obey her commands. She was frightened by his power yet intrigued by his presence. *This is his world. This is his way of helping me. I am silly, dreaming up hidden meanings in his courteous offerings.*

The sting and itch of the scratches on her legs began to worry her. He was right. They needed medication and in his world, he would know the proper treatment for her wounds.

Antoinette took the cloth and wiped away the blood and muddy stains. When she was finished, Bear held up the wooden bowl and knelt, then motioned for permission to touch her. She nodded.

Gently, he tested the area around her scratches for any sign of discomfort. He spread the newly made salve lightly over the scratches on her legs and arms, then motioned for her to remove her tunic so he could apply the salve to the wounds on her back.

Antoinette took a deep breath and steadied her nerves. *I can't let him do this. What is happening to my judgment? No, it's all right. He is a healer.* He had probably taken similar vows of service as she had. She looked once more into his deep black eyes. She had no reason to be afraid. She felt no malice, no other motives.

With the last shreds of her dignity, she turned her back to Bear, pulled the white tunic over her head and concealed her breasts in the folds of the cloth.

Bear chuckled to himself as he applied the salve and delighted at Antoinette's sighs as the cooling analgesic took effect.

I have already seen your charms, my Swan. They are indeed worth hiding.

He finished the application with a light touch of his hand at the base of her spine.

A momentary shiver ran throughout her body. *Does he also know of the power centers in the body? What new things could he teach me?*

Bear placed his leather jacket at her side and walked to the lake to wash the purple salve from his fingers. Antoinette picked up the jacket and held it to her nose. The smell of many days' wear permeated the leather and she knew she would not be able to wear the hard material close to her sensitive skin. She pulled the white tunic back over her head then donned Bear's leather jacket as her outer garment.

It would keep her warm, she rationalized, and satisfy Bear as well. Later, when he wasn't looking, she would powder it with fragrant herbs.

Bear returned to his medicine bundle and began to organize the objects, taking stock of the items that needed replacement. He would need to begin gathering roots and herbs for the winter ailments as soon as he returned to his camp. He looked at the hot sun above him. There were still a few full moons before the frost settled on the ground at night. Time enough to gather the things he needed. Time enough to introduce Swan to his people.

Bear's eyes drifted back toward Antoinette. He wondered if she would really leave her lake to come with him.

She felt the need to thank Bear for his kindness, but she was unsure of how to convey her gratitude. She realized if he had not tended her unconscious body the past night, she might have ended up as a wolf's breakfast or at the mercy of some other hunter with much less honorable intentions. The Goddess had surely granted her a blessing by sending this man to her. Though he did not know her, he had treated her as one of his people. He was definitely a healer and deserved something for his patience, something tangible to show him she would be his friend.

Antoinette walked back up the hillside, feeling the unfamiliar weight of his leather jacket on her shoulders and the brush of its hem at her thighs. It was much too big for her and she wondered briefly why she was always wearing men's cast-off clothing.

She dug deep in her knapsack hunting for her talisman. It was still pinned to the inner side of the sack, safe and secure beside Jacques' crucifix. She lifted her medicine bag from the knapsack. She would show Bear that they had similar vocations and later—

Would there be a later? she wondered. Or would he leave her there, now that she was fed and properly tended?

A cool breeze swept across the lake and small wave of panic passed over her. The turning of the seasons was fast approaching. She could not spend the winter alone. What if he would not take her with him? What would he think of her if she simply followed him home?

Certainly there would be a village where she could seek shelter or at least work for food and clothing to continue her journey.

Rummaging in her sack, her hand fell upon the dirk and she took it out. She held it for a moment then glanced at the stone finished tips of the straight arrows lying beside Bear's bow. Except for the small copper trinkets in his medicine bundle, Bear had no metal with him. He had not cut the meat with metal, but with sharp stone. The dirk, might bring him more status if his people had not learned to work with metal.

Antoinette hesitated, feeling the faint power of Lawrence Bernard's vibrations still lingering within it. There had been no time for her to banish his evil energy. She stuffed the dirk deep into her knapsack. No, it was not right to give it to Bear in its present state. She would purify it in ceremony, then she would give him the knife.

What else did she have that would please him and show her appreciation? She could not give him her flintstone, for if he left she would have no fire. She looked at the fur blanket and the deerskin cover and wondered if his people wove cloth and stitched fine fabrics as beautifully as they prepared and decorated animal hides. Then her gaze fell on the green cloak lying at her feet and she knew this fine fabric would be a perfect gift.

Bear had given her his jacket, now she would give him hers.

Picking up the cloak, she pressed it to her face. Her thoughts turned to Jacques and the many times she had watched the cloak flutter in the breeze as he stood on the deck of *La Réale.*

"*Mon amour*," she whispered into the dark fabric. "You are lost to me now. I can no longer feel your presence in my life. We were never destined to be lovers or the Goddess would have made it so."

Antoinette stared into the wind as a vision passed over her gaze. She saw Jacques, sailing toward the rising sun, his hair blowing loose from its ties as his ship reached into the wind. He was alive. She knew it as surely as she held his cloak in her hands. Their paths would cross again, though where or when she did not know. She shook her head. It was strange how her feelings for Jacques no longer tugged at her heart, only at her conscience.

With the cloak in one hand and her knapsack in the other she walked back down the hill.

"Muin, *Merci*." She smiled, offering Bear the folded green fabric. She unfolded the cloak and draped it around his shoulders with a quick twist of her wrists.

Bear smiled, his hands stroking the soft green material. He could feel great power in this clothing. He fingered the fabric and held it close to his nose, smelling the fragrant herbs she had carried in the pockets. Then he looked closely at the unfamiliar fabric.

What kind of animal had worn this skin? It was pliable and soft. Yet, there were no scrape marks anywhere and the pieces were sewn together with fine stitches of fiber. It was truly a skillful craftsman or great shaman who created this covering. Perhaps Swan would tell him how the green color was applied in such even strokes.

Bear's face brightened and Antoinette felt her heart flutter. She had made a good choice for her gift. She had pleased him.

Bear walked around the camp, spreading the cloak out like great green wings, letting the weight of the fabric tumble and fall with the lifting of his arms. He turned and danced and the robes flowed around him.

Finder, who had been watching the couple from a distant poplar limb, made a wide swoop toward the beach and joined Antoinette with a flutter of wings. Together they watched Bear as he danced to a silent rhythm.

The sun began to cast its shadow in long languid streaks. Bear suddenly stopped his dance in mid-stride. He shook his head, a bit dizzy from his gaiety, then his expression turned pensive. If he were not careful, the day would be over and he had not even begun to prepare himself for the final night's ritual.

Swan will have to understand. I need to be alone.

Bear walked over to Antoinette. She was still smiling at the pleasant sight of the strong man and his high spirited dancing. He stood calm and still, and looked down into her eyes.

"I must go." He pointed to his birch bark lean-to across the lake's edge, then he began to sign to her once more with his hands. "I must go to prepare for my night visions." He pointed to the sky. "Mother Moon will light my path to Power tonight and I must be ready to walk upon her shining road."

He turned to walk away, but undaunted by his brusque manner, Antoinette grabbed him by the arm.

"Wait, I have something to show you."

Bear looked at her hand on his arm and followed it back up to her face. He did not understand her words, but he realized the urgency in her voice.

"Please, let me show you." She gave him a long pleading glance as she pulled him up the hill towards the pallet. "I want to show you—I am a healer as well."

Bear followed her and watched as she slowly spread the contents of her medicine bag onto the leather cover. She held each item up for his acknowledgment.

"Mint leaves, rosemary, sage, hyssop, wormwood." She placed the tied bundles across the pallet like rows of marching soldiers. She pulled out a root of horseradish and scraped the skin with her finger, releasing its pungent earthy scent then she held the root up for Bear to smell.

He took it from her. He knew this root, for he used it to treat the winter sicknesses. He pointed to the sage, wondering if it was sacred to her as well.

Antoinette picked up the sage and offered it to Bear, but he shook his head, not wishing to touch her medicines for fear he might lessen their magic with his Power.

Bear knelt beside her, intrigued by the small clear containers and parchment packets. A glass vial filled with purple liquid caught his eye and he pointed to it. Antoinette held up the glass container and twisted the wax seal until the stopper slid unhindered from the neck. She placed it under her nose, inhaled the perfume, then held it out to Bear. He leaned over and sniffed the vial, then leaned back with a broad smile. It was the smell that surrounded her even now, the smell of sunshine and fresh breezes, wild lavender.

She offered the vial to Bear and he cautiously lifted it from her delicate fingers. He examined the liquid through the transparent container, lifting and replacing the glass stopper with excitement.

She knows much magic. He handed the vial back to

Antoinette and she rubbed the beeswax ring around the neck of the vial with her fingers until it was soft enough to re-seal the stopper, then placed it back among her supplies. She knew by Bear's smile that he understood. They had more in common than dreams and visions. They were both healers, both dedicated to comforting the bodies of their brothers and sisters.

They shared a long moment of silence, this time looking into each other's eyes without apprehension or reserve. They had crossed an invisible barrier of strange formality and were now simply a man and woman sharing a common bond.

Bear slowly raised his hand and stroked the side of Antoinette face with a soft feathery touch. More than that he would not allow himself to think about.

Antoinette closed her eyes at his brief caress, letting the vibrations of his touch pass through her body.

Blessed Brighid, is he the one I have been waiting for?

A second later she placed her hand to her cheek and opened her eyes, but Bear was nowhere in sight. Had he cast a spell to disappear? Or had he even been there?

Yes, she noted with a smile, he had been there, for the deer skin pallet still lay at her feet and his jacket still covered her with its warmth. She looked at the sand and saw his footprints leading around the stand of cattails to a beach and across the lake. Antoinette made a heartfelt sigh.

For the first time since Jacques held her in his arms aboard *La Réale*, she felt like an awakening woman.

Chapter 22

Melrose Abbey, Scotland

"Checkmate, mon frère!"

The white king toppled onto the chessboard with a light thud. Gaston Charboneau smiled at his flaxen-haired Scottish companion, his blue eyes sparkling in the light of a comforting fire. A single candle flickered on the table between them.

"You have won again, Alexander. You are by far my better in this game."

"Och no, Gaston. You're just rusty. Too much farming, not enough fighting." Brother Alexander handed a goblet of wine to his chess mate.

Alex was right, Gaston thought. His strategic skills had long ago disappeared, both by desire and disuse. He'd had enough of crusades and killing and though he was forced into exile by his Order, he was satisfied to watch his sheep graze on the green Pentland Hills. He lived near Rosslyn Castle, on the estate of Prince Henry St. Clair, who had also been a Templar explorer nearly a century ago. Gaston laughed to himself. He was no longer an adventurer like St. Clair nor was he a protector of the faith. He was just a protector of a flock of sheep and the warden for the St. Clair Estate.

"What has you so jovial, my French friend? Are you contemplating the sale of next year's wool?"

"Yes, Alex. In truth, I was thinking of home." Gaston ran his hands through his short silver-gray hair and stretched out his stiff legs in a long protracted yawn. "I must return to Rosslyn, now that my business in Edinburgh is complete. I need to make sure the storage bins are ready for the shipments of grain to the Abbey."

"Surely it can wait. Let me steal you away for another day or two. I grow lonesome here in Melrose for worthy chess opponents."

Gaston finished off the wine and walked to the fire, stirring it with the end of a poker. Why was he in such a hurry to leave? He looked forward to his yearly trips to Edinburgh, to his visit to Melrose Abbey and the companionship of his Cistercian friend, Alexander Seaton.

Alexander's good humor always took away the chill of loneliness. But not this year. Not on this visit. Being in Edinburgh had brought back memories of Gaston's youth, of his neglected obligations to his family. Why, he wondered, did he dredge up the past now?

"Have you heard any news from France?" Gaston asked.

"Oh, Aye." Alexander rearranged the chess pieces for another game. "The word is that His Highness will marry some duchess."

"A duchess? I suppose it could be worse, he could be marrying an Italian Countess. That is the last thing France needs."

"I agree, my friend. But the girl is French, from Lorraine or Tours... no—" Alexander held up the black queen and twirled it around in his hand. "I believe she is from Brittany. Yes, that's it. A woman from your old homeland."

The fine hairs on the back of Gaston's neck prickled with premonition. It was a feeling he despised, but always heeded.

He turned to face Alexander. Even as he spoke, he wished he had held his words, but it was too late. "Do you remember her name? This duchess?"

Alexander wrinkled his brow and stared into the fire. "Yes. It is Duke François' youngest daughter, Anne."

Gaston swallowed his wine, setting his goblet lightly on the table. He rubbed the back of his neck. The small tingles were turning into a tight-fisted grip at the base of his skull. Any minute Gaston knew his head would split with a searing pain. "I must leave in the morning, Alex. I really must get back." *As far away from the French coastline as possible.*

"Well, if you must, you must." Alex rose and extended his hand to his longtime friend. "But I insist on one more game in the morning, before you leave."

"Perhaps, my friend." Gaston took Alex's hand, clasped it in his own. If he'd known someone like Alex earlier in his life, he thought, someone strong and devoted to his faith, perhaps he would never have been exiled to the cold barren hills of Scotland.

Gaston raced the few steps to the small guest chamber, shutting the door behind him. He grabbed for the edge of his bed, just as his knees gave way. He sank onto the straw stuffed mattress with a sigh, holding his throbbing head in his hands.

Dear God, don't push her back into my life. Not after all these years. Why now, when I am finally at peace?

But Gaston knew that no matter how much he prayed, no matter how much he resisted, his sister Antoinette was destined to enter his life once more. He knew it as surely as he had spent his life trying to forget that he had abandoned his mother and sister when they had needed him.

His estrangement began with his jealousy of Antoinette. It was intensified by his mother's affection for Jacques DuPrey. With the death of his father and his decision to become a Templar, he had left Antoinette, a young girl, his father's pride and joy, to the clutches of pagans.

It was much later in his life that Gaston realized he could have changed his sister's destiny. If he had stayed in Rennes, if he had given up his own vocation, Antoinette's soul would now be safe. She would be a Christian. Her dark face would not haunt his memories or plague his dreams.

Slowing his erratic breathing, Gaston crawled into bed fully clothed. Perhaps, it was the talk of Brittany that upset him. Perhaps, the pain in his head was the result of too much wine. Perhaps, he would die by morning and not have to face the truth that payment for his mistakes had finally come due. He would not be surprised if Antoinette turned up at the Abbey's door for Matins.

No. Antoinette would not come to Melrose Abbey tomorrow. Not on the Feast Day of St. Peter's Chains, although it would be appropriate. His sins, like the chain's that bound St. Peter in Jerusalem, would bind Gaston to his sister forever.

Closing his eyes, Gaston said the litany of the Feast Day, trying to cast away the memories of his youth.

Peter, at God's word, break all the chains on earth;
you who open the kingdom of heaven to the blessed.
Alleluia. Cleanse my heart and my lips ...

But the ache in his heart increased.

☙

"What's this, Gaston?" Alexander took a mouth full of his breakfast of sausage and porridge, speaking as he chewed. "My steward informs me you will travel to France instead of Scotland? What about your sheep?"

Gaston was ill-prepared for his host's interrogation. "I received a message this morning after Matins. I must travel South. It appears my previous employers have need of me."

Alexander nodded and swallowed his last bite of sausage. He was one of the few people who knew of Gaston's vocation as a Templar, a Knight of Christ.

"This is great news, my friend. Perhaps you can sharpen your battle tactics while you are away and you can arrange a visit on your way back to Rosslyn."

"You have quite an adventurous mind for a man who leads a life of asceticism."

Alexander rose from the table and walked to his friend's side, his long white robe brushing the stone floor. "The battles within the soul are not always fought in the Field of Honor. And as a commander in God's Army, I must always be on guard for my troop's well-being."

The abbot searched his friend's face for signs of worry. Gaston returned his gaze with a smile.

"I assure you, Alex, I will not be fighting on King Charles' battlefields. This is business, not battle. I doubt if His Highness will ever be ready to mount a Crusade."

Alexander nodded. "Well, if you do get to do some fighting, I will gladly be your confessor." He slapped Gaston on the back, then grabbed him around the shoulders and drew him into an embrace. "Save your sins for me, old friend. You cannot believe how monotonous absolving my cloistered brother's simple transgressions can be."

Within the hour Gaston was riding his black stallion hard toward the English border, headed for the coast of Cornwall. He would not go into France as Alex assumed, but sail to Mont-St-Michel, the secluded island off the coast of northern Brittany. The morning message was not from Antoinette as Gaston feared, but a summons to appear at the Knights Templar Grand Assembly. Gaston had no choice but to comply. He was bound by his oath to obey the Orders requests, no matter the circumstances or timing. No matter that nearly ten years ago they had stripped him of rank and privilege and exiled him to waste away in hell.

By Christ! Gaston swore. If they wanted something from him now, they would have to pay. And pay dearly.

Chapter 23

Land of the People

It was past mid-day, time for Antoinette to prepare for her moonrise ceremony. She'd selected the forest glade with its wide circular opening as a perfect site to perform her ritual. Three rocks marked the directions of East, South and West and a flat-topped rock served as her altar to the North. Since she had no metal cauldron to symbolize the center of rebirth, Antoinette made a ring of stones in the center of the circle to contain a small sacrificial fire.

With markers in place, she spent the afternoon gathering flowers—yarrow, yellow goldenrod, sweetgrass and wild grains from a nearby meadow—to place on the altar. These gifts would be the offerings to Lugh, the Sun King, to honor his passing from life into the mystery of death.

As she walked, she wondered how people of other cultures honored the changes that nature so clearly displayed, the changing phases of the moon and sun, of summer to winter, or the passages of life and death. She thought of her grandmother, Ursule, her friends in the Sisterhood, Mère Deirdre, Anne and Jacques.

Tears pooled in her eyes and she wiped them away with the back of her hand. It would do no good to cry. She had to get used to being alone. She might not see her friends for a long, long time. Yet, in her heart, she would be with her sisters tonight. They would be celebrating Lughnasad as the moon rose. And every solstice, every equinox, every Lughnasad and Beltane—even if she never got back home—she would be with them in ceremony and in spirit.

One day, she would stand with them again and share the special moments of magic and love together. But now she was here, placed in a remote forest by the will of the Goddess. She would begin to blaze the pathway toward home with her first ritual.

Antoinette placed the harvested grains and flowers on the rock altar and looked around her sanctuary. Everything was ready for moonrise.

When she returned to the lake, the thick bearskin, the deer hide and Bear's personal belongings were gone and the fire site was dismantled and covered with sand. There was no evidence that a fire or even humans had ever marred the purity of the beach. Even the depression of footprints had been carefully swept away.

Antoinette looked across the lake at the newly remodeled lean-to hut. The deer skin cover with its broad black stripes and red designs draped the entrance and Bear sat silently a few feet away near the edge of the lake. She could see a halo of protection surrounding him and knew that he had slipped into a state of trance.

Of course, she thought. As a healer, he would also give thanks to his protectors. He would honor his own gods in his own way.

Though Bear had been kind to her, she had no time to wonder about him now, no time to dwell on the way she felt when he'd touched her or looked at her. Being near him, near his wild energy, excited her; even entranced her. Perhaps this was why the Goddess had brought her here. Perhaps she was meant to be with him.

Antoinette turned her gaze away to focus her thoughts. She could not think on her fate now. Before sunset she must bathe, wash away the worries of the day and return to the hillside glade, prepared to cast the circle.

She took off her clothing and waded into the darkening water, chanting softly as she stretched her arms out before her.

"Beloved waters of the Mother, cleanse my spirit. Blessed

guardians of the lake, fill my heart."

Her skin tingled with the cold and the beginnings of her magic. She took a final step into the frigid water, then sank slowly beneath its surface.

Wash away the anger. Dissolve the chaos in my mind.

Moments later, a gentle warmth spread within her and she felt an inner peace enfold her. She was no longer cold, afraid or lost. The glow of the Goddess surrounded her.

In a dreamlike state, she walked past her clothing and up the hillside to the glade and her circle of power.

☙

Bear considered the possibility of Swan's companionship as he put the finishing touches on his lean-to. He was not worried about her, though she'd been gone for some time. He knew she would return, for her pack lay at the edge of the forest and even though it was not covered by protective amulets it had a heavy magic upon it. She need not have bothered, for he would not touch her medicine bundle without permission, no matter how intriguing the contents might be.

The sun threw lengthening shadows across the sand. The moon would appear within a few heartbeats and Bear knew that tonight Great Power would speak to him and guide his path.

Bear sat by the lake and calmed his breathing. Yet his thoughts continued to worry him. Why had he become dizzy after his dance in his new cloak made of magical fabric? Trance had never happened quite like that before. Surely it was because he had not eaten for several days and the energy from the cloak caught him off guard. Swan's gaze had beckoned him to reach out to touch her. And that touch had re-kindled his desire to hold her close. He had been right to resist the temptation.

The cattails and poplar leaves swayed in the gentle breeze and the lake began to ripple. Bear could feel the power of the earth as the fire of the sun slipped below the horizon. The rhythmic dance of the shadows blurred into waves of muted colors—silver, gold and red—as his senses adjusted to the realms of the Otherworld.

At the edge of his thoughts he felt Swan's energy. She was somewhere near the lake. The faint fragrance of lavender mixed with the musty scent of the ground beneath him. Yes, she was walking through the woods and through his thoughts, but he would not let her pull him away. Not this time.

The breeze began a chant that flowed through him, around him. A song as ancient as the rocks, as ancient as the lake itself. The song would guide him to Great Power, if he could leave his body and float on its elusive refrain.

Bear's heartbeat slowed as he drifted into the familiar realm of another world. The pathways were opening, beckoning him to step upon them. But he could not go. Not until the moon showed her face above the lake's edge. Only then would his spirit journey begin.

ର

The twilight illuminated the forest as Antoinette walked through the soft bracken ferns. Reaching the stones, she entered the circle from the east. She laid her staff across the Southern stone, set Lawrence Bernard's dirk at the Western stone and ended her walk facing the Northern altar, now laden with flowers and grains.

Kneeling before the flat stone, she unwrapped the ceremonial tools and arranged them among the flowers and sheaves of grain.

She filled the chalice with water, then sprinkled a small pinch of salt into the cup. She stirred the water clockwise with the tip of her finger, then touched it to her forehead to purify her thoughts, then to her lips to purify her words. The sky was darkening. It was time to begin.

Antoinette stood proudly before the altar. With a graceful gesture, she offered the chalice toward the heavens to give homage to the unknown deities of her new homeland.

"Great Ones—Guardians of the earth, sky, sea and air—I honor Thee. By whatever names you are called, I invite you to witness my humble ceremony."

Closing her eyes, she envisioned the potency of the earth rising through her body, through her hands and into the chalice, charging the water with its power.

The energy of the earth swelled beneath her as she walked to the Eastern stone. She raised the chalice once more and felt the vitality and the uniqueness of each sunrise. The wind brushed against her face as soft as a whisper and a hawk made a high pitched cry in the distance.

As she sprinkled the stone with water, her thoughts turned to Springtime and the vast fields of sunflowers and the green valleys of Brittany. Yet she resisted the temptation to linger there.

The energy of the circle guided her until she stood facing South, the direction of Fire. She felt the hot, sultry Summer sun, the never ending flame of life. The sun felt different in this new land, wild as an untamed steed yet gentle as a newborn fawn.

She sprinkled water on the Southern rock and over the staff that lay before it. Both hissed with steam, and she bound the energy of the sun within her staff.

The rhythmic pull of the ocean and the tides soothed the Southern fire and she walked to the Western stone, toward the direction of Wind.

As she raised the chalice into the air her gaze was drawn to the hawk, flying high within the currents. He soared above the land, sailing on the wind. Antoinette closed her eyes and merged her sight with the magnificent bird.

The ocean and a rock strewn beach were suddenly below her. Darkening fields of flowers tilted their heads for the coming of nightfall. The lake was a shining jewel, glistening within a necklace of emeralds. She could see Bear sitting beside the lake as clearly as if she stood before him. Suddenly Bear opened his eyes. Her hawk-vision was broken and her awareness was pulled back to the circle. The hawk screamed its hunting cry, then disappeared beyond the trees.

Antoinette took a deep breath, then continued. She poured water on the ground. It splashed against the rock and she felt the cool lake flowing over her body once more. She sprinkled water across the dirk, blessing it with the swiftness of the winds. Later, she would infuse it with the power of justice.

Finally she stood before the Northern stone. Her gaze flowed up the trunk of the majestic oak rising up behind the altar. The tree's thick roots anchored it to the ground like a great ship at harbor. It had been a silent guardian of this strange land for many years and now it offered her protection.

Sprinkling the grains and flowers with droplets of water, she replaced the chalice on the altar. The energy of the directions swelling within her, she lowered her head in reverence then knelt to touch her forehead to the ground.

The circle was cast. Soon the winds of the Otherworlds would swirl around her and the gates of time and space would open before her.

Antoinette stood before the altar, her hands placed in reverence over her heart. She bent her head, braced her legs firmly on the ground and spoke to the ancient magic surrounding her.

"Guardian and protector, Great Goddess. I know not what

to call you in this new land, but I know you are here. I call upon your essence and ask that you teach me how to serve you in this new and wondrous place. Wherever I walk I will be your priestess, your daughter. You are my Beloved—my Protector—between the worlds and beyond."

For the space of a breath the energy of the Goddess soared within her, rising from the base of her spine to the back of her neck. With a quick jolt, she threw back her head and opened her eyes.

A rainbow of iridescent colors surrounded her with a swirling, entrancing, mystical light. Antoinette heard a soft, commanding voice.

You may call me by whatever name you wish. There is no time or distance between us, my daughter—my child.

The voice vanished as quickly as it had appeared, but Antoinette held on to the rapture, letting it flow through her.

Reluctantly she pulled her consciousness back into the circle and lit the central fire. The laws of Order and Chaos required her to continue the ceremony she had just begun.

As she sparked the flint against its mate and lit the dry tinder, she chanted:

> "Cauldron of Ceridwen open for me.
> By earth and breath and sun and sea.
> Thrice around,
> My will be bound.
> Son of the Sun
> Now be it done!"

As the small spark jumped to flame, the moon broke full onto the horizon. The trees blazed with its radiance, then the fire settled into its confines with a shimmering glow. Antoinette stood transfixed as it danced within the pit, flickering with the building wind of nightfall.

☙

Bear had waited patiently for the moon to rise. At the moment of its fullness it seemed as though the hillside beyond the lake had burst into a brilliant flame. He saw a bright light deep within the forest, but he knew it was not from a woodland fire. The radiance called him and he had been powerless to resist its enchanting summons. He did not remember climbing the steep path to the glade, yet now he stood transfixed before a wall of swirling light and watched the woman who stood beyond. Her body gleamed like the moon. Her breasts were full, like the Great Mother, ready to suckle the children of the earth, yet her youthful body proclaimed the innocence and virtue of all women.

Bear's presence at the edge of the circle pulled at Antoinette's thoughts, but she dared not stop the ritual. She walked toward the Western stone, picked up the dirk, holding it by the hilt. She pointed it toward the sky and blew her breath upon it, giving it the power of swiftness. Then she turned and held the blade to the radiant flame, charging the knife with power and protection. With a quick touch of the blade to the Earth, she banished the menacing forces within the metal and called forth the power of justice to dwell within the blade. When it was done she lay the knife on the altar. It could now be used for good, to kill for survival or defense. It would have great strength when used against dishonesty or injustice.

She turned slowly toward Bear. He was standing just outside the circle, his body boldly painted. A diagonal red stripe ran from his right cheek across the bridge of his nose and past his left eye. His hair hung loose and flowed like sheets of coal across his shoulders and arms. Jagged lines of red and yellow paint radiated downward from his neck and across his chest. Black bands circled his wrists and ankles. Except for a feather in his hair and a braid decorated with leather strips and small shells, he was naked.

Clad only in the garments of power and light, Antoinette walked toward him. She reached through the luminous barrier, offering her hand to him and with their fingers interlocked Bear stepped into the circle. She knew by the wideness of his eyes that he was in a deep trance and could share the power she invoked without effort.

Leading him around the circle, she stopped at the Southern stone and bid him to stay, then she crossed to the altar and turned toward him. His face was at once the vision from her dreams and the face of The Shining One, the Sun God, Lugh. The light surrounding him equaled the radiance of the sun, but it was a luminescence that came from a source deep within his spirit.

"Oh Gracious Mother of all people," she began as she offered a dried biscuit towards the heavens. "Bringer of the harvests, watcher of the Seasons. Behold your children of Earth offer you the fruits of last gleaning and the promise of new beginnings. Grant us a plentiful harvest, rich with the grains of your fields and the fruit of your trees. Bestow on your people the bounty of the forests and the seas, that we may be gracious and humble and worthy of your love."

With these words she broke the biscuit and tossed a piece into the fire. "With this offering I release my fear."

The flame reached up to meet the offering then died to a soft glimmer. Antoinette walked to Bear and handed him the remaining piece of biscuit. He followed her actions, tossing it into the fire. The fire devoured it with a lick of flame.

Standing beside him, Antoinette faced the fire and raised her arms high into the air. "We make these offerings so our dance may continue, so we may be strong."

She turned and looked at her companion. Would he follow her to the Otherworld? Would he understand her song to her gods? She began to sing.

Bear did not understand her words, but he knew the meaning of her song. The rhythm and intonation of her voice told him that she prayed to Great Power. He joined her, holding his hand out to his sides, palms upward to the heavens as he sang.

"Great Power, come to me, come to me.
Grandfather, come to me, come to me.
Mother Moon, shine on me, shine on me.
Father Sun, warm me, warm me.
Behold your child,
Behold your brother.
Power come to me, come to me.
Show me the path to awaken my spirit.
Power come to me, come to me.
Show me the path to awaken my heart."

They sang together, each in their own words, until their song became one song, one chant. Bear danced around the central fire, beating out a cadence of power with his feet. Antoinette followed his path, dancing behind him.

Power is here, he thought. *Here in the circle, flowing through me, flowing through Swan.*

Bear's feet followed a shining pathway that swirled around the fire, lighting the stones and earth before him. He could feel Swan dancing behind him and he slowed his pace to match hers. Together they circled the pathway again and again, raising the energy as they moved to the powerful rhythm. His blood pounded through his veins and his legs ached, yet he could not stop the energy flowing through him. He could not stop the rush of the wind around him, nor the fire that burned in his soul. He was like a surging river unable to stop until he merged with the sea, a snowflake that could not rest until it settled to the ground. He wondered briefly how long Power would stay with him.

They circled the fire, building the energy around them, sending the forces to the heavens. Bear spread his arms slowly and glided forward on the unseen winds of the Otherworld. Suddenly, he no longer walked on earth, but flew in the World Above the Sky. Some small part of him knew his body danced the earthly dance, but his spirit soared with Power into the heavens.

Power! he called in his mind. *Great Power—I must see the path for my people.*

Bear's spirit flew in the darkness and Power spoke to him. "I have sent you my messenger, Great Bear. You must be willing to listen. She will serve you and your people as she has served her own. She will show you the right path to guide the People into the next dance."

Bear strained to hear Power's words. "You—and you alone—can help your people to follow the path. The way is not easy. There will be hardship and loss, but the People must bend like the willows and not fear the unknown. And you Great Bear, you must be brave. Listen to your heart. You will always know the right path to travel. Go now. Power lives within you."

Bear's spirit snapped back into his body. He stopped in mid-step and turned around. Swan stood before him, her head thrown back, her arms held out to her sides. Slowly she bent her head forward and opened her eyes. They were half-lidded, glazed. She looked as radiant as White Mother Moon.

She is the Path, he thought. *I am Power.*

He reached out and placed his hands on her shoulders and with his touch a sensuous release of energy swirled around them creating a wind of shimmering stars.

Antoinette stood enraptured as she gazed into Bear's dark, magnetic eyes. Her senses reached out to find a handhold on reality, but its grasp eluded her. *He is the Sun God,* she thought.

Bear pulled her to him. And when their bodies touched a cone of fire soared to the heavens. They could not resist the passion that flowed between them. It was sanctioned by the gods, created from the sacred ceremony they shared and the desire they held for one another.

As their bodies joined—flesh to flesh, soul to soul, god to goddess—an essence, luminous and ethereal enfolded them.

Their spirits united in a single burst of ecstasy and release, a shattering climax that both sundered and made whole.

Somewhere in the silence of the forest an owl called to his mate.

Chapter 24

The heavy dew dripped off the roof of the hut and Antoinette awoke to the touch of Bear's warm body lying beside her. She still felt a heady glow from the strong Power they had summoned together.

In their magical circle, their bodies and their souls had become one. She had embraced Bear as Lugh, the Sun God. She had experienced the power of his protection and the ecstasy of her first love. Honoring the Ancient Ones by sharing a spiritual union was one of the greatest offerings to the Goddess—an offering Antoinette had willingly made.

Bear had carried her through the moonlit woods to the shelter, laid her down on the bear skin pallet and curled his body next to her before he fell asleep. His left arm still covered her protectively, his hand cupped her breast. He held her so close she could feel the pulse of his heart beat against her back and the slow measure of his breath on her neck.

The urge to press back against him, to snuggle closer into his arms, felt natural. She flushed slightly at her boldness. She had known Bear less than a day and aside from his healing powers and his kindness, she really knew nothing else about him. But in one day so much had happened. She had shared her magic and her love with him and he had opened his heart and hearth to her.

Had she gone mad with the beauty and serenity of this strange world? she wondered. How could she face him? What if he wanted to make love to her now? What should she do?

In ceremony, they had received the blessing of the Ancient Ones. The gods had sanctioned their union by allowing Bear to enter the sacred circle unharmed. The Goddess had blessed him with the rapture of her power. But now, in the light of day, it seemed different.

Bear stirred from his sleep, lifted his hand and rolled over on to his back. She heard him sigh before he rose, donned his loincloth and left the hut.

Wrapping herself in the green velvet cloak, she moved to

the doorway, and watched him walk to the water's edge where he knelt to wash the paint from his body.

He was truly a beautiful man. Strong, wild, sensitive. She could hardly believe that they had danced together, sky clad as children of the night, shared the rapture of their gods, then slept in each others arms.

She took a deep breath of the cool air and pulled the velvet cloak tightly around her as she watched him bathe. She would gather her belongings and find a way to talk to him. But not yet. Not just yet. She would watch him for just a little longer.

Bear spun a dry stick against a log until the dry tinder ignited the morning's fire, then he stood beside the fire and raised his hands in a benediction. His soft and soothing voice sang his salutation to the dawn.

"Oh, Great Father of the People,
Proud Keeper of Sun and Moon.
Bless me and all my kin.
Thank you for Sunrise to guide my path
and for Wind to lift my spirit to the sky.
Bless me, that I may walk the worlds once
more to stand beside you.
Thank you Mother Moon for lighting my path,
for healing my heart, and for sharing your
beautiful daughter Wapi'skw with me.
Thank you Mother Moon for the gifts she has given me.
May I always honor your daughter, Wapi'skw."

Bear took a pinch of tobacco from his pouch and sprinkled it into the air. "Thank you spirit helper, Muin Wap'skw, White Bear. I will not forget your protection."

Antoinette was mesmerized by the timbre of Bear's voice. Although she did not understand his words, their meaning was clear. His song was his prayer of gratitude. She sighed and stepped out into the bright morning and walked toward the fire. *Thank you also Blessed Mother. You have given me so much.*

Bear welcomed Antoinette to the hearth. He filled a small birch bark bowl with the nut porridge he'd made, offered it to her and bid her to sit beside him.

They exchanged a long smile and Antoinette realized that her earlier fears were unfounded. Bear was a shaman, a high-priest. She could tell he understood that their shared passion had been a special and sacred union. One that they might never share again.

As she watched, he took a small hollow bone from his medicine pouch and a black piece of crumbly stone. He moistened the stone with a few drops of water, running the bone pen across its surface until a thick paste formed on the black rock. Then he unrolled a piece of birch bark and laid it on the ground before him.

Bear drew a picture of a lake surrounded by tall trees. A man and woman beside it. He drew three suns in the sky and a swiftly flowing river. Two figures sat in a canoe and many figures sat by blazing fire.

She understood his drawings. It would take three days to travel to his people. They would cross a body of water with his canoe and then come to his village. Bear spoke to her in his language, explaining the drawings in detail and after some time Antoinette began to recognize the words he patiently repeated as he pointed to his drawings – man, woman, sun.

They spent most of the morning exchanging words and hand signals until Antoinette realized she had not even combed her hair or put on more than the cloak around her shoulders. What must he think of her? To sit about barely covered. But he was no better. He had not put on his leggings or even his shoes.

Antoinette excused herself and walked to the beach to gather her clothing. They were as she had left them, a few bundles of cloth lying on the sand.

Suddenly shy about her near nakedness, she stepped behind the cattails and dressed. When she emerged, Bear had donned his leggings. His arms and chest still gleamed in the sun.

Antoinette handed him the velvet cloak, hoping he would cover his shoulders, but he folded it neatly and placed it near his pack.

She pointed toward the glade, then spoke with both words and hand signals. "I'm going to get my things."

Bear shook his head and motioned for her to sit. Confused, she sat and to her surprise he picked up her foot and turned it gently from side to side. Then he motioned for her to wait.

He retrieved his moccasins from the shelter and pulled them onto Antoinette's small feet. He made a light chuckle as he laced them tightly around her ankles, cinching up the sides. They were much too large.

Antoinette practiced walking a few steps in the big shoes,

thanked him, then headed toward the glade where she dismantled the circle, scattering the directional stones. She left the altar and its flower offerings intact.

Kneeling once more before the altar, she gave thanks to the spirits of the forest for allowing her to use their sacred space. Then she collected her belongings and walked down the hillside to the lake, this time stopping to gather wild plants for her medicine cache.

Before she used them, she would ask Bear if they held the same qualities in his world as they did in hers. Considering her near poisoning with the chokecherries, she would not eat this time without asking.

ଓ

Bear spread his leather robe in front of him and looked absentmindedly at the markings. His thoughts turned to Swan. The smell of her body as he'd held her through the night still filled his senses. The muscles of his loins strained as he remembered the passion that had swept over him like an incoming tide, the rush of power and the overwhelming feeling of love that still lingered.

The night had been magical. Great Power had spoken to him and now he had much more to consider than before. He knew that he had been Swan's first lover and that the bond they had created with one another was unique. If she was willing to stay with him, he would ask her to be his wife. But it was still too early to know how she felt about him.

He traced the sunburst of red ochre painted on his power robe. It had protected him from bad weather and from bad energy, but now it Swan needed it to protect her. He had no time to hunt and render a hide for her clothing and she would not travel well without sturdy shoes.

Old Woman was already tanning a new hide and he knew she would be glad to make another robe for him when he returned to his people. Bear smiled, remembering his friend and how happy she would be to show Swan how to make clothes, to weave baskets and to tend a hearth fire.

He looked at the leather, wishing he had paid more attention to his foster mother's sewing. Swan deserved a garment of exceptional quality. As it was, she would have to wear his jacket and settle for what skills he possessed.

Bear took a piece of charcoal from the fire and drew the outline of a pair of high topped moccasins.

When Swan returned he would mark off the exact size of her foot and make her a pair of sturdy shoes. With the remaining leather he would make a short jacket to shield his shoulders from the sun and rain. The scraps would be stored for later use.

Nothing was ever thrown away. Every piece of leather and fur was precious and would be used, even to the smallest part. The animals and fish had given their lives for the survival of his people. They would be honored as long as possible.

Antoinette reappeared on the beach as Bear began to cut the thick leather with his sharpened stone knife. She saw the outline of the moccasins and guessed what he was about to do.

"Wait," she said, staying his hand from his first cut. "You don't need to do this. Don't cut your beautiful robe."

Bear shook his head then began to wear at the thick leather with his stone knife.

Antoinette smiled at the kindness of his gesture and the typical male stubbornness of his actions.

"Here." She reached into her pack. "If you insist on doing this at least let me give you a better tool."

She withdrew Lawrence Bernard's consecrated and cleansed knife and offered it to Bear, handle first.

He hesitated.

"Please, take it," she said. "It's all right. It belonged to a man I once knew. It's sharp. Take it."

Bear looked at her pleading expression and carefully reached for the small knife. Turning it over and over, he admired the fine honed edge and the highly polished wood of the handle. He touched the edge of the blade and quickly withdrew his pricked finger. It was an honor to handle such a fine instrument of power, made with strong magic.

He smiled at her, then placed the knife on the leather and cut through the hide with a swift even stroke.

"Thank you," he said in his language, nodding his approval. He cut out the moccasins and set the rest of the leather aside, then beckoned Antoinette to stand on the hide as he drew around her foot with the charcoal. He measured the length to her calves, cut the leather to fit, then pointed to the strips of sinew holding his own moccasins together.

He told her that her shoes would have to be bound together with the soft and pliable spruce roots until they reached his home camp, then Old Woman would stitch them with sinew and make the seams watertight with resin. She should decorate the sides with shells and bone or magic amulets to protect her. He knew she did not understand his words, but it comforted him to explain the ways of his people.

As he tied the final strip of hide around the moccasins, he looked up at Swan. Not too bad, he thought. Not bad at all.

Antoinette stood with the leather wrappings around her feet. They couldn't quite be called shoes, though they did protect her feet and they were more comfortable than any other shoes she had ever worn. They were marvelously soft and flexible. She walked around the beach then stopped in front of Bear.

He handed the knife back to her, handle first as she had done.

"No," she said softly, pushing his hand and the knife gently away. "Keep it—please."

Bear wrinkled his brow and lightly shook his head.

"Keep it. It was meant for you." She placed her hand on his and pushed it gently toward him. "For you – keep it."

He rocked back on his heels, contemplating her meaning.

She pointed to the knife, then to Bear.

"Knife. For you."

He smiled and pointed to his chest with the knife, repeating her words. "For—Bear?"

"Yes." She nodded and reinforced her words with a smile. "For Bear."

He pointed to Antoinette's new footwear. "For Wapi'skw?"

"*Mais oui*," she wiggled her toes inside the shoes. "For Wapi'skw."

Bear looked down at the knife, this time with new enthusiasm. Swan had given him a new and wonderful power and a strength no other shaman in his world possessed.

He watched her walk along the beach dressed in his long leather jacket and unfinished moccasins.

What other treasures would this maiden from the sky offer him? he wondered.

Perhaps her magic can heal my heart.

Chapter 25

Bear glanced at the darkening sky, then at the wind dancing across the lake. He could see the zephyr as it stirred the treetops with a whisper of its cooling breeze, then watched it traverse the surface of the water, sending small ripples to tease the edges of the shoreline. He inhaled the wind, nodding to himself.

There was a dampness in the wind, a smell of salt and secrets, and danger. Another storm was brewing in the great waters to the east.

Water fowl and sea birds huddled on the sandy beaches of the lake, leaving the windy rock-strewn seaside for the safety of inland shelter. Finder sat among them as they faced into the winds. The weather was changing quickly. By sunset the rain would be upon them.

For a moment Bear studied Antoinette, watching her face grimace with frustration, then brighten with encouragement as she struggled to pull the tough spruce roots through the side seams of her moosehide shoes. She was doing quite well with her handiwork and he was reluctant to interrupt her concentration, but time was of the essence.

She lifted her head, meeting his gaze with a broad smile that quickly turned to concern as she saw worry crease his brow. Bear's voice remained calm and steady, but she could feel the urgency in the tone as he pointed to the building clouds and then to the fire. They must gather food, he motioned. She should collect firewood and place it in the hut to keep it dry. They needed to move quickly; the storm would not wait.

Antoinette understood much of his instruction and could not help but share his anxiety about the approaching weather. Outwardly she was quiet, yet she found herself starting to panic as he grabbed his bow and quiver and began a brisk run around the lake's perimeter.

"Bear, wait!" She dropped her sewing as she ran towards him. "Wait for me."

He halted and turned at the sound of his name, then watched her balance precariously on the rocks as she crossed over a shallow part of the lake.

"I want to go with you. I want to watch you, to help you. I want to learn to hunt."

Bear looked at her for a brief moment, then turned and continued his pace. Antoinette followed, and though he did not slow his step for her convenience, he found himself taking the easiest path around the lake and toward the waterfall.

The woods grew dense as the lake narrowed. They traveled a different path, more sure footed than she had used earlier. It had seen many years of human use.

Below the falls, large boulders caught the rushing water, forming small, still pools that reflected the sunlight. Bear slowed his pace as he neared a small puddle. A rainbow trout lazed in the sun-warmed water, a captive of the rain swollen stream.

Without his fishing harpoon, Bear knew he would have to trick the fish into becoming their supper. He slipped off his moccasins and motioned for Antoinette to be silent as he eased himself down into the knee high water. His body moved in slow motion, graceful yet steady on the slippery rocks as he moved toward the fish.

Without a sound or a noticeable movement of the still water, Bear lowered his hands into the pool. He closed his eyes until his mind could see the clear beams of sunlight streaming down into the water, illuminating the tiny creatures that fed his prey. Then his body undulated like the water. His fingers floated like the blades of grass waving beneath the surface. Then he waited.

Before Antoinette could even wonder how Bear would catch the fish without hook, line or trap, a trout flew out of the water and landed near her feet, flopping and gasping in surprise.

Bear stood triumphant, a broad smile across his face, his arms and hands dripping with grass and glistening with water.

Ignoring the fish, she held out her hands to him. It was almost like magic. "Teach me. Show me how to catch fish." She motioned to the fish and then to herself. "Fish. I want to catch a fish."

Bear shook his head as he sloshed through the water toward the banks. *No.* He was lucky to tickle one fish from a pond today. Any others would have to be caught by spearing or trapped in a weir. All of the fish would know one of their brothers had been tricked out of the water today. How could he explain this to his eager student?

Bear picked up his moccasins and Antoinette grabbed his arm, catching him off guard.

"Fish!" Her words were insistent. "I want to learn, now!"

Bear looked at her for a moment. He understood the look in her eyes, they were blazing with defiance.

"*Moque!* No!" Bear pointed to the sky. "There is a great storm coming. I will teach you to fish another day."

Not waiting for her reply, he picked up the trout and shoved it into her hands, then turned on his heels and waded across the stream.

Stunned at his quick and harsh words, she watched him walk back toward the falls. Before she could yell a rude name to follow him, a rumble of distant thunder changed her mind. She looked up at the dark cloudy sky.

"*Mon Dieu,*" she said under her breath. "Does he know everything?"

ଔ

Bear did not return to camp, but detoured into the woods. He walked through the underbrush with the sure grace and stealth of a woodland creature. He smiled as he remembered the fire in Swan's eyes when she stood up to him.

She is a strong woman, he thought. Strong and fearless.

The image of her face lingered as he concentrated on hunting. He would smoke the fish over a low fire for traveling food, but they would eat fresh meat today.

Bear sniffed the air and listened to the song of the forest, tuning his senses to the environment around him. He picked out the rustling sound of a partridge scurrying through the drying leaves and underbrush. The bird's well worn path across the clearing, its spoor and the broken twigs told him his prey was within reach.

He stopped in the shadow of an oak to set his bow. Its wood was smooth and shiny from years of hunting. Nearly his height, it tapered from three fingers width at the center to narrow tips with nocks in the ends to hold the bowstring.

He remembered scraping the long slender ash limb into its tapered shape with a beaver tooth knife. He had greased it with fat and hung it to season in the dry warmth of his father's wigwam. It took many moons before it became strong and solid enough for stringing with sinew. Now, it was almost a part of him and seldom far from his reach. He cared for it daily and honored its power, thankful he had a true and trusted companion.

"Bow," he whispered, caressing the arched wood with the palm of his hand. "Spring true, my friend. Make the arrow fly with the swiftness of the wind."

He took an arrow from his quiver and paused. It was fletched with three split woodpecker feathers glued in place with spruce gum resin. The arrow, like the bow, showed the work of a fine craftsman.

"Arrow fly true." He blew on the feathers that decorated the end of the shaft to separate them. "Use my sight to find the mark and Bow's strength to speed your way. Make the kill cleanly, so our prey will not suffer."

He nocked the arrow into the bow and leaned his back against a poplar tree, listening to his heart beat in rhythm with the darkening forest. He waited for his target to cross the clearing once more.

Antoinette picked her way back up the hillside, trying to come to grips with her feeling of frustration at Bear's brusque manner. He had dismissed her request to learn to fish without even a breath of hesitation and the tone of his voice had commanded her to listen. Even if the weather was turning bad, he could have been more respectful.

She stopped at the waterfall, this time pausing to watch the water as it cascaded past the rocks on its journey to join the sea. Nothing stopped it as it fell. Nothing stood in its way. Even the immovable boulders were worn away by the relentless passage of the water.

Perhaps she should take a lesson from the water, she thought as she crossed the shallow stream bed. She could wear away at Bear's hard outer shell until he understood she was not going to be ignored. She needed to learn from him and she was not going to leave his side until she could survive on her own.

Bear was nowhere in sight when she returned to camp. She had expected him to be impatiently waiting for campfire to be blazing and for the fish to be ready for cooking.

The banked fire smoldered and she laid a log on the fire to rekindle the flame. The sky was darkening, but the thunder's rumble seemed far away and the thought of fresh watercress for dinner and a cup of sweet fern tea made her mouth water. Was there was still time to find a few plants and roots before the rains came?

Wrapping the fish in a piece of birchbark, she laid a heavy stone over it to keep away the birds, then began her search for more food. She passed bushes ripe with cranberries and red serviceberries and stuffed them in her pouch, this time careful not to confuse them with the poisonous chokecherries she had eaten the first day at the lake.

Yellow nut grass and roots to bake, blue flowered fruit and the soft leafstalks of pickerelweed filled her tunic. She dug wild cucumber roots in the wet margin of the lake and harvested the dried seed pods of the orange-flowered jewelweed. These would all be good food for traveling.

As she wandered back toward camp, she picked fresh spicy watercress and bitter speedwell from the wet lakeside.

Survival was becoming second nature and plants she

would have ignored on any other day were now seen through new eyes. Cattails with their spiked fruits and soft downy-haired seeds and the cone shaped clusters of sweet gale nutlets now meant food and not just garnish for her table. Majestic beech trees were her shelter, the bare earth was her floor and wild birds her companions.

She sighed with contentment. She was now truly living in harmony with the Great Mother's creation, not separated from Her by artificial walls or by people who only felt the wonder of the Goddess through the songs and dances written by others. She was experiencing Nature like her ancestors, living with the land and wearing clothing made from the very skins of the animals that gave their lives for food. And she had helped to fashion their skins into wearable garments. These were things she would never have experienced in Brittany in her isolated, restricted courtly lifestyle.

She thought of the country folk who lived in the small villages throughout Brittany and France. They were poor and honest, but they lived close to the land, close to the Great Mother Earth. They were hard and rugged individuals. Perhaps their way of life was what made them believe so strongly in magic, and in the saints and the ancient gods.

Yes. When she returned to Brittany, if she *could* return, she would not live in Nantes with Anne or on the island with the Sisterhood. They were separated from the land by the cold stone castles. She would find a small village near the ocean and live with the people. She would honor the Mother not only in ceremony and ritual, but in her every movement, living with Her and flowing with Her tides and Her moods.

Antoinette laid her gathered bounty and a pile of wood near the entrance to the hut and relaxed in the sunlight as her frustration towards Bear's curt actions slowly subsided.

Bear, she realized, was uncompromising, not because he was mean or ill-mannered, but because he had no other choice. If he waited or hesitated at just the wrong moment, his rhythm with nature would be broken. She must become that way as well. One with nature, one with the Goddess.

Bear found her sitting in silence, staring out at the lake. He smiled at her and at the sight of a good quantity of firewood. He waved a greeting and began to unload his catch, the small partridge and a few wild carrots and ground nuts to bake on the fire's stones as the fish smoked and dried.

Antoinette wandered down to the beach and watched Bear clean the fish. She put the berries and herbs she'd gathered out on a small piece of birch bark and placed them near his catch. He looked over them and smiled. She was not as unskilled as he had imagined.

He motioned her to come closer to the fire and began explaining that they would roast the partridge now. The fish he would cut thinly and smoke slowly over the hot coals. It would be part of their traveling food.

Antoinette found herself understanding him more and more and as she watched him skillfully render the partridge, her anxiety about meeting his people slowly diminished. She wondered if they would all be so patient with her and if they were all like Bear, hard, rugged and uniquely beautiful.

She looked at his face and his bronzed shoulders in the glow of the sunlight and wondered if he would look as striking dressed in velvets and silks. Bear set the meat to cook and took out two white cakes from his pack to add to the collection of roots and plants they gathered.

Antoinette wrinkled her nose at the strong smell of the rendered fat and her thoughts of Bear dressed in perfumed garments faded. She pointed to the fat and shook her head.

Bear shoved a cake into her hand and insisted she eat it with her food. She must fill her body with nourishment, he explained. The fat, eaten with the meat, would make her strong and give her the energy she needed to make the long trip back to his camp.

"I cannot not take you with me if you do not keep up your strength," he said. "With the uncertainty of the weather, we must leave tomorrow."

While the partridge cooked they sat in the silence of the dwindling sunlight, watching the clouds cover the remains of the setting sun. The rain had stalled in the distance, but the clouds rolled from gray to black, and the smell of wetness surrounded them. The rain would come before morning.

Bear left her side with a light touch of his hand on her shoulder as the sun slipped behind the trees. He would give thanks for the day before going to sleep.

Antoinette watched the water birds lift from the lake to fly to their nests among the treetops. She listened to the songs of the night creatures as they took their cue from the darkening sky.

A sudden apprehension filled her as she thought of spending the long night lying next to Bear. Tonight they would not be under the enchantment of the Ancient Ones. They would be just a man and a woman, alone together.

Antoinette stayed by the fire. Perhaps, she thought, Bear would understand that although she liked him, and enjoyed being with him, making love to him again might not be proper. In her heart she knew she wanted his strong arms to hold her close. She longed to hear him tell her she would always be safe and loved.

She pulled her knees up to her chest and rocked back and forth, listening to his mesmerizing chant echo across the lake. She closed her eyes in respect for the Great Mother and drifted on the rhythmic and unknown words of his prayer.

"I am part of the Mother," she repeated to herself in cadence to Bear's chant. "She is my comfort and my love."

When Bear returned to the camp he placed the fish on a wooden rack above the smoldering coals and laid another log on the hearth.

It was too early to retire for the night, he mused. And sleep would be hard to find if he shared the shelter with Swan lying so near to his side. If they were at his home camp, this would be the time for telling stories around the hearth fire, then as the night's fire slowly died, the people would retire to their wigwams to make love, to sleep and to dream of the next day's adventures.

He glanced toward Antoinette as she huddled near the fire. She did not seem like the fiery vixen he'd encountered at the waterfall, not the mysterious Wapi'skw, the Swan Woman of the lake, nor the magical Daughter of the Moon, but a woman lost in thought.

He said her name slowly, letting the word linger on his tongue. "Swan." How he liked the sound of it.

Antoinette smiled. He moved closer to her and pointed to the cloudless sky. The day-old moon would not show for many heartbeats. It was a good time to send the smoke and prayers to the heavens.

They sat across from one another and Bear laid out several objects before him: Two black bags made of mink skins and a small pouch made from a piece of white hide.

He withdrew from the longest bag a length of carved wood that resembled a hollowed out stem. From the other bag he took a small bowl made of carved bone, ornately decorated with incised geometric designs. From the third he took out a handful of herbs.

Bear sprinkled the herbs on the fire and a sweet pungent smoke lifted into the air. He waved his hands through the smoke and around his head, and passed his ceremonial instruments through it to cleanse them. Waving the smoke toward her head, he softly allowed the smudge to caress her body.

"The sage smoke will dispel any wayward spirits that linger around us," he whispered. "Tonight, I will call upon the spirits that will help us."

Bear held the hollowed stick and the bone bowl up to the heavens, then began to chant.

"Great Power, Kji Kinap, we give thanks for Father Sun and Mother Moon, for bright Morning Star who brings us love and wisdom, for Fire who lights our hearths, for Warm Wind who wakes us and Cool Wind who refreshes us, for Water who nourishes us and for Earth who lets us walk upon her face.

"Oh, Great Power, guide us as we wander the Worlds. Make our path clear and straight, and always toward the truth."

Bear lowered his arms and solemnly fitted the stem to the bowl and removed a pouch from his belt. Antoinette watched with rapt attention as he packed the bowl with dried leaves from the pouch, holding each finger full of the dried leaves first to the earth, then to the sky and in each of the four directions. The first pinch, he told her, was for Great Power; the next for Mother Earth; one for the family, one for the tribe, one for the animals, and the last pinch for all the people.

Bear lit a stick of touchwood, the wood that burns slowly, and touched the flaming stick to the dried herbs in the pipe. He inhaled deeply from the herbs, blowing the smoke up into the sky, then he turned the pipe around in a circle, toward each of the four directions.

To Antoinette's surprise he offered the pipe to her.

Cautiously, she took it and looked at the smoldering leaves in the bowl. Then she put her lips to the stem and slowly drew in the warm air. The bitter taste of smoke filled her lungs. Her throat instantly constricted and she coughed at the lack of air, suddenly unable to breathe.

Bear patted her on the back sympathetically and shook his head. Swan would need much practice to learn how to send her prayers to Great Power. He lifted the pipe from her hands and took another draw off the bowl. This time he showed her how to take it into her mouth and not into her lungs.

She watched as he lifted his head upward and let the smoke drift slowly into the air. He offered her the pipe once more.

Antoinette looked at him hesitantly, took the pipe, and this time drew in a small amount of smoke and held it in her mouth. Slowly the smoke floated upward from her pursed lips and rose in spinning curls above her head.

What a wonderful way to send offerings to the Gods, she thought. She could see her prayers lift to the heavens, dance and drift in the light breeze. If she tried very hard, she could see the fairy spirits dancing in the smoke, to disappear with a puff in the darkening night sky above her. She handed the pipe back to Bear, watching him intently now as he blew the smoke into wonderful clouds.

They passed the pipe from one to the other, until the bowl of herbs was finished.

Lightheaded and relaxed, she wondered what kind of herbs or leaves he smoked in his magic carved bone bowl. It was a strange custom, one that would take getting used to, but one she was sure she would like to take back home with her.

Bear lifted the empty pipe one last time to the sky and his voice rose softly with it.

"We are children of Great Power.
We are children of the sky.
Rain wash us, River feed us, Earth house us.
We are children of Great Power.
We are children of the sea.
Fish teach us, Thunder watch us, Bear protect us.
We are children of Great Power.
We are children of the earth.
Wind fly us, Sun warm us, Moon love us."

With the end of his song he pulled apart thc pipe, cleaned it, then put it away with a flourish of words Antoinette could not understand. "Thank you Pipe for sharing your Power with us," Bear whispered. "And Smoke for carrying our prayers to Spirit. My friend is learning to respect you; please be patient."

He smiled. He would teach her what she needed to know, but he could not think of her simply as a friend.

Bear watched silently as Swan sent her prayers to the heavens. He wanted her to be all things to him. First to be his teacher and to help his people, to stay with him, to be his wife and share his hearth. Hopefully, she would feel this way as well. He could see a small spark of interest in her eyes. And as soon as he dared, he would tell her of his affection. Perhaps Great Power would allow them to share their hearts with one another as they shared the sacred pipe.

Antoinette looked at Bear with a wistful smile. "*Merci*, Bear." She nodded, took his hand and looked into his eyes. "Thank you for your ceremony. One day, when I understand your language, perhaps you will share your pipe with me again."

"*Merci?*" he repeated. Her hand was soft and warm as he

held it tightly.

"*Oui, merci!* Thank you."

He wrinkled his brow at the strange words, and she pulled her hand from his grasp.

"*Merci.*" She paused for a moment, then pointed to her moccasins. "Thank you for the shoes, thank you for the shirt." She held the tunic out from her body and smiled. "*Merci.*"

Bear's face brightened as a flash of understanding came to him. He reached for the metal knife sheathed at his side and withdrew it in one quick motion.

"*Merci!*" he said. "Thank you for the knife."

"*Mais oui, mon ami.*" Antoinette's gentle laughter rippled through the air and Bear threw back his head and filled the silence of the lake with his laughter. For a brief moment they looked at one another, sharing the brief understanding that despite all their differences and their uncertain form of communication, they were now truly friends.

Bear raised his hand to brush away a stray lock of her hair from her cheek and gazed into her eyes. Would she allow more? he wondered. He leaned toward her and she did not move back.

A sudden flash of lightning ripped through the tender moment and Bear looked anxiously toward the sky. He inhaled deeply. He could smell the fire in the air. The rains were coming, the lightning would follow. It was time to move to shelter, time to sleep for tomorrow's journey.

"Come, Swan." He took a burning stick from the fire and motioning to the wigwam. "The storm will be here soon."

Antoinette understood him, but she could not make her legs move toward the unknown events of the night. A knot of apprehension swelled inside her throat and she motioned for him to go without her. Turning her back before he could object, she walked to the lake.

Bear allowed her the space to be alone and looked back once before he disappeared into the shelter. He held the light to the small fire he had laid inside and watched it spread through the tinder, igniting the dry twigs.

Women are so mysterious, he thought. Swan Women were proving even more difficult to understand.

☙

Antoinette stood silently watching the rising moon as it peeked through the dark clouds. "Blessed Brighid," she prayed. "This time I ask for your guidance. My heart tells me to trust Bear. He has given me clothes, food and shelter and—I cannot deny I am attracted to him."

Antoinette paused as the truth surfaced in her mind. She was afraid to open her heart again. Jacques' rejection had hurt her more than she wanted to admit. How would she feel if Bear turned away from her now? For all she knew he could have a wife and family or be pledged to a beautiful woman. She stood in the dying light of the evening amid the building clouds and resolved herself to wait until she was sure he would be asleep.

The thunder rumbled closer and the patter of rain against leaves swiftly advanced through the woods. The hard raindrops passed across the surface of the lake toward the campsite. At the last moment she turned and ran to the safety of the hut.

Huddling just inside the doorway, she watched the rain as it fell in heavy sheets, drowning out the remaining embers of the fire. She hesitated to look back toward Bear, not knowing if he would be waiting for her. But the blowing rain pushed her away from the entrance and she dropped the moosehide cover into place.

As her eyes adjusted to the light she saw Bear had taken a place behind the glowing fire on the opposite side of the small room. He lay on his side, on a woven reed mat. His eyes were closed and his medicine pouch was placed in front of him. The fur skin they had shared the night before lay near her feet and her shoulder pack stood guardian beside it.

With the fire between them, there was no doubt that this was to be her bed. Antoinette let out a sigh of mixed relief. She would sleep alone and would not have to make decisions about their relationship tonight. But neither would she sleep in the safety of his arms.

Removing her leather tunic, she snuggled into the warm bed and burrowed her head into the soft fur. She stroked the pelt with her hands, letting the fur rise and fall between her fingers as she looked across at Bear. His eyes were closed, but she could see a faint hint of a smile on his lips. He had been watching her.

"*Merci*, Wapi'skw," he whispered in the darkness.

Chapter 26

Bear drifted in his dreams until he sat with his teacher, Laughing Elk, at an Otherworld campfire.

"Grandfather!" Bear said, surprised to see the old man sitting calmly at his side. "It is good to see you. I have missed my visits to your hearth. Where have you been these many moons?"

"Muin, my son. Do you not remember burying my dried flesh and bones after winter's thaw?" The man smiled and tilted his head. Bear's forgetfulness seemed to amuse him. "It was quite a nice ceremony and I was pleased to see my wife, Old Woman, standing by your side. Nothing bothered me about my death except that she might be lonely." Laughing Elk touched Bear's shoulder with a loving gesture of close kinship. "Thank you for keeping her at your hearth."

"It was right that I do so, Grandfather. She has always been like a mother to me. I am getting fat on her cooking and soon I fear she will find me a wife to keep her company."

The spirit chuckled "You'd better watch out or she may find you one with a lonely sister. Then you will have more women than you can handle."

Bear looked across the campfire at Swan, sleeping soundly in the real world. Laughing Elk followed his gaze.

"Tell me how you feel about this woman who has rekindled the fire in your heart. I see much good in her spirit, but I also see that those who love her will bring much suffering to the People. Things will change—People will change—Power will change."

"Laughing Elk, she is not one of us, but her spirit follows a noble path. Power told me to listen to her. My heart also tells me she is important to the People. She knows great magic. I have seen her summon the sun and I believe she will help the People when the Greed enemy comes again." Bear leaned toward his teacher, whispering like a child sharing a secret. "I care for her very much, Grandfather."

"Yes, Muin. She is one to be treasured and enjoyed. But walk her path lightly, for she may also break your heart."

"Grandfather," Bear replied with a mock indignation. "I guard my heart like my medicine pouch. But—I would be happy to give her the chance."

The old man gave a deep chuckle, reverberating the

wigwam with his Spirit laugh. "If I still walked the Earth path my Son, so would I—so would I."

They sat in silence for a moment, listening to the rain soften to a light drizzle. Laughing Elk made a long sigh and turned to Bear. "You know, I don't remember anyone placing my favorite pipe alongside my bones. I've missed it very much."

"Why Grandfather, I put it there myself," Bear replied to his dream companion. "And I put a pouch of *nespipaqn* root near it so you would have something to smoke."

"Well, when I made my journey to the Otherworld, I could not find it." The old spirit looked pensively at the fire. "Perhaps you should ask Dancing Fox about my pipe when you return to the People. The winter was long and he may have borrowed it and forgotten to return it at my burial. He may want the opportunity to return it to me before it is too late."

"Dancing Fox? He was not at your burial Grandfather."

"*E'e*, I know, Muin. He was hunting herbs to burn in my pipe."

Bear paused, trying to sort out the puzzle in the spirit's words. He reached into his medicine bag, lifting out his stone smoking pipe with the alderwood stem. He secured the pipe together and handed it to his companion.

"Here, Old One, take my pipe until I can find yours. May it smoke well for you."

"Thank you, Bear." The old man accepted the pipe in his ethereal hands, nodding his thanks. Producing a pinch of herbs from the air, he packed the pipe, then lit it with the tip of his finger. He inhaled the smoke from the stem and blew it in a circle around Bear's head.

"Remember," he said. "Ask Dancing Fox about my pipe, but do not wait for his reply. Look for the pipe along the Shining River. I believe that is where he has taken it."

"Ah, yes Grandfather." Bear replied, trying not to lose himself in the disquieting contradiction of Laughing Elk's words. "Dancing Fox—Shining River—I will remember."

"Good." The old man smiled, handing the pipe back to his companion.

Bear inhaled the aromatic smoke from the pipe and watched it float up toward the smoke hole in the roof. It changed its path and swirled toward the glowing embers and the sleeping body of Swan. He handed the pipe back to the old man.

Laughing Elk took a deep draw and when he exhaled the smoke spread out to cover the room in a thick fog. Bear opened his eyes. He was wide awake yet he still smelled the sweet aroma of tobacco. Instinctively, he reached into his medicine bag, feeling for his stone pipe. It was still wrapped in the mink skin, still here in the Earth World. He would share his pipe with Laughing Elk's spirit until Dancing Fox had the chance to explain.

Bear turned on his side, pondering his dream, concerned at the shrouded messages his teacher laid before him.

I know I placed Grandfather's pipe beside him at his burial and Dancing Fox was nowhere near.

He must remember to ask Dancing Fox about Laughing Elk's message at the first opportunity. Bear tried to push the questions to the back of his mind—they could wait until morning. But the old man's words about Swan disturbed his rest. As the clouds of sleep surrounded him, he wondered what the old man foresaw in the People's future. And how could Swan break his heart when it wasn't yet mended?

White Bear Person, Muin Wapskw, Bear's spirit helper, came next into his dreams. Muin Wapskw standing at his full bear height would have engulfed the wigwam, but he sat meekly by the fire changing from his bear shape into his human shape. His pale white skin shimmered in the firelight and his once roaring voice was almost a whisper. He placed a log on the fire and held his pale hands over it to warm them.

"Hello my brother, World-Walker. I'm surprised you sleep so peacefully while the waters rise to flood the lake."

Bear's dream body jumped up and ran to the door. He looked out through the rain. "White Bear you are mistaken. The lake is not swollen. The rains have quieted."

"Look again, Muin White Bear's voice grew louder, almost deafening in the silence of the room. "Look with your mind, little brother and see past the clouds of deception. The lake is flooding, the eels will drown and none of us will eat this winter."

Bear looked out at the lake once more. This time he saw the waterfall turn into a wall of blood, flooding the woodlands as it ran down toward the sea. His words seemed to solidify in his throat as he turned to Muin Wapskw for an answer. But the white bear was gone.

Finder sat in Muin Wapskw's place and Bear opened his mouth to speak to the bird.

Suddenly, the gull shifted into the shape of a sparrowhawk and flew towards his face, its wings beating in fury. The sparrowhawk thrashed against the walls, sending birch bark and rain flying toward Bear's head as it searched for an opening to freedom.

The support poles vibrated with a loud clap of thunder and a swift rush of wind. Bear woke with rain pelting his face. It had seeped through a hole in the thatching.

Bear's heart beat wildly. Springing to his feet, he ran to the doorway, half expecting the water of the lake to be at the very threshold of the shelter. He made a deep sigh as he looked out at the unchanged scenery. The lake was still safely within its banks. Torrents of rain checked the surface as the thunder and lightning roared its temper at the dark sky.

Bear felt a shadow of dread encompass him as he turned back toward the dying fire, remembering White Bear's words. A dark premonition settled around him and he reached out in the darkness to awaken Swan. Something was wrong, he felt it deep inside his being. Something was terribly wrong.

"Swan, wake up. We must go now."

Antoinette jumped in her sleep at his sudden touch and sat up, her heart pounding as the rush of adrenaline invaded her body. "What is it? What's wrong?"

Bear searched for a way to tell her of his apprehension. He pointed to the doorway, then rushed to stuff his belongings in his pack.

"Leave. We must leave now," he said.

Antoinette looked out at the rain. "It's still pouring," she retorted, watching him scatter the embers of the fire. "If you think I'm going out there now, you're crazy."

She lay back down on the bear skin, pulling the fur tightly around her. "It's not even daylight."

How could he make her understand? How could he possibly tell her of Laughing Elk's prophecy or White Bear's warning? Bear grabbed her shoulders and turned her over to face him. "Swan, we must go."

His face was rigid with exasperation.

"All right." Antoinette sighed, throwing back the fur cover. "I don't understand, but I'll get up."

Bear rushed back to the door and looked out at the lake. The rain was still steady, but the sun was beginning to lighten the sky. He could barely see the clearing in the distance. He looked back at Swan, rubbing the sleep from her eyes. Watching her put on her moccasins and jacket, Bear remembered that part of his water repellent moosehide now covered Swan's feet.

It would be crazy to leave in the rain. Everything they had would be soaked and their leather clothing would get hard and dry. They would have to wait till the rain stopped.

Bear pushed the wet hair from his face as he turned

toward the drying fire. Swan would surely think him senseless. He had awakened her for nothing.

He scooped the nearly dead embers of the fire back together then held a clump of dried fern roots to the coals, blowing gently to rekindle the flame. He looked up at Swan, her eyes glaring now with question, then gave her a slightly embarrassed grin. Shaking his head, he pointed to the rain.

"Men!" she mumbled to herself as she rolled back into the bear skin and buried her head in the fur.

He heard her muffled words of reprimand and placed more wood on the fire.

Chapter 27

With the end of the rain, Bear dismantled the shelter and buried the fireside debris, clearing the lakeside of any trace of human habitation. He rolled up the bear skin and strapped it across his back alongside his quiver of arrows and his medicine pouch. He paused one last time at the edge of the forest, leaning against his bow as he watched Swan talking to the white gull.

"I don't know where we are going, Finder," Antoinette explained. "But Bear has shown me that we will travel through thick woodlands, far from the ocean."

She held a small portion of her morning meal out to the bird and Finder hopped from one foot to the other before he walked closer to her outstretched hand. "I'm trusting you to look after my boat and watch for ships from my home across the ocean. I just wish you could tell them where to find me."

Finder cautiously took the food from her fingers, always keeping one eye tilted up, looking at her. Then he sprang into the air and hovered over the lake for a brief moment before he flew toward the waterfall.

"Thank you for your help." Antoinette shouted into the air, waving her staff in salute. "I'll look for you when I return."

She watched Finder disappear well beyond the trees before she turned to walk across the sandy beach toward Bear. She jumped across the rocks, fording the stream. When she reached the other side she searched Bear's face for any expression that might suggest his mood or temper, but his face was cryptic. His hurried manner that morning suggested a restless anticipation, but he had waited patiently for her to make her parting gestures to Finder.

The slight movement of his hands on the handle of his bow gave away his restlessness. A slow drumming of his fingers told her he was eager to begin their journey.

This would be the beginning of a three day trip, she reminded herself. Three days of hard travel and three nights of restless sleeping, sharing the cold ground and the cold nights with only one warm covering.

Bear turned without a word as Antoinette approached, stepping quietly into the thick woodlands. This was his domain and he blended into its foliage with little effort, the leaves and trees of waning summer camouflaging his decorated clothing and bronzed skin. He made no sound in his stride, but Antoinette could tell that he had slowed his pace to accommodate her shorter legs and unpracticed gait.

She watched his every movement as he walked, following some unmarked path his trained eye could easily discern. His lithe and powerful body moved with the grace of a woodland creature, every step calculated for its weight and balance and every intake of breath used to further his forward momentum.

It seemed to Antoinette, as they traveled further from the lakeside, that Bear tuned himself to the vibrations of the forest. He became more like an animal with all his senses alert and his defenses ready. She followed silently in his footsteps as he walked his secret trail.

During the early morning's rain, Bear had made a short cape from the moose hide scraps to protect his shoulders, then braided several long strips of the leather together to form a headband to tie back Antoinette's hair. He wore a similar strip of hide across his forehead, but his band was painted and decorated with hollow beads made of etched bone and small copper colored tubes that matched the tasseled fringe on the end of his quiver and medicine pouch.

These objects, she would later learn, were symbols of his power among his people and warned strangers that he was a shaman; to speak first before taking any action.

They walked for several hours through spruce forests and birch valleys, crossing small streams and rocks as they wove their way southward. They moved farther and farther from Antoinette's boat but, she hoped, always closer to eventual safety. She did not stop to wonder who would come to rescue or even why anyone would look for her, but every step took her somewhere and she trusted Bear to lead her to safety.

By the time the sun was high in the sky her legs and muscles ached with strain. She tried to push forward until

Bear stopped, but she could not take another step. Exhausted, she dropped down beside a fallen tree, determined to rest. She watched Bear disappear in the distance. Didn't he know that she stopped? Didn't he care?

Antoinette closed her eyes in frustration. At that moment she did not care if he left her there to be eaten some wild animal. She looked up at the waning moon still visible in the western sky. Two days past full. Ten days since she left the unsure safety of *La Réale*. Ten days since she spoke to anyone who could understand her. Had it been more than a month since she walked the docks of Breton's harbors? She fought back tears of frustration and fatigue.

Bear continued some feet ahead, then turned back. She was slumped against the tree. He motioned from across the clearing. "Swan, we cannot stop here."

"I am not going any farther," she said with a wide wave of her hand and a shake of her head. "Not until my legs recover."

Bear walked back and stood over her, tall and straight like a towering spruce. She expected him to turn on his heels when he found she was not hurt. But instead he stretched out his hand to help her rise.

There was no mistaking her problem. She was tired and needed rest. But not there, not out in the open. They would rest later in the cover of the trees and share a drink of water. They must continue at a steady pace if they were to reach his canoe and cross the Great Fresh Water Lake before nightfall.

Antoinette looked at his proffered hand and placed hers in it. He gave a light tug and she rose precariously to her feet. Before she could react, Bear swung his bow over his shoulder, leaned forward and gathered her up into his arms, shifting her weight to suit his balance he walked toward the tree line.

She remembered being carried in his powerful arms once before as they left their woodland ceremony. She had been entranced then, but now she was fully aware of the stamina he possessed. Light beads of sweat dotted his brow and yet his breathing did not strain with her weight, nor that of both their belongings. She could feel the muscles of his arms and chest and the strength of his solid legs as he held her close to him, moving swiftly across the clearing.

Antoinette wrapped her arm around Bear's neck for support, feeling the smoothness of his hair, thick and straight, and so unlike her unruly curls. With her restricted view and his concentration locked on their destination, she took the opportunity of really examining his face.

His eyes were dark and bold, the color of ebony, set deeply

above high sun-bronzed cheeks. For all his rugged appearance, his skin was smooth and flawless. As he breathed, his nose flared slightly and his lips parted. His profile was strong, sensuous, and for a brief moment she wished she was brave enough to trace the line of his jaw with her finger.

Bear shifted her weight and firmed his grip on her legs as he crossed a shallow stream bed. She felt the shadow of a blush at her excitement and she laid her head against his shoulder.

Daring to look further, she continued her intimate investigation. His scent was animal, though not unpleasant. A musky, sweet aroma. A combination of all the herbs in his medicine pouch and his natural body smell. So unlike the dandies of Anne's court or the unwashed smell of the men at sea. He smelled like the earth; like the wild, fresh earth.

Bear stopped at the edge of the forest and Antoinette looked into his eyes. He held her tightly, running his gaze across her face.

Why didn't he put her down, she wondered. Please don't put me down, she prayed.

He looked at her for an instant, but it seemed to her as though he knew all the things she had only dared to imagine. His eyelids flickered, then he gently set her to stand beside him. She thought she heard him sigh—it was a small breath—but deep enough to indicate regret.

Bear pulled aside a branch to allow her to pass into the woods. Here in the valley, the woods smelled different. More like oak and ash than evergreen. It smelled of the promise of autumn and the changing of the seasons. The leaves were damp with the last of the rains and a cool mist still clung to the air.

She walked ahead of him as he guided her into the shelter of a large oak. She could tell his senses were alert to their new surroundings.

"Sit." He held up his hand in a stopping gesture. "Wait." They were short, curt words, but the meaning was clear.

Antoinette settled on the ground as Bear disappeared into the underbrush. She watched the crisscrossed patterns of sunlight play on the underbrush peeking through the leaves of the trees. Except for a bird singing a soft exaltation in the distance, the woods were silent.

Content, for the moment, she began to rummage in her pouch. Taking out a packet of berries and dried fish, she laid them before her, patiently waiting for her companion to return.

She closed her eyes and willed herself to relax. The muscles in her legs soon stopped trembling and she began to feel her strength return.

A light rustle of leaves startled her and she opened her eyes. Bear sat beside her, a soft smile on his face and a container filled with fresh water in his hand.

He took a sip of the water then handed the container to her. It was cool and refreshing and the sweetest water she had ever tasted. As she drank, she took the opportunity to look at the cup. It was similar in size to the bark cup Bear used to prepare his medicines, though this one was made of reeds woven so tightly that the water did not seep through the fibers. The design was intricate and the reeds were pliable, yet quite strong. Empty, the cup folded neatly into Bear's pouch. What fine craftsmanship and ingenuity.

Her admiration of his possession did not go unnoticed and he began a dialogue on the article she held in her hand. It had been made by a friend, he told her. Given to him for his travels to the Otherworlds, though he used it mostly in his everyday life. He told her of the fine water repellent reeds and pointed out the warp and weft patterns with his fingers, knowing all the while that Antoinette did not fully understand him.

As he spoke, she watched the movement of his hands dancing in the shadowy light, turning the empty cup this way and that. She listened to the sound of his voice and she picked out a word or two that she recognized. Slowly she noticed a pattern begin to develop in his speech. The rhythms of his language and the intonation of his voice were becoming familiar.

They must speak more, she realized. Even if they could not understand one another. She must learn to hear the words and practice the sounds.

They sat together, learning from each other the simple words of survival of their different cultures, sharing their travel food and listening to the sounds of the woodlands in the quiet moments when conversation was meaningless. As the sun passed from overhead, Bear motioned to the sky and indicated that it was time to continue. But as Antoinette began to rise, he stayed her movement with a light touch of his hand on her arm.

"Swan." He spoke her name and looked into her eyes.

Something inside Antoinette stirred and she raised her hand to stroke his cheek as one might venture to touch a wild animal, cautious yet curious.

"Swan," he whispered. "Don't be afraid of me. I will wait until we understand each other, until you tell me you want me to be your lover as well as your friend."

Antoinette heard the soft patience in his voice and there was no denying the gentleness and the longing she saw behind his gaze. She had seen that longing in Jacques' eyes.

Bear's intensity intrigued her and she let her hand linger long enough for him to reach up and place his hand on hers. Flustered and lightly embarrassed, she pulled her hand away and shifted attention to her pack.

Bear stood and hefting his belongings onto his back, took several lengthy steps into the woods. His emotions were in turmoil. He knew he must move out into the open to clear his head of Swan's fragrance. How could he even think about making love to her again? She might disappear as she had in his dream.

Old Woman would know. Old Woman would be able to talk to her. She knew the language of the Sky People and she would explain everything to Swan.

Bear took up the trail again, moving ahead as Antoinette followed behind.

As sunset neared, they crested a ridge and Bear stopped abruptly as he walked into the clearing. Before them a vast panorama unfolded. A large lake, glistened in the fading light, reflected the varied hues of sunset in its clear, cold water.

He made a discouraged sound and set his pack on the ground with a hard thud. He motioned to the sun with an outstretched hand, then to the lake and shook his head.

"It is too far to travel today. We would not make it across the lake by nightfall."

Antoinette stared at him and he took up a stick and began to draw into the dirt. He drew a canoe and motioned to the lake then pointed to the sun, lowering his hand until it rested toward the horizon.

Antoinette nodded. It was farther than they could travel before sunset. "*Oui.* I understand." She repeated his words in his language. "It is too far."

Bear smiled, then motioned to the ground near his pack. They would spend the night in the shelter of the woods. Tomorrow they would travel by canoe across the lake and then rest at his brother Two Arrows' camp. Bear's camp was one more day further west.

Antoinette laid down her gear and began to gather firewood. Bear watched her skill at laying a fire and helped her stack the firewood into shape. As he began to remove his clam shell fire box from his waist, Antoinette held out her hand to stop him.

There was no reason to keep the tinderbox a secret any longer now that she knew that he would not leave her.

Bear watched as she made a cup with her hands and struck the flint against the box. A spark leapt out to ignite the tender and she blew on the fire. Bear took a deep breath as the spark leapt into a small flame.

Antoinette held the tinderbox out to Bear and he took it, turning it over in his hands while she fed the fire small pieces of dry bark.

He ran his fingers over the intricate, inlaid mother of pearl and blue lapis decoration. Then he lifted the lid of the container. He touched the flint and striker. The stone was not unlike the flint that he carried in his pouch and used on occasion when a fire bow was too damp to set the spark. Her people's handicraft certainly rivaled the Micmac, but he reminded himself that she was from the World Above the Sky. She knew great magic.

Her people would have great craftsmen among them. People who knew the magic to fashion the sharp, shining knife now hanging around his neck. People with whom he would like to exchange many secrets.

Perhaps one day he would have that opportunity. He closed the tinderbox and handed it back to Antoinette with a nod of appreciation. Yes, he thought. He would like to meet her People.

ॐ

The fire grew brighter as they sat in silence, watching the sun slip behind the trees and the darkness descend upon the forest. The winds across the ridge blew embers up into the night sky like miniature suns trying to compete with the stars. The waning moon was still absent from the early night sky and with the blackness of the evening, the stars appeared closer and brighter.

Bear kept watch as Antoinette huddled near the fire. For all its warmth, she was shivering. She had pulled her knees close up to her chin and was, he believed, too proud to ask for covering. He unrolled the fur blanket, laid it on the ground, then moved to Antoinette's side. Placing his hands on her shoulders, he lifted her and guided her to sit on the fur.

Too cold to protest warmth and too tired to resist kindness, Antoinette obeyed.

Bear took the green velvet robe from his pack then sat beside her. With a slow gliding motion, he draped the robe around both their shoulders and pulled her close to lean against him.

She did not withdraw from his touch but relaxed into the warmth of his arms. She followed his gaze into the night sky.

During the sea crossing, Jacques had told her the names of the constellations visible in the night sky, those that moved with the progression of the seasons and the stationary North star that guided navigators on their voyages. She wondered if Bear was also guided by the stars.

In answer to her unspoken question, Bear began to whisper. She could tell from the tone of his voice and the wide movement of his arms toward the sky that he was telling her about the stars.

"All the stars have names," he said. "The North Star is *Kisiku Kloqoej*, the Old Man. He does not blink. He has three friends that hunt for *Muin*, the Bear." Bear pointed at the horizon toward the Pleiades rising in the east, "That is the Bear's Den." He motioned toward the west. "And that red star is *Jipjawej*, the robin. All the stars have names."

The soft rhythm of Bear's voice lulled Antoinette toward sleep. Bear lowered her to the pallet and slipped in beside her, covering them both with the green velvet robe. He cradled Antoinette in his arms, sharing the warmth of his body.

They would sleep now, he thought. There would be other nights together. Tomorrow there would be tiring travel. Soon they would be at his home. Soon he would speak with Old Woman and learn the secret to unlock Swan's language.

Tonight, he would have no disturbing dreams. Tonight his heart would fly with the stars as he held Swan safely in his arms. He called on his spirit helper, White Bear, to guard them while they slept.

Chapter 28

Dew soaked leaves slid under Antoinette's unsteady feet as they descended from the steep ridge. The overwhelming fragrance of evergreens filled the air as freshly fallen limbs and needles crushed underfoot. It was a bittersweet smell that reminded Antoinette of *Les Montagnes Noires*, the Black Mountains of Finistère. The silence of the woods recalled clandestine conclaves in sacred woodland clearings and *Les Forêt de Brocéliande*, the legendary forests of King Arthur and Morgaine. Breathless with anticipation, Antoinette ran to catch up with Bear as he pushed effortlessly through the spruce trees and down the mountainside.

From the ridge, the lake seemed so far away. Small waves lapped at the shoreline, rippling across the shiny surface. A light breeze flowed from the south, leaving the soft smell of wetness lingering in the air.

Bear stopped at the forest's edge as if an invisible barrier held him. With a quick extension of his arm he motioned for Antoinette to halt. She obeyed without question.

His eyes wandered up and down the shoreline. He sniffed at the air.

Was there trouble? she wondered, opening her senses to the unfamiliar terrain. She felt no danger near.

Bear looked at her and nodded, but motioned for her to stay behind as he descended the embankment to the lake. He walked a few feet along the waterline, then disappeared behind a stand of trees.

Antoinette set her pack down at her feet and leaned on her staff. She wondered how they would cross the lake and how much farther away from his camp they would be by sunset.

After a short time Bear came gliding along the water paddling a canoe. He jumped into the ankle high water and pulled the boat onto the beach.

"Come, Swan." He beckoned with a wave of his hand. "We will cross the lake."

Antoinette looked anxiously at the lightweight boat, wondering if it would make the crossing without mishap. It was about twelve feet in length and looked to sturdy. It reminded her of the small coracles used by the Bretons, but the exterior was made of a shaped tree bark and not of leather hides.

It was similar in construction to the wooden bowl Bear used to mix medicines, but instead of being folded over on the ends to keep in the water, the bark was sewn together with roots, just as she had sewn her moccasins. The seams were covered with spruce pitch, making the craft watertight. The interior structure, fashioned from shaped tree limbs, formed ribs across the bottom and up the sides. The bow and stern flared upward in rockered ends. Red sunbursts and bold geometric patterns decorated the sides. At first Antoinette thought the designs were painted, but she soon realized that the motifs were cut into the wood itself and the red coloring was the bark showing through.

The wide, broad beam of the boat sloped outward then up and in, keeping the water and spray from inside. From bow to stern, just under the rim, a pattern of crisscrossing lines trimmed the boat and matched the etching on the paddle Bear held in his hand.

Antoinette ran her hands over the decorations, hoping the marks were runes of protection, visible prayers to bless the narrow boat and its passengers.

Bear called to her from the treeline. She turned at the sound and stood motionless as her gaze traveled the length of his body. He had taken off his leggings and moccasins and stood now as she had first seen him at the lake, wearing only his loincloth.

His legs and arms shone in golden contrast to the dark greenery of the forest. His movements were swift, yet full of grace as he carried his gear toward the canoe.

Antoinette watched with anticipation as he placed their belongings inside the canoe, acutely aware of the ripple of his muscles and the ease with which he walked on the uneven terrain. She wondered if he ever tired from the fast pace of his actions.

Bear looked at her, catching her in that unguarded moment. He smiled. He knew she was watching him with more than curiosity and it made him feel good that she took notice.

Antoinette flushed at his acknowledgment of her unspoken praise and turned to unlace her moccasins. Her heart began to race at the realization of her growing desire for him. How could she think of falling in love with a savage? He was harsh, rugged, and his demeanor was nothing at all like she'd ever experienced or even imagined.

She thought of the men she knew. The men of Anne's court had been gentlemen, dressed in the most proper styles, exhibiting a most formal countenance. The priests of the Ancient Ones came from a mixture of classes, from farmers to counts. Most of the men on *La Réale* were honest, simple seamen. Jacques was a gentleman; her brother Gaston, an adventurer. All those men fit neatly into categories.

But Bear was different: he was like these men, yet he was so much more compassionate and giving.

"Help me Brighid," Antoinette whispered in growing desperation. "Help me to control this desire." Yes, it was desire. Bold and blatant and springing to life inside her. She would need to be cautious.

Bear roused her from her thoughts with words of haste.

She turned back to the boat, careful not to look into his eyes for fear he would read her thoughts.

With all the dignity she could manage, she waded into the water and stepped into the front of the canoe.

"Blessed Brighid, guide my journey," she whispered in a soft, reverent voice. A tiny smile tugged at the corners of her mouth as she glanced backward to make sure Bear held the boat securely.

Placing her weight on the branch ribbings, she lowered herself into the canoe and Bear pushed away from the shore. The boat cut through the water and the waves crested lightly on the bow. Bear guided the boat with the paddle, pulling in long, effortless strokes against the currents.

Once on the lake, his paddling became rhythmic and mesmerizing, calming Antoinette's nervous heartbeat, but not her thoughts.

For the better part of a half hour Bear watched her sitting in front of him. She was motionless, her breathing rapid, her knuckles white as they gripped the sides of the canoe. How could he explain to her that this canoe had been afloat for more summers than she had lived and that they were in no danger of sinking or capsizing unless she panicked or moved too swiftly?

Indeed, this canoe was so strong that it had been used to hunt in the great ocean waters nearby. As it grew older it had become an inland canoe, used mostly to cross the freshwater lake.

Bear gave a final stroke through the water with his paddle and the canoe glided in toward the opposite shore. He observed with amusement that his passenger relaxed her grip as the bow touched the sandy banks. He jumped from the canoe and pulled it out of the lapping waves, then extended a hand to help her disembark.

Welcoming the stability of land and the security Bear offered, Antoinette accepted his chivalry and rose on cramped and unsteady legs.

"Blessed Mother of the Waters!" she exclaimed, looking up into Bear's eyes. "Thank you for our safe passage."

Bear returned her smile with a warm look of acceptance, then motioned toward the forest.

Antoinette acquiesced and carried her gear up the beach as Bear stowed the canoe in an underbrush thicket, leaving it as a courtesy for the next traveler.

A well established path led away from the lake and the traveling proved to be much easier than before. Barberry, moccasin flowers, and sweet grass beckoned to be harvested along the way, but the few times Antoinette stopped to tarry, Bear urged her onward. The dream vision of Laughing Elk gnawed at his thoughts and pulled him homeward with an unheeding tug.

He began to muse on the dream vision as he walked. Why would Dancing Fox want Elk's pipe? And how could he have taken it after Elk's burial? Even Dancing Fox was not brazen enough to open the burial site of a shaman. Bear's spirit helper had given him words of warning, then shape shifted from bear to gull then to a hawk. None of these images made sense.

Muin Wapskw, White Bear, had never spoken to him in riddles before, nor asked meaningless questions. His advice had always been clear and direct, his words never clouded with symbols. That was Elk's way, not White Bear's.

The pipe, the waterfall, and the sparrowhawk were signs of power. He could understand about Sparrowhawk because she was still very much in his mind. The hurt in his heart was still tender. No, there must be something more. Something he was meant to know, something hidden in the symbols that he had not yet found the words to name.

"Bear," Antoinette called from a distance, snatching him from his thoughts. He turned, realizing that as his mind had sifted through the possible meanings of his dreams, he had quickened his pace, forgetting his friend behind him.

"What's wrong?" She walked to his side. "I've been calling you since we passed the last clearing. Please, slow down. I can't keep up."

Bear felt the concern in her voice and placed a comforting hand on her shoulder.

"My mind was elsewhere, Swan." He looked into her questioning eyes for a sign that she understood his apology. There was no way to explain what he himself could not understand.

Long summer shadows darkened the forest floor as they entered the last clearing near his brother's summer camp on the shores of the deep saltwater bay.

It had been several seasons since Bear shared a pipe with Two Arrows, but he knew they would be welcomed at his brother's hearth. He had bypassed the village on his journey to the Lake of the Swans. Two Arrows' people would have expected him to perform healings and tell stories and he knew he would not have been able to please them. Now, with his Power renewed, he could tell them many wonderful stories.

Yes, he thought. Two Arrows and his new wife, Little Bird, would be pleased to share their wigwam for one night. And tomorrow night he would sleep in his own wigwam, in his own village, giving thanks to Muin Wapskw for his safe return. Even though he was several days past his expected arrival, his food and bed would be waiting. Old Woman, with her keen senses, would know he was coming home and she would be overjoyed that he had brought Swan with him.

As they neared the lake, Bear stopped at a stream and motioned for Antoinette to rest and refresh herself while he prepared to enter into Two Arrows' camp. As a shaman, he would arrive with a bold flourish, chasing away unhappiness and promising magic and entertainment for the evening. The people expected this, and he would not disappoint them.

Assuming the shaman's role, he prepared his mind for the night's work. It would be a good test, he thought, to see if Power would respond to his wishes once again. He chanted, mixing up the red ochre and the black manganese dust into separate piles of thick paste on a piece of leather. He applied the paint to his face and arms in broad stripes the width of his fingers, alternating the colors.

Antoinette watched as Bear decorated his body. He was behaving much like the ancient Celts did before ceremony or battle. But the Celts were bolder with their designs, starching their hair with brightly colored mud and staining their skin with blue woad to impress audiences or frighten enemies. She was intrigued with how similar magic had remained throughout the centuries.

She understood Bear's lengthy explanation, that tonight they would stay with people, but that it was not the end of their journey. She nonchalantly watched him decorate his skin, only becoming concerned when he turned to her.

Bear's left fingers were covered with red ochre and he motioned for her to sit. It would be difficult at first to explain to his brother that Swan was a shape shifter, from the World Above the Sky. And although the idea of other beings living among the people was accepted, to actually have one enter your camp, even accompanied by a shaman, was a different matter. For now, he would explain Swan's pale skin and wavy hair as being special to her people.

Antoinette folded her arms across her chest as she looked at the red paint on his fingers.

"Is this really necessary? I'm not the local priestess. What could I do for your people? They won't even understand me."

"Swan," he said, seeing her hesitancy. "It is not proper for me to travel with a young woman. Tonight you must appear to be my wife. Two Arrows will welcome you if you seem more like one of us. If you are my wife you will be allowed to stay at his hearth and not have to sleep among strangers. Anyway, the paint will help protect you from the black flies near his camp."

Antoinette shook her head and Bear sprang to his feet. Why did she resist him? Were her ways so different? Did she doubt his Power?

Bear looked into her eyes. There was no malice behind those deep green eyes, eyes the color of spruce branches, the color of the mountains. There was no anger, no pretense—just wonder and an apprehension of the unknown.

He raised his right hand and slipped a leather head band over Antoinette's forehead, brushing a brown curl away from her face. He felt her body tense as he began to apply the paint to her face, tracing the arch of her brow and the bridge of her nose with his thumbs, then spreading the red ochre across her forehead and down her cheeks with his fingertips.

Her body bent to his touch and he heard her breathing quicken. Dipping his fingers in the pot of black manganese, he traced the lines of her jaw with a blackened finger, then reached for her bare wrist to encircle the moon shaped mark.

Antoinette found herself melting into his touch, wishing she could rid herself of the rigid barriers she tried to maintain around herself. She closed her eyes as his fingers traveled across her face and arms, reveling in the firm, sure strength of his hands. She must not give in to her desires now, she thought. She must wait until she knew what lay ahead, until she understood his customs better and, most of all, until she found out if she had a chance of returning to Brittany.

Bear finished painting her skin and let his hands drop to his sides, admiring his handiwork. One last thing remained, then she would be ready to pass for his wife. She would have to cut her hair to shoulder length. Only unmarried women wore long or braided hair.

Bear withdrew his knife. He lifted up a lock of Antoinette's hair and motioned for her to cut it. "You must cut your hair, Swan. If you are to pass as my wife, this must be done."

Antoinette took the knife from him and turned away. Breaking the tradition of the Sisterhood no longer seemed so important. Still, she prayed as the knife cut through her locks and they fell silently at her feet. "Beloved Mother, I am still your child."

Chapter 29

Nothing could have prepared Antoinette for the myriad of images that unfolded before her as they crested the ridge and she looked down onto Two Arrows' village.

Campfires burned brightly against the fading light of the sky. The aroma of cooking seafood mixed with the salty fresh breeze from the nearby ocean and the unmistakable smell of people. The smell of village life. Even the outdoor cook fires brought back distant memories of Brittany. Of home.

Antoinette fought to steady her emotions as they descended from the ridge. There were people, people who would shelter her, people who might understand her, people who might help her return to Brittany.

A sudden movement interrupted her reverie and she stopped in mid-stride. A man, tall and bronze-skinned like Bear, emerged from behind a stand of brush. His face was painted with bold black and white stripes. He wore clothing similar to Bear's. He brandished a stone headed club in his hand. His posture was poised for defense, legs balancing the weight of his body with ease.

Bear did not flinch, but calmly faced the warrior.

"What is your business here?" the scout challenged.

Bear held out his hands, palm up, in a gesture of good will. The man's face was new to him; he would proceed with caution.

"Hold, my kin friend. I am Bear World Walker, brother of Two Arrows. This is my wife, White Swan." He motioned to Antoinette, but the scout's eyes never left Bear's. "We are traveling to my village beyond the lake and we wish to spend the night at my brother's hearth."

"What proof do you have that you are Two Arrows' kin?" The man demanded an answer, yet his voice was controlled.

"Ah..." Bear smiled. "Two Arrows has a mark on his left shoulder. When he was a young boy a Great Eagle lifted him into the air. Our father, Black Stone, shot Eagle with two arrows before it would let my brother free from his talons."

The man gave a quick lift of his head. "This is a story that any warrior would know. A story told to me in my cradleboard. You must give me another symbol of proof."

"If you will permit, I will show you the twin of the Eagle's talon that I keep in my medicine pouch. My brother, Two Arrows wears the other around his neck as his chief's badge."

"You may show it." The man nodded his head. He lowered the stone club to his side, but kept his eyes locked on Bear's every movement.

Bear lowered his pack to the ground and opened his medicine pouch. He dug into the bag, withdrawing a dried eagle's talon. He held it out for the scout to examine, turning it over and over, like a fine jewel.

The scout looked at the talon and his brows raised in acknowledgment. He nodded his head. "It is similar to Two Arrows' amulet. And your eyes do not deceive me."

The man held out his hand in greeting and Bear extended his, then their forefingers interlocked in a gesture of kinship. "I accept you as Bear-World Walker, brother of Two Arrows. I am White Water, brother to Two Arrows' second wife, Little Bird." After his pronouncement his eyes strayed to look at Antoinette.

Bear stepped between them, blocking White Water's closer inspection. White Water realized his improper behavior and turned away from Antoinette. He held his hand to his mouth and a shrill whistle split the air. Soon a second man appeared in the opening, brandishing a spear. White Water turned to Bear.

"Red Feather will escort you."

Bear nodded at Red Feather, picked up his belongings, and motioned for Antoinette to walk behind him as the scout ushered them from the ridge.

She held her breath. What was happening? Bear would not knowingly lead her into danger. She watched his movements and mannerisms for any sign of apprehension as they walked toward the camp, but she saw a small smile flicker on the corners of his mouth as he turned to reassure her.

"It will be all right, Swan." He turned to meet her gaze. "My brother will welcome us."

The encampment was well structured, lying along the banks of the wide harbor like a small provincial town. Smoke drifted up from small conical shaped structures, too small to be shelters. A wigwam painted with animals and bold designs rested near the water and a much larger oval shaped wigwam, set on a slight rise in the terrain, dominated the campsite. Antoinette assumed, since they walked toward it, it was the main meeting area. She looked for stone buildings and for pale white faces, but found none. None of her people would greet her here.

As they neared the water, the smells of the camp became stronger and Antoinette wondered if Bear's people lived this way all the time, in rustic campsites without benefit of solid stone walls and furnishings. Surely this was just a hunting camp and the secure walls of a castle were within walking distance.

She looked at the people as she passed them. They were tanned and dark, like Bear, with straight black hair, mostly held back from their eyes with a variety of leather headbands. Everyone was clothed in leather garments, from decorated white doeskin to dark brown moose hide. The men were clad in leather loincloths as they worked, the women in knee length leather dresses. Strangely, no one lifted their eyes in curiosity.

They walked past a woman weaving a basket from split bark. She sat calmly and did not turn to look, but sniffed the air as they passed. Another woman tended a large cooking pot made from a hollowed maple log. A young girl fed the fire and cared for a small child.

Near the waterline, a man rendered a large animal into long strips and another woman laid the meat on wooden racks to dry in the sun. A toddler ran along the beach chasing the sea birds that hovered above the cast-off debris. It was a peaceful setting, disturbed only by the unexpected visit of new faces. Antoinette felt as though she had stepped backward in time, to an era before the invention of wheels or guns or ships that sailed the high seas; to a time when there were no such things as kings or queens or inquisitions.

Bear told Antoinette that Two Arrows' camp was larger than most of the other Micmac summer camps because two other families shared the waterfront beaches. The game and fish were abundant. Two Arrows had been granted a large hunting territory by the *sagmaw*, the chief of their People.

Together the families harvested the bay and ocean for fish, seal and whale and hunted the forests for moose and small animals. They spent their days preparing their catch for winter storage, smoking fish and drying meat on the racks that lined the waterfront. Any excess would be traded in the fall for furs and the goods they could not produce. They were a busy tribe.

The man on the beach halted his work and walked toward the advancing visitors. He stopped in front of the large bark hut, folded his arms over his bare chest and solemnly awaited their approach.

Red Feather stopped in front of him, then without a word stepped aside.

This man, Antoinette realized, was Two Arrows. He was tall

and muscular and, except for the noticeable difference in age, he was a mirror image of Bear. His broad shoulders proudly displayed two long-healed white scars that ran across his collarbone to his back. And there, suspended around his neck, hung the dried eagle's talon, the leg entwined in a lavishly braided red string.

Two Arrows' black hair grayed slightly at the temples, accentuating the years of responsibility that also showed in little creases at the corners of his eyes. His dark brown eyes were sharp and assessing as he glanced at Antoinette then settled his gaze on his brother.

A light tension crackled in the air and Antoinette's heartbeat quickened while the two men stood silent, expressionless, looking at each other without emotion.

Then the two men broke into smiles, stepped forward and embraced each other in a rough entanglement of arms and a wild flourish of words. Then, they turned and disappeared into the bark covered wigwam.

As she moved to follow Bear, a small, dark woman with glittering black eyes stepped in front of her. She was similar to Antoinette in height and age, though her complete opposite in color and complexion. A leather dress, wrapped under her arms like a blanket, fell loosely from just above her breasts to mid-calf, leaving her flawless bronzed shoulders bare. The dress was decorated with painted lines, birds and suns. Small copper beads fringed the sides.

She wore a knife sheathed and suspended from a thong around her neck and a small fur pouch lapped over her belt. She smiled and held out her hand, motioning for Antoinette to follow her as she turned toward the nearby campfire.

The woman walked with a slow, sure step, her head held high and her shoulders back. She possessed a grace quite incongruous to her rustic surroundings.

As the woman bent to lift a hot rock from the fire, her tunic stretched over her swollen belly and Antoinette realized that the young woman was pregnant.

She watched with rapt attention as the woman lowered the rock into the log kettle with a pair of wooden tongs. The liquid sizzled as the rock sunk to the bottom.

The woman dipped a bark bowl into the pot and turned toward Antoinette with a welcoming look, offering her its contents.

"I am Little Bird." Her words ran together and their velvety sound accompanied a bright smile. "I am second wife of Two Arrows." She straightened, proud of her status.

Antoinette regretted her lack of the young woman's language. She recognized the word meaning 'bird' and Two Arrows' name and assumed from the woman's mannerisms that she was introducing herself.

"Wapi'skw," Antoinette said, pointing to her chest as she accepted the hot broth. "My name is White Swan. I do not speak well."

Little Bird motioned for her to rest on a woven reed mat near the fire. "Have you traveled far?" She was unhindered by Antoinette's difficulty with her language.

"From beyond the great waters." *Farther than you can imagine.* She motioned with her hands. "From far away."

Little Bird lowered herself beside her visitor, then looked toward the wigwam. Her dark eyes flashed a hint of impishness.

"I have known Bear a long time. He has grown to be a fine man, like his brother, Two Arrows. He will be a good father." She rubbed her hands across her stomach, stretching her dress so that Antoinette could see her advanced pregnancy.

Antoinette smiled. "When will you have the baby?" she asked. Then seeing Little Bird's questioning look, waved her hands across the sky. "How many moons?"

Little Bird picked up a stick and drew a half moon and an empty circle in the sand, pointing the stick from one object to the other.

"Quarter moon to new moon?" Antoinette asked with sincere curiosity.

Little Bird glowed and nodded. Her cheeks were rosy with the glow of impending motherhood and her eyes glittered in the firelight.

"I will have a fine son for Two Arrows. Any day now." Proudly repositioning herself on the mat, she reached over and touched Antoinette's stomach with a loving gesture of an expectant mother. "You?"

Antoinette shook her head. "*Moqwe.* Oh no."

Little Bird sighed. "Ah—there will be time. The winter will be long and the nights warm in Bear's lodge." She nodded. "You will be a mother by next hunting moon."

Antoinette understood enough to know she was being consoled for her lack of productivity. She wanted to tell her that she was not Bear's mate nor did she have any intention of starting a family. But she remembered Bear's words and remained silent. The woman would not understand her anyhow.

The toddler broke away from a young girl and ran toward

Little Bird, stopping a few feet from her. He looked at her with wide, expectant black eyes and held out his hand. Little Bird dug into a nearby basket, then offered the child a piece of dried meat. He approached her cautiously, took the meat in his fat little hand and gave her a brief but thankful smile before he turned and ran back to hide behind his caretaker's knees.

"Buckskin can't wait to play with his little cousin," she remarked, awkwardly shifting her weight. "Neither can I."

The moose hide covering was thrown back from the doorway of the wigwam and the brothers reappeared. Both were smiling and now clearly reacquainted.

As they walked toward the women, Antoinette saw more of the family resemblance in their high pronounced cheekbones and striking profiles. She jumped to her feet and extended her hand to help Little Bird rise.

Two Arrows spoke to Little Bird, his voice softly commanding. "Bear and White Swan will stay at our hearth. See that they have all they need and prepare a travel basket for their journey when they leave."

Little Bird lowered her eyes in acknowledgment then turned to Bear. She looked at him from his tousled hair and painted face to his dirt-encrusted moccasins. Her eyebrows raised ever so slightly. "Will you *wash* or *rest* before the hearth fire is set?"

Bear glanced at Antoinette. They were both covered with dirt and dried paint and quite unsuitable to share a meal.

"Wash," he said with a glimmer of a smile. "Please sister, show us your bathing pool. We would not offend our host on our first visit."

Little Bird returned his smile, disappeared into the wigwam and returned moments later with an empty seal skin container to collect water. She turned to Bear with questioning look as the three of them walked away from the camp.

It was routine for the women to carry all the household belongings on their backs, balancing the weight with a leather tumpline around their forehead. With the women in charge of the goods, the men's hands would be free for hunting and defense.

"I see that you do not make White Swan carry the packs. You are a very considerate husband to share the burden with her."

Bear realized he had never once expected Swan to carry his belongings as they traveled. In fact, most of the things he did for her were not customary. He had made her clothes, cooked her food. He had not expected her to behave like other women.

Of course, he knew it was because Swan was unique. She was not like other women. She was a gift to him from another world. Little Bird would not understand their relationship even if he told her the truth. But now she sought an explanation.

"As you can see, Little Bird," he said with a soft and soothing voice. "We travel lightly, letting the trees be our shelter and the sky our roof. And—I prefer to keep my power objects within reach."

Little Bird lowered her hand to her side and clutched the medicine pouch hanging on her hip.

"*E'e.* It is wise to keep one's magic close at hand," she agreed.

The land changed from evergreen to hardwoods, from spruce forest to tall aspen, poplar and birch. The air smelled sweet and musky from the lingering dampness in the ground.

It was a pleasant smell that reminded Antoinette of the woods near Nantes, a life that now seemed a world away. It was much farther than a month's steady sailing and a few day's inland travel.

As they neared the small spring light laughter filled the air. It was followed by a loud splash of water.

Little Bird turned to Bear with a smile. "Two Arrows' oldest daughter, Morning Star, gathers reeds and watches Buckskin and her little sister. But it sounds as though she is playing more than working. My brother, White Water, is in bride service to Star. They plan to marry before winter. If their marriage is agreed upon, my family will continue to live nearby."

"*E'e,*" Bear acknowledged, understanding now why there were so many people in his brother's camp. White Water was there to prove his worth as a son-in-law to Two Arrows and to learn if his future bride would be a good wife.

"It will be good to keep such skilled hands in your camp, especially when winter comes and the baby is here."

Little Bird smiled and rubbed her stomach lovingly. Then she cupped her hand to her mouth and made a soft call that lilted through the forest, blending in with the other bird songs in the woods. A moment later the call echoed back from the spring.

"Star knows that we are coming now and will gather the children together so you will have privacy. We have all been working hard since the last storm, repairing wigwams and replenishing damaged supplies. Star will not be scolded for taking time to enjoy the beauty of the day. But now it is your turn Brother, to rest and enjoy the late evening sunshine. I'm sure you will earn your supper with stories tonight."

"Perhaps." Bear looked at Antoinette, wishing she could understand the conversation. "I have many new stories to share."

A young girl appeared from around the bend. A small child wiggled in her arms and she held the toddler, Buckskin, by the wrist. She was of average height and wore her hair long and full, accentuated by several black braids intertwined with bright strings and ornaments. She had the same overall appearance as Little Bird, but her face was delicate, almost a miniature of Two Arrows.

Morning Star stopped in her tracks as the trio appeared in her path. Her eyes widened and her mouth opened in a quick gasp of surprise at the sight of Bear's face, fiercely painted black and red, and the strange woman with light hair and odd features who accompanied him.

Little Bird scolded her with a sharp snap of her voice. "Close your mouth, Star, or the black flies will find a home. Be polite to your father's brother and his new wife."

Star blushed at the reprimand and lowered her head. The baby in her arms stopped squirming at the sound of Little Bird's voice and tucked her finger in her mouth for security. Buckskin moved behind Star's legs.

Bear stepped forward and placed a light hand on his niece's shoulder. "It is all right, Star. We have arrived unexpectedly, but it pleases me to see that my magic paint still means something to the young." He looked down at the toddler who ventured a brave look from around his protective barricade.

Star looked shyly at Bear. "Is there anything else that you require, Uncle? I will be happy to help."

"No," Little Bird said with a dismissive wave of her hand. "Take the children back to camp and tell Two Arrows I will return in a few moments."

Star nodded then slipped away from them with a light jerk on Buckskin's resisting arm. "Come Buckskin," she teased. "Or the shaman will eat you for his dinner."

Buckskin shot a wary glance over his shoulder at Bear and Star tightened her grip on Buckskin's hand, pulling him away.

"Children!" Little Bird exclaimed, then leaned against the trunk of a nearby tree to catch her breath. She placed her hands on her stomach and closed her eyes. A light grimace crossed her face. She took a long, deep breath. "Your little nephew will be quite a runner. He kicks and wiggles like a baby bull moose."

"Your time is near?"

"Yes and I am afraid that I will deliver while my mother is visiting her sister. She told me she would help with the delivery." She looked at Bear and at the medicine bundle hanging on his chest. Her eyes cleared as the pressure passed and she steadied herself. "You are a healer. You are skilled at birthing."

"Women are better prepared to handle these things. I am sure your mother will return in time to help you. What about Whispering Wind, Two Arrow's first wife?"

Little Bird glanced at Bear with a look of exasperation. "She is not at all pleased to share Two Arrows with me, nor at my having a child so soon after hers."

She placed her hand on his arm. "We get along, but I believe she fears that I will give Two Arrows the son that she cannot. She is older now and her girl baby may be her last child."

"I understand," Bear said. He looked at Antoinette, remembering the wide variety of medicines and herbs she carried with her. "Swan knows the healing magic of her people. If we are still here, perhaps she will attend you."

Little Bird turned to Antoinette, who stood beside her. Empathy filled Antoinette's eyes and Little Bird smiled.

"That would be very nice, I feel Two Arrows' son will not wait for my mother's return."

Bear motioned for Antoinette to go ahead of them to the springs. "I would speak with Little Bird for a moment. It is safe to go without me."

Without hesitation Antoinette disappeared around the stand of brush. Little Bird turned to Bear and touched her hand to his shoulder. "I am pleased to see you again, my brother," she whispered. "I am glad to see that someone has finally claimed your heart." She gave him a mischievous grin. "From the looks of it she has taken your clothing as well."

Bear chuckled. "It's a long story. Her clothing was not suited for travel and it was necessary to share mine."

"Ah." She nodded. It was all too often that clothing was damaged, by weather or age. "Where did you meet her? She is so very different. She does not look like our people or speak as we do. Where is her tribe? Is it far?"

"Yes, Little Bird, Swan is from very far away. She is the only one of her people I have met, but as you can see she has come to live at my hearth. She will soon learn the Micmac way and speak as well as you and I."

"It will be nice to have a sister my age. Perhaps you can

stay with us and witness the naming of your nephew. The hunting grounds will support many more people. We should have a proper wedding ceremony for you."

"I would like to stay. I have much to discuss with Two Arrows, but I must return to my camp and help my people prepare for travel to the winter shelter."

"E'e. I understand, my Brother. The invitation will always be open. But, right now, you should enjoy your bath."

Little Bird handed Bear the empty water skin. "Please ask White Swan to bring water when you return. We will eat after the sun sets."

ᏯᏒ

Antoinette stood ankle deep in the cool water, wiggling her toes happily in the soft mud. She had removed her leather jacket and moccasins, but retained her thin cotton tunic and contemplated her bath when Bear appeared from behind the stand of brush.

"We will wash here." He thrust a piece of soaproot into her hand, motioned for her to wash the paint from her face and arms, then grimaced and shook of his head. What a strange woman to wear so much clothing, he thought as he walked away from her.

Antoinette stared at the soaproot in her hand. "You don't expect me to wash here? Not out in the open."

She looked around the lake at the tree line. Her imagination reeled. She felt strange eyes looking back at her, watching, waiting for her to disrobe. She turned to ask where she could bathe in privacy and the words caught in her throat.

Bear stood at the far edge of the pond. Her eyes locked on the full figure of his naked body and scattered images of the Lughnasad ceremony flashed through her mind. His body then had been brilliant with ethereal fire of the Sun King. Now it was generously sculpted by the golden light of the dying sun.

A surge of excitement swept over her and she longed once more for the warm touch of his flesh and the security of his arms. She remembered the fire she'd felt inside her as their bodies and spirits had joined in passion.

As though hearing her unspoken praise, Bear turned and looked at her with a roguish grin. Embarrassed at his boldness, Antoinette turned away. Then she heard a splash.

"Come in," Bear yelled, surfacing in the middle of the pond. "Swim. It will refresh you from our long trip."

Antoinette shook her head, and rubbed the soaproot over

her arms, as though she could somehow scrub away the tingling from her flesh.

"No! I'll wash here."

"If you don't come in willingly," he teased, "I'm coming out to get you."

Bear swam toward her and began to rise out of the water.

"No!" She backed away. "No, I'll find a place to bathe. Just give me a minute."

Her eyes darted along the waterline and she leapt for the security of a stand of reeds edging the shore.

Bear shook his head and his deep laughter filled the silence of the pond. This was the first time in their long journey they had taken time to relax and enjoy each other's company. He splashed icy water in her direction.

"Come on," he called. "I promise I won't look." He did not wait for a reply, but submerged himself in the water and swam to the far side of the pond. He stood up on a sandy bank, this time in waist high water and continued washing.

Antoinette left on her white tunic and lowered herself into the water. Her muscles contracted from the chill. Her skin flushed from head to toe with tiny goose bumps. It felt terrible yet wonderfully refreshing and she was very glad Bear had coerced her into the water. Taking a deep breath, she dove under the surface and swam with full hard strokes toward the bottom of the pond, delighting in the quiet privacy of the underwater sanctuary.

Her feet touched the bottom and she gave a hard shove, springing to the surface. Relaxed now, she tread water as she scanned her surroundings.

Bear stood on the opposite bank, his back turned toward her. He worked the slippery soaproot into his long hair. The red and black paint slid with the lather down the muscles of his arms and disappeared into the shadows of the pond. The sky was darkening behind him. Antoinette sighed with contentment and lifted her body to float on the surface of the water.

"Thank You, Beloved Mother for your bountiful treasure," she whispered to the sky. She was safe and soon would be fed, warm and rested. She was with kind people and traveled with a man who obviously cared for her well being. Outside of being back home in Brittany, what more could she want? Things were so peaceful. Yes, peaceful, serene. How easy it would be to forget the troubles at home, the responsibility, the politics. She could leave all that behind. It was her friends and family that she missed. She could never forget them, no matter how appealing the lifestyle was in this foreign world.

There was a sudden tickle on her foot. A fish, she thought, kicking her foot to chase it away. She floated, looking at the sky. Until she felt human fingers wrap around her ankle and jerk at her foot.

She was barely able to take a breath before she was pulled underwater. She was quickly released and struggled for the surface. Recapturing her breath, she tread water, anxiously looking for her assailant. It had to be Bear. No one else would dare touch her.

Bear surfaced behind her and she turned around. Her green eyes flashed in anger.

He saw the wildness in her eyes. "Don't be mad, Swan. I couldn't resist teasing you. You were being too serious."

She was furious, ready for a fight, but angry words failed her as she looked into his dark eyes. They glowed with an innocent roguishness. Nothing more.

"You—you liar." She splashed water in his face then swam away. Suddenly she remembered the promise he'd made to protect her. She turned and gave him an icy stare. "You said you would never hurt me. You said you wouldn't look at me."

"Wait, Swan." Bear swam the distance between them. "What is liar?" He stopped then stood as his feet touched the rocky bottom of the pond. His broad shoulders and glistening body were magnified by thc darkening sky behind him.

Instinctively she swam away, stopping only when her feet found solid ground. She balanced herself on the slippery rocks. The thin fabric of her white tunic clung to her skin as she stood The top of her breasts barely breached the slick surface of the water. Her heart raced with anticipation.

Bear stopped a few feet from her, confused at her frantic reaction to his game. She might fly away. He must soothe her. He must let her know he meant no harm. He walked toward her with his arms extended.

"Don't be upset. I did not look at you. I did not mean to frighten you. Swan—" he said calmly, "—you are my friend."

A flood of gentleness enfolded her as she listened to his deep and resonant voice.

Seeing her relax, Bear walked closer.

"I do not need to see your body to know my desire for you. I do not need to look at you to know how much I would like to hold you."

With a slight movement of his arm he placed his palm on the space between her breasts. The cool cloth and Bear's warm hand her made her shiver, but she stood still.

Be calm, she told herself.

"Swan," he said. "Listen to your heart not to your mind."

She closed her eyes for an instant as a surge of raw energy passed through her.

His magic is strong. Ah, but I knew this.

Her mind raced to understand the emotions swirling within her, and most of all, her unwillingness to move away from him. Shamelessly, she wished he would touch her again.

He spoke softly, his words rescuing her from her inner chaos. "I do not need to fill my eyes with your beauty to know that I love you," he whispered.

The water moved in gentle caressing currents around her. The warmth of his hands encircled her waist, pressing the thin layer of cloth against her flesh and sending a shiver down her spine. She did not protest as his hands traveled to the hollow of her back, and he pulled her closer. Their bodies touched. She turned her head and leaned against his chest, listening to the pounding of his heart as he held her.

So strong. So safe.

They stood in silence for many moments, then Bear lifted her off her feet and eased her down into the water until her body floated with him as her anchor.

The hard contours, the full heat of him, fiery amid the chill, captured her. *Like fire on ice.* His skin was radiant against the twilight. *Like snow at sunset.* He smelled wet and wild.

His voice embraced her. Tenderly. Passionately. "I need to fill my heart with your love and my voice with your name." His placed his lips to her ear. "Swan," he said with a low moan. "Wapi'skw." His breath whispered warm against her cheek. "Antoinette."

Her name was almost an unfamiliar sound.

Was I ever Antoinette?

There was no need for words or space for thoughts. She could no longer resist him.

The touch of his lips to hers was intoxicating, soft and slow, belying a passion she knew he restrained. A sudden shiver sent her emotions spiraling, soaring. The kiss ended and she leaned back to look into his half-lidded eyes. They were solid black now, as black as the darkening waters around her.

Bear leaned forward and pressed his cheek to hers. She heard him breathe in her fragrance. Soaproot. Lavender. He sighed, then kissed her again, this time with a fever matching her eagerness.

His hand left her back and followed the contour of her

waist and buttocks to slide beneath the thin tunic to the top of her thighs. His hands were hot despite the chill of the water, and the hard firm flesh of his body brushed against her as he eased her weight onto his arms.

Her arms entwined around his neck, and she was aware of his warmth against her, barely noticing that he was lifting her from the water. She buried her head against the muscles of his shoulders, inhaling his fragrance.

The scent of man, of earth, of love.

Without breaking his stride Bear walked up the beach and lowered her to the damp sand. He brushed wet tendrils of hair from her face, stroking the side of her cheek with his hand. Then his hand moved to her neck.

A soft moan escaped her lips as Bear lifted her tunic, sliding his hand between the fabric and her skin. He cupped her breast gently then tugged lightly at her nipple, feeling it harden under his touch. Suddenly his lips replaced his fingers and a magical sweetness flooded through her, pulling at something deep inside her.

Waves of ice and heat fought for control, threatening to burst her heart. He was guiding her into hidden realms, yet she was grounded firmly to the earth.

Bear lay beside her and once again her body shaped to his. Movement blended with movement, so close in their dance they were almost one. He pressed against her until their legs entwined. His hands explored the curves of her body over the wet cotton fabric, first outlining the circle of her breasts then running the length of her torso to stroke the soft inner part of her thigh.

He moved slightly, pressing himself against her. His fingers traveled once more down the length of her body. Light shivers flew over her skin and gasps of surprise escaped her lips. His hand swept across her skin as though he were memorizing the sensitive areas he touched, taking time to pleasure her.

He pressed his hand against her and she instinctively lifted her hips. The tips of his fingers touched her, gently testing her eagerness.

Bear looked into her eyes. They were wide and dark, the green now hidden behind the passion that swelled within her. He knew she was ready to accept him as her lover again, she was ready to share with him the passion of his dreams.

She slid her hands under his arms, feeling the muscles of his back, wet, slick and silky smooth. She moved them downward in small circles across his spine to the small of his back and pulled him down to her.

Oh, yes. I will love you now. She would have him and all his warmth forever joined with her in this passion, this ecstasy—this bliss. Bear's love would forever banish the uncertainty clouding her heart. His strength would protect her.

Bear's hips pressed against her. Shifting his weight to one side, his hand swept the inside of her thigh, touching her gently, softly.

She is mine now, he thought. He would let her know how much he loved her. He pressed his lips to hers in a futile attempt to slow his heartbeat, to hold back the passion that coursed through him and displaced his reason.

Taking a deep breath, he looked down into her face, so trusting, so full of passion, so eager for his touch.

Antoinette felt his muscles tense, felt him shudder and take a deep quick breath. She opened her eyes and followed Bear's gaze until it settled on the small face of a child looking down at her.

Buckskin's dark black eyes gleamed in playfulness. He stood a few feet away, watching with avid curiosity.

Bear lifted his hand to wave the child away, but the little boy remained immobile, intrigued with his new friends' playful games. Bear lowered his head to Antoinette's neck and sighed. Buckskin's interruption had stolen their moment of promised passion, shattered their secluded world.

"Oh, Swan." Bear whispered into her ear, his voice vibrating with frustration. "I'm sorry."

He lifted his weight from her and Antoinette sat upright pulling her tunic down. She curled herself into a tight ball, hiding her embarrassment, hiding herself from the child and from Bear.

She dared not look at either for fear of crumbling into one of the thousand pieces of her shattered emotions. She sat with her head on her arms, shutting them out, shutting everything out.

She could hear Bear as he put on his loincloth, speaking gentle words to Buckskin. She heard no anger in his voice as he explained the danger that waited for little boys who strayed from their caretakers.

When she felt brave enough to look at them, Bear had taken Buckskin by the hand and was leading the child away from the water back toward the camp.

Their eyes met briefly, but they both knew there was nothing to be said. No words apology would be enough.

"You can finish your bath in privacy now," he said matter-of-factly. "I will see you are not disturbed."

He walked a few paces then stopped and turned. He wanted to run back to her, hold her in his arms, promise her comfort and love. But he knew that it would be senseless to even try.

"Please fill the water skin for Little Bird." There was no emotion in his voice, but Antoinette could tell that his disappointment and frustration were as great as hers. She watched him until his broad shoulders disappeared behind the brush then she looked out into the twilight sky at a single star shining on the horizon.

The chilly night wind kissed her face, cooling the hot tears that rolled down her cheeks.

Chapter 30

Bear sat with Two Arrows and Red Feather, talking and laughing beside the fire, sharing a pipe while the women cleared the supper debris and settled the children for the night. The hearth fire warmed the darkness of the wigwam. It was the central point for the evening gatherings, separating the men and women, the old and young. The youngest children sat close to the door and the oldest were sheltered well inside the depths of the wigwam.

Whispering Wind's grandmother sat farthest from the cold drafts of the entrance. Although she was nearly blind, she was still alert and quite skilled with her hands. She was a valuable asset to her people.

Two Arrows headed the men's side and, because she was the expectant wife, Little Bird shared a place next to him. Tonight, Whispering Wind sat away from the fire, nursing Two Arrows' new daughter. She would put her to sleep on the soft furs covering the edges of the wigwam.

As a visitor, and sister-in-law, Antoinette sat between Little Bird and Red Feather's wife, Smiling Eyes. The toddler Buckskin, sat next to Morning Star. He looked up at Antoinette and smiled.

When White Water returned from his patrol around the camp, he would take his place with the men. He was allowed to sit with them because he had killed his first big game. The moose meat dried on the outside racks. White Water was now considered a man and entitled to a man's privileges.

Bear touched Antoinette's shoulder as she bent to take an empty bark bowl from his hands. She glanced into his eyes, then turned quickly away. They had spoken little since their swim and what words there were felt awkward in the presence of others. What they had to say to one another would have to wait until they were alone again and back on the trail to Bear's camp.

They must talk, Antoinette thought. She must know if there were others like her here, if there was to be a way home and if not, what kind of life waited for her among his people. Most of all they needed to talk about how they felt about one another.

All evening Antoinette mimicked Little Bird's actions, serving Bear as though he was her husband. The evening progressed smoothly, until Bear touched her and she saw the mingling of desire and reserve hiding behind his easy smile. A slight flush spread across her face. She quickly looked away but caught a knowing smile from Two Arrows. Her blush turned to crimson.

Did he know? Did Two Arrows see her desire for Bear in her face? It didn't matter; tomorrow she and Bear would be miles away and she would never see him again.

The few hours since their interrupted rendezvous had provided her time to think and a dangerous amount of time to explore her feelings. Were they justified or had she merely been caught up in Bear's kindness and the passion of the moment? It was too much to comprehend, so she occupied herself by helping Little Bird string a necklace of small shells onto a piece of twisted sinew.

"Bear?" Little Bird's voice interrupted the men's conversation. "Tell us a story."

"Ah," Bear raised his finger into the air. "I have a great story to share."

Little Bird looked quizzically at the shaman. "I hope it has a happy ending."

"Oh yes, Sister. It has a happy ending, but not such a happy beginning."

Bear paused for a moment as the door covering lifted and White Water entered the wigwam. He cast a quick smile towards Morning Star, and took his seat next to Red Feather. The wigwam grew silent and everyone stopped their busy work to listen to Bear.

"One day, Kluskap was fishing in a stream that fed the Great Freshwater lake. He fished for *taqu'naw*, a rainbow trout, to roast over his hearth fire. He had been fishing for quite a while when he heard the sound of a man calling from up stream.

" 'Help! Help me! I'm drowning!' the voice called.

"Well I can tell you that Kluskap was unhappy that someone was interrupting his fishing. *Taqu'naw* had been teasing him all afternoon, never swimming quite near enough to Kluskap for him to spear, and Kluskap knew that *taqu'naw* was tiring of his game, for he was swimming closer and closer to Kluskap*'s* legs.

"Kluskap laughed, his great voice sending ripples across the water. 'Old *taqu'naw,*' he chuckled. 'You will soon become my supper.'

"Then, just as he was about to hurl his spear at the trout, he heard the man yell again. Kluskap threw his spear at the fish and missed. Now, he was so mad that he stomped out of the water and climbed on top of a big rock to look in the direction of the cry for help.

"To his surprise he saw the strangest sight. A man with a large bundle strapped to his back was standing knee deep in the swiftly rushing water, waving his hands and yelling like a green jay in a trap. Kluskap scratched his head in wonder. The man was not anywhere near drowning and this made Kluskap furious.

"*Taqu'naw* raised his tail out of the stream and splashed Kluskap with a playful spray of water as he headed home.

" 'I'll be back tomorrow,' Kluskap shouted to the fish, waving his hand in a fist. 'You'd better sleep well in the water tonight, for tomorrow you'll sleep in my stomach.' "

Bear paused in his story as everyone laughed at Kluskap*'s* boldness. He took a long draw of smoke from his alderwood pipe and slowly continued his tale.

It was a shame that Swan could not understand all of his words, he thought. For the story was just as much for her enjoyment as it was for the others.

"Kluskap took his time climbing down from the rock for he knew the man was not in danger. Slowly he walked over to the man and stood beside him, his hands resting on his hips.

" 'Friend,' Kluskap said. 'Do you have a problem?'

" 'Oh yes, kinsman,' the man said in a panic. 'I am drowning here in the water and I will never make it to the other side of the lake.'

"Kluskap looked at the man from his head to his knees, then behind him at the canoe resting on the bank of the lake.

" 'Brother, haven't you seen the canoe behind you?' he

asked.

"The man, distracted from his drowning, looked at Kluskap with a frown. 'Canoe?' he said. 'What is a canoe?'

"Kluskap raised his eyebrows. What a stupid man, he thought as he pointed to the canoe with its beautiful colored bow.

"The man looked at the canoe, but did not see it.

" 'You mean that old dry log lying there?', the man said."

"Kluskap looked at the canoe with its well crafted seams and its sturdy structure. It was big enough to carry a warrior and all his family.

" 'That is not a log, my friend. I think if you look closer you will see that it is a sturdy boat that will help you cross the lake safely.'

"The man continued to look at the canoe and shook his head from side to side.

" 'All I see is a log with branches sticking out its sides.' He turned to Kluskap with a frown. 'You should be ashamed, playing games with a drowning man.'

"Well, I can tell you that this got Kluskap really upset. The man had not only robbed him of his supper of a fat trout, now he was insulting him. Kluskap grabbed the man by the arm and pulled him out of the water. Almost as quick as a flash of lightning they stood beside the canoe.

"Kluskap pointed at the birch bark designs. 'Can't you see the long lines of the boat?'

"The man squinted his eyes and shook his head from side to side. 'No, all I see is the dark bark of a long tree. But it does have a rather unusual flare at the ends of its trunk.'

"Kluskap pointed to the paddles. 'Can't you even see the ribs or the paddles?'

" '*Moque.*' The man shook his head. 'No, only branches.'

"Kluskap was puzzled. His stomach was beginning to rumble from the loss of his dinner and he could feel himself beginning to lose his temper. Then he wondered for a moment if Kji Kinap was playing a trick with him, giving him a problem to test of the strength of his patience. He took a deep breath and threw back his shoulders.

" 'Here', he said, escorting the man over to the canoe with a gentle hand on his shoulder. 'Reach your hand out and touch the bow.'

"The man looked at Kluskap with a sideways glance, wondering why Kluskap wanted him to touch the old dry log. He thought for a long moment, then remembered that Kluskap had saved him from drowning and had no reason to play tricks on him, especially after going to so much trouble to save his life.

"The man reached out and gingerly touched the log and to his surprise the log appeared to be hollow.

" 'E'e,' the man exclaimed, withdrawing his hand like the log had bitten him. "I did not realize that the log was hollow. I could put my pack inside it, but how will it ever get me across the lake?'

" 'Look,' Kluskap said with exasperation. 'Climb in the log —the canoe—and see for yourself.'

"The man lifted one leg and then the other and sat down in the middle of the canoe, his hands instinctively resting on the sides. His eyes opened wide and he smiled at Kluskap as the canoe slowly took its shape in his mind.

" ' Why yes, friend, I see the canoe now.'

"He picked up a paddle in his hand and waved it in the air. 'And I see the paddles.'

"Kluskap jumped for joy at the man's sudden spark of enlightenment. 'Now you can cross the lake safely.'

"The man hung his head. 'I'm sorry my friend, but I don't know how to use a canoe. You see, my people have always crossed the lake when it was frozen. I have no knowledge of canoes. I am afraid that I will spill myself in the water if I try it alone.'

"Kluskap shook his head, wondering if all the man's people were so afraid to try new things. He thought for a moment about his fishing plans for the next day and quickly pushed the canoe into the water, jumping in behind the startled man.

" 'I will show you how to use the canoe to cross the river if you will do two things for me.'

"The man held on to the sides of the canoe, wide eyed with fright at suddenly being out in the middle of the lake.

" 'Yes, yes,' he said catching his breath. 'Anything that you want. I'll do anything that you ask. Just get me safely across to the other side.'

" 'Well,' Kluskap said with a slow, commanding voice. 'First you must show your people how to use the canoe.'

" 'Oh yes, Kluskap. I promise to show them.'

" 'Then, you must promise never to interrupt my fishing again.'

"The man agreed and Kluskap delivered him safely to the other side of the lake, leaving him the canoe to share with his people. But as Kluskap turned toward the lake, ready to swim back across, the man asked him one more question.

" 'Great Kluskap, how will I make my people see the canoe?'

" 'That is simple my friend," he said as he swam out into the lake. "Teach your people to see things as they really are. Tell them to be cautious, but also to be brave and overcome their fears."

"The man turned to wave the paddle in the air in thanks but Kluskap had already swam across the lake and had his spear in his hand, ready for fishing."

Bear looked around at his audience as he ended his story. Buckskin and the baby were asleep, but all other eyes were still waiting expectantly.

"Well, what happened to *taqu'naw*?" White Water asked.

"Ah, well that's another story," he remarked. "Too long to tell at tonight's campfire."

Morning Star had been silent and now she spoke. "Did the man teach his people to use the canoe?"

"Yes. He taught them to fish the great waters in the canoe and to look beyond the obvious to find the truth."

Everyone agreed with Bear and then, after some discussion between the men, Two Arrows spoke.

"It's getting late. The fading moon is in the night sky. It is time for bed." He cast a quick glance at Bear. "Since White Water will be sharing night watch with Red Feather, you may sleep in their place by the fire."

"A night watch?" Bear asked. "Since when do the people require a night watch?"

Two Arrows leaned close to his brother. "We have heard that the Kwetejk are hunting in the area. White Water is afraid that someone will kidnap Morning Star before he can marry her."

Bear nodded. His experience with Sparrowhawk had widened his outlook on their neighbors from the Shining River. "It is good to be cautious." Bear said. "She is a beautiful treasure, one that would be wasted living among the Kwetejk."

He paused and thought for a moment. Good manners required him to offer his services. He turned to the young man. "Nephew, I would be happy to stand watch with you tonight."

"Thank you, Bear," White Water replied. "If you could spare a few hours toward sunrise, I would be grateful. I promised Morning Star I would find her a fat rabbit to roast tomorrow. Red Feather has a wife to take care of and I have been taking a lot of his time."

"I will be there, Nephew," Bear said. "Just wake me when it is time for my watch."

"Then it is settled." Two Arrows rose. "We will talk in the morning."

"Yes, Brother, we will visit before Swan and I continue our journey."

"Must you leave so quickly, my brother? It has been almost a full turn of the seasons and we have not had the chance to talk."

"I have been away from my people for too long and they are waiting for me to return so we can move to our winter camp." Bear looked at Antoinette with a sideways glance. "Old Woman expected me to return a few days ago, but I have traveled slowly with my new wife."

Two Arrows looked at Little Bird, then at Whispering Wind. "Try traveling with two women, my brother. And with one of them pregnant. *That* is quite a challenge."

Little Bird turned and shot Two Arrows a derisive glare. Two Arrows smiled at her, knowing her reaction was that of a very uncomfortable woman.

"You are very lucky to have two beautiful women to take care of you, Brother," Bear said, slapping Two Arrows on the back in mock consolation. "They will both have babies to tend at the winter hearth and things will get back to normal."

Two Arrows nodded as the men walked outside to continue their conversation in private.

Little Bird laid her handiwork in her lap and spoke to Whispering Wind. Antoinette didn't understand their exchange but the grandmother, Smiling Eyes and Morning Star joined their laughter.

It was good to hear women's voices again and Antoinette found herself sharing in their lighthearted mood, raising her voice to laugh with them. It had been too long since she had allowed herself to forget her problems and laugh with others.

This is good. No, it is more than good, it is like being home.

She looked at the women's smiling faces and knew that in spite of their differences, these women were her sisters. They were women who needed their men, but could take care of themselves. Perhaps one day she would be like them, she thought. One day she would be happy and content.

Chapter 31

As morning broke, Two Arrows ferried Bear and Antoinette across the wide body of water to a rocky peninsula across from his camp. Now, in the afternoon sunshine, she and Bear walked a lonely stretch of land that offered little shelter from the strong ocean breeze. Far ahead of them a mountain guarded the shoreline like a giant sentinel, its dark green forests shrouded in the ever present mists. The sheer size of the headland made it an unmistakable landmark. It was the same headland she had seen from her beachfront shelter across the cove.

She watched Bear's green velvet cloak flutter behind him as he walked down the beach and remembered how he had explained to her that his camp lay just beyond the range. They would walk the remainder of the day and perhaps well into the night before they arrived at his people's camp to the west of the cape.

She was tired and wished she had been able to sleep the night before, but the strange smells and surroundings of Two Arrow's wigwam had kept her on edge. She and Bear had slept in each others arms once again, but they had exchanged only a few whispers in the silence of the crowded wigwam. All day there had been a strange silence between them and Antoinette wondered if Bear's feelings toward her had changed.

Absentmindedly, she rubbed the small spiraled pink and gray shells of the necklace Little Bird had given her between her fingers. Trying to stay awake while the warm sun lulled her to sleep, she recalled Little Bird's parting words.

"Swan," Little Bird had said, placing the necklace over Antoinette's head. "I hope these shells will miss their home by the sea and they will bring you back to visit us. You must come back to see my new baby."

She wanted to tell Little Bird she might not return. But her words caught in her throat. Somehow she knew she would see Little Bird once again and hold her newborn child.

Antoinette thought of her mother, but it was Ursule's face she recalled, not Marguerite's. *Where are you now, Ursule, when I need your strength? Why can't I contact you? Or Deirdre? Anyone!*

Antoinette stopped in her stride and shook her head trying to clear it. *I am dead to my sisters. They are not even trying to find me.*

Her stomach rumbled, then ceased its uproar when she remembered the hard dried meat and parched ground nuts that would be her next meal. The smell of dried seaweed and decaying fish wafted up from underfoot and a wave of homesickness and melancholy increased.

Images of Rennes filled her mind. She could almost see the lavish rose gardens and blossoming apple orchards, the fields of grain ripening for harvest. She could almost smell the aroma of Ursule's kitchen, the leavening dough, and roasting meats. She tried to remember the wonderfully tiled floors and stained glass windows that adorned her room in the Château, but she could not bring her thoughts to focus on either image.

By the Goddess, I need to rest. I need a good bowl of thick soup... a loaf of hot bread.

"I want to go home," she said, breaking the long silence they had shared during their walk.

"Swan?" The green cloak adorning Bear's shoulders swirled as he turned toward her. He saw the distant look of sorrow on her face and the darkness of the emotions surrounding her. She was falling. He rushed to her side and caught her in his arms. "Are you all right?"

Tears trickled down her cheeks and she leaned against him for support. "I want to go home!"

He pulled her close and held her tight.

"I want to go home," she sobbed, pressing her face hard onto his chest. "I want to sleep in my own bed, under a real roof. I want to see familiar faces, hear my language. I want to wear my own clothes."

The sorrow swirling around her was like a knife striking at the center of his heart. Why was she so sad? He was doing everything he could to make her happy. Was that not enough?

"You are tired, Swan," he said, stroking her hair, smoothing the fractured energy surrounding her. "We will be at my camp soon and you will feel better after you rest."

She shrugged off his touch with a shake of her shoulder, pulling away from him. "No, I must go home. I must find other people like me." There was no way to tell him how strange she felt in his world. His life was just too different. "I can't explain it to you. I'm homesick. I'm tired."

Bear searched for the right words. "I know you miss your home, but you will find a place with my people, with me. Try to be patient."

"How can I make you understand? We are from two different worlds." She moved away from him, her pent-up emotions beat against him like cold rain during a storm. "You have no concept of what my life was like, no idea what power I possessed! I helped to *rule* a country. I lived in luxury." She tugged at her rough leather clothing with disdain. "I wore fine fabrics and jewels. Not painted leather and shells."

She saw the sting from her words reflect sadness on Bear's face and suddenly she felt ashamed. She sat on the cold rocks and turned her head away from him.

"I'm just so different from you. I feel so out of place. I can't live as you do. I must go home, Bear." She turned to look at him. "There are things I left unfinished, obligations that I must fulfill. My people need me."

Words failed him. He had treated her with every courtesy and kindness he knew. His brother had welcomed her into his home without question. He had shared his love with her, bared his heart and now she was insulting him and threatening to leave. He had come too far to lose her now.

"I need you, Swan," he declared, kneeling to look into her eyes. "*I* need you now. I will make you happy. You will see."

He moved his hand to touch her but she leaned away, not wanting his comfort to confuse her further. She turned to him and a final spark of defiance leapt from her eyes.

Bear stepped back from her. She did not seem like the great woman of power, the Swan Woman he had rescued from the lake. She was behaving like a spoiled child, like a real woman.

Set fire to stop fire, he thought. He must somehow break her away from the confusion surrounding her spirit.

"You will not go!" he declared. He grabbed her arm, pulling her to her feet. The green cloak slid from his shoulders and landed on the rocks. "You will not leave until we reach my camp and Old Woman speaks to you. If you are not happy at my hearth, if my love is not enough for you, then you may go back to your world. I have no need for an unhappy woman."

He picked up his cloak, shook the dirt from it with a loud pop then turned away and walked down the beach.

Antoinette was startled by the sudden power of his words.

By the Goddess! He was leaving her, she thought. If he walked out of her life she would be right back where she started, without shelter, without hope, without him. A wave of panic spread through her. If she could not bear to part with him now, how could she part from him when the time came for her to return home?

Her heart beat frantically as she ran toward him.

"Bear," she called "Bear, wait."

He did not answer, but turned to watch as she advanced. Power spoke to him and he opened his mind to listen.

You are a Micmac leader, a shaman of your people, Power said. *If she is to survive among you, she must understand your importance. She must learn to obey your words without question.*

Bear knew the truth in those words. He had been acting like a love-sick suitor, not a shaman; not a man of Power.

Bear folded the green cloak into a tight packet and lashed it to the bundle he held in his arms. When Antoinette walked up to him, her eyes lowered submissively, Bear thrust the cumbersome pack into her arms.

"Carry this," he said unceremoniously. "If you choose to act like a real woman, then you will be treated like one."

ଓ

With the wind and sea behind them, they left the rock-strewn shoreline and climbed up a steep slope to a level plateau high above the water. They passed through a dense growth of blueberry bushes, stopping to gather a bag full of the ripening fruit before they entered the silent forests that led to Bear's camp.

At first they exchanged brief glances, but as they neared Bear's camp the tension between them lessened and they slowly began to talk. The closeness of the trees and the familiarity of the cool woodlands soothed Bear's emotions. Soon they were traveling in harmony, following a downward path that led to a narrow river.

Bear explained as best he could to Antoinette that he lived in the camp of his teacher, Laughing Elk. And although Laughing Elk no longer traveled the Earth path, Bear chose to remain with the shaman's people. He was caring for Elk's second wife, Old Woman, until she found a new husband.

Dancing Fox, Elk's son, did not like Old Woman. She returned his animosity with equal coldness. She believed that Fox was not Elk's true son, because he had none of Laughing Elk's good humor and all of his mother's ill temperament. The two were constantly at odds, with only Bear to intercede.

Fox's wife, Summer Moon, their young son and daughter, and Summer Moon's brother, Blue Heron, made up the rest of the small band that Bear called his family.

As a shaman, he traveled a great deal, but he enjoyed living next to the fresh flowing water of the Golden Stream where he could fish for *taqu'naw,* like Kluskap, and collect the wide variety of medicinal plants that grew along the stream's rich banks.

His family were hunters and trappers. They harvested game from the dense spruce forests, and traded their dried meats and beautifully cured pelts of mink, beaver and rabbit for smoked ocean fish and seal with other camps. Dancing Fox was a good fisherman—not as great as Kluskap or Bear himself—but quite skilled. Together the men fished the Golden River for salmon in the early spring and sturgeon in the summer. They set their traps for eel in the fall. The eels, high in fat and protein, provided much food for the tribe during the winter when game was scarce.

With good fortune, Bear had explained, there would be one or two full moons before the trees lost their leaves and the snows began. She would get to see the eel trapping. There would also be time to gather medicinal plants and roots before his people traveled to their winter camps.

"There are many reasons for you to stay," he told Antoinette as they walked. "My family and Two Arrows' family will share the winter camp this season. You will be able to see Little Bird once more and participate in the naming of the baby.

"If you stay through the winter and then past the spring thaw, I will take you to the summer gathering of the Micmac People where you might find someone from your world."

"Do you think there are others here like me?" Antoinette asked.

Bear nodded. "I have not seen any other people like you, Swan. But the summer gathering is large. People come from everywhere. It is a very important time."

To Bear, the most significant part of the gathering would be the assignment of new hunting territories. He would ask for his own hunting grounds, so he could take Old Woman away from Dancing Fox's hearth.

Secretly, Bear hoped that by summer Swan would be his wife. But after their most recent argument, he had little reason to believe she would accept his offer.

"Must I remain disguised as your wife when we reach your home?" Antoinette asked.

Bear wondered if she had been listening to his thoughts. "We will see," he replied, steadying the uncertainty in his voice. "I wish Old Woman were here. She would know what to say to you."

He knew Old Woman would accept Swan. She would realize immediately that Swan was not of this world. That she was a special person.

"Old Woman? Is she your grandmother?"

"Oh, no." Bear chuckled. "She is old enough to be my grandmother, but she was the second wife of Laughing Elk and I have taken responsibility for her. It is too far for her to return to her family near Land's End. It is too many days' walking for her aged legs. Though I would never say *that* to her face."

Yes, Bear thought. Old Woman would know immediately that Swan was not of their world. They would get along perfectly. Dancing Fox, however, would be a problem. He had never been a great believer in the power of the Otherworlds and would be suspicious of the pale stranger. He would certainly question her origin.

The evening was well underway, but the night sky still held the red glow of the late summer sun. Antoinette watched Bear, learning the way he read the signs of the forest. Occasionally, he would stoop to the ground and pick up a handful of dirt, rubbing it through his fingers as he smelled the earth, breathing in the familiar scents of home. He showed her different plants, edible and non-edible, growing along the hillside. Once he showed her an almost invisible marking on a tree that pointed to a ridge and to a different pathway. He showed her how to look for broken twigs and crushed leaves, both signs that people had recently passed along the same path. He made her stop to listen to the small animals as they scurried through the underbrush.

Bear stopped as they approached a small stream. He made a soft call that sounded like a loon, then waited for a reply.

After a long pause he repeated the sound and waited again. When no reply came, he led Swan across the stream, stopping once more a few feet inside the woods. He raised his hand to his mouth to call again, but caught sight of a quick movement on the ridge above them. Without a word, he grabbed Antoinette by the arm and pulled her to the ground.

He placed his hand over her mouth to smother the words of resentment he knew were sure to surface.

"Shhh," he whispered into her ear, not daring to move his head to reaffirm his fears with a second look. "Make no noise."

Bear held Antoinette against him and he could feel the quickening of her heartbeat and the fast cadence of her breathing as she stifled the sudden panic that rose within her. He tightened his hold in an effort to reinforce the necessity of remaining still. After a few moments, he felt her relax into his arms and knew that his silent message had been received.

Slowly, he slid from her side. Pressing himself into the thick underbrush he slithered up the slope to scout the ridge.

Four Kwetejk warriors walked on the crest above them. All were dressed in dark leather clothing, their faces fiercely painted and their shoulders smeared with red ochre, a sign of hostility—a sign of danger.

Bear felt an evil wind in the air. They did not attempt to hide their loud movement through Bear's tribe's hunting grounds. The presence of armed men should be challenged, but he would not engage them at Swan's peril. His mind raced as he tried to still his rapid breathing.

Why were Kwetejk warriors hunting so far from their camps? he wondered. Why were his neighbors dressed so defiantly? Nothing could have happened in the short time he had been away. Two Arrows had set a watch to guard his daughter, but he had not mentioned any problems with the Kwetejk. What could be wrong?

He remembered his trouble with Sparrowhawk. It had been almost two seasons since she left his camp. Repercussions from her visit would have been resolved through diplomacy and not through revenge.

Bear watched the men move along the ridge, away from his camp, away from them. When they were out of hearing range, he moved.

"What's happening?" Antoinette asked in a low whisper.

He heard the slight tremble in her voice and reached out to reassure her, placing a hand on her arm.

"They are not my people. They are Kwetejk. I don't know why they are here," he said, hoping she did not see through his thin facade of calm. He would have to leave her alone, it was too risky to take her into his camp without knowing the full situation. "There is a place nearby where you will be safe. I want you to stay there until I speak to my people."

Antoinette followed him up the hillside to a hidden footpath that led to a towering cascade of rocks. Bear lifted a low-lying tree limb, swept aside a tangle of vines, and then disappeared into an engulfing darkness. After a few seconds he returned and motioned for her to follow him.

A memory from childhood filled her senses. A smell of musty earth, of herbs and smoke. A smell of magic and mystery lay hidden in the silence.

Bear lit a strip of leather, laid it in an oil filled clamshell, and a small flame filled the darkness with a soft sputter. He held the flame to dry kindling and the silence was replaced with bold crackling as a fire flared upward from the hearth.

They were in a cave. Antoinette's gaze swept the length of the rock wall. Breathtaking images of painted animals decorated the walls. Bands of double curves, red spirals and exploding suns filled her field of vision.

From the expression on her face, Bear knew she felt the power of his sacred space and the energy of his herbal stillroom lingering with his magic, his shaman's secrets.

He glanced around the cave. It was just as he left it. A low rock ledge supported a row of small baskets, some with lids, others, open-topped, were filled with herbs and medicines. A second shelf displayed a variety of dried animal parts, feathers and fruits. A niche ran along the far side of the wall. Bear walked to it and placed his sacred pipe on the ledge. He sighed, and turned toward Antoinette.

"You will be safe here. Muin Wapskw, White Bear, my spirit helper, guards this place and Laughing Elk's spirit says he will protect you while I am gone."

He moved to leave, but Antoinette grabbed his arm.

"Bear, I'm sorry if I have caused you this trouble."

"I am sure it is none of your doing, Swan." He took her hand and placed it above his heart. "There is something you should know."

"It can wait." She lifted her finger to his lips to silence him, ran her hand across his cheek, then stroked the line of his hair. "We will talk when you return."

He shook his head, halting her hand as it moved to caress his shoulders. He took a deep breath and steadied his words.

"No, I must tell you something I have never told anyone. I cannot see what lies ahead. Last Winter many of my people went hungry. A few of the old ones died. I could not see what the future held for my people. I could not call the animals to the hunt."

Bear strained to control his heartbeat. He needed to tell Swan about Sparrowhawk and the other problems she had caused him.

"I could not read the signs," he said. "Great Power would not speak to me. That is why I went to the Lake. To seek Great Power." He glanced toward the cave's entrance with uneasiness then focused his attention on Antoinette's face. "Because of your strength, my quest was successful. Now I can feel the danger in the air and I fear for my people."

"Bear, you cannot always know the future. You must understand that Great Power...even the Great Goddess will never let us know everything."

He shook his head. "I would never have lost the power to walk between the worlds if I had thought of my people first and not myself."

"A wise woman once told me that sometimes the gods test the truth in our hearts by sending us impossible tasks, ones that we are destined to fail no matter what we do."

"Do you believe that?" he asked hopefully. "Do you believe Great Power was testing me?"

"*Oui.*" She nodded. "My Goddess is testing my strength. She is testing my faith. Unwisely I sought to know my destiny and the Goddess allowed me to see you in my visions. They set me on this path and I haven't a clue where it will lead me."

Bear leaned down and pulled Antoinette close. "I hope it will lead you to my hearth," he whispered, inhaling the sweet fragrance of her neck and hair.

Antoinette rested her head on the hard-muscled flesh of his chest as his arms encircled her.

"Perhaps it will."

He pulled back, searching her eyes. "Would you stay with me? Would you marry me and become one of my people?"

"Don't ask me those things." She glanced away. "Not yet." *I must know if I can return to my home.* "There are things I must finish before I can chose my own path."

Bear lifted her chin and brushed her lips with a light kiss.

"I will wait," he said.

He looked into her eyes. The firelight reflected tiny golden stars in the corners of the green pools of darkness. Stars he knew shone only for him. Stars that would light his way back to her arms in the darkness of the night. Her lips were full and soft and she yielded without resistance to his kiss. Her body, pressed to his flesh, promised more than he could easily resist. But with great effort he pulled away. There would be time later to fulfill their unspoken promise of love.

He turned toward the cave entrance. "If I do not return by the rising moon, you must not follow me. You must return to Two Arrows' camp with the morning sun and tell him what we have seen."

Then he was gone.

Antoinette ran to the cave entrance and lifted back the greenery. "What do you mean?" she whispered. But he had disappeared into the thick underbrush and the darkness of the night.

Bear could not answer her, for *Muin* Wapskw's words rang in his ears, their meaning clear as they resounded in his mind. Why had he not understood the cryptic message earlier?

The eels will drown, we will have no food for winter.

The eels were his people, drowning in danger. A waterfall of blood, a flood of danger threatened them.

He raced down the pathway, his black hair flowing behind him like a rampant fire.

It was almost beyond hope that his family had not come to harm.

Chapter 32

They were looking for him. Something in Bear's gut told him so, but there was no time to question why as he inched through the underbrush toward his camp.

Thick fog hovered over the damp ground, shrouding Bear protectively. The air was still, the vibrations foreboding. Where was the smell of cooking food? Where were the lamenting sounds of the night birds? The return call to his welcoming signal?

A hollow ache lodged in the pit of his stomach and he fought the instinctive impulse to run. He couldn't leave; these were his people and they needed him.

The wigwams were a soft blur hiding within the heavy mists, yet he knew he was near his camp. He saw the sweat lodge, the small birch bark hut used for cleansing the body and spirit, just to the left of the path. It stood near a small run that fed into the Golden River, set apart from the main wigwams. Bear passed the structure, looking into the room with a quick glance. Nothing seemed amiss.

A cold shiver ran up his spine as he passed the stretching frame used to cure animal skins. He had helped lace the wood fibered cordage through the edges of a large deer skin a few days ago. When he left, the skin was stretched across the rack and Old Woman had just begun the long hard rubbing of the surface that would make the leather pliable and nearly white. Now the rack was empty, the cordage cut and dangling from the frame like dead vines. It was not Old Woman's hand that had taken the skin down.

Bear recalled that one of the Kwetejk warriors had carried a white bundle tied across his shoulders. It was surely Old Woman's moosehide.

He closed his eyes, trying to recall the other men in the Kwetejk band, remembering now that one carried a fishing spear, another a long bow.

No! By the Thunders! Don't let it be true.

Alarm coursed through him and he ran, unhindered now

by the thickening fog, ignoring the foot path, cutting across the stream toward the dwellings. His heart pounded in his throat, the bitter taste of bile rose in his mouth as he neared the camp.

Quiet! Caution! His instincts commanded him.

Bear knelt low in the cover of an aspen tree, quieting his breathing and sharpening his senses. Silence. The sound of his blood pounded in his temples, echoing like thunder. No movement broke the unearthly stillness and it seemed to him in those long moments of apprehension that even the river rushing past his camp had ceased to flow. He steeled his nerves then ventured into the clearing, but it was not enough to stop the pain flooding through his heart.

The small camp that once adorned the peaceful banks of the river lay empty and in ruins as if a summer gale had ventured deep within the forest, selectively destroying those things made by human hands, leaving the natural surroundings untouched. Bark had been ripped from the wigwams. The lodge poles, pushed over, lay upended in the dirt like the beached rib bones of a dead animal. The entire area had been stripped clean of goods worth taking. Broken baskets, smashed drying racks and debris were scattered throughout the clearing. A fire still smoldered in the center of the camp and half burned belongings draped the logs like refuse.

It was not the act of a tribe preparing to move, but a senseless deed of vengeance. All the signs confirmed his fears. His people were gone. There was no way to tell if they were dead or alive.

A piece of half-cooked meat floated in the heavy wood cooking pot, a layer of congealed fat skimmed the top of the water. The last remnants of a meal buzzed with feasting flies and gnats. Bear kicked the foul smelling pot and the contents slid to the ground, sending the tiny scavengers flying in a haze above it.

Bear ran to the river's edge, looking for any evidence that his people had escaped. Perhaps they had escaped.

Then he saw his canoe. Its bow was splintered into kindling. A gaping hole in the upturned bottom displayed the work of human anger. He ran his hand over the edge of the remaining wood. Memories of working shoulder to shoulder with Laughing Elk as they fashioned the canoe shattered like the remains of the boat. Gone. Beyond repair.

A feeling of dread hung in the warm air and Bear's blood slid through his veins like icy shards. The hand that had destroyed the canoe had also brought death. He thought of Old Woman and ran toward the area she used as her power place, upriver, a short distance from the camp.

Let it not be her bones that I find, he prayed as he ran toward a stand of rock that jutted out into the water. The death of anyone would be a great loss, but hers would be the hardest to accept. *Let my senses be wrong.*

Bear stopped as he neared the outcropping. He heard a choked cry, a barely audible groan, then realized it came from his throat.

A body lay slumped, face down at the base of the rock. Bear approached slowly, assessing the situation. As he neared the body, he realized that it was too large to be Old Woman's. Nevertheless, it was one of his people. He turned the lifeless body over.

It was Dancing Fox. He had died from a head wound. His skull was smashed like the fragile bark of a canoe. His eyes, still wide in death, were fogged and caked with blood, his face frozen by his fear. Fox's hands had been severed from the wrists, his tongue cut from his mouth. Fox's death was not an act of war: it was a ritual killing. A death of dishonor. Fox's spirit would dwell in turmoil forever.

Grandfather was right. Bear knew the truth of Laughing Elk's words. Dancing Fox had stolen his pipe. He had betrayed the honor of the tribe and someone, either Kwetejk or Micmac, had paid him for his lies and treachery, taking his tongue so he could not lie in the afterlife and removing his hands so he could not steal anyone else's Power.

Disgusted, Bear let Fox's body fall back, face to the ground. Burial for the traitor could wait. He turned his back on the dead Micmac leader and stepped away.

Now, more cautious of his surroundings, Bear circled the camp with a sharper eye. His mind raced to put all the visual clues in order. There were no other bodies, no other signs of death, no sign of struggle. Near his wigwam he found a few possessions cast into the underbrush: a reed mat, a broken snowshoe, Old Woman's tattered leather shawl.

He crouched to the ground and buried his face in the soft chamois, praying the well worn leather could somehow reveal the recent tragedy's secrets, but sorrow paralyzed him.

"How could I have been so selfish as to leave my people?" he cried.

There was no time to listen for Power's answer. A sudden blast of pain exploded in his body and he turned toward a sound that echoed in his ears like a thousand buzzing flies. An arrow ringed with magic markings lodged half-way through his right shoulder.

Bear reached to pull the arrow from his body, but his knees collapsed, his weight pulled him to the ground.

He struggled to pull out the silver knife tucked inside the high top of his moccasin, but his arm would not move. His fingers faltered on the cold handle. Sensation was leaving his limbs. He tried to move his head, his hands, but he was helpless. His eyes blurred. What magic had captured his body so skillfully, to make it disobey his will? Even the strongest poisons did not act so quickly. It was a great shaman indeed who had made this arrow so powerful.

Someone came toward him. Bear whispered a charm to move his lips to dispel the evil spirit approaching him, then prayed to Power. *Let me die with honor.*

The warrior hovered over him and Bear focused to look his killer in the eye. He was at the mercy of a Kwetejk warrior, his face painted black and red; A Herald of Death.

What cause did they have to destroy his camp? To kill his people? He wanted to ask, but his thoughts would not become words.

Would he be mutilated like Dancing Fox? What would the warrior take as proof that the shaman Bear World-Walker had been killed? His heart? His hands? How long would it take before his spirit could walk the earth again?

Somewhere beyond the fog clouding his mind, Bear heard the warrior speaking. His words were like distant chants hiding within the mists.

"Sparrowhawk, shamaness of the Kwetejk, sends greetings to you, Bear-World Walker, and with them your death."

The warrior placed his foot on Bear's shoulder and withdrew the arrow with a quick jerk. A sharp nerve-wrenching pain roused Bear to instant awareness.

The warrior continued his message, his words practiced, precise. "You have outlived your usefulness. You are no longer needed among the living. Sparrowhawk would have shared her power with you, but you were unwilling. Now there is no room for your Power. Sparrowhawk has learned your magic."

Bear did not understand. He had shown Sparrowhawk kindness and love. She had been a bright and eager student. Perhaps too eager. She had been too interested in the dark side of Power. Had the dark magic taken over Sparrowhawk? It happened sometimes, to shamans that misused their magic. The darkness blocked out the light and the shaman became the victim of that darkness. But why would she desire the destruction of his people? Why would she want to kill him?

"Dancing Fox will welcome you in the Ghost World." The warrior motioned toward Dancing Fox's inert body with the arrow. "He served his purpose. He told us of your absence."

Bear could feel the wild tension in the warrior's body. He was about to strike.

"Fox wanted Power." The warrior laughed. "Sparrowhawk gave it to him swiftly." He spit on the ground toward Fox. "We have no respect for traitors."

Great Power—Muin Wapskw, Bear prayed. *Do not let me die with this burden on my spirit. Do not let me die with this crime against my people unavenged.*

The warrior bent close to Bear, so close that he could smell the dry earthy scent of the war paint on his face and feel the passion of his anger. The warrior slashed through the shoulder band of the medicine pouch and pulled it roughly from Bear, then snatched the stone knife from the leather sheath hanging around Bear's neck.

It does not matter, Bear thought. *My magic will not work for him, it will fade as I die.*

The warrior raised Bear's sharp stone knife high into the air to deliver the final death blow. Bear tried to still his thoughts, closed his eyes to focus on the bright light that would lead him to the Ghost World where his spirit could rest. It would be his heart that the warrior claimed as his prize. He could no longer feel his body.

But instead of the light, he saw the image of Swan's face hovering before him. He smiled, remembering the warmth of her body lying beneath him, the soft fullness of her lips, the smell of her hair. She was safe. Hidden in his spirit cave. She would honor his wishes and return to Two Arrows with the rising sun.

Somehow I will send my spirit to guide her back to her people. The warrior can have my heart. My spirit does not need a heart to love Swan.

A low rumble shook the ground. Bear knew his earthly body had given up its fragile hold on life. He must be dead. The dull pounding in his head did not bother him. The rumble turned into a roar and Bear forced himself to open his eyes once more. The warrior disappeared into the heaviness of the fog and he knew the warrior moved swiftly through the forest, taking his prize back to Sparrowhawk.

How long will it take for me to die? Bear heard the low rumble once more and turned his eyes in its direction. His spirit helper, Muin Wapskw, sat by his side, not in his human shape this time, but in his Bear Person body. Large and white. He licked his paws like a cub.

"I knew you would come to take me to the entrance to the Ghost World and lead me to Papkutparut, the Guardian of Souls," Bear whispered. He focused on the low rumbling of his spirit helper's voice. It would guide him to the Ghostworld. But human sounds distracted him, kept him from his journey.

He heard Muin Wapskw's voice, calling him back from the edge of the pathway to death. "Brother, World-Walker. You have fought bravely. You have honored your people and regained your power. But, it is not your time to die."

He would have laughed if he could have moved his lips. *You are wrong this time, Muin Wapskw. I can see the Ghostworld before me.*

Suddenly the earth moved beneath him and he opened his eyes. Trees blurred above him and he could hear sticks and leaves crushing under him. Something or someone dragged him by his ankles, dragged him away toward death.

Chapter 33

Antoinette pulled the green cloak around her shoulders as she stepped from the cave into the foggy night. The warm fabric gave little comfort to the cold fear that besieged her. She stared into the grayness of the mists, clutching her staff for security. She sighed. When the moon rose in the sky tonight she would not see it for the mists. The comforting stars would be hidden. There was nothing bright to drive away the eerie chill of loneliness she had placed upon herself by following Bear's wishes. All she could do was wait. Wait and be patient.

After their earlier disagreement, she had vowed to obey Bear, but now a foreboding knot of anxiety tightened around her chest. She returned to the dark security of the cave.

I cannot go. I gave my word. She settled herself on a low rock with a swirl of her cloak. *I must not leave.* If she could reassure herself he was safe, then she could relax and be patient. Indecision gnawed at the edges of her mind. *He is in trouble. I can feel it.*

Antoinette reached for her knapsack. It was time to call on the Gods to share their sight. She dug through the bundles of dried herbs, stones and assorted items she'd gathered over the past few days and withdrew the silk shawl and her ceremonial belongings from the depths of her bag. She reached for her dagger, a candle and a chalice to fill with water.

To find Bear, she would need a power object on which to focus her thoughts.

Her gaze found the niche carved in the wall that held his ceremonial pipe. She hesitated, then reached for the pipe, cautioning herself about the risk of handling someone else's power objects. She had held it before with his permission. Surely he would allow her to touch it in his absence. He would understand her need to know where he was. Reassured, she took the pipe from the recess. Ignoring the light tingling of warning it emitted, she slipped his pipe and stem from the mink pouch and laid them before her on a makeshift altar made from a flat stone.

She lit the candle, then filled the chalice with water until it nearly overflowed. She set the candle to cast a glow over the surface of the water, then touching the water with her dagger, she closed her eyes and took several deep breaths. Cautiously, she placed her hands over the chalice and waited for the familiar prickle of magic to awaken in her fingers.

"Blessed Mother of all, diviner of the future. I would summon Your sight to fill my bowl."

Recalling Bear's actions at their pipe ceremony, Antoinette took the two pieces in her hands and offered them to the heavens. "Great Power, I search for your child Bear World-Walker, my—" Antoinette hesitated. What should she call Bear? He was more now than just her companion, more than her friend. Her thoughts flashed through the last few days, recalling images of the lake, Bear fashioning her clothing, his arms holding her close as they lay on the beach, his eyes, his lips. There was no use denying what the Deities already knew.

"Kji-kinap! I search for Bear-World Walker, my lover," she pronounced, joining the bowl and the stem of the pipe together.

At her words, soft waves of energy trickled along her arms and Antoinette lowered the pipe, then packed it with tobacco from the pouch. She lit the touchwood and inhaled the bittersweet smoke, then blew it over the chalice. She focused her vision, not on the surface of the still water, but deep within the cup.

With vision like an eagle, she saw a clearing shrouded in mist and a river flowing swiftly beside the remains of an empty village. Closer, she demanded, concentrating her sight to slice deeper into the smoke.

She felt the knife edge of death before she saw the body

lying face down in the dirt. Her body stiffened with panic then she realized it was not Bear's lifeless form, not his clothing, not his shape.

"May you rest easy," she whispered to comfort the dead man's spirit. She wondered who among Bear's people had met such a violent death. Clutching Bear's pipe close to her heart, she willed her vision farther into the camp.

She saw burned structures, an overturned cooking log, and scattered debris. Then she saw Bear, struggling to move, scarcely breathing. He was calling her name, not with words but with his thoughts. She saw blood seeping from his shoulder. She winced in sympathetic pain. The image disappeared and she looked out into the darkness of the cave.

Antoinette forced herself to follow through with the end of the ritual, thanked the Gods for sharing their sight and respectfully returned the pipe to its pouch and its resting place. She poured the water on the ground to return it to the earth and packed away her chalice in the soft confines of a piece of leather. She wrapped the silk scarf around her waist and, without hesitation, tucked the dagger inside the belt.

There would be danger; she had seen it. Danger and death. If her magic failed, her aim must not.

ꟹ

The fog thinned as Antoinette walked toward the encampment, following not so much the well trodden path, but the smell of the rain-dampened hearths and the loud rushing sound of the river. As she moved, she realized just how much she had learned from Bear the past few days. Her senses were alert, her body was fully at her command. Her inner vision was much clearer than it had ever been. Was it because of the new simplicity of her life, now that she no longer muddled her mind with the petty workings of kings and queens? Or was it because she now relied more on her senses now for survival?

She wondered if she would maintain these attributes. If so, then she would have the advantage if she ever saw Cardinal Visconti again.

A sound whispered through the fog and the hair on her arms and neck stood on end. Aware of the dangers lurking around her, Antoinette stepped off the path and into the shadow of a dogwood tree, pressing tightly against its trunk. She laid her forehead against the rough bark to clear her mind and still her rapidly beating heart. She took several deep breaths, calming herself.

She summoned the sight once more and looked past the mists surrounding the camp. Bear was on the ground. A thin blue light hovered close to his body, shielding him from the gray, swirling shadows of death that hovered above him, caressing his body in anticipation. He was still alive, barely.

She took a quick step forward, then stopped cold. A wave of fear assailed her. It did not come from Bear. Her vision was instantly replaced by sensations emanating from across the clearing. Fear. Anxiety. She knew these emotions came from a man, but where was he?

Turning back toward Bear, she saw his life energy begin to flow out of his body as the gray mist absorbed the protective blue energy around him. She had to act now, even if an unknown danger also threatened her. Hopefully, she could summon a mystical energy that would magnify the emotions and perhaps the man would shift his attention to her long enough for her to get Bear safely away.

Antoinette stepped into the clearing, held up her hands and silently called on the Goddess to cloak her in an ethereal shield of power. Almost at once she was surrounded by a glamour of protection, increasing her visual presence with dramatic waves of golden light and glowing color. Adrenaline pumped through her veins and she walked toward Bear, stopping as she neared his side.

He was unconscious. She could see the life energy swiftly leaving his body from the center of his stomach where a thin blue line paled with gray as it ascended upward into the mists. Without hesitation she raised her arms once more. This time she spoke in the ancient language of her people as she called down the Goddess.

"*Salve! Regína, Mater misericórdiae, Albina Magna Mater*; Hail! Queen, Mother of Mercy, Great White Goddess."

The flooding rays of light surrounded them and she lowered her arms over Bear's body. His draining life force momentarily ceased its flight. The gray cord dissolved back into the mists and the blue glow once again hovered over him.

Quickly, she swung the cloak from her shoulders and laid it on the ground and pulled Bear's body onto it. With the strength of the Goddess still coursing through her, she dragged him from the clearing and into the shrouding mists. They were well into the darkened woods before the energy left her and she crumbled to her knees beside him.

"Blessed Goddess!" she whispered as her senses resurfaced. She stroked Bear's face, feeling the warmth of his body taking hold once more. "*Mon amour*, you must live."

Bear opened his eyes at the sound of her voice. He looked past her with a vacant smile. Death was still too close.

Antoinette took the dagger from her waist, slipped the leather tunic over her head and with one swift stroke, cut a length of her linen undershirt and held it against Bear's seeping wound. The gush of blood stopped with the pressure and she wrapped another strip of linen around his chest.

Wiping sweat from her brow, she leaned back and to look at her handiwork. It would do until she could get him to safety, treat him with her medicines and make a poultice to keep the wound from festering.

She laid her leather tunic over Bear's chest, tucked the velvet cloak around him, and waited, listening for any sounds of danger. When she was sure it was safe, she dragged Bear onto the path. But where could she take him? It would be impossible for her to pull him up the hillside and back into his cave.

She saw a small wigwam concealed in the forest underbrush and she dragged Bear towards it. She had seen a similar sweat lodge in Two Arrows' camp and knew that it would provide shelter. They would be safe, at least until the sun rose.

The lodge smelled of smoke and the musty fragrance of burned herbs and leaves. Not unpleasant, but pervasive. But there was no other choice.

Once inside, Antoinette lowered the leather hide that covered the entrance. Fumbling in the darkness she found her flint and the wax candle she kept in her pocket, lit the candle and then held it to illuminate Bear's face. He looked worse than she had imagined. She lifted his eyelids and his dark eyes stared blankly back into hers—unknowing and unaware.

She slid her hand along the vein in his neck. *He cannot be dead*! She felt a pulse, then she took a deep breath of relief. His heart still beat, but his energy was barely detectable; his pulse was slow and irregular. Not a good sign. She felt his head for damage and examined his body for hidden injuries. Other that the scrapes and bruises from dragging him, he was whole. The wound was not near his heart and though she could see torn muscle and tissue when she lifted the compress, there were no other wounds. Whatever was causing his unconsciousness was more than the damage done by his assailant.

Antoinette shivered as an ill-seasoned rush of cool air crept under the heavy leather door covering. Bear needed warmth, but with the danger of being discovered, a fire was too risky.

He also needed treatment, for more than just his wound. If they were to seek a safer refuge by sunrise, he needed a tonic or stimulant to restore his consciousness. She would have to go to the cave to retrieve his warm bear skin covering and brew the medicines.

"I wish that I could see your bright smile once more, my love." She traced her finger along the hard edge of his chin. The salty taste of tears slid slowly down her cheeks, wetting the edges of her lips. "Hold on until I come back. I can't lose you now." With one last look at his face she snuffed out the candle with her fingertips. "You cannot die," she whispered as she slipped out of the sweat lodge and into the night. "I love you."

Chapter 34

Sparrowhawk looked at the medicine pouch and stone knife lying at her feet. She touched the pouch with her toe, flipping it over to feel the bulk of its contents. The lingering force of the magic within it gave her a tingle of warning. She let it lie.

Picking up the knife, she balanced the weight of the stone in her hand, then handed it to her assistant, Black Otter, who stood behind her.

They were Bear's possessions, to be sure, but it was not proof enough to show his death.

"Is this all?" she asked, glaring with reproach at the warrior who stood before her. "Did you bring his heart?"

The Kwetejk warrior swallowed his words as he looked at the woman standing before him. Any explanation he gave the shamaness would not be sufficient to suspend her wrath.

Unwilling to be captive by headband or string, an unruly mane of fiery red hair circled Sparrowhawk's face. She accentuated it with a melange of hawk feathers and dangling copper beads. Her eyes glowed with a savage inner fire. Her sharp features were enhanced by dark charcoal lines painted above her brows. She was as tall as any man in the tribe, twice as fierce with her tongue and equally ruthless with her magic. She was a woman to be feared. She *was* Power.

"I tried."

"You—tried?" She leveled her gaze into his eyes as she stepped over the medicine pouch.

The warrior took a hasty half-step back.

"You tried?" Her voice pierced the edge of anger, but her body remained outwardly calm.

"Yes." The warrior threw his shoulders back, attempting to regain his dignity. As he traveled to return to the Kwetejk camp, he thought about the bizarre magic he had witnessed in the Micmac camp. The events still bewildered him. Perhaps Sparrowhawk would understand his actions, even if he did not.

"After the raiding party left, I waited in the forest. As you predicted, the shaman came. I loosed the arrow, hitting him just above his heart. He fell to his knees as your magic took control of his body. I delivered your message to him as he lay dying in the dirt."

He held out the arrow, returning it to the hand that had fashioned its magic. Its tip was still stained red with Bear's blood.

"Did he understand you?" Sparrowhawk asked coolly. "Did he say anything?"

The warrior shook his head. "He did not speak, but I know that he heard my words. His eyes betrayed his thoughts. Your magic was fast and his body would not listen to his mind."

"Why didn't you strike then and take his heart while he still breathed?"

The warrior hesitated, then blurted out his tale. "A white bear—big and fierce, walked from the mists. It sat beside him."

Sparrowhawk's eyebrows raised as she realized Bear's spirit animal Muin Wapskw, had come to defend him. She should have known Bear would not be easy to kill. He had taught her well and she had searched long and hard for the right magic to subdue him. The nerve deadening poison she used would slowly kill his body. Without an antidote it would leave his mind awake, though delirious and undirected. If he did not die from his wound immediately, he would spend many days in agony.

"Continue," she commanded, restraining her anger at the warrior for his lack of courage.

"The bear would not let me near him. I waited, hoping the white bear would finish him off and I could somehow retrieve his heart. It grew dark. The mists began to rise like ghosts from the river." The warrior swallowed the hard lump that lodged in his throat, unsure that the shamaness would believe his next words. "Then the mists gathered and a woman appeared from within them. The white bear disappeared."

Sparrowhawk's attention focused on his last words.

"A woman? We brought all the women of Laughing Elk's

camp here to serve us." She looked with disbelief at the warrior. Dancing Fox had not mentioned a female traveling with Bear. In fact, he had told her Bear was celibate. He had not been with a woman since she had left him. It was a good time to take control of Bear's magic, when he was weak and impotent.

"Describe the woman," she commanded.

"She was pale and fair. Her skin shimmered like fine doe skin. She wore a magic cloak that flew out from her sides in great green wings."

The warrior closed his eyes as he remembered the strange apparition walking through the mist-shrouded camp. "Her hair floated free from her shoulders, like waves of dark light. When she stood over Bear's body she raised her arms and gathered a great energy from the sky."

The warrior hesitated, searching for words to describe the magic he had seen the woman call forth. "She called to Power and Power came to her, like it comes to you in your sacred circle, blazing with color and great magic."

"You speak falsely!" she retorted. She signaled Black Otter to restrain the warrior. "What woman do you suppose has powers as great as mine?"

"Wait! Sparrowhawk, let me finish. The witch woman was not one of the people. She did not speak as we do, but I know that I heard her call on Power. She said things to Power, then the magic swirled around her like great clouds of dust."

Sparrowhawk gestured with a wave of her hand and Black Otter released the warrior.

"Tell me exactly what she did? Leave nothing out ."

The warrior looked at Sparrowhawk with growing uneasiness, unsure that he could remember the motions he witnessed.

Sparrowhawk nodded, confidant that no one could possibly know the depth of her magic. Bear's detailed knowledge of medicines and poisons had been the only thing she'd needed to complete her training. With his death she would be the most powerful shaman of all. Not even Bear-World Walker, if he lived, could control the Power she intended to summon.

The warrior began his pantomime, pretending to cast out offerings, turning and twisting his body in imitation of the ritual he had witnessed. Finally, he stopped and raised his arms into the air,

"*Sal-ve*!" he shouted. The words fell like rough jewels from the warrior's mouth. "Hail!"

A cold chill raced up Sparrowhawk's spine as the ancient

magic invocation was spoken.

The words echoed inside her brain. She knew these sacred words of power. The were foreign, strange words, not unlike her own secret incantations.

"Speak no more!" she commanded. She reached for the talisman of protection that dangled from her waist, her heart racing with apprehension. She wrapped her fingers around the cool flat metal and drew strength from its angular shape.

"Tell me what happened to this woman. What happened after Power came?"

The warrior panicked, realizing with horror that he should never have told her about the witch. He should have swallowed his fear and tracked her into the forest. It would not have been as difficult as standing before Sparrowhawk. But it was too late to look back and he could not afford to let Sparrowhawk see his weakness.

"Power circled around the witch. She took off her wings and laid them on the ground. She lifted Bear's body onto them, wrapped them around him and pulled him deep into the mists. It was like the great mouth of a whale swallowed them. I—I could not find them."

Sparrowhawk turned away, afraid her face would reveal her agitation. She stared into the crackling fire. His story was too unbelievable to be false, too alarming to be true. There was no Elder to explain how another shamaness could call Power to do her bidding so precisely.

Her thoughts turned back to the warrior. He would have to be killed. He knew too much. "Place him under guard," she said to Black Otter. "Let him speak to no one."

Bear's cache of herbs and medicinals was extensive. Many were similar to those Antoinette had used in Brittany, but there were a few she had never seen, and all too many that might be deadly or dangerous if used unwisely.

She hoped Bear, like most healers, had a system for sorting his curatives. Antoinette arranged hers by their use. She could close her eyes and visualize the tiny rows of dried herbs lining the rafters and shelves of her stillroom. Hops, cloves, pennyroyal for toothaches; horehound, ginger, sassafras for sore throat; chamomile, catnip and peppermint for nerves. Their uses often overlapped, but that was the way she had arranged them since she began her vocation as a healer.

Antoinette looked over Bear's pharmacopoeia and tried to

envision how he would arrange his scullery. By color? By use? By their strength or by their names? She ran her eyes over the tangle of branches, leaves and bark piled in one corner of the cave. Beech, oak, willow, sumac; all medicines from trees. Plantain, sweetflag, fleur-de-lis, cattail, all dried and neatly arranged on a birch bark platter. All these plants were found near the wetlands. Dried garlic, fieldcress, and wild onions nestled side by side in a carved wooden bowl; these were used for seasonings. A pattern was beginning to develop.

Bunches of dried grasses and vines hung from animal bones that had been driven like nails into the cave wall. Dried eels and skins stuffed with fat hung alongside dried strips of sinew and leather. A wide variety of berries lay separated on small flat pieces of leather, ready to be stored. A wooden container filled with acorns sat beside a woven reed basket of hazelnuts. It was orderly, but bewildering.

Picking up a piece of partially dried and thinly sliced root, she held it to her nose. It smelled like dragon's root, but she couldn't be certain. She touched it with the end of her tongue and a sharp, biting sensation enveloped her mouth. Instinctively, she spit out the bitter saliva. Yes, she determined. Bear had an order to his keeping room, but it was known only to him. She had best leave the unfamiliar plants alone.

She set to work, rekindling the small fire to burn in the hearth pit. With difficulty, she located a wooden cooking pot stashed among the various furs and rushes in the back of the cave. Placing several small rocks into the fire to boil the water, she began her search for the herbs she required for her potions.

The yarrow was easy to find, with its distinctive flat topped white flowers and rough angular stem. It hung upside down on a long twist of rope, beside other flowering herbs. She added barberry and hyssop from her medicine pouch to cook with the yarrow, knowing that blending these herbs would make a strong stimulant to strengthen Bear's blood.

Externally, she would need to cleanse Bear's wound and make a styptic to stop the bleeding. Nettle, heal all, or sweet dock would be best. She would purge his injury with a solution of pounded alum root and water, then dress it with a softened nettle leaf poultice.

Antoinette watched her potion as it strained through a scrap of her linen tunic and into a birchbark bowl. Drop by drop she was painfully aware of the precious time she spent away from Bear's side. What would she do if she returned and found him dead? Where would she go? How would she live without him?

She briefly closed her eyes as a moment of weariness and uncertainty overcame her. "Help me Brighid," she prayed. "Help me to save him."

Antoinette awakened to Bear's plaintive moans and knew they were cries of inner torment. Throughout the night, she had helped him sip the stimulant and she prayed to the Goddess to keep him alive long enough for them to get to safety. Antoinette hoped he would be strong enough by daylight to walk and lucid enough to understand their precarious situation.

When Bear finally settled into a light fevered sleep, Antoinette left him to guard the entrance of the lodge. The fog had cleared. The sky, lit by the small crescent of a waning moon, was now rich with stars, resplendent in a darkened night. The Pleiades had progressed to the west. In a few hours it would be dawn.

A cool wind raised tiny goosebumps on her arms and she wished even harder that she had a fire to keep Bear warm. Without hesitation, Antoinette knew what had to be done. There was no more she could physically do for him and she could not bear to think that he might actually die.

Standing, she raised her hands to the sky in supplication.

"Great Mother protect him," she sighed. "You have given me so much. You have allowed me to feel your presence in my life and you have given me someone to love who also loves me. Bear is a good man. Please show him your mercy, your compassion. Spare his life. Speak to his God, speak to Great Power and sue for His favor. Surely your persuasion would do better than mine. I ask for nothing else. Nothing more for myself. I will do your bidding without question."

A knot of apprehension swelled in her throat as she said the final words. They would seal her fate, but it was the most precious sacrifice she could offer to the Goddess. "I will no longer ask to return home. I will not ask to share your power. I will only ask for your blessings."

At her words a star fell from the sky, burning brightly as it descended from the heavens. She knew that the Goddess had accepted her promise.

ᘛ

Bear made it though the darkest part of the night. But Antoinette was cautious as she continued her vigil. Her dagger was a constant companion at her waist, a reminder of the dangers of his unfamiliar world and a symbol of the inner strength she must find. Bear's knife lay by her side. She was prepared to face Bear's enemy. If he came back and tried to kill Bear, she would not give up without a fight.

In the pre-dawn hours, the forest began to awaken. A small fox passed by the lodge, waking Antoinette from a light sleep. It looked at her with curious eyes and instinctively she clutched her dagger.

Not today, my friend. Bear-World Walker will live. You will hear his name on the lips of your grandchildren. Go! She waved her arms and the fox slipped into the underbrush with a *swoosh* of its russet tail.

Antoinette stretched out her tired limbs. Hesitating before she went back into the lodge, she lifted her hands, feeling the warmth around her, breathing in the air to taste the winds. No disruptive forces surfaced in her senses, except for Bear's uneasiness. She whispered a brief thanks to the Goddess for the night's protection and returned to Bear's side.

As the sun crept above the horizon, Bear began to respond to her touch. With Antoinette's help, he sat up, then stood. His healthy glow was paled by the poisons running rampant through his body and his usual strength had disappeared. His eyes were glazed with fever and his body was hot to the touch.

Her heart ached to see his agony. She knew, as she looked into his eyes, that she loved him with all her heart. She could never willingly leave him.

As they reached the security and comfort of his cave, Bear turned to her. "Merci," he whispered. Then his legs buckled and he slipped down onto a cushion of soft fragrant spruce branches covered with a leather hide. "*Merci,* Wapi'skw."

Antoinette bent down and brushed tousled hair from his face. He looked at her with wide, clear eyes. It was a look of love and gratitude. A look that needed no words for her to know his meaning. He loved her.

She leaned over and gently kissed him. He tasted of bitter tonic, smelled of fever. He moved to return her embrace, but his arms would not support his weight and he sank back onto the pallet. His eyes fluttered once, then closed as the sickness overcame him again.

It was as though an inner fire burned in his body, stealing his warmth, stealing his life. His body shook and shuddered in a macabre dance.

Antoinette turned away in anguish. She had watched him too many times throughout the night as the tonics battled the poisons in his body. She had held him close until the tremors passed and there had been nothing she could do. She knew the poisons must run their course and leave his body. Time, care and patience were the only antidotes.

Antoinette rushed to the fire and blew on the tiny embers until they blazed against the tinder she held. "Blessed Brighid," she prayed. "Send your sacred fire to quickly burn away his sickness." She could ask no more.

Looking at the charred stick in her hand, she walked toward the cave wall above Bear's bed. Slowly, she drew the outline of a dragon across the broad expanse of rock. Curling flames leapt from its mouth and its expansive wings spread in an arc of flight, protecting Bear with a mystical canopy. She stepped back to look at her artwork. Sacred drawings were common practice and well-known to the Sisterhood. They should work just as well here as in the caves of Brittany and France.

She turned from her drawing and walked out of the cave and into the light of a bright day. She needed fresh burdock leaves to dress Bear's wound and she should check the traps she'd left near the stream. But she could not leave him. Not yet.

Chapter 35

Antoinette sat with Bear throughout the morning, watching for signs that his strength was returning. Around mid day his fever broke and he had fallen into a restless sleep. Now he was sleeping soundly and she felt confident that she could leave his side.

Covering her tracks and watching for danger, Antoinette made her way down the hillside and to the edge of a stream. As she took a drink of the clear sweet water, she began to realize why Bear's people had chosen this quiet valley for their home. It was secure from summer squalls and nestled between two small mountain ridges, yet it was a simple walk to a river and only a few hour's walk to the ocean. The glen was abundant with plants, herbs and wildlife. Bird songs drifted sweetly on the soft, fresh evening breeze. It was a serene and idyllic surrounding.

Bear had explained to her that his people lived in bark covered wigwams and did not built their homes to last more than one or two seasons. When they traveled, they moved on foot or by canoe. There were no horses, no carriages. Now she knew that Two Arrows' village had been typical of the native people's lifestyle. There were no stone buildings, no monumental cathedrals to either gods or kings, nor walls for protection or bridges to cross.

The still pool of water reflected her body. It was tanned and firm, stronger, thinner than ever before. It seemed as though everything about her had changed. Even her strong desire to return home.

She wondered how Anne was dealing with the changes in her life. Dealing with King Charles and his entourage would definitely be a formidable task, but Anne's life would never be as challenging as living in Bear's land.

Lost in her thoughts, Antoinette bent to wash her face. She heard the sound of a twig snap and the high pitched whoop of a war cry. Jumping to her feet, she whirled around.

Two fiercely painted warriors stood before her, their muscles strained against their painted skin. Feral eyes glared at her. She raised her staff.

"Stop!" she commanded.

A warrior moved. She swung her staff in defense. The warrior grabbed it from her then threw it aside.

Before she could move, a dark fist met her jaw and the ground rose up to meet her.

Antoinette regained consciousness and tried to move, but she was tied securely. Strips of braided leather dug into the flesh of her wrists and bound her arms behind her. Her limbs were numb, her back ached and her jaw throbbed. Lying on her side in the darkness she could neither see nor cry for help, for her mouth was gagged with a piece of deer skin tied behind her head. Leather ropes encircled her ankles and a loop connected them to her wrists. The ropes tightened every time she tried to move.

Gathering her senses, she rolled onto her stomach and relaxed her muscles on the hard, packed ground.

She recalled the men that had trapped her and her heart beat with a renewed panic. Her assailants had worn their hair pulled back from their faces. They were tall, muscular and fast. They were warriors, clad in loincloths and moccasins with their shoulders and faces painted red and black, but they were not Bear's people. She knew it in her heart. The gentle people she had met in Two Arrows' camp could never be so vicious without warrant, they would never have treated a woman with such disrespect.

Were they the warriors Bear had seen on the ridge the day before? Why had she not felt their presence in the woods? The men knew the magic of disguise, for neither the birds nor the animals had revealed their presence.

She recalled her first encounter with Bear, in the glade above the Lake of the Swans. He had blended with the underbrush, so well that even Finder had not seen him. For all her magic and intuition she had been easy prey.

Had she always been so trusting? No, she answered herself. Not in many, many years.

She stifled a wave of nausea, remembering the first time she had been so naive. She had been six or seven years old, hardly worth the trouble to notice. But her brother, Gaston, had noticed her. He had tricked her into following him into on of the high towers in Chateau Rennes, then he locked her in a room and told their mother that she had gone to bed.

When the servants found her the next day Antoinette had soiled her clothing and her dignity had been destroyed. Gaston was reprimanded and forgiven, but his cruelty toward her continued until he finally left home.

Antoinette pushed her brother's image from her mind. He was no longer her concern. Yet she wondered if her childhood experiences had not, in reality, brought about her current opinion of men. She liked wielding her woman's power and she had no tolerance for egotistic, overbearing men.

Indeed, she had resisted them all her life. She had been able to control them, even Cardinal Visconti. When he had pushed her, she did not back down, she had resisted and called his bluff. Lawrence Bernard had caught her off her guard. She had not expected his violence toward her. But neither men were her problems now. They could not reach her here. Visconti could not save her for his own fires of redemption. Someone else now held her life in their hands.

As the ache in her shoulders faded and her eyes adjusted to the dim light, she began to recognize her surroundings. From the smell of smoke and herbs, she knew she was being held in the old sweat lodge near the stream. She could hear low voices murmuring outside, the crackle of a fire and a faint rhythmic clicking of stones hitting wood.

Click—pause, pause. Click—pause, pause.

It was as if someone beat out the seconds of her life, slowly ticking them away. Like a slow dance macabre.

Death. Soon to find me. Death. Soon to come.

Her mind turned to thoughts of Bear, weak, alone and dying. Perhaps dead already and without her to ease him over to his Ghost World, his land of the spirits.

She had not meant to be gone more than a few minutes. Now she might never see him again. What if he somehow roused from his sickness? He would not know where she was, he would worry; and if he was strong enough, he would try to find her.

Oh Goddess! she thought in panic. Don't let him come. Don't let him try.

Her despair soon turned to tears. The warm wetness ran from her eyes and slid across the bridge of her nose to puddle near her cheek.

Crying is forbidden. She heard Ursule's reprimanding voice in her mind. *Crying is for babies. Crying makes you weak and vulnerable. Don't be like your mother. Crying over things you should not have done, things you can't bear to remember. Won't help anything. Won't make the wrongs right. Act, child. Don't cower. Don't be afraid.*

What an odd thing to remember, she thought. The last time she had been censured for crying she was surely no more than ten years old. Was it Ursule's constant reprimand, magnified by a child's fear of failure, that caused her to push herself so hard?

Antoinette laughed at the irony. It was a bit late to realize her life had been directed by fear and arrogance. No matter. It would all be over soon enough.

Her head began to pound again and her jaw throbbed as the feeling slowly returned to her face. She turned her head, placing it against the cool comfort of the tear-dampened ground. The same ground on which Bear had lain so close to death only a few hours before.

"J'taime, mon coeur," she whispered, hoping her words would carry past the barriers of distance.

She lay quietly now, having put the ghosts of the past behind her, listening to the clicking of the stones until her heart began to beat with the syncopated rhythm.

Click, pause, pause. Click, pause, pause.

The men laughed and talked and Antoinette tried to separate their voices, wondering if there were more than the two at the stream. She might have a chance of escape with one or two men guarding her, but more would be nearly impossible. If they were men like Bear, they would be swift hunters and expert trackers. Why would these men want to capture her? Why didn't they just kill her?

The clicking stopped and her heart froze. She searched for the familiar shape of her dagger. The metal pressed against her stomach, sheathed in its soft leather pouch and hidden within the folds of the sash around her waist. If she could somehow free her hands and get to her dagger, then she could protect herself when they came for her.

But could she use it to kill? Could she act against her healer's oath, without hesitation, without fear?

Footfalls approached and she rolled back to her side, feigning unconsciousness, desperately trying to slow her heartbeat. From underneath her dark lashes she saw a shape block out the firelight. The scent of sweat, smoke and moldy leather filled the room.

Repressing a cough, she remained still, commanding her breath to be slow and even. Stall for time, she thought. Need time to think.

A hand brushed the hair from her face then wandered down her bare arms to test the bonds behind her back. The fingers were rough and callused and she begged her body not to betray her with a shiver of disgust.

Don't touch me.

As though the warrior heard her unspoken command, he abruptly withdrew his hand, rose slowly and left the lodge.

I touched his mind. He will be easy to control.

The men began to talk and the slow clicking began again.

Antoinette let out a long held-in breath. *I must waste no more time.* She tested the strength of her restrictive bonds. There was perhaps four or five inches of rope stretching between her wrists and her ankles, but lying on her side, she still could not move.

Summoning her strength, she tensed her body and swung her legs upward until she rolled once again onto her stomach. Inching her way over the hard ground, she struggled against the tightening ropes, until she lay in the long, dark shadows cast by the men around the fire. She took several deep breaths and lifted her head. There were two men, sitting with their sides to the lodge, a bright fire glowing full behind them. A large wooden bowl balanced between them and Antoinette watched as one man tossed the bowl's contents up into the air. The objects landed in the bowl with the now familiar click, pause, pause. Click! Pause, pause.

The warrior passed his hand from side to side over the shallow bowl as if waving away an evil spirit. He made a disappointed grunt then handed the bowl to his companion. After several shifts of the bowl between the men, Antoinette realized that they were playing a game. A game that might give her the valuable time she needed.

Lying on her stomach, she could just touch the ends of her feet. But she knew the strength of the leather rope. Even if she could reach the knots, she would never be able to untie them. They would have to be cut. Cut with her dagger.

Slowly, she rolled over and looked around the dark lodge. If there were some way to loosen her sash, some way to free the dagger from her belt she could escape. As if beckoned by her thoughts, the fire flared to light the shape of a narrow pole that ran along the inside of the lodge. It had sprung loose from the bark covering and had not yet been repaired. She had used the pole to hang up pieces of clean linen as she dressed Bear's wounds, never thinking it might later help to save her.

She began to visualize the possibility of using the sharp point of the pole to tear her sash. Perhaps she could lean against the rough point and free the knife. It was risky, but worth a try.

Rocking her shoulders and hips back and forth, she inched toward the far wall. She felt as though she had been stuffed into a leather bag and made to swim without using her arms or legs. She rolled onto her side and attempted to raise to her knees, but the ropes pulled her tightly downward. It was simply impossible to flex her muscles far enough to obey her will.

She tried again, but the awkward momentum caught her off balance. She fell backward, letting out a gasp as her side hit the hard ground.

The clicking stopped. So did her heart.

Not yet. Not yet.

Catching her breath, she forced her body up again, then fell forward as her unbalanced weight threw her haphazardly toward the wall and she landed on her shoulder. She held her breath as she listened for the warriors, hoping they had not heard her movement. The game continued.

The pole was still inches away. She bit her lip against the pain and rose to her knees, edging toward the pole. By the Goddess! It was going to work!

The fabric tore as she rubbed against the rough limb and the dagger fell to the ground at her knees. Unable to retrieve it from its sheath, she rolled back to her side and then edged her way to the wall until the dagger lay within her grasp. Methodically Antoinette used her fingers to work the dagger from its leather pouch then held the blade's sharp edge to the leather at her wrists. Just as the leather began to yield she heard a shuffling movement outside. A flash of light forced its way into the darkness and she froze like a rabbit in shock. The dagger was hidden in the shadows beneath her. She was motionless.

"I've won you." The warrior shoved the flickering torch into the ground beside her head. It was the man who had struck her unconscious. "I've won you for the night."

"*Wait!*" Her green eyes raked his face like sharp talons and he chuckled low in his throat.

"Sparrowhawk warned me of your magic, but I'm not afraid."

Antoinette could not understand his words. He ran the back of his hand along the side of her face and down the length of her long slender neck. Picking up the string of shells lying across her breast, he turned them to sparkle in the firelight.

"A work of fine craftsmanship," he remarked, lifting them over her head and hanging them around his neck.

Antoinette glanced at the delicate shells against the dark war paint, then forced herself to recapture his gaze. *Unbind my ankles! Unbind my legs!*

The warrior ran his finger across the leather covering her mouth. "I wish I had the courage to free your mouth. I'm sure your voice is sweet and warm. But—that is the only thing that the shamaness commanded of us. To keep you silent."

Release my legs!

His hands ran down the length of her leather-clad torso, touching her with a rough passion that sent her mind into a swift rage. *By the Gods, loosen my legs!*

Suddenly, the warrior withdrew his sharp bone knife from the sheath at his waist and looked at her with a fierce, savage desire. "I want to feel your legs wrap around me as I claim my prize."

Without looking, the warrior reached behind her and cut the leather strip that bound her wrists to her ankles. Slowly she straightened out her legs, keeping her arms behind her. He sliced the leathers on her ankles until the bindings fell free. The warrior stood and removed his loincloth. There was no mistake about his intentions. He meant to claim his victory without delay.

Antoinette stayed the dagger in her hand, forcing herself not to panic. *Wait,* her inner voice commanded. *You have one chance.*

The warrior pushed her legs open and knelt between them, anxious and ready. "I have heard that once you mate with a witch, you will be as powerful as she is." He shoved her leather tunic up and over her hips, running his fingers along the soft line of her thigh.

Her body trembled with disgust. Still your mind, she told herself. *Don't react. Be ready.*

"I want your power." He leaned forward, his face inches from hers. "Give me your magic."

The hard bones of his rib cage jarred her arm as she struck upward with a force she did not recognize as her own. Flesh ripped and tore. The dagger made its way to the warrior's heart. His full weight fell forward onto her. He was stunned and gasping for breath. Antoinette shoved the dagger harder, until the hilt could go no further.

Hot blood gushed over her hand as the life force fled from the warrior. Ignoring the bile rising in her throat, she shoved him aside.

Firelight grazed his angular face, casting a gruesome shadow across his eyes. She watched in shock as the man writhed in a silent dance of death.

Antoinette sprang to her feet and looked at the dagger, bloodied and silver, clutched in her hand, flickering its triumph in the dying firelight. A knot swelled in her chest. She had willfully taken the life of another human, broken her oath to the Goddess and dishonored her healer's pledge. Regardless of the man's savagery, he was dead and his death could not be condoned.

She threw the dagger down in disgust, it was a useless instrument now. No longer sacred. She could not touch it again. She pulled the gag from her mouth and turned to run from the lodge then stopped, remembering the other warrior. Her task was not finished yet. She must escape. But she knew that she could not kill the other man. She would not take another life, no matter what the cost.

The torch flickered once then extinguished, and Antoinette stood in the darkness, listening to the blood pounding in her temples. She looked at the dark shape of the dead warrior. It was only a matter of time before his friend questioned his absence. She could not stay in the sweat lodge another moment. She would have to run.

Peering out the entrance, she saw the second warrior standing away from the fire, urinating into the stream. His back faced the lodge. Taking advantage of the opportunity, Antoinette dashed from the lodge. The warrior turned at the sound and stared at her fleeing shape. He secured his loincloth, grabbed his war club and ran toward the lodge. Realizing that his captive was more important than the well being of his companion, he began his pursuit.

Antoinette had learned much from following Bear and made her way swiftly through the darkness, slowing only after she reached cover. She urged her mind to mingle with the night creatures, then she picked up a clump of earth and rubbed the blackness over her body, disguising whatever smell of sweat or death lingered around her. She yearned for the contents of her backpack, but they sat by the doorway of Bear's cave.

Where would she go? she wondered. If she made her way back to Bear's cave, the warrior would follow her. If she went toward Two Arrows' camp, she could bring help for Bear.

Her gaze focused past the tall treetops as she tried to find the North Star to set her route for the coastline. Barring recapture, she would make it to the shore by mid-morning. When she reached it she would go westward to Two Arrows' camp.

The leaves rustled. She stayed her movement, willing herself to become part of the forest. Her eyes adjusted to the darkness and she saw the warrior standing not an arms' length away. Her heart froze as his eyes swept the vacant space above her head, but he quickly turned and continued his search. She waited for what seemed like a lifetime, watching the man's shape fade into the night. Slowly she rose from her camouflage. Antoinette swallowed the despair in her heart and drew in a deep breath. Her only chance lay at the shoreline and it was time to go.

Chapter 36

Mist. Fog. Swirling clouds of gray changed to white, flared to crimson, faded to nothing. Walking—running.

"I can make it! I can see it!" Bear's spirit body pushed forward through the heavy mists of the Ghost World. He ran toward the spiraling cone of energy surging before him. Its center, illuminated by transparent colored lights, pulsed with his heartbeat, opening and closing like an underwater flower. At first he was alone, then Dancing Fox ran beside him.

Bear looked over his shoulder and smiled. "This is my race, Brother," he said nonchalantly, pulling ahead of his companion with a burst of speed.

Dancing Fox laughed and fell behind. With a wave of his arms and an unspoken command, Fox shifted his shape to that of his spirit helper, Crow. Crow flapped his wings, growing larger with every stroke, multiplying his body to resemble the Thunders, the Great Power Birds that rule the sky. A sharp gust from their wings threw Bear off balance for a moment, then he lifted his legs and let their wind push him onward.

Bear threw back his head in a triumphant peal of laughter. "I know it is you, Dancing Fox. You cannot fool me with your disguise. Don't you know that the Thunders protect me?" Bear spread his arms like wings and rushed forward. "You will not leave the Ghost World holding onto *my* moccasins."

Dancing Fox returned to his human shape and faded into the mists. Bear's feet hit the ground and he ran once more, timing his footfalls and his breath with the slow pulse of the light, counting the heartbeats between the flares until the right moment. Without thought, he leapt into the light. His body floated, drifted on a sea of emptiness, an emptiness that went forever.

Without warning his body became heavy and he fell, feet first, as though a giant hand pulled him. Struggling through the mists, he grappled for handholds on vacant air. Then his feet touched wet sandy ground. A dark red sea rushed furiously beneath his feet and immense waves licked at his moccasins like a dog at her pups.

"Papkutparut," Bear called. "Guardian of the Ghost World, why have you brought me to the edge of the waters of death?" Bear looked for his abductor, but all around him was red sea and red sky. The waves lapped higher, teasing his legs with a warm stain of crimson, murky and full of mystery. He opened his mouth to speak but was silenced by a bolt of lightning that sent the sea steaming in its wake. He was sure that the Thunders were nearby, protecting him with their power.

Bear turned to walk to the shoreline, then stopped in mid stride. It was gone. A rising tide surrounded him, thickening into a mire of red seaweed at his waist. He moved, struggling through the congealing ooze as it rose ever higher, reaching his neck, then his chin. He looked at the darkening clouds above him and prayed to his power animals to protect him even as the thick mud covered his head. He was trapped in hard packed clay ready to be baked by the heat of the rising sun.

"Guardian! Why do you bind my spirit with the earth?" Bear cried aloud, shouting to the heavens. There was no answer. He tried to move, testing his fingers; they were stiff and unresponsive. He wiggled them again and felt the dried mud begin to crumble. He moved his arms, then his legs, and like a chick bursting its shell, he broke free with an explosion of red sparks and flashes of lightning.

A red powder covered Bear from head to toe and he shook himself, sending clouds of dust floating into the air. Bear looked at the red ocher around his feet and remembered the painted shoulders of the Kwetejk warriors. A sudden sense of foreboding filled his senses.

"Swan!" His voice was frantic, her name catching in his throat as he moved. He must get to Swan. She was in danger.

Bear turned to run. A wall of fire suddenly blazed before him, singeing his hair. He jumped back. A wall of rock blocked his path. Instinctively, he raised his arms to shield his eyes from the searing heat. With a sudden flash he found himself pinned to the wall by bands of shifting light encircling his wrists and ankles. Tiny blue balls of fire danced painfully across his body, weaving a fine net of threads around him, yet they did not burn him.

"Keeper of the Spirits," he called. "Reveal yourself or give me death so I may get on with my mission. I tire of your game."

A deep voice echoed around him, "Muin, Bear World-Walker, I am saddened that you have lost your sense of humor. There was a time when you would not give up so easily."

"There is now much more at stake, Papkutparut. You know that my people are in danger. Why distract me from my path?"

"Because you have become blind to the truth. You must open your eyes."

Bear struggled against his luminous chains as he spoke.

"What do you mean?"

"You are seeing with your heart, Muin. Not with your eyes or your senses. You ignore the answer that sits before you."

Bear did not respond, but focused on the taunting blue flames, sending thoughts of ice and rain to douse their tiny fires.

The fire around his feet leapt and blazed like an inferno and Papkutparut's voice boomed in his ears. "Listen, World Walker! The woman you call Swan, has the knowledge to help your people. "

"Papkutparut, it is not for me to question, but Wapi'skw? You call her a woman. You are mistaken. She is from the World Above the Sky."

The Guardian laughed and the wind whipped Bear's hair off his shoulders, stinging his face like sharp spruce needles. "You are a man, Muin. A foolish man who sees only goodness in women. You stand at the entrance to the Ghost World ready to die for your folly."

Bear thought of Sparrowhawk and the magic arrow. The black faced warrior's words flew back to his mind: 'You have outlived your usefulness...no room for your Power... Sparrowhawk has your magic.'

Images of Swan and the sound of her voice touched his mind with the warm kiss of the wind. "But Swan has been good to me," he pleaded. "She loves me. She loves the People."

Papkutparut's voice silenced him and quenched the heat of the crackling flames. "Her people will destroy your way of life. This you must know."

"Yes," Bear hung his head, remembering Laughing Elk's words. "So I have been warned. But I know what great magic she can share with my people. I have seen the difference in her power. It comes from within her and shines from her heart like a great star."

"Ah! You are in love, World-Walker, and it has blinded you to the truth. She is a woman, a woman of flesh and blood. A woman only, not Wapi'skw, not a Swan Woman."

Bear turned away from the faceless voice, wishing he could hold his hands to cover his ears and shut out the truth of the Guardian's words. Swan had done nothing that his magic could not match. She had not called upon Great Power to do her bidding. She had behaved like a woman, with a woman's hopes and a woman's needs. But she was a special woman who shared his love.

"Why do you tell me these things? Why do you not let me die with Swan's memory warming my heart?"

"Because, Muin, you must look with clear eyes to see the way for the People. Many have already fallen. You are their hope for awakening."

"Me?"

"Yes, Muin. You are among the last of your People who have the courage to accept the changes happening within the Worlds. You must show the People that they can live in peace as One People, that they must face the coming changes together."

Bear did not want to delay while Swan and his family were in immediate danger. Beyond his ability to save the People, he knew that he had something that Papkutparut wanted and offering it to win his hasty freedom was worth a try.

"Guardian," he said with respect. "If you set me free now, if you grant me leave to find Swan, when it comes time to help the People, I will accept your guidance without question. And when next you call me to the Ghost World, I will gladly accept your invitation.

"E'e! Yes, World-Walker." Papkutparut assumed the shape of a man, two heads taller than Bear and half again as broad. He stood beside Bear, placing his hand on Bear's shoulder in kinship. "That is a bargain well made."

The blue flames released him and the Guardian's cold, gentle hand turned him to face the foggy ocean.

"There are other things you must know before you leave." Papkutparut pointed to the horizon. "You must look beyond the obvious, you must look past the mists to see the truth."

Bear widened his eyes and looked at the water, now calm beneath his feet. His gaze followed a strand of foam up and out to the edge of the earth.

"You must look past the mists to see the truth. Look into the unknown without fear."

Bear strained to look at the dark clouds and, as if by his will alone, they parted. A large island loomed before him, floating towards the shore on a murky line of tide. Tall trees with white leaves fluttered in the wind. Bears of all shapes and shades, from brown to white, climbed to sit atop the swaying boughs and lined the shores of the island like puffins at roost.

He turned to ask Papkutparut the meaning of the vision, but the Guardian was gone. Instead, Swan stood beside him, glowing in her white tunic. He reached to touch her. "Swan," he whispered, forgetting the mysterious island as he walked toward her image. "Have you come for me?"

He slid into her arms, but at her touch his eyes opened in panic. Instead of the warmth of her flesh, Bear felt the cold shards of a winter storm. His breathing quickened as his consciousness snapped back into his earthly body. He began to lift himself from his sick bed, then fell back with a thud. A stab of pain screamed from his shoulder. He closed his eyes. Nauseated and confused, he lay motionless while the pain subsided and his heart found a slower rhythm. Then he opened his eyes. Beams of light filtered in through the cave entrance and Bear knew instantly where he was.

"By the Thunders! I'm back among the living." His voice, only a whisper, echoed off the stone walls like ripples on still water. "Swan?"

He tried to move again, this time prepared for the pain in his shoulder. He gritted his teeth and succeeded in lifting his weight to an unsteady sitting position. The room tilted and he closed his eyes. He felt stiff and useless, like a deerskin that had been tanned and hung out to dry too long in the sun.

When the room ceased to spin, he opened his eyes. He looked around the darkness, taking a quick inventory of his surroundings. His belongings were carefully laid out; his clothes, his moccasins and his weapons. The green velvet robe lay haphazardly at his feet, thrown off during his fever. Now he wished he could pull it up to cover his shivering body. *Where is Swan?*

Vague memories of her flashed through his mind. *Where is she? Probably just outside. But what if she left me for dead?* He couldn't blame her if she had.

He shivered as a chilled breeze whispered into the cave. Swan had been gone for some time or there would be a warm fire blazing in the hearth instead of cold ashes.

Bear stared at the dark roof the cave, trying to still the ache in his shoulder and to quiet the myriad images that flashed through his mind; the times he had held Swan close to him, the sweet memory of discovering their love on the banks of the pond, teaching her the ways of the People. Was Papkutparut right? Could Swan be a woman?

Spirit or woman, I love her and she would not leave me. She must be in trouble. She would not leave me cold and alone if she thought I had any chance of living. I must find her.

His thoughts jumped to Dancing Fox's mutilated body and he winced at the possibility that Swan and his adopted family shared the same fate. He remembered hearing Swan's voice in the Ghost World, but he had not seen her Spirit or the Spirit of Old Woman.

A smile broke across his face. Old Woman would surely have come to greet him if she had been there. She would have teased Papkutparut until he let him go free. Old Woman was determined and cunning, and Bear knew in his heart that she was alive and walking the Earth World with Swan. He must find her as well, to help him interpret the rest of his vision.

Bear lifted himself to his knees. This time the cave did not spin. He reached for the water skin near his side and drank. It tasted lifeless and flat and he wondered how long had he been fevered. The inside of his stomach seemed to touch his ribs, and he knew that he had not eaten anything in days.

Bracing himself against the wall, he rose to his feet. He focused on the cold hearth and staggered toward it to retrieve his flint and stone from the storage ledge.

He thought of his medicine pouch and wished for the contents, the rare medicinals and magic amulets it contained, but it was gone. Gone with the warrior who had left him for dead.

As he lit the dry punk, he remembered Muin Wapskw and held the small flame up in salute. "I know that you helped me, Brother. Thank you for my life."

Bear touched the wood and the small flame consumed the dry tinder. Slowly warmth crept through his body, reviving his senses and clearing the fog from his mind. He sat beside the small fire, watching the crevices in the dark and ominous cave walls turn soft and flowing.

His eyes adjusted to the light and his gaze immediately focused on the charcoal drawing above his bed. The dragon's wings undulated with the flickering firelight and he knew that only Swan's hand could have drawn such a magnificent creature, a flaming Thunder Brother to guard him on his Spirit Journey. It was Swan's work, for she was the only person besides Laughing Elk who had visited his cave. He closed his eyes as he thought of her drawing the protective totem. He would tell her that the Thunder Brothers always fly together—there would be two images, not one. Perhaps she would draw another one for him.

The small rocks heated quickly and Bear made a strong broth, soaking dried strips of meat in the hot water. It would renew his strength, however it would be several hours before he would have the stamina to venture outside the cave and begin his search for Swan.

An undisturbed sleep overcame him and he woke with a cleared mind, but a restless spirit. He tested his strength, then paced the ground near the dying fire before walking to the cave entrance.

He pushed back the green camouflage and stood in the

doorway, his body a golden bronze against the dark night. A faint sliver of the moon hovered in the dawning sky and Bear knew from its shape he had been sick for one, or perhaps two, days. A stray beam from the firelight fell at his feet and his eyes locked on Swan's knapsack lying near the doorway. His hopes for her return dissolved. She would not have left for long without taking her knapsack.

He looked at the pale crescent moon suspended in the dark sky and the bright shining star cradled in its upturned arms and made a silent promise.

"Swan," he whispered. "I'm not going to lose you now."

Chapter 37

Sleep!

Sometime she would have to stop running and sleep. Morning was approaching and the sunlight was certain to betray her tracks. Antoinette's stomach rumbled and she realized that the few berries and nuts she had eaten over the past day and night would not sustain her much longer. Reflexes slipping, she stumbled several times as weariness descended. She needed to rest, but she dared not stop. Surely the warrior would come after her to avenge the death of his partner. The image of the dead warrior towering above her and the feel of his blood sliding down her hands caused her to shudder with a renewed surge of guilt. The face of the warrior would never leave her mind and his spirit would follow her into the next life. It was not an easy future to look forward to.

She stopped in the dark shadow of a tall spruce tree and leaned against it for support. Checking the stars to regain her bearings, she found the familiar starry tail of Scorpius in the south and turned toward the eastern horizon. It would not be long before the sun peeked over the edge of the earth and she would once again be the object of pursuit. She closed her eyes for a moment sluggishly placing one foot in front of the other as she walked. A sudden gust of wind dropped a shower of dew upon her and she gasped, realizing that she had allowed her mind to drift. She could have been killed in that instant by the warrior's swift hand and never known her death. When her heartbeat quieted, she sent her awareness into the silence of the pre-dawn forest. She felt that her hunter was not far behind.

The terrain was level in the high upland clearing. A stand of hardwood trees surrounded her and beyond the clearing the dark outline of spruce and fir trees rambled toward the horizon.

Black flies buzzed her head, biting at the exposed skin of her forearms. She stopped at the base of a tree and listened to the sounds of the forest, hoping she could still trust her senses. There was no movement. She hesitated. She had been fooled before.

A bird flew from the treetop and landed on a nearby berry bush. She took it as a sign of safety. She walked from the clearing to the edge of the woods and began to gather berries from the low lying bushes.

Hearing a sound, she turned, instinctively reaching for her dagger. It was missing.

The warrior stood motionless, his jaw clenched, his eyes narrowed and set. He looked at her with was she recognized as fear.

In the light of day she looked quite different from the natives, ghostly and pale compared to a people so tanned and rugged. Using the split second of his uncertainty, she threw up her arms and screamed in the worst guttural French she knew, then she turned and ran.

Less than a heartbeat later the warrior regained his wits and in two long strides grabbed her by the arm, spinning her around to face him. In the long night of running, Antoinette had promised herself that she would never again be taken prisoner. She would die rather than submit. She fought with a wild strength. She would be free or have him kill her now.

Antoinette's nails raked the side of the warrior's face. A stream of blood swelled from the ragged gash and his confident grin turned thin-lipped, sneering with disgust. With blurring speed he pulled her wrists together in one rough hand. He stopped as he saw the birthmark on her wrist, then spat on the ground. It was a small ritual, but enough for him to believe it would dispel her magic.

He smothered her against his massive chest with his other arm. She felt his breathing as unsteady as her own. A thread of terror ran through her as she looked into his eyes, dark and black, dilated with rage. Different from the other warrior, different from Bear.

A growl rumbled in his throat and she watched his mouth form slow, angered words. She wanted to scream, to block out the harsh sound of his voice, but her throat was tight with fear. Turning her face away, she stared into the rising sun.

She thought of her pact with the Goddess. Nothing for myself, she remembered. If she was to survive, she must use her own strength for defense. She waited for his death blow, but instead she felt the skin on her neck prickle as he slowly moved his head, smelling her hair, inhaling the musky scent of her body. She felt his heartbeat quicken, not with anger but with desire. His body stiffened and a hard pressure became firm against her thighs.

A flood of panic rose from deep inside her, spreading quickly through her senses. She kicked wildly, struggling against him, then sank her teeth into the soft flesh of his chest. Instantly he released her and she broke free.

His fist slammed into her stomach and she fell to her knees.

It was over.

Bear was strong enough to stand, restless and eager to begin his search for Swan. Her well disguised path was no match for his tracking skills. They led him to the stream where he found her staff and the smoldering remains of a fire. Deep depressions in the sand nearby showed signs of a fight. A rush of adrenaline pumped through Bear's veins and a cold sweat broke out on his forehead as his mind saw images of a struggle.

It was too soon to be walking, too soon to be tracking. The poisons were still working in his system. Relax, he told himself, kneeling down to examine the tracks. He had to calm his mind.

He forced his eyes to focus on the story in the sand. Swan's irregular shaped moccasin print was heavy, as if she had let her weight down on the balls of her feet, then taken a step back. There was a distinct shape of a hip and a hand where someone had hit the ground. The other tracks were from a man. Light-footed, shallow depressions of a hard soled traveling moccasin started from the underbrush with a swift run and ended with a quick stop.

Bear imagined Swan falling victim to a warrior's swift attack. His chest felt as if it would burst. He turned to follow the tracks that led to the sweat lodge. The chill of death increased with Bear's every step and he feared he might find Swan inside, raped and murdered. Cautiously, he stepped into the lodge.

A Kwetejk warrior's body lay face up, a blackened wound gaping in his side. He was naked. Swan's shell necklace hung around his neck. His loincloth and Swan's dagger lay beside him.

Bear let out his long held breath. Swan had managed to kill her abductor. Why had she not returned to the cave? There must have been more than the single warrior.

Bear looked at the man carefully as he removed Swan's necklace and retrieved the dagger from the floor. The dead man was not the same warrior who had wounded him with the arrow. That menacing face was forever burned into Bear's memory. The face and the voice. But the dead man was Kwetejk and far from home.

Bear left the lodge to examine the camp fire near the stream. A second set of smaller prints told another story. Their owner had paced back and forth near the fire, heavy-footed, uneasy. The cooking spit and half of a roasted partridge had fallen into the pit. An old wooden waltes bowl and several marked bone disks and markers lay beside the ashes, along with other debris from Bear's camp. Swan must have stumbled onto the small raiding party and become their captive. She had summoned great courage to kill the man in the lodge.

There was no time to waste. He had to release the haunting spirits of the dead and begin his search for Swan.

He walked the length of the camp to the outskirts of the village and pulled what was left of Dancing Fox's body back to the sweat lodge. He laid it alongside the warrior. With the violence of death lingering in the walls, the lodge was now useless as a place of solitude.

Taking a smoldering ember from the hearth he lit the dried birch bark and flames danced from pole to pole in a blazing funeral pyre. The fire would send the men's spirits to the sky and destroy their bones so they could not come back to haunt the people. They would have no link with the Earth World. Papkutparut would soon deal justly with them.

Bear raised his arms to the sky. "Fly swiftly, Spirits of the dead. Fly to the Guardian with open hearts. Papkutparut, do not spare your wrath."

Turning his back on the billowing smoke, Bear followed Swan's trail. As he had expected, her tracks were followed by those of a hard soled moccasin.

Chapter 38

Antoinette was harnessed, her wrists tied at her waist and her voice silenced once again by a gag. She and her captor traveled fast through the remainder of the hardwood forest. As the hillsides began to smell of spruce and evergreen, they turned not Northward, as Antoinette had intended, but South to run along the high ridge of the fog shrouded cape.

From the height of the promontory, she could see the outline of a tiny cove similar to the one where her journey in this untamed land had begun. She imagined the red seaweed dancing against the rocks in the shallows of the tides and the white birds diving into the waves hunting for food. She wondered if her boat still lay in wait somewhere on the shore and if Finder flew nearby, guarding it for her return.

The wind blew with a sharp bite, bringing her thoughts back to the high cliffs on which she stood. A wild sea beat its turbulence against the rocks below but for all its briskness, the air was heavy with impending rain. Thick clouds hid the horizon in a colorless haze and Antoinette wondered if this was the beginning of the change of seasons. How long had it been since she first met Bear? How long since their celebration of Lughnasad? A week? Time had almost blurred to nothing but the chilled wind reminded her that the seasons would change even if she did not take notice.

Awed by the majestic sight of the vast waters, the warrior stopped. Together they looked out to sea. Antoinette's gaze wandered to the distant ocean swells that tumbled like blue and green ribbons against a blackening sky. She searched the horizon for white sails or dark hulls, but saw only the distant white caps tossed by low winds. How ironic it would be to see ships now, when she had no way to signal them.

Gray harbor seals floated on the crests of rolling waves, keeping a safe distance from the rocky shoreline. It was easy to see how an anxious seaman could mistake their sleek, curved body for that of a mermaid and their low moaning sounds as a woman's lament, beckoning them to cast their ships against the treacherous shoals. She wondered if there had been others here like her, people from a civilized world who had looked out across this same sea, longing for their homes, their families and their lovers.

A fragment of a song drifted through her mind.

For whom will the Mother Ocean make welcome?
Those who know Her secrets.

How easy it would be to lunge just once and take her captor with her to a watery grave. Unbidden, the image of Bear's face flashed before her and a band of longing wrapped itself around her chest. Could she die so easily, without knowing if he still lived? Could she die so willingly, without hearing the sound of his voice one last time or feeling the touch of his body?

She turned her thoughts not to her death but to life, and searched for a flicker of Sight that would tell her of Bear's fate. Surely, if he were dead, she would feel the loss. She felt nothing. No pulse of his life, nor vision of his death. Nothing.

A swift jerk on her tether yanked her forward, pulling her from the edge of her emotions. The warrior led her downward and away from the cliffs and into the fog. What little solace she had gained quickly disappeared.

As the long day drew to a close, Antoinette tried to understand why the warriors had kidnapped her. Perhaps she was destined for a life of slavery; perhaps the warrior's leader, like the Turks, kept a harem of women for his pleasure. She was not meant for the warrior, for he had not touched her since their fight, and from the discreet distance he kept, he was unlikely to do so.

Whatever the reason, they wasted no time. They traveled down, and down. As the gray twilight slipped into blackness, they crossed a small creek bed. Ahead the forest glowed with an eerie hue of red and orange, an unnatural color silhouetting the trees against the darkness of night.

Mixed smells of habitation assailed her nose with a gut wrenching tang. Fear rose from her empty stomach. The warrior hastened his pace, dragging her behind him. She stumbled once as the landscape changed from forest to rock-strewn valley, and the warrior turned to catch her fall.

Pulling her by the leather harness laced across her chest, he settled her feet on the ground. His brows formed a disconcerting frown, sending a chill down her spine. He did not intend to lose her now, would not allow her to foolishly hurt herself. He turned without a word and led her at a slower pace.

It was the drums she heard first, low and rumbling, striking a slow, irregular cadence that offset her heartbeat and echoed through her body. A distant flute joined the discordant melody, both sad and enchanting, sending a chill of warning to the very center of her being.

Fear and despair accosted her, leaving an ache in her soul. The same twinge she had felt when she stood before Cardinal Visconti.

She stopped, planting her feet firmly on the ground. It was not a noble village of Kings or Sultans into which they walked, instead it was a dominion of evil.

A burst of energy surged through her, exploding in her head like a bolt of lightning. Cold probing tendrils menaced her thoughts and she shook her head in apprehension. Someone was trying to force their way into her mind. She closed her eyes to push the intruder away.

Whoever you are, you will not enter my mind! You will not gain entry to my soul.

The warrior jerked on the reins of her harness.

Antoinette stood fast, willing her shaking legs not to falter and her thin veneer of stamina not to crack. She threw back her shoulders in defiance. *I will not walk in trussed like an animal, sent to slaughter.*

The warrior turned to her. His face betrayed the sharpened edge of his own fear, then his cold, hard gaze ran the length of her body, fixing once again on her eyes. Antoinette lifted her head and met his gaze, searching his face for any sign of her future, but his features had tightened and his emotions were unreadable.

He slid his stone knife from its sheath and she took an undetectable half breath as he closed the short distance between them. With a quick upward thrust, the knife came up between her breasts and sliced through the leather bindings of her halter. Then he cut through the leather covering her mouth. She wet her lips and said nothing.

The warrior was silent for the space of a heartbeat. Antoinette smelled the fear in his spirit.

Whoever waited for her also waited for him.

Chapter 39

Château Nantes - Brittany
September, 1491

The trees cast faded colors against the bright Autumn sky, blending their foliage with the muted gray walls of the Château. Late summer had taken its toll on the once lush gardens of the ducal estate.

Anne strolled in the gardens as she waited for the King and his court to arrive. Her face clouded with uneasiness. Was she ready to challenge the men who sought to manipulate her? One who fought for his country and one who fought for his faith? Could she convince them that her goals were compatible with theirs? She wanted peace and security for the Bretons, and the ability to promise them freedom to worship without oppression from the church or a strong-handed monarch.

These were powerful men. But they were only men. Men much like any others with desires and goals. First she would appeal to their individual interests, then offer them assistance in exchange for their acquiescence. She would pray to the Blessed Mother to guide her words and temper her emotions. This would be a difficult day.

The peal of bells from the Cathedral of St. Peter broke her thoughts, announcing the arrival of the king and his entourage. There was no more time to worry. Charles would expect her within the hour.

Anne remembered their last meeting. Charles had been pleasant and accommodating, but tonight Cardinal Visconti would be with him. That would make the audience much more difficult. Protocol and strategy required that she meet with him, even if she did not wish to have him in her home.

Better to get it over with.

Anne turned away from the bleakness of the gardens and walked to the Château. *I must get Visconti out of Brittany as soon as possible.*

Charles turned to face his future bride. A twinkle glinted in his eyes. “We are pleased you have set a date for our wedding. December is such a quiet time of year; it will make a good event and it will please the people.”

Anne calmly returned his smile. He was making this audience with the Cardinal much less painful than she had imagined. They had been talking for some time and no one’s temper had flared. But that was all about to change.

She turned to Visconti. “Your Grace, I know you have great plans for my future husband. I hear that he will lead a crusade to claim the Holy Roman Empire.”

Did she notice a tensing of his jaw as she spoke? Neither man commented on her pronouncement.

“I believe you will be requiring funds for such a noble endeavor,” she continued. “And with a few concessions from both yourself and the king, I am willing to assist you.”

Visconti spoke with a calm voice. “M’lady is well informed of the desires of the crown. I am not in a position to offer concessions from the church, however I would like to hear what you wish to offer.”

“We have discussed my wishes for Brittany’s independence. If I can be assured of the Bretons’ autonomy, I will put the treasury of my realm at the King’s disposal.”

Visconti looked stunned. “M’lady, I am surprised at your frank offer and the directness of your presentation. Clearly you have thought on this matter. What you offer will most certainly advance our goals. What are your conditions?”

Anne’s voice was velvet-edged, full of depth and authority. “The Bretons must be free to worship as they please, whether it be in the groves of the forests or the Churches of Notre Dame. There must be no more witch hunts.”

Visconti’s face was without expression, but Anne could see she had struck a nerve.

“M’lady, if it were up to me, I would accept your offer right now. Alas, I must seek the council of others. Let me assure you I will suggest acceptance.”

Charles was pleased with Anne’s air of self-confidence and her generous offer. She was going to help him gain his dream of re-claiming the throne of Charlemagne, and soon she would sit beside him, regal, proud and almost an equal. He turned to her with an excited smile, taking her hand in his.

“Anne, you won’t be sorry you have decided to put your

trust in me. I promise Brittany will have its autonomy from the Crown. And France will defend your borders and coastlines as if they were her own."

This was almost too easy, Anne thought, returning Charles' smile. Why were these men agreeing to her wishes? She was certain Visconti could call off his Inquisitors without further approval. So why was he being so shrewd? She must make him commit to her demands.

She tuned to Visconti with the quiet firmness she had learned by watching Antoinette deal with the opposition.

"I know, Your Grace, that you have the authority to withdraw your Inquisitors. You need not discuss this with anyone other than Della Rovere."

Momentarily speechless, Visconti struggled to control his surprise. How could the duchess know these things? Was that witch of hers back among them? He had not been able to find her. Perhaps the duchess had been more successful. His gaze swept the room for intruders.

"M'lady, I don't know what you are implying. Cardinal Della Rovere has nothing to do with my orders from His Holiness."

A stern look of skepticism crossed Anne's face. "Come Cardinal, we must speak frankly and demonstrate some trust if we are to work together toward mutual goals. I do not care about the workings of the Holy See. It is beyond my power to shape events in Rome. I seek to do what I must for my people. And I do not require a confession of your intrigues."

Visconti began to answer but she held up her hand.

"I have something else to offer you that I am sure will make you change your mind."

Both men sat silently as they waited for her pronouncement.

"If, Cardinal Visconti, you promptly call off your minions and pledge your word before your king that this will be done—I will openly and wholeheartedly embrace the Church and the Blessed Virgin." She held her hand out to Charles, signifying a bond between them. "Together Charles and I will lead the people by example into this new era that we are creating."

Charles stifled a grin at the cunning Anne demonstrated and the look of astonishment on Visconti's face. He had never been able to penetrate the layers of deception that surrounded Visconti, nor catch him so off guard.

Visconti looked at Charles, but received no signs of encouragement. Were these two regents conspirators? Could he take the chance and turn away Anne's offer to embrace the church? That in itself would lead many of her people away from their pagan superstitions. His mind raced in panic. What would Della Rovere do?

He took a deep breath and bowed his head in acquiescence. "I accept your offer M'lady. You shall have no further problems with the Church."

Anne made an inaudible sigh. So it was done. Now, she would seal her pledge with a promise. She rose from her seat and smiled at the two men. She was careful to suppress any trace of triumph from her voice.

"Then let us work together. I will begin construction on a chapel to the Blessed Mother within a fortnight and, Your Eminence, you will travel to Rome to see that the proper steps are taken to withdraw your investigators." She gave them no time to refute her request as she walked toward the doorway. "Now, Your Highness and Your Grace, I must prepare for tonight's events."

There was a moment of strained silence between the men as they sat stunned at the young woman's daring and courage.

"Well!" Charles exclaimed with a wry smile. "What do you think of my future queen, Your Eminence?"

Visconti was not so amused. "How can she know so much of our plans? I assume you have not spoken to her of them."

"Certainly not, Your Grace. Though perhaps you forget that she is a ruler of her own country and she has informants just as we do."

"Do you trust her not to spread our plans to Maximilian?"

"You need not worry about that. She has had no contact with him since the marriage was annulled." Charles paused to reflect on his wine, turning the thought of Anne's loyalty over in his mind. "No, you need not worry about her silence. She has pledged to abide by her words. She can be trusted."

"Perhaps you have not felt the sting of her deception as I have. The fiasco at Rennes with her advisor, Antoinette Charboneau, did little to endear me to her."

"Ah, yes. Antoinette. I assume that with the acceptance of Anne's offer, you must call off your search for the woman."

"It will take time to cancel my orders, Your Highness. Why, for all I know, she may be in the custody of my men at this very moment."

"Do you have her then?" Charles brows raised in genuine surprise. If Antoinette had been found, then the marriage date could be advanced.

Visconti shook his head. "I regret she has skillfully eluded my men."

Charles stifled his disappointment. "I have promised Anne

that I will not interfere in her efforts to find her friend. And it appears, Your Grace, that you have also made the same promise."

Visconti lifted his chin, meeting Charles' eyes with an icy gaze. "As I said, Your Highness, it will take some time to recall my orders. Who knows what may happen before they are received?"

Chapter 40

Land of the People

The warrior moved behind her, prodding her forward with the edge of his knife.

Antoinette flicked back her hair with a shake of her head. Resolute and courageous, she faced her destiny with what dignity she had remaining.

The village lay along a wide and running river. Many wigwams lined the bank, their bark coverings shimmering silver and gray. A hush loomed around the empty dwellings. It was not from these simple homes that Antoinette's trepidation came.

A bonfire blazed from a small island in the center of the river, throwing a plume of dark smoke and luminous sparks into the starless sky. The drums were there, the noisemakers, the flutes, all echoing their haunting refrains throughout the silent valley.

The warrior led Antoinette to a canoe and settled her onto the hard wooden ribs of the boat. The sounds grew louder, almost deafening, as they approached the island. The refrain of the flutes rose and fell in hard high pitched scales that amid the thunder of the drums and the stamping feet made the air thick with magic. The wild scream of a bird of prey pierced the air and the low plaintive howl of a wolf followed. The fact that the sounds were from human voices made Antoinette's skin shiver. It was almost like crossing from one world into another. From the light of life to the darkness of death.

Several hard strokes of the wooden paddle took the canoe across the water and they landed with a scrape of bark against the rocky shore. The warrior shouted orders to men gathering about them and without decorum pulled Antoinette from the canoe and pushed her toward the fire.

The drums pounded in her body, lodging their beat in the back of her throat and the high whistle of the flute threatened to split her eardrums. A wave of energy hit her as they neared the blaze and she stopped, mesmerized by the flames.

Dark silhouettes swayed with the tempered rhythm, circling the fire, concentrating the restless energy as the people of the village danced to call Power. The shadows they cast against the ground, were those of animal, bird and reptile.

Antoinette stepped back as their thoughts filled her mind. Their Power was real, dynamic and explosive, and she felt herself slipping into their illusive realm of trance.

The warrior shoved her forward, startling her out of the momentary ecstasy, shoving her past the fire. For all the heat of the flames, Antoinette felt sudden chills invade her heart, chills from a cold hand that stirred the air.

The drumming faded to a slow beat, and a rattle shook in the distance, beckoning the spirits to stay near. A quiet hum sounded from the people, as one by one they left their trance to watch the warrior and the pale captive approach a birchbark lodge.

The warrior spoke briefly to a man guarding the entrance to a large oval structure and without hesitation the guard held back the white hide covering the door. He motioned their admittance.

The interior of the room was dim compared to the brightness of the bonfire. As her eyes adjusted, Antoinette began to see her surroundings. The high birch bark walls were supported by lodge poles, driven deep into the ground and arched to meet at a ridge running the length of the room. A dark sooty ring, like an all-seeing eye, loomed above her, and her gaze followed a thin flume of smoke as it rose and disappeared through the hole in the ceiling. The room smelled of burning hemp, tobacco and mint, whale oil and musk. The intoxicating aroma made her head spin.

As they walked further into the lodge, Antoinette's fading energy quickened with her heartbeat.

At the far end of the room a small iron brazier glowed with the embers of a slow fire, smoldering the bitter incense that drifted to the ceiling. Behind it on a raised mound of earth stood a crude altar, draped by a length of stained yellowed linen. A once gilded goblet sat in its center and a rusted broadsword crossed its front.

Behind it all, a tattered square of cloth hung from a broken length of wood. A faded remnant of red whispered from the background of the fabric, the symbol hidden in the shadows.

Could it be a sail? she wondered. Were these items just flotsam and jetsam from her people's passing, curiously displayed as honored relics?

The drumming began again. This time it was one drum, beating a slow and syncopated tap, suspending her breath on its echo and calling her thoughts away, forcing them to wander.

A sudden burst of smoke and sparks from the center of the room snapped Antoinette from her lethargy. She blinked her eyes, and a woman, fiery red from head to toe, stood defiantly before her.

Antoinette recognized the old magician's trick, a mixture of sulfur, coal and powder thrown into the fire to surprise wary spectators. Its suddenness, combined with the image of a fiery Goddess of War standing before her, stole her breath. *Macha — Morrigu—Ceridwyn.* Antoinette drew in what breath she could from the stale air around her and prepared herself for the touch of the Goddess, but the distorted image wavered and she saw only a woman.

"Who are you?" Antoinette demanded. She spoke Bear's language, but her voice was weak from so long a silence. "Who gave you the right to drag me here, bound and gagged like a common prisoner?"

She stepped toward the shamaness, then a heavy hand fell on her shoulder, staying her movements.

"Silence." The red woman waved her hand then turned to the warrior with an air of indifference. "Is this woman the all powerful witch that beguiled you and killed your brother?"

"Yes, Sparrowhawk," the warrior replied. "But she is no woman, for I swear I have seen her use magic. How else could she kill so strong a man as Hunts-By-Night?"

There are many subtle ways, Sparrowhawk thought, as she turned from the warrior to look more closely at Antoinette.

The woman stepped from the earthen dais and walked toward her captive with the slow fluid grace of a cat stalking its prey. Antoinette raised her head in defiance, her eyes never wavering from the red image coming toward her.

Sparrowhawk extended a long finger and ran it down the length of Antoinette cheek, then turned to the warrior. Her brows arched as she looked at his fresh scrapes. "I trust you have not damaged her."

The warrior lowered his head in obeisance. "No, Sparrowhawk."

Sparrowhawk laughed. "Hunts-By-Night was foolish to bet

his manhood against a witch's powers."

The warrior looked at the shamaness with fear in his eyes. How could she know that his companion had won the witch as his prize and died trying to claim her? He opened his mouth to reply but Sparrowhawk silenced him with a backward wave of her hand.

"You have completed your duty. You may join the others."

The warrior breathed a sigh of relief and turned to leave. He hesitated in his stride and turned to the shamaness. "Sparrowhawk," he said, rubbing his chest with painful remembrance. "Be warned. The witch's teeth are as dangerous as her spells."

Sparrowhawk threw back her head and laughed as the warrior disappeared behind the leather doorway. Then her gaze focused into her captive's eyes.

Antoinette could feel the woman invading the private recesses of her mind. She did not resist, but let Sparrowhawk see that she had no magic to threaten her.

"I know you are hiding your power from me." Sparrowhawk spoke now in the Micmac language. "But I will have it from you. I will take your power, as I took Bear's. Then you will die."

She walked over to the altar and caressed the goblet and the rusty sword, running her hands over the metal with the tender touch of a lover.

"You see, only one of us can hold Power. There can only be one of us."

She waved her hand and her bodyguard, Black Otter, stepped from the shadows and grabbed Antoinette, holding her body tightly as Sparrowhawk picked up the goblet and walked toward her. She forced the bitter liquid into Antoinette's mouth. Her throat worked involuntarily. Antoinette coughed and spit out what liquor she could into Sparrowhawk's face.

Stunned at her captive's defiance, Sparrowhawk wiped away the residue of the potion with the back of her hand. Antoinette braced herself for violence, but Sparrowhawk's voice held no malice when she stepped forward.

The smell of incense and evil preceded Sparrowhawk and Antoinette lifted her arms to push away the image that wavered before her.

Sparrowhawk grabbed Antoinette's arms and looked at the crescent moon mark on her wrists. *She has the mark of the prophecy.*

Digging her pointed fingernails into Antoinette's pale flesh, Sparrowhawk lifted her chin and looked deep into her captive's eyes.

"Rest now, my little witch. Rest and prepare yourself to meet your lover in the Ghost World." Sparrowhawk smiled and her face turned harsh and hollow. "I have seen Bear's spirit in my dreams and witnessed his agonizing death. He will not be able to save you."

Antoinette remained silent.

"Take her to the others!"

Sparrowhawk's command echoed throughout the room and she vanished behind a flume of smoke. Black Otter pulled Antoinette from the lodge.

The drumming continued, though now it seemed far away. The drums were no longer calling her. A heaviness centered in her chest as she thought of Bear, dying alone and without her, and she felt overwhelmed by all the events of the past few days.

"No!" She clutched her head with her bound hands. "No, he can't be dead. I would know." She thought of the shamaness and her crude disappearing act.

She's bluffing. She doesn't know. Blessed Mother, I don't know if I can fight this evil by myself. I need your power, but I will not beseech you. Give me your blessings. Guide my thoughts when the time comes. Welcome my soul when I stand before you in death.

The draught from Sparrowhawk's goblet blurred her thoughts and the myriad questions that flooded her mind.

What wrong had she done in her life, Antoinette wondered, to have her destiny place her here, before a woman who revered old and weathered debris as sacred relics? Where had they come from? How long ago? Had there been others like her to stand upon these shores?

A glimmer of hope coursed through her. Perhaps they still lived here, further inland or near deeper water. Yes, they would come and rescue her and take her back to Bear—take them both back to France. Or Bear would come for her, save her again, hold her, make love to her.

"No!" she cried to the images surrounding her. "He's dead. She said he was dead."

People from her past, wild shapes of animals and men danced before her as she walked with Black Otter past the fire. She held up her arms to force the images from her eyes, but Black Otter pulled her hands down.

Suddenly, Jacques stood before her with outstretched arms, beckoning her to dance with him. She made a move toward him, but strong arms pulled her back and Jacques' face faded into Bear's face, Bear's hands, Bear's body.

Black Otter shoved her through the stockade doors and locked the gate.

"*Mon amour—*" she cried to the air. Her awareness slipped away as she held onto the rough spruce poles and lowered herself to the ground. "*Mon coeur et mon âme.* My heart and my soul, I will be with you soon."

ଓ

Swan's path had been difficult to follow. It pleased Bear that she had learned to disguise her tracks so well. Then his enthusiasm turned to anguish as Swan's tracks became clearer and a second set of heavier footprints shadowed hers.

At the edge of the hardwood clearing he saw where the hunter and the hunted had first struggled. He followed the tracks until they cleared, then he knew Swan walked behind the warrior. Her footfalls were uneven. She had been taken captive. What would he find when he caught up with them?

Bear tried to remember the different discussions he'd had with Sparrowhawk, about her people and her camp. The Kwetejk were not originally from the land of the Micmac, but lived along the shores of the great river whose waters rushed in and out with the powerful tides, exposing the shores like freshly skinned meat.

They did not speak the People's language, indeed the name Kwetejk meant 'those who do not speak as we do.' No, Bear thought, they do not speak or live as my People.

Sparrowhawk claimed that her people were the first people made by Kji-kinap and that Kluskap was the father of them all. Kluskap made their forests first and the magic place where the great waterfall reversed its flow and the shining rocks that sparkled with the gold of the sunrise and the blues of the sky.

The Kwetejk were the chosen ones, she had said. The Kwetejk were the bright stars in Kluskap's heart. Not the Micmac, not Bear's people.

A long hard winter with little game and many deaths had forced the Kwetejk to leave their river home and seek refuge among their brothers, the Micmac, securing hunting grounds from the Micmac Chief for the rest of that season.

When the shamaness of the small Kwetejk band died, it had been proper for Bear to share his knowledge of medicine and magic with Sparrowhawk. He could not understand why she wanted him dead but he knew why the warrior wanted Swan. She was a woman of great Power. Any warrior would see these things and want her for himself. But where was the warrior taking her?

Sparrowhawk's people were more suited to fish the rivers for trout and salmon than risk the dangers of the deep salt waters. If he were their leader, he would choose to make camp in familiar surroundings, next to a river or a stream. The direction of the tracks was leading him to the next river not more than half a day's travel. Barring any unforeseen problems, he could be there by the next sunset.

It had to be Sparrowhawk's doing, Bear reasoned as he walked through the seemingly unending forest. The plunder and destruction of his camp, his brush with death and the abduction of Swan by a Kwetejk—these things were not happening by chance.

Bear held back the curse that formed on his lips. There was no use thinking wasting thoughts on why these things were happening. He must plan what he would do when he found Swan.

The tracks led him to the high promontory of the smoking mountain where he watched the sun slip behind a hazy bank of clouds. A shiver of premonition crept over him and Bear forced himself to look past the breakers, out to where the land met the sea. His eyes settled on the vacant horizon and he breathed a deep sigh of relief. There were no islands, no white trees to menace him today. It was not time. They would someday appear, of that he had no doubt.

A low fog built with the cooling air and spread across the distant inlet like a flock of graceful birds flying to roost. It would soon engulf the mountain with its chill and dampness, blocking out the night sky and whatever tracks might still be visible in the evening light. Bear turned toward the forest where the tracks led into the dense fir and spruce trees. He would follow them as long as the twilight filtered through the trees and begin again with the morning sun.

Before he left the security of his cave, Bear had taken the time to prepare himself for an unknown amount of travel and he had packed his pouch with a good supply of dried meat and fruit.

He knew that Swan would want her shoulder pack. Like his medicine pouch, it held her magic and secrets of who she really was and memories of her life before they met.

Without his medicine pouch he felt almost naked and clung to Swan's pack as if it were his own, pulling strength from its closeness. Propriety prevented him from investigating the items inside, but he felt justified using her tinderbox to start his fire because she had once offered it to him as a gift.

Now, the bright flames of the small fire gave him comfort against the stillness of the foggy night. Alone in the silence of the forest, Bear pulled his smoking pipe and tobacco from his pack and stood, holding the tobacco up to the sky.

"Father Sun, unending Bringer of Light, nourisher of the People. I give thanks to you for my strength, for my health, for lending your light to show me the path to find Swan, for the shelter of the trees and the bounty within.

"Mother Moon, companion to Sun, giver of sleep and rest, to you I give thanks for the flow of my life, for the constant reminder that all things pass to nothing and then are renewed. May my strength and power be renewed with your growing light.

"Earth, most generous of parents to such wayward children as we People, thank you for your patience as we tread upon your heart.

"*Muin Wapskw,* White Bear, Brother, I will need your strength in the coming days. Strength to face whatever lies ahead, strength to accept my path, wherever it might lead.

"And Laughing Elk, always with me in Spirit. I will need your wisdom."

Bear sat before his small fire and filled his pipe with the mixture of *nespipaqn* root and herbs and held a flaming touchwood stick to the bowl. The sacred smoke rose around his face, then drifted to the heavens, taking his worries and his prayers to Great Power.

Soon the evening fell into a full and heavy darkness, and Bear rolled himself up into the green velvet cloak and covered himself with a thick spruce branch to disguise his scent from nighttime scavengers.

The fragrance of the evergreen mingled with a sweet aroma that lingered in the weave of the cloak and Bear began to think of Swan. To hold her close, flesh to flesh and breath to breath, to make love to her as he had in ceremony, to have her near him, smelling her womanness and hearing her silvery voice imitating his words; these things gave him comfort, but he knew that he would not sleep.

The sounds of the night, of restless creatures, filled his mind with wakefulness as he lay in the darkness, willing sleep to come.

Chapter 41

A wet cloth brushed across Antoinette's brow.

"Here, young one."

Antoinette gazed into the face of a beautiful Micmac woman. "Open your eyes and welcome the sunrise. You are lucky to see it after your visit with Sparrowhawk."

The woman spoke a patois of mingled French and Micmac. She tossed her jet black hair back from her shoulders then ceremoniously spat onto the ground, warding away the evil name of the shamaness who held them both prisoner. "She must want your power very badly to let you live."

Antoinette sat up and held a hand to her aching, spinning head. She felt as if she had been dragged behind a horse and left to wither in the hot sun. Her mouth was dry and tasted of bitter herbs and fermented fruits. No doubt Sparrowhawk's intoxicating potion would linger in her system to nauseate her through out the day.

She accepted the wooden cup of water offered in the woman's soft brown hands and looked into her eyes before she drank. Then she realized the woman was speaking French.

"You speak the language of my people," Antoinette said.

"Not well." The woman waved away the compliment with a lift of her hand. "I learned it as a child from an old man who came to live in my village. It has been many moons since he died or since I have spoken the man's words."

Antoinette experienced a moment of mixed emotions at the revelation that there had been others of her kind to live among the People. Perhaps there was still a chance of being rescued. The woman smiled and Antoinette felt an instant rapport with her, the same feeling of friendship she had shared Little Bird.

"Are you from Bear World-Walker's tribe?" Antoinette asked.

"I see my foster-son has told you about us. If he told you he liked my cooking, he lied."

"*You* are Old Woman?" Old Woman met her glance with a tilt of her head, patting her on the shoulder as if she were a baby. "Bear told me you were old and wise."

"Sometimes men can see the truth," Old Woman said. "You must be Swan. I was told that you were stubborn and willful. Very suited to Bear."

"Bear?" Antoinette asked with alarm. "Is he here?"

"No, but Power tells me that he is very near."

Antoinette's heart raced with excitement. If Old Woman was right, then Bear had made it through his sickness. But he did not know what was happening. He could be walking into a danger he had no way of fighting.

"Then who told you about me?" Antoinette asked. "Who told you that I was stubborn and willful."

"Ah, yes," Old Woman said matter-of-factly. "Finder told me. I use his eyes and his ears where I cannot use mine. He is my spirit-helper."

Bear had told Antoinette of his power animals and spirit-helpers. They gave him his otherworldly support and strength, much like the elementals gave to her.

"But I named the bird Finder. Do you call him Finder as well?"

"No, his spirit name would not fall well from your lips. It is better you call him by your chosen name."

"So, you have been watching me."

"Only so much as to give you a little help now and then. To turn you in the right direction when you walked astray."

"Bear has seen Finder. Did—does he know Finder is your spirit-helper?"

Old Woman laughed and her straight white teeth gleamed in the sunlight. "Ha! He has been too preoccupied with you to remember something so insignificant to him."

"Then it was you who led me to Bear?"

"Oh no, my dear. I merely followed you as you chose your own path."

Fate, Antoinette thought. Her fate and her destiny.

"What is happening here?" Antoinette asked.

"Too much." Old Woman shook her head in disgust. "The shamaness drugs the people with her potions and her words. She speaks of a Great Power that will come to guide the people into a new way life. A Power that will bring riches and prosperity. The people will not have to work so hard for their meals but will have it served to them on plates of shining metal instead of wood. And that they will dress in fine tanned hides as thin as tree leaves and bathe in waters spiced with flowers and oils."

Antoinette cringed at the description of her old lifestyle. Was it possible Sparrowhawk had learned these things from some shipwrecked sailor?

Old Woman lifted her eyebrows in a light mischievous

smile. "One of the men, a Kwetejk who brings me fresh herbs and tonics, says she has always spoken of this Power. But it is only since she came from our camp that she has used her words and her magic to persuade her people.

"My friend tells me the madness was the same with her mother and her mother's mother. They were all known for their prophecies and their witchcraft, but it always came to nothing. They were not as strong as Sparrowhawk," she whispered, half expecting someone to be listening to their conversation. "They did not have the magic of the Micmac to make them powerful. Sparrowhawk is different, her magic is corrupted. She uses Power for her own gain."

"You see so much, Old Woman, I am surprised that Sparrowhawk lets you live."

Old Woman smiled and Antoinette blinked her eyes. She looked at Old Woman again and this time Old Woman was withered like an old crone, crippled and aged. In the next instant Old Woman resumed her natural shape and the radiance of her good health.

"Sparrowhawk is blinded by her power," Old Woman said. "She sees me as I wish her to."

"I see where Bear has learned much of his magic."

"Oh, I spent many years with Laughing Elk before he died. You cannot live with a man so long and not learn many of his secrets."

Antoinette smiled at Old Woman's casual remark. It was no wonder Bear put so much faith in the woman. She was a sparkling treasure of wisdom like her grandmother, Ursule, though with a lighter countenance.

Old Woman helped Antoinette to sit up and they talked together in a low whisper. Her tone became serious.

"Do you know the power behind Sparrowhawk's magic?"

"I think so. I have seen the symbols and objects in her lodge before. Many of them may have come from my land, brought by my people. I cannot tell how she uses them. She did nothing last night but appear and disappear like an old magician."

Old Woman chuckled. Sparrowhawk had learned that from Bear, and Bear from Laughing Elk. "Simple trickery," Old Woman said with a wave of her hand. "Good enough to fool the inexperienced. She said no magic words? Made no spells or incantations?"

"She said that there could be only one of us to hold Power. Only one of us to wait." Antoinette looked at Old Woman's face as it turned from youth to aged and back again.

Something changed in her spirit; a shift of time or a shift of consciousness, Antoinette could not tell. When Old Woman spoke again it was with a solemn voice.

"We must prepare you to be victorious. You must be the One Who Waits."

"Prepare for what? What or who am I waiting for?"

Old Woman did not answer.

☙

The drums beat a steady rhythm throughout the day as if calling the night to come quickly, to sweep down from the heavens and surround the camp with a heavy darkness. The sky remained gray with heavy clouds. Once or twice its rays broke through the mire, giving a promise of morning.

Sparrowhawk sat in the darkened lodge. She lit a bundle of herbs with the end of a flaming tapered reed and placed them in the iron brazier at the foot of the dais. Small copper beads tinkled against the shells interwoven in her hair as she lifted her head to watch a trail of smoke rise in a wispy thread.

She waved her hands in the vapor, pulling the pungent smoke around her face, inhaling the trance inducing opiate. Lifting her rattle of deer claws, suspended on a single antler, she shook it into the smoke, chanting in a tongue that was ill suited to her voice, speaking words that she had learned as a child from her mother and grandmother—the meanings lost long ago but still powerful enough to do her bidding.

"Come to me. Come Old One. Give me your knowledge. Come, give me your Power. I wait for you."

The drums beat, the sound of birchbark rattles and the lamenting voices of her people began to pull at the edges of Sparrowhawk's consciousness.

It was time, she realized. Time to begin the ritual, time to bring the false shamaness to stand before her. As the sun reached its zenith and flooded her lodge with light, she would steal the witch's Power and with it her magic words. Sparrowhawk rose and let her heavy robe fall to the floor. Her tall nude body shimmered translucently in the faint smoky light, painted yellow and red and striped in black. A necklace of white caribou bones encircled her neck, reaching to the tips of her round firm breasts. A white belt glittering with mirror-like stones and fine sand-polished gems encircled her waist, resting atop the soft swell of her hips as a protective shield for the center of her power.

She was thin and graceful. She cultivated her shape and

painted her body to enhance her mysterious nature. Her stature was well above most of the men in her tribe and she was well aware of the impact she had on the few who dared to share her bed.

There had been many suitors—both men and women of her choosing—who fell trance to her violet eyes and found pleasure from her seductive body and generous lips. She found few who pleased her. Bear should have been one of them, but an intimate union with a shaman like Bear would have been risky. She needed his Power in other ways. The witch on the other hand, might be an interesting conquest—before she died.

Sparrowhawk walked to the altar and surveyed her first gift to the Old One. A white doe lay draped across the low altar now, the goblet near its head and the rusted sword beside it. It struggled against its bindings, its eyes clouded with a sedative to keep it still until just the right moment. The moment that she would send her supplications to the Old One.

She ran her hand down the length of the deer, feeling the warmth of the animal's life, the rise and fall of its labored breath, the softness of its fur. She could smell the animal's fear as she stroked its neck and underbelly. So flawless. So white. She would make a new gown from the hide.

Sparrowhawk practiced how she would kill the deer as her first sacrifice. She would swiftly bring the ritual knife down to cut through the life giving vein in the deer's neck. It would jerk once or twice, then its body would be stilled as warm blood flowed onto the altar, into her cupped hands and onto her breasts, arms and legs.

She would take Power from the animal to strengthen her own, covering herself with the swiftness and agility of the deer. Then she would watch as the blood pooled and dried on the ground at her feet. Watch as the blood mingled with the witch's blood and took her prayers to the Old One.

Yes, with the witch's death she would be able to speak the witch's magic words to the Old One and he would hear one voice, her prayers.

She dipped three fingers into the pot of Sikwan, the red ochre paint and drew a wide chevron on the deer's white skin. She pulled her crimson stained fingers across her cheeks, down her neck and across her necklace and breasts, imagining the magic growing within her. Before the real blood flowed the red ochre would seal her Power; it would draw the Spirit of the Old One to her, like the tides to the shore.

"Come, Old One. Bless this sacrifice prepared for the glory of Your Holy name."

A sudden chill wrapped around her and she rubbed her hands down her arms to warm them. She looked up to the roof and saw the sunlight begin to slip from behind the clouds. It was nearly time to begin.

Summoned by her thoughts, her attendant Black Otter lifted the door covering and stepped inside the lodge. His gaze strayed to the bound animal and then to the ochre reddened body of the shamaness. His fearful look told Sparrowhawk that her magic was working. He would help her with her task today. She would reward him with her body tonight.

Sparrowhawk nodded. "Bring her."

"If she has mastered the skills she learned from Bear, you must watch her hands." Old Woman was insistent. "She will use them to distract you as she wields her magic. You must not look too deeply into her eyes, for I have heard that she can burst your heart with her glance."

Antoinette stared at Old Woman in disbelief. What kind of power did Sparrowhawk hold over her people to make them believe she was unconquerable?

"Certainly she did not learn that from Bear."

"No," Old Woman laughed. "Not from Bear, but from some other shaman who willingly shared his secrets and no doubt gave his life in the process."

"Why didn't she kill Bear, if that is her way?"

"I believe that she intended to return to our camp and claim him as her suitor, once she had entranced her people and made them believe that we were their enemy. Dancing Fox told her that Bear was gone and the warriors came to our camp to ambush his return. She killed Dancing Fox because he was a traitor to his people. Now she is vengeful towards Bear because she has found that he did not share all his secrets.

"I knew that Dancing Fox was jealous of Bear's power and status. But no one would listen to me, an old woman."

"You spoke of your camp. We found no one there. It was empty."

"When we were attacked I sent Dancing Fox's wife, Summer Moon, and their children to tell Two Arrows of our troubles, hoping that Bear would be visiting his brother. But you were already gone. Two Arrows brought White Water and Red Feather with him. They were captured and are now in the men's stockade."

Antoinette cringed at the thought of the brave chief, Two Arrows, caged as a prisoner. “And what of the others? What of Two Arrows’ family?”

“The women will hold watch at the fishing camp and wait for the men to return.”

“But Little Bird is expecting a baby.”

“Don’t worry. Little Bird is a strong woman. She will be alright. She was chosen to marry Bear before he became a shaman and decided not to take a wife.”

Antoinette wanted to know more, but this was not the time to ask about Bear’s past. She needed to know more about the Frenchman Old Woman had seen in her childhood.

“Old Woman, you speak my language. Have you known many people like me? Are my people living among the Micmac?”

“No, the pale man was the only one I ever saw. I heard stories of men who lived here in my great-grandfather’s time, white skinned men from a place called Norvegia. They were the friends of Kluskap. Some were red-haired like Sparrowhawk.

“Others lived here during my grandfather’s time. They wore white robes and carried sharp knives and long bows. They were a people like you, Swan. People who fought for what they believed in. Like you must when Sparrowhawk challenges you.”

Antoinette rode the shiver that ran the length of her spine. Her people had been here before, long ago, and no one remained to take her home. There would be no one to save her from her fate.

“I am not a fighter, Old Woman. I don’t have the training.”

“Perhaps it will not come to that. Your magic will protect you. Just hold fast to what you believe and call your Power to defend you.”

“But Old Woman... I have no Power.” She recalled her pact with the Goddess. “Not anymore.”

Old Woman saw Black Otter approach the stockade and she sprang to her feet, standing before Antoinette as the warrior crossed to them. “Of course you have Power, Swan. That is something that no one can ever take from you. True Power comes from here,” she placed her hand above Antoinette’s heart. “No, shamaness, no man or woman can ever take it away. That is the mistake Bear made. He confused a broken heart with loss of his Power. He forgot that he is a man first, and then a shaman.”

Old Woman lifted a bag from around her neck and looped its leather cord over Antoinette’s head. The bag was made of leather, delicately interwoven with quillwork and moosehair.

"Quickly! Black Otter comes." She placed her hands on Antoinette's shoulders and looked into her eyes. "I give you my medicine pouch and my Power. Use it to increase your magic, draw strength from your spirit-helper and from Great Power."

Black Otter threw open the gate and grabbed Antoinette's arm, pulling her away from Old Woman's embrace.

Remember, Old Woman's voice echoed in Antoinette head. *You have Power. Call upon it to defend yourself, to defend the People."*

Black Otter cast a quick glance at Old Woman and she smiled at him with a tilt of her head and a youthful, suggestive grin.

He sighed in disgust at the withered old woman he saw and turned away, ushering his prisoner toward the oval lodge. Old Woman smiled as she collected her few belongings and walked past the unlatched gate.

Chapter 42

Antoinette's heart raced in panic as she walked toward Sparrowhawk's lodge. *Was this happening?* Could she have come all this way and crossed over an untold distance of ocean and land only to face someone else who wanted to suppress her faith in the Goddess and the Ancient Ones?

She laughed at the irony. This time she had nothing to give and not even the Power of the Goddess to call upon for protection. It would do Sparrowhawk little good to interrogate her, she would learn nothing.

Black Otter walked beside her. He grimaced as they passed his people and there was a sad look about his eyes. It was a brief expression, but Antoinette saw it. A small lift of his brows revealed his distaste for their indulgence in the shamaness' potions.

Antoinette took advantage of his agitation to speak, calling him by name. "Black Otter."

He turned his head to look at her, but did not stop their momentum towards the lodge.

"Do you see what's happening to your people?"

A wave of grief passed over his face. She knew he understood. She reached out to touch Black Otter's mind as she had the other warrior. *Your people are not the same since*

Sparrowhawk returned.

Black Otter loosed the tight grip on her arm and she knew that he was not altogether sure of the thoughts running through in his mind, but his eyes remained focused on the lodge.

Your people are captives. Look at them. Their freedom is gone. Their spirits are in turmoil. They need your help. You must stop Sparrowhawk's reign of sorrow. You must free your people's tortured spirits.

Black Otter stopped in front of the doorway and turned to face Antoinette. He had gone quite pale, she thought, as gray as the birch bark covering the lodge. His eyes were dark and full of fear, as if his very thoughts had sealed his fate. When he spoke his voice was a whisper, hollow and resigned.

"I can do nothing as long as she lives."

He tightened his grip on her arm, turned, then lifted the hide covering, pulling Antoinette behind him as they entered the darkened lodge.

The atmosphere was thick with the pungent herbs still smoldering in the iron brazier. Antoinette turned her head away from the trance inducing smoke as Black Otter led her to stand on a woven reed mat in front of the dais. With a quick jerk of his hand, he shoved her to her knees as though their brief understanding had never occurred.

She glanced up at him once more, looking for any sign of help in his face, but it had gone cold. His eyes focused on the dais before him.

Antoinette followed his gaze and saw the deer—an obvious sacrifice—and Sparrowhawk, who knelt before the crude altar, concealed in a robe that hid everything except her crimson hair.

The robe was covered with shards of rock crystals and iridescent shell bangles that spiraled in overlapping layers around the garment. It shimmered in the growing sunlight which crept in from the ceiling's smoke hole.

Sparrowhawk rose to her feet and turned toward Antoinette. Amid the sound of her clinking armor, she was like a dragon uncoiling from a long sleep, her belly red with fire, her tongue poised to strike with a deadly flame.

Shaking the vision from her eyes, Antoinette looked around the room for a way of escape. There were no other doors or windows and the exit was barred by Black Otter who stood silent and entranced.

Sparrowhawk raised her arms to the sky, and turned to the altar. The crystals in her robe sent shafts of glittering light to fall against the dark walls, across the deer and the faded fabric draping the wall behind her. Her harsh voice echoed in Antoinette's spinning head.

"*Lóripat. E'spirí, Spirí, Santo, Santo, Santo!*" A single drumbeat repeated the cadence of Sparrowhawk's last words and she raised the goblet to her lips and drank deeply from its bowl. With a silent step from the dais, Sparrowhawk crossed the short distant to Antoinette.

Antoinette felt the presence of Black Otter standing close behind her, and she stifled her impulse to run. It would be no use, she realized. Though she was no longer bound, there were many warriors and a cold, deep lake between her and any hope of safety. She lifted her eyes to focus on the shimmering being, no longer resembling a woman, who now stood before her.

Rays of the growing sunlight filtered through the smoke that now filled the room and enhanced the mystic quality of Sparrowhawk's body.

The smoke. I must not breathe the smoke, I must not be afraid.

"What...what do you want from me?"

"The witch has found her voice," Sparrowhawk turned to Black Otter. "Let's see if she can use it to postpone her death."

She walked to Antoinette and placed strong hands on her shoulders, raising her to stand. Antoinette's eyes were level with Sparrowhawk's chin and she had to look upward to meet her gaze.

Sparrowhawk's face looked transparent and Antoinette struggled to focus on her mouth and not her eyes, remembering Old Woman's warning, but her words sounded strange and the sound did not move in time with her lips.

"I want your words of Power. I want to know what magic you use to summon the Spirits of the Other Worlds, what words you say to call the Old One to do your bidding."

"I don't know what you want."

Sparrowhawk stepped closer and Antoinette leaned back from the impact of the woman's energy, brushing against Black Otter's chest.

I must not be afraid. I must trust my heart.

"You do not speak the truth," Sparrowhawk snapped. "What words did you use to steal Bear from the warrior's death knife? What magic allowed you to kill a strong man like Hunts-By-Night?"

"I have no power—no special magic." Antoinette thought of her promise to the Goddess. *No, I have no special magic. But I have Faith.*

She straightened her shoulders. “I receive my strength from the Goddess and the Ancient Ones. The warrior, Hunts-By-Night, was foolish. His lust was the weapon that killed him.”

Sparrowhawk’s lips turned up in a derisive grin. “I knew he would not waste an opportunity to sample your magic. I should have known better than to send him to capture you after I whetted his appetite for Power with a taste of my own. It’s too bad you killed him, he was a most capable lover.”

“It is not my habit to bed with my enemies,” Antoinette said.

Sparrowhawk cast a sideways glance at her and stepped closer, raking her gaze across Antoinette’s body.

Antoinette moved back and leaned her weight into Black Otter’s hands. Why was she becoming so dizzy?

“From the look of you, it does not appear that you are in the habit of bedding anyone. Bear did not lie with you.” Sparrowhawk looked at Antoinette’s drowsy lids, waiting for the intoxicating smoke from the brazier to overcome her. Black Otter lowered Antoinette to the ground, leaning her against the altar. He reached for the goblet and placed it against Antoinette’s lips.

“Drink. It is only water,” he whispered.

Too tired and thirsty to resist, Antoinette drank the water and her head cleared enough to focus on Black Otter’s face. Why was he helping her? Would he come to her side when Sparrowhawk challenged her? Could he resist the power of his mistress’s magic?

Black Otter stepped back into the shadows.

Sparrowhawk walked to the center of the lodge, waiting for the light. It would soon be time to begin the ritual. She shook her head in disgust as she spread out her robe to catch the light. “I had hoped for a much longer discussion.”

Undaunted by her captive’s unwillingness to speak, Sparrowhawk continued her ceremony, kneeling once more before the altar. She leaned forward, placing a reverent kiss on the deer’s forehead. The doe struggled. A faint whine wheezed through its muzzled jaw.

Sparrowhawk took the goblet and lifted it high into the air. “*Oramus Te, E’espiriti Santo.*”

Black Otter’s voice repeated her phrases.

In the recesses of Antoinette’s clouded mind she remembered hearing the cadence of the words before, witnessing a similar ritual. It was familiar, disconcerting, disorienting.

Sparrowhawk dipped a hawk's feather into the remaining water in the goblet, flicking the clear liquid out over the deer and toward Antoinette. Suddenly, the sunlight broke through the clouds and reflected in magnificent splendor on the crystal robe. Hundreds of lights filled the dark room, casting refracted rays of color on the walls.

Sparrowhawk's voice began. "Asperme, Dómine..."

Antoinette stood. A single beam of light focused on an eight pointed cross gleaming red and ominous on the remnants of what she now realized was indeed a tattered sail. It hung from a ship's broken spar. Long forgotten words surfaced on Antoinette's lips and the two women spoke almost in unison.

"Asperges me, Dómine, hyssópo et mundábor; lavábis me et super nivem dealbá bor. Miserére mei, Deus, secúndum magnam misericórdian tuam."

Antoinette turned from the sail to look at Sparrowhawk, whose face had grown as pale beneath the red ochre as the bright light reflecting in her eyes.

"How dare you speak the words of the Old Ones," she snarled. "How dare you call Him to you with my Holy magic."

With clarity, she recognized that the words Sparrowhawk tried to say was the litany of the Mass, the Christian Mass Antoinette had learned as a child.

The altar, the ritual. Sparrowhawk had taken the Christian ceremony, the magic of the shamans and the Power of her people and fashioned it into something of her own, something distorted beyond recognition. Now she called upon some evil power do her bidding, attempting to use all the secrets of her teachers as her magic stepstone.

Antoinette looked once again at the sail and thought of the trappings of the crusading Knights Templar and the Navigator's Guild, sending their men to the far ends of the earth to save heathen souls. She took in a quick breath as her head cleared. The men of her brother's order, the Knights of Christ, were explorers. They sailed to far off lands and possessed secrets still unknown to the Catholic Church. Bear's land was surely one of the secrets.

Enraged at Antoinette's defiance, Sparrowhawk grabbed the rusty sword and hurled it in front of her, missing Antoinette's arm by the blade's width. Antoinette ran for the doorway. "I will be the One Who Waits." Sparrowhawk screamed. "I will be here when He returns from the Land of the Kings." Sparrowhawk threw off her robe and ran toward her.

"By all the Gods and Goddesses," Antoinette cried to the madwoman with a sudden realization. "Are you waiting for the

Templars to return?"

ௐ

Bear ran toward the sound of drums echoing in the forest. They grew louder and more frantic with every step. He felt the beat of Antoinette's heart with every beat of the drum.

The clouds parted and the sun began to stream through the mists with bright rays of light, showing him the way, leading him to Swan. His blood pounded as he wove his way through the trees, dodging limbs and jumping across the shallow streamlets that led to Sparrowhawk's village.

There was great tension in the air and he knew whatever Sparrowhawk intended to do, it would be done as the sun reached its height. He had taught her that much, to use the sun and hollowed out moon to enhance her strength. To have them stand witness to ceremony was to use the greatest power.

He slowed his pace as he approached the village. His gaze swept the cold campfires and the vacant dwellings, then darted across the lake to the island. He focused on Sparrowhawk's lodge.

There was no central fire and the men and women neglected their work and their children.

This is where Sparrowhawk has set her Power, he thought. This is where she will meet her death.

Bear edged his way past the wigwams and slipped into the cold stream, holding his pack and gear high above his head. The water was swift, but his footing held and soon he was on the shore. Dripping wet, he crossed unnoticed to the edge of the camp.

One man guarded the stockade that held Bear's people. Micmac men, but no women. He saw a mark of two scars across the shoulder of one of the men and knew Two Arrows was among those captive. Red Feather and White Water sat with their backs against the heavy spruce poles. Bear whistled the green jay's call and Two Arrows turned, slowly and cautiously.

Two Arrows' eyes narrowed and he saw his brother just beyond the clearing of the camp, hidden well within the brush. He tilted his head in recognition, turned his back to the guard and began silent hand signals of warning to Bear. *The shamaness holds Swan in the lodge, much danger, hurry!*

Bear inclined his head, then slipped from view.

Awakened from the lethargy of his captivity, Two Arrows reached through the lodge poles of the stockade and pulled the unwary guard toward him. The neck snapped like a dried twig.

Bear closed in on the lodge and circled around to the back, hoping to enter through the small doorway common to all shaman's lodges, a secret place to exit and enter unnoticed. It was there as he expected. He stepped forward to enter the doorway but his path was blocked by a warrior with a war club in his hand.

It was the warrior of his nightmares, the warrior with the arrow painted black and red, the warrior of the hard soled moccasins.

"You see I do not die easily." Bear smiled.

The warrior took a swing at him with the heavy war club and Bear jumped away, rolling past him then springing to his feet with the grace of a lynx.

"I do not wish to kill you," Bear said breathlessly. "But there is much bad blood between us. You have tried to kill me and you have taken my woman."

The warrior remained silent and lunged again with the club, striking the air furiously as Bear stepped aside. Angered, the warrior drew his stone knife and threw the club aside, moving to close the short distance between them.

Bear took a fighting stance and pulled Antoinette's knife from his moccasin. He saw the brief flicker of the warrior's glance from his eyes to the knife and back again. They held each other's gaze, then the warrior lunged. Both men were evenly matched and held away each other's weapon.

Bear summoned his power and shifted his weight to the side, throwing the warrior to the ground with a swing of his hip. Then he was upon him, knocking the stone knife from his hand and sending a swift blow to the warrior's jaw. Bear pulled him to his knees.

Bear stood behind him and offered a silent prayer to the warrior's spirit as his knife bit into the warrior's throat and he fell lifeless to the dirt.

Suddenly, Black Otter stood before Bear. He recognized Black Otter as the brave who first brought Sparrowhawk to his camp. Bear lifted his bloodied knife in readiness, but Black Otter held up his hands in a gesture of peace.

"I have no quarrel with you, Shaman. It is Sparrowhawk who must answer to your knife."

Bear looked at the unarmed brave suspiciously. "Why do you turn traitor to your mistress?"

Black Otter took a deep breath. His eyes strayed to the outer edges of the camp and to his listless, hopeless people.

"She has held my people captive for too long and I find

myself powerless to defend them."

"Then help me! Where is she now? What is her weakness?"

Black Otter's face was grim. He tilted his head toward the small doorway. "She is in the lodge." Black Otter looked at the small knife in Bear's hand. "It will be hard to kill her with that as your weapon."

Bear moved to push him aside, but Black Otter grabbed his arm, holding him back. "Her weakness is her vanity. If you kill her, will you give my people back their hopes and their lives? Will you let us go back to our homes on the Shining River? Or will you kill us all?"

Bear looked hard into Otter's eyes. He was a beaten man to beg for his people so, but Bear knew he would have done the same. "It will be done as the Chief decides." Bear said, pushing past Black Otter to enter the lodge.

The sail blocked his way and he ripped through the threadbare fabric like a fragile spider's web, rending it in two.

The two women stood face to face in the harsh sunlight streaming into the lodge. Bear moved toward them from the earthen dais, but a familiar voice stopped him, speaking from the shadows.

"My son, it is their fight. You must not interfere."

Bear rushed to Old Woman and stood beside her.

"You are alive," he said. "I had thought she would have killed you first."

Old Woman smiled up at him from beneath her wrinkled lids. "She would not look at me for fear she would see herself as old and useless."

Bear turned back to the two women. The atmosphere crackled with loosened magic and Power.

Sparrowhawk was breathless with rage.

"How dare you question me." Sparrowhawk's shape shifted.

Antoinette stood dazed and confused as she watched the shamaness spread her arms and take on the image of her namesake.

"I am Sparrowhawk. I am the One Who Waits."

The hawk swiped at Antoinette with its red talons, and she ran to the wall, grabbing the rusted sword and swinging it at the flying bird. The hawk's piercing scream rent the air and turned into a hideous laugh as Sparrowhawk resumed her human shape.

"You see, little witch. I am the great shamaness and I am many things."

Antoinette caught herself looking into Sparrowhawk's violet

eyes. *I must break the contact between us or I will be killed.* Willing her arms to move, Antoinette lifted the heavy sword and held it up.

"Stop!" she commanded. "You have no power over me. You cannot control my mind or my thoughts."

Sparrowhawk took a step forward and her body shimmered. Antoinette blinked as the shamaness changed her shape to the image of Bear. His voice echoed in Antoinette's mind, "What about your heart, my love?"

Antoinette lowered the sword as Bear's image approached her. "Come to me, my love. Let me lie with you again," the image said. "Let me feel the warmth of your body around me."

"No!" Antoinette screamed, throwing down the sword and grabbing her head in pain. "Get out of my mind! You are not Bear! You can never be Bear!"

Sparrowhawk's shape shifted again and this time Antoinette saw Jacques, beckoning her to come into the safety of his arms. His white cotton shirt flowed in the ocean breeze.

"*Ma chère, je comprends.* You do not need to be afraid."

Antoinette took a step forward, then saw Jacques disappear. Suddenly she stood on the edge of a great precipice. She looked down at the void below her, at the rocks crumbling beneath her feet, and she felt her body pulled forward by a relentless power. Her knees threatened to buckle beneath her and she reeled back. Her stomach lurched as her head spun with vertigo.

A sharp voice snapped her awareness back to reality.

"Antoinette!" She heard Bear's strong voice from beyond her thoughts and she opened her eyes to stand face to face with Sparrowhawk.

Sparrowhawk turned and grabbed Antoinette by the hair, shoving her against the wall. But Antoinette spun around and drove her full weight into Sparrowhawk's chest. The shamaness stepped back in surprise.

"If I cannot kill you with trickery, then it will be as my sacrifice to the Old One." Sparrowhawk stepped to the altar, and from beneath the folded linen, withdrew a golden dagger shaped like an elongated cross, polished to a high sheen.

Antoinette could see the light reflecting from its long, pointed blade and choked back a quick breath of fear.

It will be the cross that kills me yet.

"The Old One left this as a reminder of his return," Sparrowhawk cried.

Antoinette summoned her wits and her courage. "Sparrowhawk, you follow a false God. Can't you see that these are the relics left behind by men who came to conquer your people? Don't you know that they would never allow a woman to hold Power, they would never allow you to speak to the Old One, the One God they call Jesu Christe?"

Sparrowhawk's eyes were wide with anger and she looked up to the sunlight now fading into the clouds.

"You cannot speak His name."

"They believe only a man may speak to the Old One." Antoinette taunted her, turning knowledge into a weapon as she edged her way along the wall.

"You know the litany. *Deum de Deo; lumen de lumine, Deum cerum de Deo vero.* God of God; Light of light; true God of true God; Who for us *men* and for *our* salvation, came down from heaven. For men, Sparrowhawk. Not for women. Not for us.

"It is Albina Magna, the Great Goddess to whom I pray, not to the god of Old One, not to the god of the Christians. I am no threat to you."

"You speak the lies of the Micmac, lies to deceive me."

"I know these men, Sparrowhawk. My brother is one of the followers of the Christian god. They have forgotten you. They turn their eyes to the east where there is gold and riches beyond belief. You have nothing here that interests the Kings of my world; they will not come back."

"No!" Sparrowhawk screamed as she lunged at Antoinette. "The Old One promised to return. He left us in charge of the talismans as keepers of the secret. You will not fill me with your lies."

Sparrowhawk grabbed at Antoinette and pulled her to the ground. Their bodies locked in fierce combat as they turned over and over, the dirt flying in clouds around them. Sparrowhawk raised her arm and the golden dagger flashed near Antoinette's face. With a quick burst of adrenaline, Antoinette shoved Sparrowhawk away and sprang to her feet.

Undaunted, Sparrowhawk backed Antoinette toward the center of the lodge. Her eyes were shifting pools of indigo, threatening to drown Antoinette in their raging tide of anger.

Don't look into her eyes, Antoinette remembered.

"Now, you will die and I will have your power," Sparrowhawk said, pointing the dagger at Antoinette's heart.

Standing in the shadows, Bear made as if to move once more, but Old Woman shook her head and held his arm.

"It is for Great Power to decide who lives this day."

Unwilling to stand by and watch his friend and lover fight unarmed, Bear took Antoinette's athame and slid it across the ground. It stopped within inches of her feet. She watched the sun gleam on the dagger's silver edge.

From the corner of her eye she saw Bear and Old Woman standing before the torn sail, and the sight of Bear's living, breathing form filled her with a sudden will to survive.

With her gaze never leaving Sparrowhawk, Antoinette reached down for the dagger. Could she kill again? Could she kill to save her life? Could she kill to save Bear's people?

Her fingers folded against the cold handle and she felt the life energy of Hunts-By-Night lingering on the blade. She raised the knife. It was now as her protector. She pulled Hunts-By-Night's power from the knife and took a low, fighter's stance, shifting her weight to the balls of her feet. She swung the knife hard to the left, but Sparrowhawk parried her thrust and pulled away.

Sparrowhawk spun around and stepped into Antoinette's next swing, checking the move with the hilt of her dagger. The blade flew from Antoinette's hand. Sparrowhawk grabbed her tunic and pulled Antoinette close, locking her arms in back of her and spinning her around to face Bear. The sharp golden blade dug into Antoinette's neck and she choked back a cry of pain.

Sparrowhawk stepped backward with her hostage until the sail was behind them and behind it her means of escape.

"Look at her one last time, Bear," she cried. "Look into your lover's eyes and witness her death."

Bear moved from the shadows into the light, his eyes pained and helpless. There was nothing he could do for her. No magic. No words. Not even his Power could save her now.

In that instant, the shaft of sunlight surrounded Bear like a burning flame and Antoinette recalled the warmth of his arms around her, and his all-encompassing strength of his love. A sudden rush of power surged through her body and without thinking she made a hard elbow jab to Sparrowhawk's stomach, spinning away from her as the woman labored for breath. They parted, then Sparrowhawk surged at her, wild and furious.

Alert now to Sparrowhawk's tactics, Antoinette anticipated her lunge and jumped aside.

Sparrowhawk fell to the ground, pulling the ragged sail down around her.

She lay silent for a long moment and Antoinette stepped back, poised for her assailant's next move. Sparrowhawk was still. A crimson stain spread onto the white sail, filling the faded red of the cross pateé with Sparrowhawk's bright blood.

Bear turned Sparrowhawk over on her back. The cross,

once gleaming with the high polish of gold, had been driven deep into her chest by the momentum of her fall.

Sparrowhawk slowly opened her eyes and looked at Bear.

"Enjoy your woman now, great Shaman, for the Old One *will* return. He will claim the spirits of the People. He will come and he will take from you what you have taken from me. He will not let your White Swan live and worship a false goddess."

There was the ring of prophecy in Sparrowhawk's words, but Bear refused to acknowledge the curse.

"What would you have me do to rest your Spirit?" Bear asked.

Sparrowhawk looked into Bear's eyes and for a brief moment he saw the innocent face of the young maiden who had so recently broken his heart.

"My Spirit will never rest," she said, closing her eyes as death swept over her.

The drumming stopped and a rush of wind swept into the lodge, cleansing the air of Sparrowhawk's corruption.

Bear lowered the dead woman to the ground then rushed to Antoinette. He pulled her into the safety of his arms and turned her away from Sparrowhawk's body.

He lifted her chin and placed a soft kiss on her lips. If she would still have him, he would never leave her side again. Nothing else mattered.

Old Woman walked from shadows, looked at Sparrowhawk, then crossed to the altar. She cut away the deer's bonds with Antoinette's discarded knife, then ushered the animal to the rear doorway, giving her a swift slap on the rump. She turned to Bear. "You know what you must do."

Bear shook his head. "I will leave that to you, Old Woman. I have had enough destruction for one day."

Sparrowhawk had been right, Bear realized. Her spirit would never rest. Old Woman would burn the shamaness' body, grind her bones to dust, then cast the fine powder into the air where it would wander forever on the winds of time.

Chapter 43

It was resolved that Sparrowhawk and not the Kwetejk people were to blame for the destruction of Bear's camp. Two Arrows, as elder of the small Micmac tribe, decreed that Black Otter and his people should leave the Micmac lands and return to their homes.

Chilling winds blew strong from the north, ushering the turn of the seasons, changing the days of late summer and the ripening time to the moose calling time of autumn.

Old Woman did not want to live in their old campsite near the river, but Bear needed to remain near his cave, so when Two Arrows offered the hospitality of his camp as temporary shelter, Bear gladly accepted his kindness. Time would distance the energy in the old camp and he knew that by Spring Old Woman would be ready to return to her old home and rebuild.

Bear's encounter with Sparrowhawk had strengthened his resolve to speak to the Council of Elders before the next Summer gathering. He must tell them of his vision and of the dangers that lay ahead for the People, and place before them a plan to unite the tribes in readiness. Leaving his family in Two Arrows' care during his journey, he could travel unhindered.

But foremost in his thoughts was his desire to marry Swan and begin his life again, without the shadow of Sparrowhawk hovering in his heart. He and Swan had renewed their strong friendship. They lived as man and wife among the People, yet they had not given in to their desire for one another since that first night.

Bear stood on the banks of Two Arrows' camp and greeted the new moon with a single request.

"Mother Moon, grant me the love of Swan to warm my hearth and to share my bed."

"Since when does a husband ask the Moon for the love of his wife?" Two Arrows stood beside Bear as both men looked out into the clear blue sky and the faint shape of the growing moon. "You would do better to ask her yourself, brother."

"Ah, I am afraid that I have not been entirely truthful, Two Arrows. Swan is not my wife. We have not made the marriage before witnesses."

Two Arrows looked at his brother with a raised brow and folded his arms, waiting for Bear's explanation.

"I was afraid that you would not accept her so easily if she were not my wife. She is so different from the People that I did not know how you would feel." Bear could not confess his belief that Swan was from the World Above the Sky, a Swan Person come to bring him a message from Great Power. "It was foolish of me, I know."

Two Arrows shook his head. "I am hurt that you would think so little of my character. Do you believe me so ill tempered as to cast her out without a word? The same blood flows in both our veins, little brother, yet you do not know me. Little Bird told me that something was not right between you." Two Arrows chuckled. "I should have believed what my eyes revealed. A blind man could see the look of unsatisfied desire in your eyes."

Bear felt a light flush spread across his cheeks. "Perhaps I thought that by claiming her as my wife, it would make her love me. Now, I am afraid that since I have nothing to offer her, except the food I catch and the warmth of my arms, she will not want me."

"When has love not been enough to start a bond between a man and a woman? Has she asked more than that of you?" Two Arrows placed his strong hand on his brother's shoulder. "After all that you have been through together, I think that she is quite satisfied."

"But she wants to return to her people in a place far away. A place I cannot go."

"Have you asked her to stay with you? To stay here?"

Bear tried to remember when he had last asked Swan to stay with him. "Yes. Before her capture. But not since we have returned to your camp." He hesitated, frowning as he turned to his brother. "She has no family. Whom do I ask for her hand?"

"You must ask Swan, my little brother. Mother Moon can do just so much."

☙

Alone on the rock-strewn beach, Antoinette watched the waves lap onto the shoreline. She had come full circle, returning to the edge of the vast ocean that separated her from her people and from a lifestyle she would never again experience. Except for the few things in her backpack and the amulet still sewn in the fabric of her tunic, there was little to remind her of her past life.

Antoinette placed small strips of birch bark and wild flowers on the slow drifting tide as delayed offerings to the Mother for her safety and her life. There was much more to be thankful for and much more she needed to understand, but she was not ready to rekindle her magic by calling upon the Ancient Ones. Not just yet.

She had promised the Goddess she would not ask to return to France, and indeed she would never request it. Now she wondered if she could go home if the opportunity arose. Could she leave Bear and the people she had come to love and respect?

The knowledge that men from her land once lived among the Micmac, had once walked the shores of this exotic and untamed land, filled Antoinette with anxiety.

Evidence of Templars and their presence in this land was information the Mère Deirdre should know. The Sisterhood would not want their antagonists to establish a stronghold here where people lived free with nature, unhindered in their beliefs. It would be a travesty to inflict them with the heavy trappings of the Christians or, for that matter, the Goddess and the Ancient Ones.

It was probably only speculation on her part. She had no real evidence that the Templars actually had an outpost here or that they left behind people like Sparrowhawk to await their return.

Distanced now from the encounter with the shamaness, she began to wonder if the trappings Sparrowhawk revered were indeed the remains of an aborted crusade, or if the poorly memorized Latin was simply the hopeful prayers of a lost priest. Even Old Woman questioned the truth and had asked Black Otter to explain the oddity of Sparrowhawk's ways.

Sparrowhawk's mother and grandmother had been powerful women, he told her. They had also waited for the Old One to return, passing the obligation to Sparrowhawk when they died. She kept the ceremony of the Old One alive, though by that time it had become distorted and confused and there were few followers left. Sparrowhawk's lust for Power drove her to learn the dark side of magic and the use of potions, not for healing, as they were meant, but for controlling her people. She apprenticed with many shamans. She searched for the power to Walk the Worlds from Bear, but soon realized his power could not easily be stolen. In the end, it was simply greed that had turned Sparrowhawk into such an evil woman.

Sparrowhawk had spoken of a prophecy. Someone was expected to come from far away and interfere with the Old One's return. If the Old One was a Templar, then Antoinette had fulfilled the prophecy. There would be no one left to wait, no one to keep that faith alive.

Antoinette shuddered as she remembered Sparrowhawk's last words. *He will come and he will take from you what you have taken from me. He will not let your White Swan live and worship a false Goddess.*

Antoinette's relationship with the Sisterhood confounded her further. Besides spending her early childhood with her mother learning the ways of the Christian church, she'd had intense training with the Sisterhood. She'd been estranged from her brother, who was both a Templar and a navigator.

Could her journey aboard *La Réale* have been planned by the Sisterhood from the beginning? If true, it was frightening to think she had been so wantonly manipulated.

In her turmoil, she began to wonder what her true destiny really was. She remembered the dark eyes of her dreams and of Bear and his expressions of love. Suddenly everything became clear.

It did not matter, in this world of nature and raw survival, what passed between the followers of one god or another. The future with Bear was hers to explore and the sparks of love they had kindled had waited long enough to burst into flame.

Ursule's words echoed in her head. *Listen to your heart.*

She knew as she watched Bear approach her, his tanned skin and black hair brilliant against the blue of the sky and the deep red cliffs of the cove, that she was meant to love and be loved by him. All the powers of kings and rulers could not stop their destiny together.

Free from danger, free to be herself, she would live life to its fullest. Together, she and Bear would explore the passion that waited for them.

She rose to greet him. When he stood inches away, he raised his hand as if to brush the wind-swept tendrils of hair away from her face, but instead drew her to him and held her tight against his chest.

Bear kissed her eyes then gently kissed her lips.

His love flowed through her. There was no need for false modesty or restraint. She was his and would be his. Here, on the rocky beach or later, there would be nothing to stop her.

Bear looked into her eyes. The power in his gaze entranced her and the longing in his voice braced her against the sudden chill of the air. He lifted her hand and placed a small carved bone object in the center of her palm.

The delicate sculpture of a white swan in flight glowed with an iridescent radiance. Antoinette's heart rushed to her throat. She opened her mouth to speak but Bear stopped her words placing his fingertip to her lips.

"Sing me the song that lives in your heart and I will teach you the ways of love. Be my wife, Wapi'skw, and we will learn to walk the worlds together. We will become one in spirit."

Antoinette clutched the ivory pendant in her hand. In its simplicity it was more beautiful than Anne's silver brooch, more precious than the gift of the Goddess, for it was crafted by the love of its maker.

She held the charm to her breast and looked up at Bear, gazing into the dark sensuous eyes of her dreams, into the intoxicating depths that called her to find her destiny.

There was no reason to refuse him.

"*Oui,*" she said softly, not trusting her voice to make more than a single sound.

Bear touched her forehead with a kiss as tender and light as the ocean breeze and led her away from the shoreline.

ଔ

They were to be married when the Hunting Moon rose in a little less than two weeks. It left little time to arrange the wedding feast, but with many willing hands and many joyous hearts to share the work, things fell swiftly into place.

Little Bird gave Antoinette her wedding dress of white deerskin, lavishly decorated with rolled copper beads and oval seashells. It fit Antoinette as though it had been made for her. As her bride's dowry, Two Arrows presented Antoinette with a white rabbit skin. Finer than any of Anne's ermine robes, it was made from long strips of skin, twisted and woven together to make a square blanket with fur on both sides. It was warm, yet lightweight and nearly windproof.

It was a tradition that the groom's wedding garments be new and made by the bride's hands as a symbol of her worthiness and her ability to care for her new husband.

Old Woman gave Antoinette a white deerskin, exquisitely tanned and flawless in its grain.

"This skin was hard won by Bear," Old Woman said, "and tanned by my hands. The meat was tender and fed many people at our fire. It would do my heart, and the deer, a great honor to have Bear wear it on his wedding day."

Antoinette accepted the gift with pride. With the help of Little Bird and Old Woman to guide her hands, Antoinette began the loving task of fashioning Bear's wedding garments.

The days passed and the moon grew through the starry nights. The men hunted and fished, and the women readied for the feast, preparing the camp for the many visitors that would arrive.

The morning of the wedding dawned with a clear and cloudless sky. A fresh breeze blew off the water and with it the smell of an early autumn drifted through the camp.

Old Woman woke Antoinette and led her to a wigwam where she would cleanse her body and relax before the wedding ceremony. It was a circular sweat lodge, made from poles that were bent to form a low arch. The poles were lashed together with roots and the entire structure was covered with bark and lapped with tanned skins, then stretched and sealed with pitch to make an airtight roof.

Antoinette and Old woman took off their clothing and entered the misty room. The clean smell of evergreen and a cloud of warm air hit Antoinette's nose. Almost at once she felt the steam's therapeutic effects. Steam rose from a pit in the center of the room where hot rocks were doused with water.

Old Woman settled on the leather floor covering and took a deep breath. "I look forward to the spring, when the sweats will be cooler. The summer is not the best time to steam like a clam."

Antoinette laughed. What a joy it was to find someone like Ursule. A sister companion who was wise in the ways of the heart as well as the mind. She knew that she would learn many things in the years to come. Her mind flashed forward and she thought of herself older, wiser and imparting knowledge to the younger women, perhaps her daughter, or granddaughter. A prescient shiver crossed her body and she turned her mind back to her impending marriage.

"Friend, tell me of my husband. I would know all that I could about his life and his ways."

"Ah," Old Woman made a long deep breath. "There are many things that you must ask him yourself. I can tell you of his youth and his life since I married Laughing Elk."

The old woman folded her legs under her and tossed a ladle of water onto the hot rocks. The sweet scent of wild cherry rose with the steam and Antoinette breathed in the new fragrance with gusto.

"Bear has always been different," Old Woman continued. "A caring man. Laughing Elk used to say that Bear would one day become the greatest shaman of our people. He had the power to walk the worlds with effortless grace, and he had the gift to treat the sick at heart as well as those with the sickness of the body and soul." Old Woman smiled. The atmosphere lightened. "You have felt his gift."

Antoinette nodded, remembering Bear's gentle touch.

Old Woman's brows lifted. "It is a good sign. His heart has healed. I thought Sparrowhawk had killed it completely."

Old Woman sighed, then took a deep breath. "When Sparrowhawk left, something in Bear died. He has been lost and confused. It is painful when an important part of your life is suddenly gone."

Antoinette thought of Ursule, Anne and Jacques. Tears swelled in her eyes. Yes, she knew that feeling quite well, that emptiness that could never be filled.

Old Woman placed her hand on Antoinette's. "Bear loves you. And he has searched long and hard for someone like you. It appears, my daughter, that you have filled that empty space in his heart."

Antoinette was silent, wondering now if she would live up to Bear's expectations.

Oh, Goddess. Am I doing the right thing?

Before she could speak of her fears Old Woman laid a gentle hand on Antoinette's knee. "It is natural to be frightened on your wedding day. It is the beginning of a new life, when you will no longer be alone. You will have a helper and a friend who will be by your side. You will have someone to care for. But being a shaman's wife is different from being married to a fisherman or a trapper. A shaman's wife must have patience and understanding."

Old Woman's mind drifted for a moment, then she resumed her conversation in the middle of a thought. "One time Laughing Elk brought me an old flea infested fur. Oh, it smelled to the sky, and dried meat hung from the skin. It was all ragged and torn. Good for nothing but burying."

She laughed. "I wouldn't let him bring it into the wigwam. He said, 'Old Woman, how do you know that this isn't a handsome young warrior, waiting to turn back into a young man and do your bidding?'

"Well, he had a point. Who was I to argue with a great shaman? I did not have the sight to know what spirit man or beast hid within the fur. I packed that fur and carried it over many miles, from winter camp to summer camp and back again, and it never turned into anything other than the old skin it was. It just hung outside the wigwam, ugly, dried and smelly." Old Woman put more water on the rocks and stretched her legs, settling back on the floor. "When Laughing Elk died, I buried it."

Antoinette laughed, realizing she would have done the same thing. The tension in the air became lighter and Antoinette's anxiety over her marriage dissolved.

They spoke of other things, sewing, cooking and the afternoon's marriage ceremony. More hot rocks were brought into the wigwam and the women sat a long time in silence, inhaling the steam that had turned sweet and pungent. It seemed to penetrate into Antoinette's very being. She closed her eyes and after a few minutes, Antoinette found that she was alone.

A new container of liquid and freshly heated rocks were brought into her and she poured a ladle of the syrupy water onto them. The mixture bubbled and seared as it hit the hot rocks and this time the smell of fir and pine mixed with the freshness of the cherry and sugary maple. Underlying it all was the bitter aroma of burnt honey. A familiar tightening at the nape of her neck told her that she was slipping into the world beyond her senses.

Her eyes stung from the pungency in the air and she stretched out onto the low pallet in an effort to escape the rising heat. Just a moment's rest, she thought. It would clear the fog that swirled into her mind.

Day-dreaming of Bear in his youth, she watched the shapes of the mist dance against the roof of the wigwam until her eyes closed.

She was on *La Réale* again and Jacques stood by her side, dressed in the leather marriage garments she'd made for Bear. He wrapped his arm around her waist, pulling her close to him. He pointed to the horizon with an outstretched arm.

"This new world is yours, *ma chère*," he said. "Keep it for the children."

He kissed her with a deep passion that caught her breath. Pulling back, she looked into his eyes. "A kiss for the bride," he said, placing a light kiss on her forehead. "A kiss for the future."

Antoinette wanted to tell him of the love she had finally accepted in her life, but with a whirl of his long cape he turned away and pressed through a crowd of men dressed in chain mail and metal.

Antoinette pushed against the armored wall of human flesh, beating against the hard shields of the warriors. "You must understand," she shouted. "I had no choice."

A warm hand touched her shoulder and she opened her eyes with a jerk. She was back in the wigwam, the mists had cleared, the rocks no longer steamed.

With a warm smile, Old Woman offered her a cup of broth. Antoinette began to speak, and Old Woman silenced her with a shake of her head. "Drink this now. We will talk of your dreams later. You must prepare for your wedding. The guests are arriving."

Antoinette took a few minutes to still her heartbeat and to clear away the cobwebs of her sleep. Despite the dream, a deep calm spread through her like the warm winds of the first days of spring. It was time to set aside her past and begin a new phase in her life.

ଓ

Birch bark canoes lined the banks of Two Arrows' lake. From the narrow river canoes to the long ocean-going boats with the high rockered ends, they were all decorated with the familiar double curved motif, sunbursts and personal totems, each as different and individual as their owners.

Antoinette had donned her white leather gown and draped the white rabbit fur robe across her shoulders. Anne's jeweled amulet hung in the center of her white leather headband, glistening in the sun like a radiant star. Old Woman led her toward the welcoming smiles of Bear's friends and family.

Two Arrows stood before the large wigwam, the eagle's talon and bone necklace adorning his chest and a white caribou cape hanging loosely around his shoulders.

With a great shout, he called the wedding party together. The marriage couple, the men, Old Woman as acting Mother of the groom, and Little Bird would share the marriage meal inside the wigwam. The other women and children would join the festivities when the ceremony was over.

The wigwam floor was laid with fresh fir boughs and a variety of newly dusted skins. A fire burned clean and bright in the hearth that separated the men from the women and thc bride from the groom. Two Arrows, sat at the head of the gathering.

Antoinette and Bear, separated for the better part of a week sat across from one another and tried to hide their desire to be alone. That would come with the rising of the moon. They could be patient.

The meal of roasted meat, boiled clams and smoked fish was served and when everyone had their fill, Two Arrows spoke.

"Kinsmen, we have come to witness the marriage of my brother, Muin, and Wapi'skw, who has come to live among us from far away. I ask that you welcome her as one of the people and accept her ways as she lives among us."

There was a general murmur of acceptance from the gathering and Two Arrows lit his pipe and settled into his oratory of Bear's lineage. Antoinette had been prompted by Old Woman in the proper etiquette for the bride, to be demure and silent. She kept her eyes lowered and only looked directly at Bear when everyone applauded his merits or the attributes of his ancestors.

Bear's gaze never wavered from Antoinette and every time their eyes met, she could read his thoughts as if they were her own. *Soon we will be in each other's arms and the rest of the world will simply fade away.*

Finally she heard the words *noogumich*, Grandmother Ursule, and all eyes turned to her. Antoinette lifted her head and listened to Two Arrows words.

"Ursule was White Swan's teacher. She was a healer and a great shamaness, honoring Mother Moon and Father Sun, as the People do. She counseled the great chiefs of White Swan's tribe and held high status among her people. Ursule was blessed with one daughter, Swan's mother Marguerite. She chose a solitary path to follow Great Power. Swan has come among us to share the ways of her people so that we may better understand the ways of others. Learn from her, my kinsmen, and the people will be strong."

Everyone smiled and nodded, leaving Antoinette a little embarrassed at the grand overture in her honor.

Two Arrows looked at Bear. "Now, rise and show us that you would have this woman as your wife, Bear."

Bear stood and for the first time Antoinette dared to look at him. She had spent many hours sewing his wedding garments, yet only now saw the results of her labor. She had been given the freedom to pattern her designs as she saw fit and now she marveled at the vibrant colors against Bear's darkly tanned skin.

The leggings of white leather were tied at the waist and fringed with strips of leather down the sides. Shells, copper beads and hollow bird bones interlaced the fringe and rattled gently as he moved. Red and yellow suns burst from below the knees and black and white waves undulated at the cuffs. The leggings were finely crafted, however the jacket revealed the love in her heart.

She painted the bodice with black double curved lines and yellow and blue stars, and at the cuffs of the sleeves, rows of red spirals interspersed with yellow crescent moons. Across the back, she traced the dark outline of Muin Wapskw, the Spirit of the White Bear and painted it white.

In her honor, Bear wore his hair unbraided and adorned his headband with a swan's feather—a statement of his love for her. He held a bowl of roasted meat and offered it to her with his head bowed in reverence.

"I promise to provide meat for your hearth and shelter for your body. I will give you my love and my heart. If you will have me for your husband, I promise to respect you and place the honor of your family above mine."

With a smile, Antoinette accepted the offering and set it beside her.

Old Woman began to drum on a small wooden box and Little Bird chanted the words to an old wedding song, shaking a rattle filled with stones. Bear began his wedding dance. He danced in a large circle around the hearth fire, the leather fringe on his leggings rattling with the treasures of bone, copper and shells.

The blood coursed through Antoinette's veins, beating hard with every stroke of the drum and every impact of Bear's feet against the ground. She was swept away by the beauty of his dance. Suddenly he stopped. With a flick of his wrist, he withdrew the silver dagger from his side and the men gasped at the sight of the shining metal. Bear held it for all to see.

"This is my knife. A gift from White Swan and a treasure from her people."

Slowly he cut a lock of hair from his head and handed it to Little Bird as a sign of his pledge to the bride's family.

Little Bird stood next to Bear and motioned for Antoinette to stand beside her. She took a stone knife from her sheath and cut a short braid from Antoinette's hair and handed it to Bear. She positioned Antoinette to stand by Bear, then guided them both to lie on the ground, side by side, their hands interlocking.

Old Woman continued her chant and the men rose to dance around the wedding couple shouting, "*Ahe! Ahe!*"

They were now man and wife. Antoinette looked at Bear. He returned her gaze with a slow secret smile.

ଔ

The wedding party continued throughout the day, moving outside the wigwam to include the other guests. There were jokes and laughter, mostly about Bear's wedding night duties and Antoinette's impending nuptial bliss. Everyone danced and ate until the sun slipped behind the darkening treetops.

It was the custom to usher the newlyweds to their marriage bed as the night descended, but Bear requested that they be left to themselves. Alone and together they would give thanks to Mother Moon as she rose full into the night sky.

Unnoticed, they slipped into the forest and up the ridge to a small clearing overlooking the ocean. Bear had prepared a simple lean-to of spruce poles and fir boughs for their bridal chamber and laid a fire for their ceremony.

Drums beat in the distance. This time they spoke not of despair but of a joyous celebration of life.

Antoinette took off her fur robe and stood before the unlit fire, waiting until the moon danced at the edge of the horizon. She touched the dry tinder with her flint and stone, slowly coaxing the fire into a brilliant flame. Bear stood behind her, wrapping her in his arms as they watched the Hunting Moon rise, luminous and enchanting in the dark evening sky.

Strangely, Antoinette did not feel the need to magically summon Mother Moon, for as her lover held her in his embrace, she felt the glow of the Goddess spreading from his heart to encompass her entire being. The Mother would be with her tonight and she would honor the Mother through her love for Bear.

As if reading her thoughts, Bear stepped back and led her to sit on the soft rabbit skin robe. She found herself extremely conscious of his body as she watched him add wood to the fire. When he removed his jacket and placed it around her shoulders, she felt as though he had wrapped her in the warmth of his flesh. The heady scent of his manliness surrounded her and a delightful shiver ran through her limbs.

Bear stood in the moonlight and turned to face the moon. His hair draped in dark rivulets across his shoulders and his chest was painted with the ritual red, yellow and black of his shamanic symbols. Tiny beads of sweat glistened on his chest and the white leather of his leggings and loincloth reflected the brightness of the moonlight, bathing him with an otherworldly sheen. He swayed with the beating of the drums, and as Antoinette watched him begin his dance, her awareness took a precarious leap into the realm of his magic.

Fire swirled as he spun around it, each salamander of flame rising higher with the motion of his seductive dance. He called the moon and his body glowed in its cool light; he beckoned fire and his body flared red with the ochre of the land and the blackness of coal from the earth. He summoned the sun and yellow spirals streaked from shoulder to shoulder in radiant flames that twined the fire centering the circle. He was at once the fire of the sun, the moon, the earth and man.

Antoinette watched in awe and reverence as his body told the story of love between Sun and Moon. She sat motionless and enthralled as he moved through his intricate ballet with the grace of a deer and the fine quick movement of an eagle in flight. The slow drumbeat from the distant camp and his soft low chanting slowly lulled her to the edge of his world. A world where they would soon be united in spirit as well as body.

Every sway of his hips and undulation of his body pulled her deeper and deeper, until she was no longer Antoinette, but the Great Mother ripe with the bounty of earth. He was Great Power waiting to cool the fire of her senses with his passion.

She could feel her body ignite with the thought of holding this fiery creature of passion next to her. And though she had made love with him before, slept in his arms for nights on end, tonight would be different. Tonight there would be no restraint. He would caress her and share the wondrous secrets of love.

His dance slowed to a steady rhythm as she stood to meet him. His dark eyes caught hers, and she stepped into his arms, melting to the gentle touch of his gaze.

He lifted his hand to untie the loops that fastened her dress and his fingers unwrapped her leather gown. He cast it aside. The long bone buttons and hollow copper beads tinkled as it hit the ground.

A cool breeze swept Antoinette's body, kissing it with the moist night air. She closed her eyes, awaiting his warm touch against her chilled flesh. The heat of his hand would surely melt away the confusion in her soul.

He did not touch her, but with a surprising grace knelt before her. Without a word, he placed a gentle kiss on the tops of her feet. His lips were warm. Flares of desire shot through her, running up her legs and ending in the small of her back. Before she could recover, he moved to kiss her knees. He placed a soft feathery kiss just below her navel.

She felt both ice and fire running through her veins and floated on golden waves of passion that spread over her like a winter storm. Instinctively, she spread her arms and he placed a tender kiss on her breasts.

His arms encircled her. Their lips met. The full heat of his body pressed against her as he pulled her into a long lover's embrace. Antoinette's world spun madly. Bear whispered to her, but his words were lost in the ringing in her head. He lowered her and the soft fur of the pallet reached up to caress her skin with a thousand small sensations. The scent of crushed cedar boughs enveloped her.

Bear took off his white leggings, then his loincloth, and stretched out beside her.

"Be calm my love." Bear kissed the hollow of her throat and stroked her shoulders. "We have the rest of our lives to learn about each other. Tonight will be special."

He traced his fingertip across her mouth and down her chin then followed it with kisses, ending on the swell of her ivory breasts. He captured her lips again. This time she returned his kiss with a growing hunger, so desperate, so passionate, that he pulled away.

Bear closed his eyes and took a deep breath, stilling his mind, slowing his heartbeat. He would not rush his love. Tonight, he would give her the pleasures she deserved. But she was so ardent, so willing. His desire for her was quickly overriding his senses. There was no denying that desire spiraled through him. She had aroused an ache in his heart and body that could only be quenched with his release.

Just a little longer, he told himself. He must wait, bring her to him slowly and not let her building desire vanish too quickly.

Bear leaned back on his arm to watch the slow rise and fall of her breasts, tracing each orb with his finger until they were firm. His body pressed against her and she turned toward him in response. He stroked the smooth contours of her back, the increase of her hips, riding the curve of her waist with his hand to end on the length of her thighs.

He had never felt a woman's skin so soft, so lustrous and firm. Now he wanted that softness around him, to smother him with its sweetness. He pulled her on top of him and she sat astride his hips, her torso shielding his eyes from the brilliance of the bright moonlight. Her pale skin and lustrous hair shone golden against the sky. She moved her hands to caress the hard muscles of his chest.

Kissed by Mother Moon, he thought as he watched the tiny crescent mark on her wrist move back and forth. Kissed and blessed by Mother Moon.

He touched her breasts one by one to his lips, placing a gentle kiss on their small red tips. He laid her down on the fur, following the path of his hands with kisses until he reached the soft mound of her womanhood.

His touch roused her to heights beyond ecstasy. A liquid fire chased the very blood from her veins, replacing it with the coolness of the ocean tides. She hungered for more, much more. She would have him inside her now. She would force him to put out these flames of passion, the sweet torture that consumed her.

Entangling her fingers in his hair, she pulled him forward until he yielded his treasure. The intense heat of his body stretched the length of hers. Instinctively she opened herself to accept him. He was the God of passion and fire, the Horned One, Opener of the Gates of Life. She was the Silver Huntress, the Goddess of Night, the Maiden of the Moon.

"Now, my love." She pushed him up from her chest to look

into his eyes. They were dark and filled with the wild hunger he struggled to control. There was no one, nothing to stop them. “Love me now.”

Bear closed his eyes and took a deep breath grasping for a last hold on his senses. It was no use. He must yield to the searing passion that so desperately drew him to her. He sensed her need and held her close, watching a sudden wave of expectancy pass across her face, then just as quickly turn to wonder. He whispered soothing words to her but they were lost to the wind as his body took control.

Antoinette rode on the waves of their passion and the long moment of ecstasy that exploded around her. She let her body find the rhythm that bound them together.

We are one spirit, she thought as they lay together with the moon showering Her blessings upon them. Antoinette stroked his hair, watching the dark strands glisten in the moonlight as she traced the geometric designs on his arms and chest with the tip of her finger. W*e are one.*

Oiseaux en Vol

Birds in Flight

Chapter 44

Mont-St-Michel
Brittany/ Normandy Coastline
October, 1491

"She is your sister."

"By Christ! Don't I know that?" Gaston Charboneau sat across the table from René d'Anjou, French Administrator for the Knights Templar, the once honored mystic crusaders.

A line of sweat ran the length of Gaston's spine, soaking through the heavy linen of his white mantle. He ran his hands through his short cropped hair with distraction. This interview was much more difficult than he could ever have imagined. Even though it was D'Anjou that summoned him to Mont-St-Michel, Antoinette was not a topic Gaston ever wanted to discuss.

"You, of all people, René, should know better than to condemn a man because of his associations."

René shot Gaston a withering glance and Gaston knew he'd hit a weak spot. René had been associated with the ill-fated Joan of Arc in his youth, involving himself in her crusade and finally traveling with her to Orléans. Even now, as an old man, the visions of her death made his heart ache.

He'd had second thoughts about sending Gaston to find his sister, but he knew Gaston's sworn to obey the Order was steadfast. He folded his hands in front of him.

"Your tongue has loosened with your wits, Gaston. How long have you lived among the Scots?"

A shadow of annoyance crossed Gaston's face. "You know very well I have lived near Rosslyn at the Order's request for the past few years."

"Why have you never asked for a review of your case? You were one of our most honored knights."

Gaston answered indulgently. What could he lose? The Order had already exiled him to the realms of Nowhere. Out of trouble and out of sight. "I prefer the smell of sheep to the courts of the Kings."

René grunted and shook his head. Any other man's contemptuous tone would have sparked his anger. Not

Gaston's. It was difficult to be upset with someone who possessed such piercing honesty.

"Nevertheless, Antoinette is your sister and she has gotten herself involved in our affairs."

"I don't mean to question you, René, but what has this to do with me? I've had no contact with my family for at least eight years. I wouldn't know Antoinette if I saw her."

René smiled. "They say Antoinette is very much like your mother. And like you, outspoken and headstrong."

Gaston's bitterness spilled into his voice. He waved his hand dismissively into the air. "Still, I wish to have no dealings with her. Why tell me about my family now? Why, after all these years?"

"Because your sister has become involved in a most dangerous and serious mission."

Gaston stirred in his chair. His attention wandered to the construction site below the large open window. The afternoon sun cast long rusty shadows on the granite walls, darkening the doorways beneath the cloistered walks. Did he really have to become involved in the Templar's intrigues again? Couldn't they just leave him alone to live out his life in his Highland retreat? Right now the wet and gloomy hillsides appealed to him.

He did not listen to René's words until he heard a name he had not heard for years. Gaston's thoughts broke like thin ice, slicing his heart with sharp and craggy angles.

"I know you were once friends with Jacques DuPrey."

Gaston's jaw tighten at the sound of Jacques' name, but he feigned indifference, turning his gaze back to the construction of a building below René's window.

"Yes, we attended school together in Navarre and later in Sagre. That was also many years ago." By Christ and Mary, he swore under his breath. The Order could not know of his argument with Jacques. "What has he to do with this?"

"It appears that Antoinette was aboard a French ship under the command of Jacques DuPrey. The ship was not bound for England, as the roster stated, but out to sea to transfer goods to the out-bound fishermen. We are concerned because DuPrey was also commissioned by the Order in Sagres to determine the accuracy of a chart made over a century ago by our brother and protector Prince Henry St. Clair. We believe the Sisterhood planned to steal the chart to prevent us from expanding our mission to the New World."

"This is absurd, René. Antoinette is a young girl. She would know nothing of intrigue or espionage. I can't believe that

Jacques and Antoinette even know each other."

René looked at Gaston from the corner of his eye.

"Perhaps not," René said. "Or perhaps they know each other too well."

Gaston's blue eyes turned sharp and silver. For all the hatred he held toward the man, Gaston could not believe Jacques would forswear his oath to the Order.

"What do you mean? That Jacques could somehow be connected with the Sisterhood? Impossible!"

"Yes, I agree. It would be stretching the problem to an extreme. It seems that there was an attempted mutiny by a few men aboard the ship but Jacques was able to overcome them and return to France. We believe that their leader was placed aboard the ship by someone in Rome. We have him in custody. Unfortunately neither the chart nor your sister returned with *La Réale.* Jacques is being detained until either Antoinette or the charts are found."

Gaston's mind tumbled in confusion. "Does he know who she is? Where she is?"

"Yes. He knows she is your sister. He claims he set her adrift off the coastline of what he believed to be the New World. He believes she may still be alive, yet insists she knows nothing about his mission. He has his log book but swears he gave the chart to Antoinette for safekeeping."

"Do you believe him?"

"Yes, he had always proven to be an honest man. He has accomplished much for the Order during his career. Nevertheless, we want Antoinette returned to France, even if the chart is gone forever. We do not want her to remain in the New World. It would not do for the Sisterhood to establish a foothold where we already have a claim. "

Gaston's heart skipped a beat. "What are you telling me, René?"

René d'Anjou looked his protégé firmly in the eyes. "I am telling you that Jacques has confirmed the way to the New World. And, I am ordering you to go there and to bring your sister back to France."

Gaston was speechless. The old man could not mean he must personally sail away from the sight of land and safe harbor. The Order of Christ had exiled him inland, abandoned him. He'd left sea and sail behind. Now, he owed them nothing. Nothing at all.

"And how is this to be done?" Gaston asked calmly. "I am no longer a navigator. How will I know the way if there are no charts?"

"Whatever mistrust you have with DuPrey must be set aside. You are to travel to Amboise to speak with him. He is more than willing to find Antoinette. It seems he formed some kind of attachment to her while they were aboard ship."

Gaston rose from his chair, his mind racing at the possibilities of René's words. "What?"

René laid a soothing hand on Gaston's arm. "Don't worry, my friend. Jacques cares for the girl and would like to know she has not come to harm."

"*Nom de Dieu*!" Gaston's face flushed. He ran his hands across his face. "You know it has been many years since I've spoken to Jacques DuPrey. We have no love lost between us."

René poured Gaston a goblet of cider and thrust it into his hand. "*Mon ami*, when your life and your mission depend on someone, it is best to find out all of his strengths—and his weaknesses. Jacques has devoted his life to Christ's work, to our work."

Glancing at the signet ring on René's finger, the ring bearing the symbol of the Knights Templar, the grail and sword, Gaston wondered if the Order trusted him as much as they did Jacques.

He looked into his old friend's face and breathed deeply. "I cannot speak to Jacques. There is too much pain in our past."

"You have no choice, Gaston. He is the only one who can tell you where Antoinette may be. We are arranging his employ on a ship through Anne de Bretagne. Jacques need not know of the true cause for Antoinette's return until you are under sail. Then you may tell him whatever you wish."

Gaston closed his eyes, gathering his thoughts. He really did not want to know more than what was absolutely necessary, and there was no desire left in him for political intrigue. Perhaps there was some way out of this mission.

"What if I refuse to go?" he asked.

"You have little choice in the matter," René said, as if the answer was obvious. "Remember you gave up the freedom to choose your destiny when you swore on the Blessed Virgin's Heart you would obey and defend the Holy Secret. Till death, wasn't it?"

So, that was it, Gaston thought. No choice. Death or dishonor. Two sides of the same coin. A coin that had been tossed for him before.

"We are prepared to offer you something in return, Gaston. Something we know you still seek."

"I have given up on my desires, René."

"Have you given up your desire for freedom?"

"What do you mean?"

"We are willing to grant you full return to France and reinstatement of your rank. If you do this for the Order, you can come home to France."

Speechless, Gaston stood. The Order had found his only desire. The privilege to live in his homeland. He nodded, then without a word, he turned and walked swiftly from the room.

There were many miles to cover before the sun set and the tides rose to cover the causeway between Mont-St-Michel and the mainland of Normandy. Brittany, home, was only a few leagues and one mission away.

Chapter 45

Land of the People
Summer 1492

Three turns of the seasons had passed since Bear gave his husband's pledge to Swan. Seasons filled with love and laughter. Two Arrows' new son was now six moons old. The baby was named Raven.

Within two moons the trees would begin to change their colors and the cool breezes of Autumn would blow into Bear's camp. And with the wind's song, Bear hoped to hear news of a child growing inside Swan's belly.

Bear walked the high plateau near the sea, thinking of this. It would be a blessing for the tribe to have another child among them.

His child would learn the shaman's way and Swan would teach him the healing arts and magic of her ancestors. Bear would teach his child how to read the message of the sun and the changing of the seasons. He would show his son or daughter how, at the beginning of summer, the sun rode farther to the North at its wakening. And how, like today, when a ribbon of colors thrown against an azure sky lingered long past the sun's setting, it was the sign to prepare for the mid-summer gathering. These things Bear would teach his child—a child destined to lead the People.

Bear pushed away thoughts of what might be and walked along the high ridges of the promontory, gathering the cranberries and blueberries that grew sweetest along the hillsides. In a short walk through his medicine field, he gathered sweet fern and pansy, sweetgrass and clover, flowers and herbs that could only be harvested in the high days of summer. A pouch full of berries would be a grand prize and more than enough to make his new wife happy.

It took very little to make Swan happy. A flower growing near the wigwam door, a squirrel taking food from her hand, a bird singing high in the pines. He could not remember ever knowing a woman to take such pleasure in little things. Laughing Elk's spirit was right when he told Bear that he had a treasure in Swan.

During the few months they had shared a hearth and the pleasures of marriage, they had learned each others language well. With Old Woman's help, Bear now understood Swan. He had learned some of the ways of her people. He could see in his mind the great rulers of her world when she described their clothing and their habits. And he visualized the enormous stone lodges where her people lived, though he wondered why they would choose to stay in one place all their lives.

He imagined the fields of grains and fruit trees purposely planted by Swan's people. They did not move with the seasons; they did not live among the wild creatures. Their men had lost their ability to tell the direction of prey by the smell of the air or the taste of the earth.

There were many animals he had never seen: the moose without its antlers that carried a man upon its back, and the tamed birds that lived in cages—it seemed absurd, yet possible. Even with all Swan's explanations and drawings, he could not imagine the great canoe that brought her to his world. He was glad, however, that it swept her away from the most evil of men and left her in his land to be his wife. He knew Great Power had blessed him with his bounty. Great Power had given him happiness during the past turning of the seasons.

Two Arrows offered the hospitality of his camp to Bear and his family. The fall hunting had been good, yielding many moose and caribou to feed the tribe during the mild winter. There had even been a marriage between Two Arrows' daughter Morning Star and White Water.

Bear was reluctant to give up his cave and the campsite near the river; it was too good to be abandoned. So, as the heir to Laughing Fox's hunting territory, when the spring sun thawed the rivers, he had taken Swan and Old Woman back to the camp in the valley between the mountains. The destruction still lingered, but the sorrow and death had passed with the seasons.

Bear made short day trips from his camp, traveling to sit at council, to hunt and to restock his medicinals. He would return to his camp to share meals, to be with Swan and Old Woman, then he would retire to the quiet cave where he worked his magic long into the night.

It was a good life Great Power had given him, and in return he had been charged with a mission. In a few weeks, at the annual summer gathering, Bear would present the Tribal Elders with a plan to unite all the people in peace; Micmac, Maliseet and Bethouk, as well as their Abenaki brothers across the ocean to the West and the Montagnais and *Kwetejk* to the North. Together they would work to rid all People of the enemy that grew among them—the enemy of greed that had devoured Sparrowhawk, Dancing Fox and many others.

He would tell them of Laughing Elk's words of warning, that Power would change, that the Worlds would change. And as much as he regretted his duty, he would also reveal Sparrowhawk's prophecy of doom: that the Old One would return and claim the spirits of the People. And if he could not make the great Chiefs understand, if the people were not willing to fight the Old One together, then Bear would help the People make the change as best he could. Like the hatchling shoved from its nest, he had no choice.

The shadow of the late evening fell on the high cliffs as Bear returned to his home in the valley. He stopped to enjoy the colors of the darkening sky and to smell the strong salty scent of the sea.

A distant image pulled his gaze away from the beauty of the twilight and his eyes searched the horizon. Every time he glanced away, his gaze and thoughts involuntarily returned to the low cloud that floated where the sky kissed the sea. A single cluster in a cloudless sky, a strange, unnerving image moved across the water.

He studied it, watched the soft and billowy white tufts of air grow in size with increasing speed. He lowered himself down to the edge of the precipice and watched from behind a bush as the cloud came nearer. It was something he had never seen before.

A lump grew in Bear's throat as the prophecy of his vision unfolded with uncompromising clarity. A dark island moved toward the shore. Tall trees grew like sharp spears from its center. But they were not quite trees, not quite spears. And the clouds were not at all like clouds. Unlike the animals of his vision, the creatures in the clouds were men, climbing the trees like overgrown squirrels, shouting to each other as the island stopped in the outer edges of the cove.

The island turned toward Bear. He saw the white clouds full on, flattened like a white moosehide hanging in the sun. A red symbol glared from the center of the largest hide, red and bright, the color of blood—the color of Power. It was the same symbol he had seen painted on the hide behind Sparrowhawk's altar.

Had Sparrowhawk's hide also come from a great canoe like this one? A canoe Antoinette's people called a ship. Yes, she had said it was a ship that carried her across the sea and brought her to his wigwam. Now the ship was back.

Blood pounding in his veins, Bear laid his head on his folded arms, trying to calm the grief swelling in his heart. With happiness filling his new marriage, he had tucked the prophetic vision into the depths of his mind. Now it had become a reality that he was not prepared to face.

Bear watched the shadows scurrying back and forth in the darkness of the ship. Had Sparrowhawk's Old One finally returned? Had he come back before Bear could unite his people, before he could enjoy a rich and full life with Swan?

The sky grew dark, yet Bear kept his silent vigil, straining to see the outline of the ship against the moonless sky. He watched as the white hides were rolled and strapped to the trees, the red symbols disappearing into their folds like great red tongues in a dog's mouth. He waited, listening to the constant banter of a language he could not quite understand. The sky grew black and the men aboard ship became silent.

No one left the ship, no one swam to shore. Then he realized the Old One or his emissary would wait until sunrise, when the light of day could show him the way to Swan's wigwam.

Panicked, Bear sprang up and raced down the hillside. He must go to Swan; hide her and Old Woman in his cave until before the sun rose and betrayed the well trodden path to the sea. Hopefully the Old One would leave quickly and empty-handed.

ଔ

Gaston stood motionless on the rolling deck, listening to the slow waves echo from the shoreline and return with a whisper to lap against the hull of *Le Bon Breton*.

Gaston turned to Sebastian. He had accompanied the

voyage as Anne's representative. "I hope this landing proves more bountiful than the last time we went ashore. Bird eggs and clams will not pacify our crew much longer," Gaston said. "I lose faith that we will find Antoinette."

"Jacques is sure we are near the area where he set her adrift. He said he saw a high promontory in the distance before he cast her boat away. Even though there was a storm raging, the tides were advancing and the currents were running steady and westerly. There was dark smoke rising from high cliffs like a signal plume. We saw smoke this afternoon, just there." Sebastian stretched his arms out over the railing, his hand following the curve of the promontory on the western horizon.

"So far, this is the highest peak along the coast and the only one with the dark mists," Gaston agreed. "I will fire the signal guns."

"Wait." Sebastian said. "Should we wait until morning? We don't know what waits for us on these shores. It may be as bleak as the last landing or there may be savages lying in wait." He touched Gaston on the arm, cocking his head toward the hatchway. "Come, Jacques is waiting below to plan tomorrow's actions."

Gaston turned from the railing and took a deep, painful breath. His body stiffened with regret at what he might have to do, actions that might cause a breach of trust with both men. The troubles that had plagued him from his youth had been dimmed by the passing of the years and during the crossing he and Jacques had made their peace. A few words had healed a lifetime of pain and misunderstanding but now their friendship might be shattered once again.

"When we find Antoinette, we will bring her back to France," Gaston said.

"I thought that was the reason for our trip."

"You don't understand. If she doesn't come willingly—" Gaston hesitated, knowing he must be blunt and to the point with the man. "—we will have to take her back as a prisoner."

Sebastian stepped away from his companion. "What? You are mad, Gaston. The travel at sea has taken your wits. Jacques would never hear of it. Anne would have your head when you return to France."

Gaston turned once more to gaze at the dark and shimmering surface of the water.

"If this was a simple mission, they would not have sent me. Whether you believe me or not, I love my sister and I will do my best to keep her from harm." Gaston paused, choosing his words carefully, he stepped toward Sebastian. The sound of the wooden deck creaked under his weight. It was time to know if Sebastian would be on his side when the time came for action.

"What do you want more than anything, Sebastian?" Gaston place his hand on his companion's shoulder.

"What do you mean?" Sebastian's looked at him curiously.

"I know that you dream of becoming a navigator. There are positions open at Sagre. If you aid my mission, I will see that the Order of Christ accepts you into their fold. You will have a ship of your own to command within the year."

Sebastian's eyes brightened then dimmed.

"I will have no part in her mistreatment, Gaston. But I will help. Not for any reward. Only for my love for her ladyship, for your sister and for my adopted homeland."

"Then you will back me up, if need be?"

"Yes, Gaston. If it will bring Antoinette home alive, I will support your cause."

As the men turned away from the darkening shoreline, they did not see the silhouette on the mountain top rise against the glowing night sky. They did not hear Bear's fervent prayers to Great Power as he disappeared into the thick forest.

ଓ

"You are late, my love." Antoinette rose from her seat in front of the wigwam, walked toward the fire and briskly stirred the contents of the wooden cooking pot. "I began to worry for your safety. Old Woman has eaten and gone to bed. I will have you all to myself tonight." She turned, offering the bowl of hot stew to Bear, then stopped short as her gaze fell on him.

He stood some few feet away, looking at her with a vacant stare. His arms hung limply at his side. He was short of breath and the sweat of a hard run beaded on his chest.

"What has happened?" She ran to him, unable to read the emotions on his face. "Are you sick? Hurt?"

Bear took a long deep breath and swallowed the tight knot in his throat. "He is here."

"What do you mean? Who is here?"

"He has come in a great ship." Bear pulled her close to him, disregarding the soup bowl in her hands. Her hair smelled like the lavender he'd picked for her that morning. "The Old One has come."

Antoinette face flushed with excitement, her green eyes flashing gold in the firelight. She pulled away from him and ran to the doorway, missing the sadness and tears swelling in

Bear's dark eyes.

"You saw a ship? When?"

Bear held her by the shoulders and turned her around to face him. "It is the Old One," he said with a hard voice. "He has come to kill you."

Antoinette shook her head. "Nonsense. The Old One was only a creation in Sparrowhawk's twisted mind."

"The hide that pushes the ship is the same, Swan; the red symbol on it is the same."

"Symbol?" Antoinette's face turned from expectancy to alarm as she realized the meaning of his words. "A cross— there is a red cross on the sail?"

Bear bent to the sand and drew the symbol of the cross pateé. "There are many men. Men of your kind."

Antoinette steadied her voice, taking a step back from his drawing. "Where? Where are they?"

Bear hesitated. If she wanted to find them she could. Once she had the power of sight and he knew she could summon it again. "The ship is in the cove by the smoking mountain. I watched it well past sunset. No one came ashore."

Antoinette nodded. "Yes, they would wait until morning."

Distracted, she turned and walked to the fire, dropping the contents of the bowl back into the cooking pot. She stirred the stew with a long wooden paddle, then ladled out a hot portion to cool in a birch bark bowl. She thought momentarily of Jacques. Could he have come back for her? Or were Sparrowhawk's dying words proving to be true? Were the Christian Knights and the followers of Christ about to invade Bear's land?

Her long hair, grown now below shoulder length with the passing seasons, whipped against her face as she turned toward him. "Take me to the ship."

Bear threw off his pack and crossed the short distance between them, grabbing her in his strong arms.

"No." He smothered his words into the curve of her neck. "I will take you to the cave."

He held her head between his hands and kissed the lids of her eyes, her forehead and her lips. "I will not let the Old One have you. He will not take you from me."

"Nor will I go with any man, my love," she said, gazing up into his eyes. "But I must know who will stand on our shores in the morning light. I must know if they are truly my people— if they are Bretons or Englishmen, Spaniards or Portuguese explorers or if they are crusaders for the god they call Christ."

"It is a long walk to the coastline, perhaps two or three

hours." Bear pulled her once again to his kiss, smelling her hair, feeling her warm body against his. He stood on the edge of losing her and wanted desperately to hide her away. "It is too dark for us to travel this moonless night."

"Then we will go as soon as the dawn breaks," she said, oblivious to his caresses. Her thoughts were at the cove. "I want to be there when their boats come ashore, to see their faces and hear their words before we stand face to face."

Bear ran his hands along her back and down to the round swell of her buttocks. He could command her not to go and he knew she would obey him, but she would never forgive him. Perhaps he would drug her soup, tie her up, do whatever it took to save her from destruction. The overpowering need to protect her filled his heart.

"Come, let us go to my cave, we will discuss this later." He edged her away from the campfire, and out into the night.

"But you have not eaten," Antoinette said. "The stew is hot." She pulled away from him, reaching for the newly filled bowl, but he stopped her.

"I do not need hot food to serve my body now, *chère*." The words of her people slid effortlessly from his lips and Antoinette's heart melted at the warm touch of his hand around her waist. "I need to hold you now. I need to shut out the painful thoughts of tomorrow."

"But the fire," she protested. "the food."

Bear cast a quick glance behind him as Old Woman peeked out from behind the deerhide covering the wigwam door.

Ignoring Old Woman's shaking head, he turned Antoinette toward the pathway. "The food will keep till morning."

଼

Old Woman stood at the entrance to Bear's cave, her traveling pack strapped to her back and her walking staff in hand. She rapped with her staff on the cave wall.

"I would go now, Bear. It is time to go."

Bear threw the green velvet cloak around him, covered Antoinette with a hide and walked to the cave entrance. He glanced at the small sliver of moon hanging in the distant sky behind Old Woman's head.

"What in Great Power's name are you doing here?"

"I am ready to go see the friends of Kluskap."

"What? Old Woman, we are sleeping. What do you mean?"

"I mean I want you to take me to see the great canoe. I want to see the men who come to our land."

Bear clutched his robe with one hand and ushered Old Woman into the cave to stand by the warmth of the fire. He held his finger to his lips and motioned toward Antoinette across the room.

"Old Woman, I do not intend to go back to the cove," he whispered. "I will not take Swan and I will not take you."

Old Woman turned and began walking to the entrance. "Then I will go by myself and I will see the friends of Kluskap before my eyes are too clouded to see the pathway before me."

She was strong and stubborn, always one step ahead of her fate. Bear often wondered if Papkutparut would have to trick her to get her beyond the doors of the Ghost World when her time came to depart the living.

Defiantly, he stretched his arm across the doorway. "Old Woman, Grandmother, these men may not be the friends of Kluskap. It may be the Old One returning to kill Swan. You were there, you heard Sparrowhawk's words."

Old Woman spat on the ground at the mention of Sparrowhawk's name. "She knew nothing of the great path of our people. She was a sorceress, a witch, not a shamaness. She could only vomit the words of her mothers and the potions of living death." Old Woman spat again and set her stride, heading for the doorway.

"Wait, grandmother." Antoinette spoke from the shadows of the cave and walked to Old Woman's side, smoothing her hair. "I will take you with me. If Bear refuses to face his destiny, then we will let him hide like a rabbit in winter."

With a quick side-step, he stood between the doorway and the two defiant women. His eyes filled with sadness. "Neither of you have cause to belittle my honor. It is not my destiny I wish to defy, Swan, it is your own."

"You would have me hide like a mouse from a fox?" Her words were clear and forceful and without anger. "I cannot run from my fate, any more than I can stop myself from loving you."

Bear understood Antoinette's analogy. There were some things that must be done. Some things that would not let you rest until the task was complete.

"What about you, Old Woman? Why do you not heed my wishes?"

"Because I am old. When my eyes are gone and my limbs can no longer carry me about, I will have nothing else to live for. I promise to die quietly, but when that happens I want to stand before Great Power and proclaim that I have been a part of my people's destiny."

Bear searched one face then the other and knew there was nothing he could do except give in to their desires.

"If you truly wish to risk your lives then I must be there to protect you." He walked toward the two women and spread his arms wide to gather them to him. "You must surely know you are my heart and soul. I would be nothing without either of you." He made a deep sigh.

How easily I am persuaded by the women I love.

ଓ

The signal cannon fired at first light, breaking the silence of the cove like a thousand Thunder Brothers raging through the sky. Bear, Antoinette and Old Woman heard the shot as they left the cover of the forest and stepped into the thick morning mists shrouding the shoreline. The ship was nearly invisible in the fog but Antoinette knew the furled sails hid the red cross pateé of the Knights of Christ, the explorers of the seas.

Disturbed at the loud explosion, Bear held the women back with an outstretched arm, but Old Woman pushed past him and stood looking in the direction of the sound.

"Kluskap's friends have rude voices. They will wake the Spirits of the Dead."

Images of the death and the destruction of a hundred years of war and pain filled Antoinettc's thoughts and, in a brief moment of panic, she wondered if she was making a horrible mistake, insisting she meet the ship.

"It is a cannon, Old Woman," she said. "A great weapon used for war. These men are not gods. They are warriors and conquerors."

Old Woman nodded in understanding. The loud voice of destiny, she thought. *I will hear it again before I die.*

Bear felt the shock of the sound through his feet and Laughing Elk's words echoed in his mind.

"Swan, this is not good. Laughing Elk told me your people will bring much suffering to my land."

Antoinette gazed out at the ghostly shape of the ship in the cove. If Laughing Elk's spirit had also seen the future of his people, then their destiny could not be stopped. It could only be varied to suit their needs.

"I have seen the future as well," Antoinette confessed. "But if we are not the first to meet them, there will be others. Perhaps people from a tribe who do not understand. Would you rather have the workings of the future at your command or in the hands of others less capable?"

The moment of his people's destiny rode hard on Bear's shoulders. Somehow, he must summon the courage Papkutparut gave him and look into the unknown without fear. He remembered the Guardian's words. *Swan has the knowledge of your people's future. She can help you.*

He turned to Antoinette, his eyes full of resignation. He would do as she wished.

"If you will stand by my side," Antoinette pleaded. "And be my strength, we will see this through together."

She closed her eyes as he pulled her into his arms. It was the beginning of the change she had dreamed about. Once the two cultures made contact, nothing would ever be the same again for Bear's people, nothing would ever be the same for her and Bear.

"Let us wait until the fog lifts," she said. "Let me see if these men are friends or enemies. Then I will know if it is right for us to meet them."

The small boat slipped like a wraith through the thinning fog. The sound of paddles pulling against rolling waves carried across the silence of the cove to Bear's ears. Five men stepped off the landing boat and stood expectantly on the rocky shoreline. From their perch atop the low tree sheltered cliff side, Antoinette, Bear and Old Woman watched as the men advanced.

Although she could not see their faces, Antoinette knew by their dress that they were Frenchmen. Safer by far than if they had been Spanish or English.

They landed and two men advanced across the beach. Ship hands unloaded empty barrels. Antoinette squinted, trying to see their faces. Her heart quickened as she recognized Jacques' silver hair and Sebastian's easy stride.

"They are my friends," she said and began to move toward them.

Bear reached out to stop her, holding her wrist in a tight grip. "If they are your friends, they will want to take you home. Are you sure this is what you want?"

Antoinette's emotions tumbled. Jacques had finally come for her. She wanted to run to him, to hold him and tell him she was alive. She wanted to hear a comforting familiar voice from home.

Tears welled in her eyes and a tight knot lodged in her

stomach. What was she to do? She could not, in good conscience, just walk away from the new life she had begun. She searched Bear's face for any trace of understanding. She would never be able to explain everything to him and she could not tell him about her love for Jacques. Besides, Bear was right. It was not a coincidence these men had landed in this cove, near the area where she had been shipwrecked.

"I must speak to my friend. He has crossed the ocean and risked his life. He has made a dangerous journey to look for me. But on my oath, my love, he will not take me back. I am your wife and my place is by your side."

Bear released her, then took her hand and laid it flat upon his chest. His body was warm, his skin smooth. She could feel the vibration of his voice through her fingers as he spoke.

"You have brought my heart back to life and now it beats with yours. If you must speak with them, I will stand by your side. I will listen with my ears and not with my heart. Then if you wish to go with him, I will not stop you, for I have no need of a wife who is unhappy at my hearth. But you must know that I will kill anyone who tries to take you against your will."

Antoinette withdrew her hand from his chest. There was no way to be certain Jacques would not try to take her away. She knew Bear was as good as his word.

She stepped out into the open, then remembered she was dressed like Bear and Old Woman, in leather and moccasins. Bear's face was painted with red ochre. Even his height would startle a Frenchman. The crewmen would be well armed. The situation was dangerous.

Antoinette told Bear and Old Woman to expect the men to be surprised at their appearance, then she led the way into the open cove.

The men turned one by one and the sound of steel sliding against steel echoed through the silence as they drew their swords. At once Jacques recognized Antoinette and at his quick order, the men lowered their weapons.

Jacques lifted his head and his gray eyes locked with hers. He smiled and began to run to her, but she lifted her hand urging him to remain still. The expression of joy on his face made her heart sink. He still loved her. Distance and time had made no difference.

Her gaze traveled to the shoreline and she saw Sebastian and another man standing by the small boat. The man was meticulously groomed. His skin was fair despite the fact he had been aboard ship for many weeks. He wore a long tunic of white linen, emblazoned with the red cross pateé. It was only when he turned that she realized it was Gaston, a pale phantom from her past, a man opposed to everything she believed and who held no love for her.

For all intents and purposes, Gaston was Sparrowhawk's Old One, bringing his word of the One God to Bear's land. The future of Bear's people had been set in motion.

Jacques stepped forward, cautious of the stern glance in the eyes of Antoinette's companion and of the silver dagger suspended from a leather sheath around Bear's waist.

Antoinette smiled, then handed her staff to Old Woman who stood behind Bear. With all the courage of a warrioress going into battle, she walked to Jacques and stopped a few feet from him. How could she tell him that she had waited until all hope of rescue was gone? That she had fallen in love with a man who shared her beliefs? And above all else, that some part of her still loved him? There was no easy way.

"Anne sent us," he said, knowing Gaston's presence as representative of the Templars unnerved her.

She looked past Gaston to Sebastian and he waved to her. Stepping back, she stood by Bear and placed her hand on his arm. "This is Bear World-Walker and his foster mother, Old Woman. I live with them in their camp."

Antoinette watched Jacques' gaze level on Bear and from the forlorn look in Jacques' eyes, she knew he was beginning to understand. Bear wore Jacques' green cloak. The woman to whom he had pledged his love and crossed an ocean to find stood proudly beside another man.

"The Micmac have taken me to live at their hearth. They have accepted my ways and I live among them as a free woman. There is no Church to question my faith. Only the forests and my kinsmen are my concern."

Antoinette turned to Bear, knowing he understood the strained emotion in their words, if not the entire meaning of their conversation. She looked at Jacques, tears welling in the corners of her eyes.

"I have a new life."

"Is it one you truly desire, Antoinette?" Jacques asked. "What of the Sisterhood?"

She heard Jacques' unspoken words. *What of us? Why would you choose to remain here instead of going home?* His gaze told her that his heart was breaking.

Antoinette began to answer, but Gaston stepped to Jacques' side. They were an oddly matched pair: one dark, the other fair. Jacques was an explorer. Gaston was a Templar, sworn to conquer all pagans and infidels. And she knew he was here for reasons other than simply finding her.

"What brings you so far from home, Gaston? There is nothing here to conquer," she said, quick and to the point.

"We've come to rescue you," Gaston said.

"You? Where were you when Ursule took me from our mother?" Antoinette's voice was cold and biting. "Where were you when Visconti threatened me with the Inquisition? You did not come to save me then!"

Gaston took a quick breath at her retort. "You were not so important then."

"Me? Important?"

"Yes," Jacques interrupted, stepping between them. His eyes searched hers, looking for some trace of hope that she would reconsider her decision. "Anne has sent us for you. You can come home now. She is Queen of France and has retained full control of Brittany. It is safe for you to return."

Antoinette's eyes flashed to Gaston, but his face was stoic, his countenance unmoving. "What about Visconti?" she asked. "I still have him to consider."

"You need not fear the Church. My Order will deal with the Cardinal," Gaston said. "The Church we can restrain, but we cannot protect Anne from her husband."

"Our past together has been troubled," Antoinette replied. "Why should I trust you now?"

Gaston waved away her words. "We were children, Antoinette. I have changed. You have changed. I give you my word that you will have my protection."

"You must come back, Antoinette," Jacques said. "If not for yourself, then for Anne. She needs you now more than ever."

Gaston took a step forward and Antoinette stepped back. Her heart quickened as the long-forgotten fear of him returned. She half listened to his words as she struggled with her memories. "What?" she asked. "What did you say?"

"If Jacques will not speak for himself," Gaston repeated. "Then I will."

Antoinette wondered just how much Gaston knew of her relationship with Jacques. Did Jacques tell him of their brief encounter?

Jacques raised a hand to silence Gaston and pulled him aside.

"No. This is not the time or place."

"By God, man!" Gaston shrugged off Jacques' restraint. "You've traveled a thousand leagues from home to find Antoinette. Can't you tell her how much you love her?"

"She knows," Jacques replied. "But it must wait."

Antoinette looked at Jacques once again. Surely the pain in his heart was as unbearable as her own. She searched for a way to tell him that she still cared.

"Antoinette, listen to me," Gaston pleaded. "I swear by the Blessed Virgin, that Anne needs you."

She drew back from her brother's words. "What has Brittany to do with me now?"

Sebastian stepped forward. "Your presence can keep Visconti from harming Anne."

"What about Charles?" Antoinette asked. "Doesn't he love her? Can't he protect her?"

"He cares for her, however Visconti wants Brittany's wealth. He will do anything to get it," Sebastian replied. "He would even persuade the King that he no longer needs Anne by his side."

Antoinette looked from one man to the other. It was all too much. The politics, the intrigue, the lying and treachery. Afraid her knees would give way, she stepped back. Bear's warm hand on her shoulder calmed her.

"I cannot go back," she said with renewed strength. "I have made promises. I have a new family." She turned to Old Woman and stepped back to stand beside Bear. She placed her hand on his arm. It was as rigid as the knife at his side. "Bear is my husband."

Gaston's face flushed. "You cannot mean you have bedded with this—this savage. This red man." His hand flew to the hilt of his sword. "You would choose to live with these people rather than to serve your Queen?"

Jacques stayed Gaston's arm before he could unsheathe his sword. "It is not for us to judge the worth of these people. If she has chosen to live with them, then we should abide her decision."

Bear did not understand Gaston's words, though he understood the malevolent tone in his voice. He stepped protectively in front of Antoinette.

Gaston lifted his hand. "I will have no quarrel with you, red man, if you let my sister go."

Antoinette touched Bear's shoulder, letting him know it was all right. Then, she walked past the men and down to the shoreline. She felt like the red seaweed swaying back and forth against the tides, belonging sometimes to the sea and sometimes to the rock it clung to.

She turned back to look over her shoulder at the men and the old woman standing expectantly on the beach.

Bear moved behind her, defending her as she stood alone.

She owed so much to him. He had given her hope when there was none to be found. He taught her to rely on her inner strength, and most importantly, to trust her heart to love. She could never leave him.

She was ready to give her reply. "I—"

Bear held up his hand, requesting silence. Then he walked toward the men. To their surprise, he spoke in passable French.

"Power tells me you are men of honor," he said, filling his deep voice full of authority. "You speak many truths but you listen with your head instead of your heart." He nodded toward Gaston. "You should respect your sister and keep your eyes from betraying your fear."

Gaston stiffened at Bear's insult, yet he remained still.

"You have my permission to hunt and fish these lands within a day's walk," Bear continued. "Further than that I cannot guarantee your safety. You may sleep on these shores tonight and we will let you know by the rising of the next sun if Antoinette will return with you."

Respect and admiration flooded Jacques' face as he listened to Bear. He nodded, accepting Bear's decree. This was not a simple savage who stood before him. This red man spoke the King's French better than most Bretons. Though he was rough and rugged, wildly painted and dressed in skins and furs, he showed a keen understanding of the makeup of men. Jacques wondered if all the inhabitants of this land were so defiant, so straightforward and wise.

Without further word, Bear took Antoinette's trembling hand and slowly led her past the men. Old Woman silently followed them back to the cliff side.

"Very well," Gaston shouted to their backs. He took a quick deep breath and, venturing forward, slid his sword into its sheath with a swish of metal against leather. "I will wait until tomorrow's high tide for your answer."

Chapter 46

Antoinette was solemn as they walked the path homeward. The burden her brother laid on her shoulders troubled each footstep and Jacques' love weighed equally heavy on her heart. Each step away from the coastline, away from her brother, from Jacques and the promise of home, filled her with even more questions. Questions she must resolve and act upon by the mid-day's changing tide.

As if echoing her worries, Old Woman's words broke the cumbrous silence. "I am not pleased with Kluskap's friends."

"Nor am I, Old Woman," Bear said. "You would think his messengers would have better manners. The gray haired one has a noble heart. The pale one intrigues me. He has eyes like a fox."

Antoinette nodded. "Like a fox at hunt. Headed straight for its prey."

Why was Gaston here? she wondered once again. After all the years of separation from his family, why would he come out of seclusion? She was not important enough for the Order of the Knights of Christ to send one of their best crusaders on such a dangerous journey and Jacques could have pleaded Anne's case to her. There was something else that Gaston wanted.

Antoinette thought of Sparrowhawk's relics and her last words. The Old One had left her ancestors in charge of the goblet, the sword and the cross. The Old One was a keeper of a secret. The Templars had once been to these shores.

She remembered Jacques' chart, the chart Lawrence Bernard had nearly killed them for, the fragment of a chart she now carried in her backpack. The parchment was old, the lines drawn in outline. On *La Réale's* voyage Jacques had been re-enforcing the lines, filling in details. A sudden phrase passed through her thoughts.

"My purpose here is to confirm a safe route for future explorers," Jacques had told her. He was not discovering a new route but mapping a known one.

Yes. The chart surely belonged to the Templars and pointed the way to this land. Gaston needed the chart to prove the Templar's claim to the land, and he knew it to be in her possession. She would not speak of the relics or Sparrowhawk's strange Christian cult, she decided. Not until she knew what Gaston really wanted. Perhaps she could convince him that she knew nothing. She would quietly give the chart back to Jacques. She would only tell him of Sparrowhawk.

The Sisterhood must also be told about the possibility of an old Templar outpost. They would want to take steps to stop them from having a stronghold of worship in this new land. There would be no way for the Sisterhood to learn these things unless she could get Sebastian to tell Anne. Anne would let Mère Deirdre know, then Antoinette's duty to the Sisterhood

Sisterhood would be complete. She had given the Sisterhood her youth and they would have use of her no more. She could live with Bear in peace.

As much as Antoinette missed Anne, she did not need to be at her side. Anne would see that the Bretons kept their heritage and retained their unique way of worship, even with men like Cardinal Visconti snapping at her heels. Anne would also know to guard herself against the King.

Antoinette did not believe Gaston's lies, that his Order could control Cardinal Visconti. He would pursue her, even if she had the immunity of the Crown and the assistance of the Knights of Christ. She would be as helpless as a field mouse in a snake's lair with the Templars protecting her. Better to face the Cardinal and his Inquisitors. At least he had human weaknesses to exploit.

But lingering above all her considerations about returning to France was her relationship with Jacques. It was almost unbelievable that he had come to find her. He must love her very much to risk another ocean crossing. But did she love Jacques enough to give up her freedom and her husband? If he realized she had truly found happiness, Jacques would understand. He would want her to be happy.

Bear walked ahead of her, clearing a broken limb from the pathway. If she could not leave him, she thought, perhaps Bear could go to France with her. But he would be lost without his freedom, powerless among the men in silk and shining armor. Besides, he would never leave his people. Not for her. Their care was his vocation; she was merely his wife.

The gods were unfair to make her choose between her life with Bear and going home. Either way, one of the men she loved would suffer and neither of them deserved any more pain on her behalf.

Antoinette wondered if her brother would understand her reasoning if she did not return to France. Knowing his temperament, Gaston would not accept her refusal without violence. Could Jacques talk Gaston into sailing without her?

First, she would make Gaston believe she was not a threat to him or his mission. Then, she would somehow explain to Jacques that as much as she loved him, she could not leave her husband. She was not the same woman he had known aboard *La Réale*.

Relieved of her burden, Antoinette walked toward Old Woman and Bear, who had moved some distance ahead. "I have made my decision."

Bear stopped his trek and looked into Antoinette's eyes.

"I would hear your words with respect, Swan."

"I will not go," she said with a calm voice, feeling more positive about her decision even as she spoke. "I am not going back."

Bear checked his emotions, turning instead to look toward the hidden pathway to his cave. "I will speak to Great Power at sunset about your decision. Please come to the cave when the moon rises. We have much to discuss."

Antoinette was unprepared for Bear's indifferent reaction. She watched him walk up the hillside alone, then she turned to Old Woman.

"What does he mean? I have made my decision."

Old Woman shook her head. "A shaman must always have the last word. That is the way it is." She made a chuckling snort and spoke low under her breath so only Antoinette could hear her. "Makes them feel they are in charge of destiny."

Bear watched the fire cast its light against the cave's walls. It was magical, almost like the light of a setting sun caressing the darkness with its golden glow. Magical and mysterious, like Swan casting her light of love into the darkness of his heart.

It was impossible to think of Swan leaving him. Their life together had just begun. There was so much more they had to discover, about each other and about love. She had taught him about her people and their ways, but not enough to save them if the white men declared war. He had heard their thunder sticks and Swan had told him of the great death and destruction they could bring.

It was not that he feared the white men. They were just men, with desires and troubles like himself. He would deal with them in his own way, if they threatened his people. And their presence here was a threat to Swan. What they said—what they wanted of his wife—*that* put fear into his heart. And the way the gray haired man looked at her—he was surely in love with Swan.

If Swan's pale-haired brother spoke the truth, if her friend and ruler's life depended on Swan, then she must go to her. Swan must protect her, even if it meant Swan must leave his hearth forever.

How distant could this France be that she could not come back to him? He had traveled west to the great river and still returned home. Bear heaved a deep sigh, removing his pipe from the niche in the cave wall. Tonight he would smoke the *nesquipapin* root mixed with the sight giving herbs and ask Great Power to help him make the right decision. Perhaps Great Power would also tell him why his heart was breaking, why he must sacrifice his beloved.

Bear threw his green velvet cloak around his shoulders and walked outside his cave to witness the setting sun. He held his pipe and tobacco to the sky with extended arms.

"Ho! Great Sun. Ho! *Nichekaminou*, Great Power. Ho! I thank you for the bright days and plentiful game you provide for my people. We are grateful for your kindness. We are glad to be your children and to walk the pathways in your light."

Bear lowered his arms and opened his tobacco pouch, and sprinkled several pinches of the herbal mixture into the air as a gift to the Sun, as a gift to Great Power. He let the dry leaves drift outward on the wind.

"Tonight I smoke to find Truth." Bear packed his pipe with the tobacco and lit it with a smoldering firebrand. He drew in several puffs of the smoke and blew it at the sun. "Smoke with me, Great Power, and share your wisdom."

Bear sat down at the entrance to the cave and smoked his pipe without further overtures to the sun. It was time to listen and time to wait for the visions. He closed his eyes and turned his attention to the sounds of the night.

The slow trickle of the stream bed below the cave sang to him. The night wind whispered high in the trees and the owl called its mate with a low trill. With the last light of day, he heard the low rumbling growl of his spirit helper, Muin Wapskw, taking the human shape of a warrior as he sat down beside him.

Bear opened his eyes. Muin Wapskw lifted the proffered pipe from Bear's hands and took a long draw of the tobacco. "Brother," he said blowing smoke into the air and nodding his head. "The smoke is good. You have made a fine mixture, not too bitter and not too sweet."

Bear smiled at his friend. "I would please Power with just the right blend. Better to have a happy guest than a disappointed one."

Muin Wapskw smiled and handed the pipe back to Bear.

"You call on Great Power to confirm your decision or to give you alternatives?"

"I would know what is right, my friend. My decision has much more significance than just my happiness. It must be the right decision or we will all lose honor."

Muin Wapskw tilted his head, his long brown hair falling over his naked shoulders and hairy chest. "Do you remember your marriage pledge to place Swan's honor above your own?"

"Yes." Bear frowned. "I remember. But is there ever a time when personal honor must be set aside for the sake of the people?"

"Do you not mean for the sake of your desires?"

"Ah, that too, Muin Wapskw." Bear nodded. "There is no denying what I truly want is not virtuous. I wish to hide Swan from the white men, to forget they ever came among us. But I cannot."

"What is best for Swan, Brother? What is best for her?

"I want to think her destiny is here with me. If I could speak to the one called Jacques who looks at Swan with love in his eyes, I know he would tell me the truth. He knows what waits for her in her land."

Muin Wapskw handed the pipe back to Bear. "If you believe this would help to clear your mind, you must go to him in your spirit form. He will hear your voice in the Spirit World. Call him to you."

Bear closed his eyes and leaned against the cave entrance, feeling the coolness of the rock seeping through the thin velvet fabric of his cloak. He took a deep breath and waited for the familiar sensation of his spirit lifting from his earthly body. With a quick thought he traveled to the cove, to the ship and stood before Jacques' sleeping body. He took swift account of the small enclosed room. He must be watchful for a powerful shaman could trap his spirit in this small box.

"Jacques." Bear spoke in his spirit voice. "Join me in the Otherworld."

Jacques' pale shade rose from his sleeping body and stood beside Bear. He seemed younger, more handsome and his stoic countenance was much milder in his spirit body.

"What brings you aboard this ship, Red Man? Surely you know there are dangers here for you."

Bear snapped his ghostly fingers and the two men were at once standing on a small island at the entrance to the cove. "We stand now on neutral ground. And we must agree to use no magic to harm each other's spirits."

Jacques could see his ship tugging against the hard set anchor. He turned expectantly to Bear.

"I agree."

"I would speak with you, Gray Hair. I would know what waits for my wife if she goes back to her homeland."

Jacques' expression was indifferent, but Bear felt the other man's emotions as he spoke. "You would know my falsehood if I did not tell you that she faces many trials and hardships. Her life will always be full of dangers, whether she is here with you or there. I know you can see how much she means to me. I assure you, if she returns I will do everything in my power to protect her. She has her own destiny, but I believe it lies in her old world and not with you or among your people."

Bear sighed. "Perhaps her destiny is with you after all. I have not seen her growing old at my hearth. I have not seen her future past the rising of tomorrow's sun."

Jacques took a deep breath. "Then you already know she must come with me on tomorrow's tide."

Bear looked hard into the eyes of his Otherworld companion. The energy around him was easy to read in the spirit world. "I fear if she does not go with you, she will come to greater harm."

Jacques was surprised at Bear's insight. "You are right, my brother. The master who Gaston serves requires her to return. If we do not bring her back, many white men will come to your land."

Bear laughed. "They will come anyway, Gray Hair. I have seen this future for my people. The white men will take the land from us like the sea takes the sand from the shores."

"I cannot control the sea, Bear. But I can hold back the tide. If you send Antoinette back with me, I will see that many seasons pass before the white men come again. I will not tell them how to return. You will be an old man when you see ships like this again in your coves. You will have many years to prepare your people."

"You have so much power?"

Jacques shrugged. "I am not invincible, but, yes, I have much power over the travel of the water."

"To control such things, you must indeed be a friend of Kluskap." Bear said with dubious respect. "Are you a friend of Great Power?"

Clothed in his spirit body, Jacques could not lie. He was indeed a servant and friend of a great power, the servant of Christ, and the great power of the Holy Spirit.

"Yes, I am a friend of Great Power. And I speak the truth when I tell you I will do my best to protect Antoinette if she returns with us. She means much to me and I want what is best for her."

"Be at peace, my brother," Bear said. "We will see what tomorrow brings."

Bear looked at Jacques. His spirit body radiated the white light of truth. Suddenly, he waved his hand into the air and their spirit bodies vanished from the small island.

Jacques woke in his bed, sweat pooling along his spine.

ଔ

The rekindled fire threw a fine light on Antoinette's body as she walked into the cave. Bear rose as she approached and pulled her into the safety of his arms. He wanted to hold her forever, to hide her away. He knew she would be gone with the morning tide.

She tensed and pulled herself away from his embrace, crossing the room. A sadness surrounded her as she turned to face him. Her eyes burned with a far-away look. She was almost crying, her voice barely a whisper. "I cannot leave you, my love. You are my life now. There is nothing left for me in my old world."

"You have a friend and a brother who think you would be better living with your own kind."

"They are no longer my people, Bear. I no longer see the world through their eyes. Here I am free, and that freedom makes me like you, one with Power and the Goddess. No one tells me what I must believe. No one declares what I may do or say."

Bear took a step toward her, his hands held out in supplication. "Will the freedom you have found be diminished if you return to your people? Can anyone truly take it away from you, now that you have heard the song of truth and carry it in your heart?"

"No." She shook her head. "Nothing can ever diminish the bond I have with the Goddess and the Ancient Ones. But there are some who would use my faith to imprison me, perhaps kill me for my beliefs."

"Your friend Jacques says his master will protect you."

Her eyes widened in surprise. "You have spoken to Jacques? Her eyes swept the edges of the cave as though she believed him to be hiding in the shadows.

Bear crossed the room. "I have spoken to him in the spirit world and I believe he tells the truth. The life of your friend is at stake. You must honor your vow of service to her." He forced the words from his mouth as he touched her. She should know the truth as he did. "Jacques has also told me that if you do not go with him, your life is in danger."

Antoinette laughed and reeled away from Bear's extended

hand. "You men and your honor. I am sick to death of the battles and sacrifices that have been made for honor. Is love not a higher ideal? Should love not be set above honor?"

Bear held his hand out to her once more in a gesture of love. She acquiesced and placed her hand in his, feeling the warmth of his touch. She laid her head on his shoulder. His heart beat hard against hers.

"Love *is* the highest ideal. But you would love me less if I did not respect you. You would think less of me if I did not care for my people or yours."

Antoinette could not answer him. These were the things she valued in him. Honor and integrity, the virtues that made him special.

Bear looked into her eyes, focusing his emotions for fear they would betray his pain. "If you truly want to embrace my people, you must respect our ways. You must fulfill your duty to your people, to your ruler and your friend."

"You do not understand, Bear. If Anne knew I had found peace and love in my life, she would not ask me to return."

Bear stepped back from her, holding her at arm's length. Antoinette's eyes filled with tears waiting to flow onto her cheeks. "If you do not go, the possibility of your friend's death will always overshadow your life. Do you think you will ever be truly happy knowing your return might have saved her? You must go back. I have seen your destiny."

Bear's words struck like an arrow in her heart and she tore away from his arms with a choking cry. She could no longer deny the truth he spoke. She had also glimpsed her destiny, growing old alone in a cold stone castle. And she would do everything in her power to change its direction. Turning away from him, she stared blindly at the glowing fire.

"If I go with my brother, it may be many seasons before I can return." She thought of Cardinal Visconti, the Templars and the Sisterhood, and all the people she must confront. "There are many dangers. I may never come back."

"You will come back to me. I have seen it." For the first time in his life Bear did not speak the truth, and he was amazed at how easily the white men's talent for lies rolled off his tongue. Their poison had already taken hold on his integrity.

But he thought of witnessing Swan's death at her brother's hands and did not retract his words. He closed the harsh distance between them with a silent step and brushed the hair from the back of her neck.

His breath quickened against her skin and tingling fingers

of fire spread through her limbs. He kissed the edge of her bare shoulders, running his hands down the length of her arms, reaching his hand around her to cradle her breast.

The touch of his warm lips and his tender caress pulled at the center of her heart. It tugged at the spark of new life that grew inside her. There was more at stake than just their love. She could not tell him of his child. Not until this impasse with her brother had ceased to be of importance.

Antoinette spun around in his arms, melting easily into his embrace. She felt the smooth firmness of his skin beneath her fingertips as she curled against the contour of his body.

"My love, I cannot live without you," she said firmly. "There is one alternative we have not discussed. If the life of my friend is so important, will you go with me to France and help me save her?"

Bear stopped his caress and looked at her, his dark eyes wide with question. The idea was so absurd it had never crossed his mind. None of his people had ever crossed the unending waters.

Undaunted, Antoinette continued. "You could learn the ways of the men who will someday visit your land. Perhaps it is your destiny to meet them now, on their own soil."

"I had not thought to go with you." Bear stepped back into the security of his cave. "How could I leave my people, or Old Woman? It is not something I have seen in my future."

"Think of it, Bear. With a great shaman standing before him, my king will see that the People are strong and should be left alone. That you are not savages."

Bear wandered to the edge of the room and looked at the baskets of herbs and medicinals lining the walls. There was so much work to be done before the fall hunting, so many people to care for within a day's walk. He wondered briefly if Old Woman could care for the people while he was away. No, she was too old to take on the responsibility. There were surely others more skilled than he who could tend wounds and heal sores.

In seven sun rises, Two Arrows would travel through Bear's camp on the way to the summer gathering. Old Woman would be safe alone until then and Two Arrows would surely take her into his hearth again. She still had many years to serve the tribe.

Two Arrows knew his plan for the Micmac's future. He could tell the Elders about the white men and Sparrowhawk. The Elders would listen to Two Arrows just as they would his own words.

"I have never walked in your world, Swan," he confessed, moving toward her. The long tail of his velvet cloak brushed the ground beneath his feet. "But it may be time for such a journey."

Bear reached out to her and she moved swiftly into his arms. The heat of his body penetrated the thin leather tunic between them and she felt secure once again.

His hands slid to the hollow of her back and pulled her into a kiss that came from the depth of his heart.

"Yes, Swan." He lifted his head to look into her eyes. "I will go with you to this distant land and we will speak to your chief together."

Antoinette smiled, assessing his words. They may not be able to change their destiny, she thought, but they could certainly arrange to face it together.

Bear lifted her light body from the ground and crossed the short distance to their sleeping pallet hidden in the alcove beneath the dark charcoal dragon Antoinette had once drawn to protect him. His hands moved almost magically, undressing her while he covered her exposed skin with his kisses.

In the short few months they had been married, he had learned how to please her with his touch. Now her body ached with a fire only his love could subdue.

He felt her desire and moved with her as her body arched toward him. Without breaking his flow of kisses, he buried himself in the softness of her flesh.

A blinding light exploded behind her eyes and she fell like a shooting star, riding the wind of her lover's passion, moving with him on the pulsing waves of their twinned heartbeats, spiraling upward toward the edge of ecstasy.

A slow rhythm bound their union and together they ascended into realms beyond that of flesh, each meeting the full force of their love with shared desires.

Antoinette looked into Bear's eyes. They were dark and seeking, reaching into the depths of her heart with every thrust of his body. She could not pull away from his gaze as their passion reached its crescendo. His love and his eyes burned into her soul, branding her heart with his love. The thought of being with Jacques vanished from her mind. He would forever be a dear friend and nothing more.

When she and Bear made love again, in the silence of the dark moonless night, it was a love made with a quiet sense of longing. A slow dance. A joining of spirits that took them closer to the dawn.

Antoinette and Bear watched the sun rise from the western edge of the cove, the ocean's dark blue waters vivid against the black ragged cliffs. Dark purple wisps of clouds danced in the air as the sun lifted silently into a crimson painted sky.

Then, like a slow breath from the Gods, the wind lifted the thick veil of fog to reveal the rugged rocky coastline and a ghostly ship anchored in the harbor. A boat loaded with barrels of fresh water and rendered game being rowed out to the anchored ship. Antoinette knew if Gaston saw her, he would accompany the next boat to shore. She was not yet ready to face him. Not just yet.

They waited until mid-day, then they descended the steep embankment prepared to tell her brother her plans.

Seabirds scavenged at a large form draped across the rocks some few feet up the beach and Bear walked cautiously toward it. The birds scattered as he approached, revealing the entrails and hide of a deer discarded in a haphazard pile. Black flies covered the carcass, buzzing as they enjoyed their feast.

Bear was appalled at the disrespect for the creature. It was an unspeakable action toward an animal that had given its life for food. How could these white men be so indifferent? This would make him more cautious with Antoinette's kinsmen. He would explain to them about the reverence they should show the animal's spirit. If they did not have the capacity to understand, he would take care of the animal's remains himself. It would not do to leave the deer's spirit to wander.

Bear and Antoinette made their way along the cliff to the rock- strewn beach to wait for the small boat to return with Jacques and her brother. This meeting, she determined, would be to tell them of her plans. She would ask for one more day to gather her belongings and for Bear to prepare his people for his absence.

She was anxious about their reaction to the idea of a 'savage' traveling with them. They would have to accept him if they wanted her to even set foot on that ship.

A chill of uncertainty swept over her. Her courage wavered as she watched Sebastian and Gaston row to shore. She did not blame Jacques for not wanting to see her again. She had hurt him beyond measure by choosing another man.

She turned to look at Bear. His countenance was

unshaken, solid. He stood proud and confident and she drew strength from him.

The two men disembarked and exchanged a simple nod of greeting with Bear.

Sebastian stood quietly at Gaston's side, his hand never far from the hilt of his sword. It was obvious he was making an effort to remain calm.

Gaston broke the silence and addressed Bear. "Thank you for your fresh water and game. My men were careful not to take more than we needed. We have enough provisions to make our return trip in safety."

Bear pointed to the carcass of the deer. "The white brothers have forgotten to honor the spirit of deer by returning his bones to the earth. It is disrespectful to leave the remains of any creature scattered on the beach."

Gaston quirked his eyebrow questioningly, then turned to Sebastian. "See that the men clean up their mess. We do not want to insult this man." His voice was courteous, but his patronizing tone could not be disguised. "Please forgive any offense. We were not aware of your customs." Gaston turned to Antoinette. "Have you decided, sister?"

"Yes, Gaston. I will return with you under one condition." She spoke with a quiet, confident firmness. "My husband will go with me. I must have your word and an oath against your faith that you will not harm him. He is a great leader of his people. You must treat him with respect and honor."

Gaston scowled. "Antoinette, you know his presence in France would not be acceptable. Look at him. He is wild, a painted savage."

His words were frank and full of censure, and Antoinette glowered at her brother, trying to overlook his lack of discretion.

"I know it is in your power to protect us. And I will only go if Bear accompanies me."

Gaston looked at Antoinette with a deceptive calmness. His gaze flitted to Bear and a hint of a smile crossed his face.

"I believe you have made a wise decision, Sister. Your husband is welcome on my ship. And I will do my best to show you both the respect you are due."

The eyes of a fox, Bear thought. The smile of a serpent.

Antoinette felt a warning but her voice remained controlled, her features composed. Suddenly she was anxious to escape from her brother's gaze. "We will be ready to sail with tomorrow's tide."

Gaston nodded. "Good. We will take the extra time to

provision the ship for two more passengers." With a swish of his long cloak, he turned away and walked to the boat, motioning for Sebastian to follow.

"Gaston, Bear and I are married, that is a bond that you cannot break. You will see that he is not as you think. He is a great healer and a wise man among his people."

When he spoke, Sebastian's words were in Italian, meant only for Gaston's understanding, but his explosive tone could be understood in any language. "It is impossible, Gaston. We cannot take this savage aboard our ship." Sebastian stroked his hand across the scabbard of his sword. "He would slit our throats before the ship is out of the cove."

Gaston's face remained somber. "I do not doubt it. But we will wait to deal with him once we are at sea. The ocean will welcome even a heathen's soul."

Antoinette was shocked. They had no idea she could understand their words as clearly as her native Breton. They would never accept Bear. But it would do no good to tell Bear of her brother's deceit. Not until they were away from the men and he could not harm them. She must let her brother think her willing to abide his wishes.

Bear's gaze moved from man to man. He did not understand the words but their intonation was unmistakable. He spoke calmly in Micmac to Antoinette.

"Your brother's words are full of hatred."

Antoinette kept her fear restrained. "Yes, they do not realize their folly. They speak of your integrity. They fear that you will kill them at the first opportunity."

"They may be right. I no longer believe any of their words." Bear looked piercingly at Sebastian. He could see Sebastian's emotions ready to explode. He had to protect his wife. He stepped between Antoinette and the young man. "We must not go with them."

Sebastian realized Bear's reluctance and drew his sword, throwing the scabbard aside. Bear drew his knife, pushing Antoinette protectively behind him. Gaston stood some few feet away, motionless and silent.

"You have shown your false faces to me, pale ones," Bear said. "I would be a mindless animal if I let my wife walk into such an obvious trap." He waved his arm toward the ship. "Go from my land and take your ship back to your chief! My People will be ready to greet him when you return. But tell him to send honorable warriors who will speak the truth and fight like honorable men." He looked toward Gaston and pointed to Sebastian. "Tell your ruler to keep his unweaned pups at home."

Sebastian's eyes flashed wild and furious. He lunged toward Bear.

"No!" Antoinette screamed, running toward them. "This is not right. I want no bloodshed here." She turned to Gaston. "Why have you lied to me?"

"I did not lie, Antoinette." Gaston advanced toward his sister. His voice was deceptively calm. "It is true that Anne needs you. And it is true that we have been sent to find you."

Without waiting for her reply, Gaston reached for her and swiftly pulled her toward him. He drew his pistol and brought it to her heart. "What I have not told you is that you have no choice except to return with us."

Bear whirled toward Gaston, stepping away from Sebastian in one movement. He stopped short as he saw Gaston's weapon glistening in the sunlight.

"Tell the savage not to move," Gaston ordered.

Antoinette said nothing. The mustiness of Gaston's clothing and the hard muscles of his arms caught her breath as he pulled her tightly to his chest and backed down the beach. Bear took a long stride toward them.

Malevolence glared from Gaston's eyes and the point of the gun pressed harder. "I regret that you cannot come with us, red man. It would have been interesting to see how you survived the courts of France."

A hush fell over the shoreline as though even the sea feared to breathe. Bear stopped his advance, his mind weighing his next move. At all costs he would save Swan, even if it meant his death.

The jagged rocks echoed Gaston's words as he yelled to Sebastian over his shoulder. "Make ready to sail!"

Without hesitation, Sebastian sprinted to the boat and pushed it into the water.

"Gaston, don't do this," Antoinette cried. "Don't take me away. You cannot know what you are doing."

"It's too late," Gaston said.

Bear bristled with rage, his mind frantic at the impasse. He could not rush Gaston for fear of harming Antoinette, and Sebastian was now out of reach. In the time it would take for Bear to draw his bow and arrow, Gaston could kill Antoinette.

Somehow, someway, Bear knew he must bargain for his wife. He could not allow her to be taken. He lowered his knife, yet kept it firmly gripped in his hand. "Brother, why must you take your sister against her will? Why do you betray your family and your people with such dishonorable actions?"

"I have no family." Gaston's voice grew hard and bitter. "I left my family long ago. The Knights of Christ embraced me and I owe my allegiance to them. They have given me my task and I will not fail them."

Bear took a cautious step forward, his gaze resting now on Antoinette's face.

"Come no closer!" Gaston warned. "I do not wish to kill you, but I will. Throw down your weapons."

Bear stopped, tossing his knife and bow to the ground. Antoinette was led through the water, thrust into the swell of the boat and tied fast to the ribbing. Was there nothing he could say, no magic he could summon to serve his purpose?

As if following his bidding, a rogue wave splashed high around Sebastian's waist, threatening his balance on the slippery seaweed covered rocks.

Great Power had heard his plea and called Mother Ocean to aid him. Summoning his strength, Bear lunged at Sebastian and fell with him into the water. The quickness of Bear's action and the violent splash pulled Gaston's attention from Antoinette and he rushed to his companion's aid.

Antoinette watched helplessly as the three men struggled in the foaming, spitting sea. By the gods, why had she spent her magic on Sparrowhawk's defeat? She had made a pact with the Goddess; she had no power, no right to call upon the Goddess to help her husband. Bear would have to fight alone, unless she could persuade Gaston by appealing to his greed.

"Gaston," she screamed, struggling desperately against her bonds. "Stop. I will tell you what I know of your Order here."

Gaston swung the hilt of his gun full force to Bear's head. The sound of the hard wood and steel striking against unshielded bone sent a chill through Antoinette's body. She watched Bear's body slip once beneath the waves, then float passively in the water. Gaston lifted his pistol, cocked the firing lever and aimed at Bear.

"No," Antoinette cried. "Give him the dignity of dying by the Mother's hand. I will tell you anything you want to know. I will give you a chart that Jacques left with me."

Every second that passed seemed like an eternity. Bear's limp body floated onto the slippery rocks. Gaston lowered his gun.

"Where is it?" he demanded, across the roaring surf. He rushed back to the boat, ignoring Sebastian's lament as he fell into the boat.

"Tell me where it is," Gaston threatened. "Or I'll kill the rest of his people."

Antoinette nodded toward the beach. “It’s in my pack, stuffed inside a sealskin pouch.” As Gaston turned she glanced at Bear’s body now lodged between two large boulders. She could not tell if he were alive or dead. She reached out with her mind, trying to bridge the distance between them with her thoughts, but could not touch him in the chaos of emotions.

Gaston sloshed through the tide. He hefted her pouch above the waves and slung it inside the boat. She heard a glass vial break on impact and grimaced. Hopefully it held only powder and not a liquid that would ruin everything, especially the parchment she had bargained for Bear’s life.

“Gaston, why do you do this? What have I done? There must be more to this than you have told me.” Her thoughts spun to Sparrowhawk’s goblet, also hidden in her backpack. “Is my abduction the Templars’ order? Because of their settlement here?”

Gaston looked at her with surprise. If there were men, his brothers, alive in this wretched land, he would be obligated to contact them. Perhaps he would need to take them or at least a message back to René. He swung his legs into the boat and began an eager rowing against the incoming tide, matching Sebastian stroke for stroke.

“What do you know?” he demanded. “Are there other white men here?”

Antoinette was silent. She looked back to the shoreline but could no longer see Bear among the jagged rocks. She looked the other way, not wanting to witness his body floating out to sea.

Gaston grabbed her arm in frustration, roughly turning her to face him. “What do you know? I demand that you tell me.”

Antoinette glared at him. “What will you do? Kill me? Take me back to the Inquisitors?”

“Antoinette,” Sebastian pleaded, “when we are home, you will see that this is the best thing for you. You need to come back with us. You were turning into one of them.”

“Far better than to turn into one of your kind. Callous and cruel.” She turned to Gaston. “I know of your life. You have been alone too long and your faith has twisted your heart with hatred. You have never loved anyone, nor any cause. And I do not believe you have the ability to do so.”

Her venom-laced words severed the last vestige of Gaston’s endurance and he drew back his hand as though to strike her. They glared at one another for along moment. Sebastian stopped rowing and they drifted toward the ship in an awkward silence.

"You have not changed, brother," Antoinette said, "Sadly, I find that neither have I." Her hands bound behind her, Antoinette raised her face into to the sky. "Beloved Mother, I beseech you. Hear my plea. Send your strength to sustain me, and bring justice to these men. Let their own actions thrice be known, and thrice be used against them."

Gaston shook his head at his sister's irreverent incantation and laughed scathingly. Sebastian made the sign of the cross on his chest.

"Your charms have no effect, Antoinette," Gaston said. "I am a servant of Christ and he protects me against the evil in your words."

Cold and angry, she looked into his eyes. "We will see, brother. We will see."

They reached the ship and the men lifted Antoinette aboard. Gaston ushered her below deck and tied her to the central beam running the length of the main salon. He tossed her pack beside her.

"I will find suitable quarters for you as soon as I tend the anchor, and then we will have a look inside your pack."

She did not answer. There was too much pain to hold back her sorrow any longer. Hopefully Jacques had no part in her abduction. He would surely release her when he heard of Gaston's deeds.

"Blessed Mother, protect Bear as he travels to his spirit world," she cried in a lamenting whisper. *Protect my unborn child as I bear the pain of Bear's death.*

She wished she had told Bear of the daughter she carried, but with the landing of the ship there had been too much confusion. Now the baby would be born in Brittany and away from the family Antoinette had claimed as her own.

Her melancholy was shattered as Gaston reappeared through the open doorway. He seemed not to notice her tear-stained face.

"We will lie at anchor a bit longer. A sea fog has rolled in and the men are reluctant to leave the safety of the cove."

The momentary reprieve gave her a glimmer of hope. The gods were listening to her. Perhaps she could still convince Gaston to release her, to let her return and search for Bear.

"The map you treasure points to nothing. The people have no gold, no riches to fill your pockets. Only rocks and shells and smoked fish."

"I will let my superiors decide if this land is worth the effort."

"You have no idea what a mistake you have made," she said with contempt. "By killing Bear, you have angered not only my gods but his People."

"Yes." Gaston sighed and shrugged his shoulders. "I am sure that I will regret his death the rest of my life."

Antoinette turned away but he stood towering over her. He lifted her chin with the tips of his fingers, forcing her to look into his cold blue eyes.

"Do you know what I will gain by returning you and the chart to the Templars?" He did not wait for her reply. "I will win back my honor. I will be able to live in freedom. I will ride the countryside of France and the lands of my ancestors in peace. I will no longer be in exile."

"Your freedom is won at too high a price. Will it be worth living with my death on your conscience?"

"No," he said, leaning away from her. "I am not as cruel as you would have me be. You will not die. I have bargained for your life. You will be secured in a nunnery with our mother, to live out your years safe and secure behind walls dedicated to the Blessed Virgin."

"It matters not to me," she retorted. "You have already taken my life and my will from me." She dared not tell him she carried Bear's child until she could no longer keep it secret.

Gaston shook his head. "Little sister," he said, softening his voice. "I am sorry we must be at odds with one another."

"You lie. You have never cared about me. You left us to seek your fortune. You set Marguerite against me. She hated me so much that she sent me away." Antoinette reared back in disgust. "You are too much like our father."

Gaston turned away. Unknowingly, she had deepened a wound that would never heal. Guillaume had been the reason for Gaston's exile. Defending his father's name, Gaston had killed a fellow knight. Brother killing brother was a crime punishable by death or exile. Caring too much for life, Gaston had chosen the latter and more times than not, had wished otherwise.

Antoinette's insight rang true. He had hated the baby growing inside his mother's womb. It had taken what remained of Marguerite's attention from him. He had plotted and planned, in his adolescent mind, how to punish Antoinette. And now, it seemed, he had succeeded. However the taste of his success was bitter. He could not hate Antoinette, the woman. A strong woman who had found a way to survive the hardships of life.

For all their differences they were too much alike.

He unfastened her bindings. "You will not speak our father's name in my presence," he said derisively. "You did not know him as I did."

"And I am glad for that." she said. "I pity my mother for having been made to endure his bed as often as she did."

Gaston disregarded her incisive comment, but she had touched a nerve still raw with pain. He lifted her to her feet and directed her to the doorway leading to large captain's quarters at the stern of the ship.

"I will see you are given every comfort possible aboard the Queen's vessel," Gaston said as he walked toward the cabin door. "Sebastian will not mind sharing his room with me. As soon as we lose sight of land, I will tell Jacques you are aboard. Then you'll have freedom of the ship and his bed if you wish."

When Gaston left the room Antoinette walked to the large windows at the rear of the cabin and pushed them open. A thick billowy fog surrounded the ship in a heavy mantle of gloom, effectively hiding sheet from shroud.

With the fog *Le Bon Breton* dared not move without risking damage to her hull on the rocky cove entrance. The ship would have to wait until the mists completely disappeared and the tides changed again, some five or six hours away.

She could barely see the beach and the rocky shoreline. Was Bear's body out there, floating in the tide? With remorse, she sank onto the bed beside her, pulled her knees up to her chest and closed her eyes.

"Great Goddess, forgive us all," she whispered.

It was a great feeling of loss that awoke Antoinette sometime later. When the door to her quarters opened, she drew in a long silent breath. Jacques' unmistakable silhouette framed the doorway. Tall and lean, he was dressed in a plain colored tunic and britches.

"I believe we need to talk." His voice was soft as he closed the door behind him.

Antoinette sat up, her heart pounding erratically. This time it wasn't fear that coursed through her veins, but a great sadness. It seemed strange that she should face him now. "I didn't expect to see you until we left the cove."

He cast her a smile, then walked to a small table and calmly poured two cups of wine. "I didn't expect to see you at all. I just learned you were aboard. Will you believe me if I say that I'm sorry it has come to this?" His voice was calm as he offered her the wine.

For the moment Antoinette felt better knowing that Jacques had not conspired against her. He still cared about her.

"But—I did not come here to make you sad," he said. "I came to apologize. For everything."

When she did not reach for the wine, Jacques set it on the table in front of her and took a long drink from his cup. "I don't blame you. You have no cause to trust me. I am as guilty as your brother for wanting you to come home."

She shook her head. "I trust you Jacques. It is Gaston that concerns me."

"Oh," he whispered. "Gaston. He will not harm you. He is content to believe there is a Templar colony inland. He wants you to take him there tomorrow."

He waved his cup toward the rear window and the dark night beyond it. "Was the land as beautiful as I imagined it to be?"

She nodded.

"Was your husband good to you?" he asked after a long silence.

Antoinette closed her eyes, blinking back the memory of Bear's body washing against the rocks. "Yes. I have lived in paradise and known the love of another good man."

"I wish it had been me." Jacques' eyes glistened in the candlelight.

"At times when I was alone and frightened, before I fell in love with Bear, I wished for that also."

"And now?" He looked at her expectantly.

"Now it is too late."

"Perhaps when you are over your grief at his death, it will be different."

"Jacques," she said hesitantly. "I carry his child."

"I understand." Jacques said calmly.

Antoinette's eyes welled with tears and she let them fall onto her cheeks. "The child will be grow up without knowing its father."

"You did not fare badly being raised by your mother and Ursule."

"I do not wish that fate on my child. I do not want her to be a pawn of the Sisterhood. And that is what she will be if I return to France. A first born daughter to follow the path of unyielding service to the Sisterhood."

"You will be under Anne's protection. She will not allow

your child to be taken away."

Antoinette laughed, then stepped forward and took the wine from the table. She swallowed the contents of the cup in one gulp.

"Anne is as much a puppet as I," she said. "We are all fools to believe we control our lives."

She reached within a fold of her clothing and withdrew the silver pendant Anne had given her. She crossed the short distance to Jacques and placed it in his hand.

"If I do not make it back to France, give this to Anne. Tell her I was content." She reached to her neck and caressed the crucifix beneath her shirt. "I will keep your cross as a remembrance of your love."

Reluctantly, Jacques folded his fingers over the pendant then gathered Antoinette in his arms. Too exhausted to protest, and thankful for his compassion, she let his strength enfold her.

"I will take care of you and your child, Antoinette," he whispered. "If you will allow me."

The door opened behind them and Gaston walked in. He gave them a wry smile "I see it did not take you long to get reacquainted. I will leave you alone as soon as you give me that map."

Antoinette stepped away from Jacques' comforting embrace. "You will not find your Arcadia here, Gaston. You are too late. The men you seek—the Templars—they are no longer alive."

A red flush spread across Gaston's face and Antoinette could feel the energy crackle in the air around them.

"You have no concept of the conquests of our Order," Gaston said. "The Templars have been here for over a hundred years. By now, there will be settlements reaching to the western boundaries of the New World."

"You're wrong." Antoinette lifted her chin in defiance. "I witnessed the death of your last true believer. A mad sorceress who did not even know the name of your god."

"A woman?"

"Yes. She claimed to be the High Priestess of an ancient god. A god who left his armor and sword to rot on a pagan altar."

Gaston shook his head and smiled obliquely at Jacques. "Lies. All lies of a desperate woman."

Antoinette walked to her pack and withdrew a leather parcel, then moved within arms length of Gaston and shoved the bundle into his hands. "Here, this is proof of my word."

Hastily, he pulled at the leather bindings. A gilded goblet studded with jewels sparkled in his hands. He let the leather drop to the floor. His eyes grew wide in amazement.

"My God! This is the goblet of St. Katherine, the original chalice that was used over one hundred years ago in Rosslyn Castle. We use a replica of it in our mass." He had held a similar vessel in his hands not a season ago. He grabbed Antoinette's arm, nearly lifting her from the floor. "Where did you get this?"

Antoinette summoned what courage she had and spit into his face.

He cast her aside and she fell against the table, knocking the wine and cups to the floor. Jacques rushed to her side. Gaston drew his sword.

"You will tell me!" Gaston threatened. "And you will take me there."

"I will tell you nothing." Her breath came in gasps. "And I will take you nowhere."

He took a menacing step forward and for a brief moment Jacques thought he would run them both through.

"Hold!" Jacques demanded. "For God's sake. This is your sister. Your flesh and blood."

Gaston looked at him as though caught in a trance. "She would keep from us the very thing we came here to find."

Jacques was resolute. "Lay down your weapon, man. You have promised her your protection."

Gaston held the goblet up and shook it into the air. "This is proof that we have been here. Proof that St. Clair was here."

"No, I do not believe it is proof," Jacques insisted.

"Have you forgotten the main purpose of our Order, Jacques? The New Jerusalem is to be colonized in the New World."

Bracing his feet on the deck, Gaston firmed his stance. "I demand you take me to this place. Where is the map Jacques gave you?"

Antoinette found her voice. "I have the map, but the place you seek does not exist."

Jacques turned back to her. "Is this true?"

"Yes. Just as it is true that no one wants me to return to France alive. Not your Order, not Visconti, and most definitely not Charles. We have all been used once again to fulfill someone else's desire."

"You know nothing," Gaston said.

"I know more than you wish me to know. I can read it on your face. You want to be free, to live your life as you wish, without the Order to summon you at their slightest whim."

"You know she is right," Jacques said. "Who among the Order has not wished for his freedom?"

Gaston's face tightened, his thoughts taunted by Antoinette's insight. Jacques saw his chance and closed in quickly. He knocked the goblet from Gaston's hand. With a clatter of metal on wood, it skidded across the floor, landing near the open window.

Without thinking, Antoinette rushed to retrieve it. She did not see Bear emerge from the shadows until he was standing beside her. She froze.

Was this Bear or Bear's spirit? she wondered.

Then he reached out and touched her cheek with his wet finger and she knew he was solid human flesh. She flung her arms around Bear's neck and he pulled her into the shadows.

"How —" she began.

Bear tilted his head toward the window. "A rope leads to the waterline."

She looked beyond him. The stern anchor line was just below the window. It kept the ship from drifting sideways and into the rocky outcroppings. She should have thought about it before as a means for her escape.

Flesh hit against flesh as the men struggled behind her.

"Take her to safety," Jacques shouted.

"You're not dead," she cried, realizing that Bear was actually standing beside her.

"Not that I can tell," he replied. "And I would like to keep it that way, so hurry. We must go as Gray Hair says."

"How did you find me?" she asked.

"Later," he demanded, pulling her toward the window. "We must leave, now!"

Antoinette reached for her pack and stuffed the goblet deep inside, then looked over her shoulder. "What about Jacques?"

"It is his fight. We must not interfere."

Antoinette nodded. She understood. The blood bond of family had been broken with her kidnapping. Bear no longer considered Gaston as his kinsman. If Jacques did not kill Gaston, then Bear surely would.

"Jump!" Bear insisted. "Jump or I'll push you in. Swim away from the boat. The water is deep, but Two Arrows waits in a canoe. He will row out to pick us up."

Antoinette looked out into the mists. She could only trust there was water somewhere below her. She kissed Bear on the cheek. "I'll always love you."

Bear smiled, then put his hand on the small of her back

and pushed her out the open window. She fell into the darkness of the icy water.

The chill as she plunged deep below the surface reminded her of Ursule's root cellar, cold and silent, a place to hide from danger. Then the tranquillity was broken by the sound of musket fire spitting in the stillness above her. She dove deeper and swam with all her strength.

Mother Ocean did not fight her this time, but worked with her, pulled her toward shore.

Someone shouted, "There they are! Fire again!"

She heard others shouting as she surfaced. Bear surfaced beside her, then shoved her behind him with a swift swirl of his body. Musket shot impacted the water only inches away. They were out of range, swimming out of the fog that surrounded the ship.

Two Arrows appeared beside them and lifted Antoinette out of the water. "We must hurry, brother." He helped Bear into the small boat. "White Water is waiting for my signal."

"Give it," Bear commanded, catching his breath in long, strained gasps. "We cannot wait any longer."

Two Arrows lifted a birch bark horn to his lips and blew a harsh bellowing vibration into the air. Atop the precipice, where Bear had first sighted the intruders, small fires lit the sky. Antoinette heard the zing of arrows as they flew toward their target, hitting their mark with astonishing accuracy. Within seconds dry canvas sparked to raging flame, lighting *Le Bon Breton* from bow to stern with an eerie yellow glow.

"No!" Antoinette yelled. But she knew it could not be helped. The ship had to be destroyed or others would come. Still she felt a deep sorrow for the lives of the men aboard. Especially for Jacques and Sebastian.

She wished she could have reasoned with Gaston. It was too late. They would have to resolve their problems in another life, in another time.

Bear joined Two Arrows in his swift paddling and they were soon standing on the shore.

"The great canoe will burn to the waterline," Two Arrows commented, pulling their small boat onto the land.

Bear nodded, bringing Antoinette into the protective fold of his arms. "Papkutparut will have many souls to welcome this night."

Two Arrows pointed to the shape of a small boat pulling away from the ship and through the fog. "But not everyone aboard."

Antoinette could barely see through the mist, but

instinctively she knew it was Jacques and possibly her brother who risked death upon land instead of at sea. She looked into Bear's eyes for signs of his intentions.

Two Arrows pulled out his knife. "Brother, let me avenge your honor."

Bear moved back from the beach, shoving Antoinette behind him. He drew his weapon and stood firmly beside his brother. Antoinette knew she could not stand by and watch her brother and friends slaughtered. Sebastian had always been by her side. Right or wrong, Gaston was still her kin. And Jacques had always offered her kindness.

The gods were giving them all a second chance. She must make Bear listen. She stepped in front of him, her arms outstretched in supplication. "Husband. These men have paid for their treachery with their vessel and the lives of their own kind. Must they die now because they have acted upon unwise orders from their chief?"

Bear nodded his head. "It is our way, Swan. These men will bring their evil among us if they live."

How could she make him listen to her? She had to make Bear understand why the men had to be spared.

"Who will believe you when you tell this story at the summer campfire?" she asked, making a desperate appeal to his common sense. His emotions were too enraged. "Who will believe that the white man has come among us, or that he will come again?"

"What do you mean?" Bear asked.

"Their lives will be useful to you at the gathering of Elders," she said. "Living, they will be proof of your fears. Dead they will only be rotting corpses in your memory."

"The woman speaksthe truth, Brother," Two Arrows whispered. "Take them prisoners now. We can kill them later."

Bear knew the wisdom of Antoinette's words, but he also knew the ruthless heart of her brother. He might consider sparing Gray Hair's life, only because he had once cared for her.

"Keep guard, Two Arrows," he warned as Gaston disembarked from the small boat and walked slowly toward them. "The tall one is like a fox and the dark one is unpredictable. Gray Hair can be trusted."

Bedraggled, Gaston stumbled to the beach and fell on both knees. His white garments and face were blackened by smoke, his hair streaked with ash. He had no weapon.

"You have won, Red Man." Gaston looked over his shoulder at his ship, burning now with uncompromising flames. "We are at your mercy."

"Your friend and Gray Hair?" Bear asked, motioning with his knife. "What of them?"

Gaston coughed his words, glancing back at Sebastian and Jacques. "Let us go and we will leave you in peace."

Bear narrowed his eyes. It was strange for a man of Gaston's nature to submit so easily to a conqueror. "Why does a warrior like you surrender so willingly?"

Gaston ran his hands through his short cropped, hair. He laughed hollowly. "It simply doesn't matter anymore. There is no way to return to France. I have been betrayed by my superiors. The map... the ship...my mission, all have failed. There is no reason to return."

As though echoing the finality of Gaston's words, *Le Bon Breton's* hull burst into flame. Gaston laughed once more. This time it was with the crazed laugher of a desperate man. "I am in exile again."

Antoinette moved from Bear's side and stood over her brother. How pitiful he was. He was no longer the tyrant of her childhood but a lonely, broken man.

"Have mercy, my husband," she pleaded. "Every man should have a second chance to make amends. My brother has not taken the lives of your people. He has wounded your warrior's pride. In my land the stories of your People are ones of frightful savages. Gaston knew no better."

Bear firmed his lips and looked at his brother. Two Arrows shrugged his shoulders and made no comment.

"You are too sympathetic. Your judgment is clouded by your kinship."

Antoinette searched for words to make him understand. She searched for something that would make him trust her wisdom.

"When has my perception been wrong, Bear? Have I not proven my wisdom and insight to the People?"

Bear nodded. She had certainly overcome the obstacles Great Power had put in front of her.

"Have I ever asked you for anything that was not right or proper?"

Bear shook his head.

"Do you trust me?" she asked.

"Yes. But what path are you walking?"

Antoinette smiled. "I believe that I have judged well by making you the father of my child."

Bear looked at her with amazement, then pulled her into his arms. "How can I argue with you?"

"Don't try," Two Arrows said casually. "You will only cast your words to the fish."

Bear ignored Two Arrows' attempt to lessen the tension. "If there was some way to know your brother would bring no harm to our people I would gladly spare his life."

"What would you have me do, Bear? I can no longer see into the future. I have no right to ask my gods for as much as a whisper from the heavens."

"Look!" Two Arrows arched his arm across the void of the night sky, suddenly brilliant with bands of color. "It is *Wakatisk.*"

They gazed to the glittering expanse of sky above them. Bright spirals, tumbling rainbows of mist swirled overhead. Red, lavender, blue, lights mixing, spinning wildly in a patterned rhythmic dance as it flashed brilliant across the heavens.

"It is the Breath of Kji-kinap," Bear whispered reverently. "*Wakatisk.* A rare sight so late in the summer." The air popped and crackled with distant rumblings. "Listen, Swan. Power is singing to you. It is the whisper you were afraid to ask for."

Antoinette looked into the sky, marveling at the beauty displayed before her. She could not deny that a song of hope stirred deep within her heart, a rhythm that echoed the heartbeat of her unborn child. It was much more than a sign. She could feel the gift from the gods electrifying her with a renewal of power.

"Will you accept it as such, Bear?" she asked.

He slid his arm around her waist. His body had warmed from the chilling swim and she found comfort in his touch.

"If I could change into a being of the night sky, I would honor you as Great Power does tonight." He kissed her lightly on the forehead. "But you will have to take me as I am."

"Does that mean yes, my husband?" She was determined to have his word.

"I will have a pledge from your brother, from Gray Hair and the others who survive," he said sternly. "An oath that binds their lives to their word of honor."

"You shall have it." Antoinette explained Bear's conditions to Gaston and to Jacques, who had moved closer.

Jacques reached out and handed Anne's jewel pendant to Antoinette. "Give this to your daughter."

Antoinette looked one last time into Jacques' eyes, filled now with a different kind of love. A love she knew could never be taken away. When he stood beside Bear she noticed the drastic contrast between the two men. They were so totally different, she wondered if their cultures would be able to exist side by side.

"Swear before me Gray Hair," Bear began in his native tongue. Antoinette translated Bear's words. "Swear before whatever creator you honor that you will live among us in peace and that you will respect the ways of your new land."

Jacques looked at Antoinette standing resolutely beside her husband. Antoinette and Bear were a formidable pair. Like the wind and the sea. But he would always love her.

"Yes." Jacques spoke the words of loyalty as Antoinette continued her translation. "I swear by the Blood of Christ that I will honor your ways and your people."

Gaston took the oath as well.

"Know, Gaston, that you are bound to me, as brother to brother." Bear said. "Know also that I will defend you as I do my kinsman." Bear grabbed Gaston's forearm and stepped forward, locking him in a tight grip. Then he lowered his voice so only Gaston could hear him. This time he spoke in French.

"Do not doubt my knife is sharp or believe I sleep without guard. For, though I will not take revenge this day, I will never forget it."

Gaston looked into Bear's dark eyes. He knew this man, this warrior, would not hesitate to act upon his words. Bear was far more honorable than himself. He nodded and firmed his hold on Bear's arm. "I will never doubt your knife's true aim or your intentions."

The skies flared above Two Arrows as he escorted Sebastian up the beach at the tip of his knife. Sebastian was limping, his clothes torn and burned. He refused the offered assistance of Two Arrows' arm for support.

"Would you have the young one's oath now, brother?" Two Arrows asked as they came near.

Sebastian's face glared with contempt at his captors. He shrugged off any further attempt to move him forward.

"No." Bear shook his head. "Not today. I would take no false oath of allegiance from him. He must see his own path clearly before his words can be trusted."

Though he did not agree, Two Arrows understood the meaning within Bear's words. Bear had promised Antoinette to spare her brother and Gray Hair's lives, but only after their oath of loyalty to the people. If Sebastian would not give it, then Bear would be forced to kill him. After making peace with one man, it would not bode well to kill his friend.

Two Arrows refrained from comment. Things should be done swiftly, completely. This was Bear's responsibility and not his. There would be time to question the wild one, but it should be soon. Trouble was a good name to paint across the pale one's face.

As though echoing Two Arrows' cautious thoughts, *Le Bon Breton's* hull gave up her resistance to the sea and sank beneath the water, giving out a low groan of release.

The sky flared once more above them. This time a myriad of colors sparkled in the starlit sky.

Bear asked Two Arrows to guard the men and he led Antoinette up the winding path to the rocky precipice above the cove.

"You must promise me you will seek out your Goddess and not deny your voice to the Ancient Ones any longer," he whispered standing behind her. His hands wrapped protectively around her stomach. "Our daughter must have knowledge of your Goddess. She will need to be as wise and strong as her mother. We will need the strength of all our children, for your people are the first of many strangers that will stand on these shores."

"I have seen this as well, Bear," Antoinette admitted. "And I have seen that there will be time to prepare the people, time to teach them we can all live in peace."

"Perhaps Great Power is showing us the way to take the first step, to nurture a new garden seeded from the best of both our peoples."

Antoinette whispered. "Yes. Our daughter will be born of both worlds. And she will walk within them unafraid."

Bear turned her to face him and whispered. "She would do well to find a love as infinite as ours, my Swan."

A ribbon of color reached down from the sky and swirled around them. Antoinette gazed up into Bear's eyes, lit now with the heavenly fire. He lowered his lips to meet hers, and with his kiss, bound their prophecy for the future.

~ *Ka'iya* ~

Aleta Boudreaux is descended from four generations of artists. She holds a degree in Fine Arts and has been a student of metaphysics, studying comparative religions and philosophy, for the past 20 years. She lives near the Gulf of Mexico with her family and is an avid blue water sailor when the weather is calm.

Her husband, Hamilton, is a direct descendent of adventurers who came to Nova Scotia in the early 17th century.

Aleta's current projects for Laughing Owl Publishing include: ***SEPTERRA,*** a heroic fantasy set in a shape shifting world, ***BENEATH THE CRESCENT MOON,*** a romantic dark fantasy set in New Orleans and ***BY COMPASS AND SQUARE,*** *a sequel to* ***SONG OF THE WHITE SWAN.***

FURTHER READING

INDIANS and HERBOLOGY

Smith, Dwight L. Editor, *Indians of the United States and Canada: A Bibliography*, Santa Barbara, ABC-Clio, 1974

Lacey Laurie, *Micmac Medicines - Remedies and Recollections*, Nimbus Publishing, 1993

Hutchens, Alma, *Indian Herbology of North America*, Shamballa Publications, 1973

Gaddis, Vincent H., *American Indians, Myth and Mysteries*, Radnor, PA., Chilton Book Co., 1977

Elias, Thomas S., *Edible Wild Plants- A North American Field Guide*, Sterling Publishing Co, 1990

Graves, Richard, *Bushcraft, A Serious Guide to Survival and Camping*, Schocken Books, NY, 1972

Wallis, W.D. and Wallis, R.S., *The Micmac Indians of Eastern Canada*, The University of Minnesota, Minneapolis, 1955

White, John Manchip, *Everyday Life of the North American Indian*, New York, Holmes and Meier, 1979

Whitehead, Ruth Holmes, *The Micmac, How Their Ancestors Lived Five Hundred Years Ago*, Nimbus Publishing Ltd.,1983

Whitehead, Ruth Holmes, *Stories From the Six Worlds - Micmac Legends*, Nimbus Publishing, 1988

Whitehead, Ruth Holmes, "I Have Lived Here Since the World Began" an essay from *The Spirit Sings*, Toronto, McClellan and Stewart, 1987

Whitehead, Ruth Holmes, *Elitekey - Micmac Material Culture from 1600 AD to the Present*, The Nova Scotia Museum, 1980

Whitehead, Ruth Holmes, *Six Micmac Stories*, Nimbus Publishing and the Nova Scotia Museum, Halifax, 1989

Whitehead, Ruth Holmes, *Nova Scotia Protohistoric Period 1500-1630, A Curatorial Report*, Nova Scotia Museum, Halifax, N.S., 1993

Micmac - ETV Series, Nova Scotia Department of Education, Halifax, Nova Scotia

NAVIGATION

Belgrave, John, *Astrolabe - Mathematical Jewel*

Aspley, John, *Speculum Nauticum on the Sea Man's Glasse*, London, 1624

Bauer, Comm. Bruce A., *The Sextant Handbook*, International Maine Pub. Co., Camden, Maine, 1986

Ferris, Timothy, *Coming of Age in the Milky Way*, Bantam, Doubleday, Dell Publishing Group, Inc. New York, NY, 1989

Hammick, Anne, *The Atlantic Crossing Guide*, International Maine Pub. Co., Camden, Maine, 1992

Landström, Björn, *The Ship: An Illustrated History*, Doubleday, New York, 1961

Quinn, David, *North American Discovery- Circa 1000-1612*, University of South Carolina Press, 1971

Villers, Captain Alan, *Men, Ships and the Sea*, National Geographic Society, New York, 1962

DRUIDIC AND CELTIC STUDIES

Graves, Robert, *The White Goddess*, Faber and Faber, 1961

Herm, Gerhard, *The Celts: People Who Came Out Of The Darkness*, Barnes and Noble, New York, 1993

Nicols, Ross, *The Book of Druidry*, Aquarian Press, London, 1990

Mathews, Caitlin, *Elements of the Celtic Tradition*, Element Books, Dorset, England, 1989

Mathews, John, *The Celtic Shaman: A Handbook*, Element Books Dorset, England, 1991

Ross, Ann, *Pagan Celtic Britain*, Routledge and Kegan, London, 1967

Starhawk, *The Spiral Dance: A Rebirth of the Ancient Religion of the Great Goddess*, Harper and Row, 1979

KNIGHTS TEMPLAR

Baiget, Michel, *Holy Blood and the Holy Grail,* London, 1982

Bradley, Michael and Dianna Theilmann-Dean, *Holy Grail Across the Atlantic,* Hounslow Press, Ontario, Canada, 1988

Burman, Edward, *The Templars, Knights of God,* Destiny Books, Rochester, Vermont, 1986

Sinclair, Andrew, *The Sword and the Grail,* Crown Publishing, New York, 1992

DISCOVERY OF NORTH AMERICA

Quinn, David, *North American Discovery, circa 1000-1612*

Holbrook, Sabra, *Founders of North America and Their Heritage,* Antheneum, New York, 1976

EUROPEAN HISTORY

Academe Francaise, *The Lives of the Kings and Queens of France,* Knopf, New York, 1979

Brudel, Ferdinand, *Structures of Everyday Life, Civilization and Capitalism, 15th-18th Century,* Harper and Row, New York, 1981

Galliou, Patrick and Jones Michael, *The Bretons,* Basil Blackwell, Inc., Cambridge, Mass., 1991

Manchester, William, *A World Lit Only By Fire: The Medieval Mind and the Renaissance* - Portrait Of An Age, Little,Brown and Co., Boston, 1992

BRITTANY

Bell, Brian, Editor, *Insight Guides -Brittany,* APA Publications, HK, 1989

Caffee, Gabrielle, *The Breton and His World,* Madaloni Press, Mobile, AL, 1985

Marriott, Michael, Editor, *Berlitz - Discover Brittany,* Berlitz Publishing Co. Ltd, Oxford, England, 1992

Brittany, Passport Books, NTC Publishing Group, Lincolnwood, IL., 1993

LAUGHING OWL PUBLISHING, INC.

Call 1-334-865-5177 to order by phone and use your major credit card. Or use this coupon for mail order.

____ **Glencoe: A Romance of Scotland**
0-9659701-3-2 $8.00 US 12.00 CAN
by Muireall Donald. Historical Romance. In the late seventeenth century, two clans embodied the essence of rivalry and revenge. Meg Campbell and her ancestral enemy Niall MacDonald must battle clan dishonor and old sorrows as they unwillingly fall in love amid the last snows of a bitter Highland winter.

____ **The Beloved** (Available January 1998)
0-9659701-4-0 $8.00 US 12.00 CAN
by M.D. Gray Occult. Adam was the man of Shona's dreams. But when the forbidden sensuality of their past lives came crashing into the present, she awakened to the terror of her lover's demonic possession and her own enthrallment to the ecstasy of his touch.

Name____
Address____
City __________ State__________ Zip_______________

Please send me the LAUGHING OWL books I have checked above.

I am enclosing	$________
Plus Postage and Handling	$ 3.00
Sales Tax (Alabama residents add 6%)	$________
Total Amount Enclosed	$________

No cash or C.O.D.s.

Send check or money order to:
Laughing Owl Publishing, Inc., 12610 Highway 90 West, Grand Bay, AL 36541.

Valid in the United States and Canada only. All prices and availability subject to change without prior notice.